Rainbow Majesty

Ann Ulrich Miller

Rainbow Majesty

Ann Ulrich Miller

Earth Star Publications
Pagosa Springs, Colorado

FIRST EDITION
First Printing June 2010

Library of Congress Control Number: 2010929245

Earth Star Publications
216 Sundown Circle
Pagosa Springs, CO 81147

Please check www.earthstarpublications.com
for updated address information.

ISBN 978-0-944851-32-6

Printed in the United States of America

Cover photo by Tom Raven, Otaki Beach, New Zealand
www.flickr.com/photos/tomraven
email: tomraven@whitebuffalo.net

DEDICATION

To all the light workers on Planet Earth

Other Books by Ann Ulrich Miller

Throughout All Time, A Cosmic Love Story

Under the name Ann Carol Ulrich

Intimate Abduction

Return To Terra

The Light Being

Night of the November Moon

The Mystery at Hickory Hill

The Secret of the Green Paint

The Pouting Pumpkin Mystery

Future Books by the Author

The Legend of the Lantern

The Root Cellar Mystery

Sonata Summer

Visit www.AnnUlrichMiller.com

Author's Note

Inspired by my many years of living in the North Fork Valley of Colorado, I wrote this book after I relocated to southeastern Ohio in 2007. Bringing the characters to life in the beautiful place that I missed was a comfort to me in the year and a half I spent caring for my terminally ill husband.

The Rainbow Majestic Lodge was inspired by a landmark up Stevens Gulch Road, eighteen miles north of Paonia, which is known as Electric Mountain Lodge. In March 2005 there was a gas explosion that caused the lodge to burn to the ground, which resulted in the death of three children. The tragedy was a shock to the community. Since then, Electric Mountain Lodge has been rebuilt, although it is not as large or grandiose as the original.

Light workers are a special breed. I have had the pleasure over the years of getting to know many of them, and consider myself to be one as well. People ask, "What *is* a light worker?" I suppose there are many definitions. The simplest answer I can give is this: "A light worker is someone who wants to make our planet a better world."

Marcia McMahon describes light workers as those who "hear the Sacred Voice of the Divine, known as the Still Small Voice of God. ... They never exclude others' understanding that they also are a part of Divine Source and each person's work is valued and cherished for their spiritual gifts. Their laughter and sunshine brightens any room. They bring the Masters with them to any party. They have moved beyond churches and temples, holding their sacred energy within."

Acknowledgements

My undying gratitude goes to the following individuals for their encouragement, support and loving guidance in this rewarding project of Love and Light ...

Suzanne Ward, Judy Horky, John Cali, Chrystle Clae, Ildi Ingraham, Honey Lee French and Arda Golden Eagle Woman.

Also my unseen helpers in the other Realms, including my guides and angels, friends in spirit and my soul mate.

I especially want to thank a special person in my life who has helped open my eyes and my mind to new ways of thinking. Thank you, Doug, for being you and letting me be me, as well as your refreshing, realistic perspective, your sharing, your caring, and your knowing that you always have my love.

Rainbow Majesty

1

Through misty eyes I stared at the casket in front of me, on braces that would soon lower my mother's remains into the ground. It reminded me of another coffin, one that had been draped in the American flag. Two years ago I stood in this same cemetery—crushed by grief—my sobs unstoppable. The memory of that day remains imprinted in my mind forever.

The pungent, wet-earth smell of freshly upturned soil was like it had been the day Sean had been honored by a twenty-one gun salute. That June morning the sun had shone through the clouds for a brief minute, mocking my inconsolable sorrow. Today a fine mist hung heavy in the air around me. Beneath my high heels, wet grass brushed my ankles from the morning's rain.

People headed to their cars parked along the curb of the cemetery drive. Church women wearing rain scarves stepped into the vehicles with their dark-suited husbands. Many had been busy the night before with pies and hot dishes, soon to partake of their labors in the church basement.

"We'll see you at the church, dear," called my mother's cousin Phyllis, who dabbed at her eyes with a lace-edged handkerchief. Her gray, wiry hair was stuffed into a black felt hat that matched her dress.

Neighbors and relatives murmured words of sympathy or placed a comforting hand on my shoulder. Tears did not stream from my eyes like they had at Sean's funeral. My mother's death had been a welcome relief from suffering.

"How are you holding up?" The man's voice from behind caused me to turn around. Mike Rollins stood there, dressed in his black trench coat, his short black hair ruffled from the wind. Specks of rain stuck to the lenses of his thick-framed glasses. There was a telltale red dot on his neck from a razor nick.

Mike's tall presence was a welcome shield against the sudden emotions that seized me. His hazel eyes with the thick brows usually carried a certain formality in his expression, but now his voice softened as he leaned toward me. "Juniper, it's time to go back to the church. Let me take you."

As if I didn't have any say, Mike took my arm and walked me past the slowly moving vehicles to his parked minivan. At least for the moment, I was relieved that somebody else was taking charge. I'd had to carry the reins for quite a while, and when Mother had died close to a week ago, a flood of decisions had come down on my head.

At least now the funeral was over. I had held up okay until the memory of Sean's coffin had unleashed my emotions. I really didn't want to go back to the social gathering the church women had arranged. I just wanted to go home, to be alone and unwind.

In the car, Mike turned on the windshield wipers and let out a sigh. "Well," he said as he pulled out into the stream of traffic, "what now, Juniper?"

I could only stare at him. This evoked the slightest twinge of a smile in him, causing his chin to look as square as his head.

"You're the one with all the answers," I said, and turned to gaze out the window. I didn't want him to notice my trembling lip.

"If you mean the will ..." Mike began.

I swallowed my pain, then took a breath to compose myself. At least Mike had the decency in this moment not to bring up Sean. "My mother obviously did not believe I am capable of handling her affairs," I said in a stronger voice than I felt I possessed. "So she named you as executor."

"Look ... Juniper ... I'm not pleased with how this turned out any more than you are." Mike signaled to change lanes. "Why Margaret named me personal representative of her estate is beyond me."

"You have to understand," I told Mike, "my mother was not an easy person to live with these last two years. In fact, she was downright hateful toward the end. She kept threatening to throw me out of her will and it looks like she has succeeded."

"No, Juniper," argued Mike. "She did not throw you out of her will. You're very much a part of the estate. And if I've got anything to say about it, you're going to come out of this just fine." He sighed, then added, "But it's not like Margaret had a ton of money stashed away, or investments—or even real estate of any value."

Yes, I thought to myself as we drove downtown toward the

church, *it all hinges on what Mike is going to say about my mother's estate and what I get out of it.* I knew she didn't have a lot—just the house, which wasn't much—and a heap of medical bills that would have to be paid before I, as her sole beneficiary, would ever see a penny of it.

"There shouldn't be a problem with keeping the house," said Mike as if he were reading my mind. "I think once we ..."

"Mike, please, I don't want to discuss Mother's will right now, if you don't mind." I did not feel like dwelling on business matters at a time like this. I hadn't expected this rush of grief over Sean to surface like it had. Soon we would arrive at the Presbyterian church annex and I'd have to face all those friends and relatives who were going to smother me with sentimentalities. *Oh, what a wonderful woman Margaret Sutton was ... oh, your mother this ... your mother that ...* and I would have to smile and pretend that I agreed with them.

Then there would be those who—behind my back—would whisper among themselves, *It's such a shame ... after losing the man she was going to marry ... the poor, poor girl ...*

The truth was, my mother and I had been in a struggle for years, and yes, her Alzheimer's had been the enemy—not *her*, per se—but even before the Alzheimer's grew worse, Mother and I had our differences. I had agreed to come live with her— and take care of her—because she had asked me. At the time, I needed the distraction.

By late afternoon I was back home. Mike had dropped me off after I assured him I was all right and did not need his companionship. It had been a long day. I was tired and turned the telephone's ringer off. I couldn't deal with any more well-meaning relatives.

The evening descended on me and I felt the weight of it as though the walls were closing in around me. I had no interest in television. I picked up a magazine or two of my mother's, but nothing grabbed my attention. Stacks of Mother's magazines lay all around that she had received and never read. Toward the end she'd forgotten how.

I dreaded going to bed too soon. Being mid June, the days were long and it didn't seem right to retire before dark. Outside I heard the neighbor's lawn mower running. Mostly I didn't want to lie in bed, thinking. I didn't want to face what was ahead ... *my future*. I had put it off for two years, and now—sooner or later—I would have to make some decisions about what I was going to do with my life.

I was single and had not finished college. What did I have to offer the world? And what was out there for me? Even though I had spent the better part of my life right in this house in Great Bend, Kansas, I knew I didn't want to stay here. I didn't know what it was that nagged at me, but I knew eventually I wanted a life. I wanted to discover Juniper Sutton.

Two full years of my life had been devoted to taking care of a dying woman who didn't even know I was her daughter the last weeks of her life. As hard as it had been, I hadn't wavered from my self-imposed duty. She was my mother, after all, and it didn't matter if she had treated me like dirt. I kept telling myself she was not responsible.

The next morning, after a halfway sleepless night, I fixed a grapefruit for breakfast and downed a cup of coffee and a cinnamon roll, one left over from the funeral. The sun was out today. I peeked out the kitchen curtains and saw the heavy flow of traffic in the work rush. Perhaps soon I would be in that rat race again, commuting to some office job, or perhaps working in a retail shop like before. My job at the book store had been all right, and although it hadn't paid much, I had enjoyed the people I met and especially liked browsing through the aisles of books.

At the book store is where I had met Sean Kimble. He had come in several times and seemed to linger around the organic farming books. About the third time he was there, we began talking, and I found out he worked as a salesman for the farm supply store in Great Bend. He was interested in agriculture and wanted to have his own farm and raise organic food. Sean was lean and somewhat tall, with a narrow nose, and hair so blond it was white. It wasn't long before he found out I was available and we began dating.

I was living in my own apartment at the time. After high school, I tried attending college. I had always been interested in plants and animals, and wanted to major in wildlife biology. I hoped to one day get a job working outdoors. I had never had the opportunity to enjoy the outdoors really, but somehow it appealed to me. But I found the science classes too challenging, and instead of applying myself and studying harder to make it, I quit school and went to work in the office of the Division of Wildlife. I worked about a year, and then budget cuts occurred and I had to find another job. The book store hired me right away.

Sean asked me to marry him after we'd been dating a few months. It was shortly after that when Sean had an argument with his boss and quit his job at the farm store. I was shocked when he told me he had signed up to join the Marine Corps. His argument was that he needed money to buy the farm and fulfill his life-long dream. He was willing to sacrifice a few years of his life for his country in exchange for getting something in return.

I pleaded with him not to go. We'd find another way to raise the money. But he wouldn't listen. Shortly after he went to boot camp, Sean was deployed and sent to the Middle East to fight. He was there a total of seven months, and then he lost his life in Iraq.

I was devastated. It was right at that time when my mother asked me to come home and take care of her. Rather than go to a nursing home, she wanted me to stay with her. I know my mother was frightened to death of what would happen to her, and I was in such turmoil over Sean's death that I would grasp at anything. The diversion seemed to be a reprieve.

Mike Rollins had been a family friend for many years. His parents were prominent members of the community and had been good friends to my mother. She and Mike's mother had become close during their volunteer work at the hospital. Mamie Rollins was active in the League of Women Voters, and always tried to get Mother to come to the meet-the-candidate nights. Mike's father was Mother's physician. Dr. Rollins had always been gentle and patient, coaching me on what to expect next with Mother's condition. They had sent Mike off to college to be an accountant, and now he had his own business and was doing very well for himself.

I noticed that Mike made himself available to us quite often in the past year. If we ever needed anything, he was quick to come over and help solve the problem, whether it was fixing a leaky faucet or changing a yard light. During the big snow-storm that hit us in November, Mike had arrived with his snow blower and cleared our walks.

Mother doted on him and I often got the feeling she treated him as though he were the son she'd never had. He was the one who discussed her finances and helped get her affairs in order before her mental state deteriorated. She would get into fights with me and then call Mike the next day to rewrite her will. I always assumed he came over just to humor her, and he assured me nothing was changed. But at some point they had managed to name Mike as Mother's executor.

I finished my coffee and cleared the dishes into the sink. After I got dressed, I walked into the room in which my mother had spent her last weeks. It had been too difficult for her to climb stairs, so we had fixed up a small room off the living area with a hospital bed and television. I cleared some of the reading material from her bedside tray, then decided to go through the desk. The rolltop oak piece of furniture had been one of her favorites, where she used to sit and write her bills and correspondence.

I rifled through one of the drawers and found stationery, blank envelopes, a set of felt tip pens and a small address book. There was a collection of bank statements, receipts and postcards she had saved over the years. In the next drawer I found a bundle of old letters tied together with a piece of blue yarn. A small box with a lid contained a stash of old photographs. I lifted the box out of the drawer and sat in her rocker to see what it contained.

There were some old pictures of relatives. I recognized my mother in a couple of them. She had kept a picture of this house as it was when she had first bought it twenty-two years ago. That had been right after my father died. I smiled at the cute snapshot of our dog, Porgy, a cream-colored cockerpoo we had when I was young. When Porgy ran out in the street one afternoon and got hit by a car, Mother put her foot down and said we would have no more pets.

I sighed, sad now that she had been so stubborn and not let me have an animal to raise. I had always envied my school friends who had dogs and cats. Even a caged bird would have been a companion to a lonely girl without siblings or a dad.

Then my eyes fell on a photograph of two men standing over a deer. They were dressed in outdoor clothes, heavy jackets, boots and stocking caps. One of the men cradled a rifle in his arms as he admired a beautiful buck that had been propped up to make it look as though it were still alive. I immediately turned the picture over and saw the writing on the back side, which read, "Fred and Nathaniel, Majestic Mountain, Colorado."

Flipping the picture over again, I studied the faces of the two men. The one holding the rifle was my father, Nathaniel Sutton, and the other man had to be his brother, my Uncle Fred. I knew that Dad had a brother who lived in Colorado. I didn't know much about him because Mother refused to talk about any of the relatives on my father's side. I also knew that something tragic had happened, resulting in my father's death twenty-two years ago. I had been only five at the time. There had been some kind of hunting accident, and Mother had told me Uncle Fred was to blame. Whenever I would bring up the subject, she would dismiss it immediately and scold me.

"Juniper, some things are just better left alone," she would say. She had brought me up with the idea that hunting was a shameful pastime and all hunters were ruthless killers. This prejudice had been instilled in me, and yet my views had been challenged when Sean confessed to me that he enjoyed hunting and always looked forward to deer season in the fall.

Studying the faces closely, I saw the resemblance of the brothers. My father had been a man of medium height, with reddish-brown hair and a mustache, green eyes and a cheery face that was round and flushed much of the time. My early memories of him included a happy-go-lucky man who laughed a lot and enjoyed life. He had always loved the outdoors. Uncle Fred looked older, with a stern face and a beard. I could tell he was proud of my father's trophy in this photo.

I set the photograph on my lap and stared at the mirror on the wall beside me. My own long hair was light-colored with a tinge of red, kind of frizzy and thick, which I usually kept pulled back, ponytail fashion. My bangs were parted to one side, emphasizing my slender face. My eyebrows were naturally light and finely arched. My green eyes had the same sparkle in them as my father's had, and my high cheek bones had long ago lost the faint freckles I had detested in my childhood.

I went through the rest of the photographs, and then started to replace the box. Before I set it back in the drawer, I pulled out the picture of my father, my uncle and the deer, and decided to hold onto it. I knew that my parents had lived during their first years of marriage in Colorado Springs where I had been born. So, naturally, I was interested in Colorado. I knew they had chosen the name Juniper for me because of my father's favorite tree, which grew in the high country near one of the places he liked to hunt.

A loud knock on the door jarred me from my reminiscence. I placed the photo on top of the desk as I went to answer it. Mike stood outside, dressed in black slacks and a white short-sleeved shirt with a paisley tie.

"You didn't answer your phone," he told me. I couldn't tell if he sounded annoyed with me or was just mocking.

"Come on in, Mike. I turned the ringer down last night. I guess I forgot to turn it back on." I immediately went to the telephone in the hallway and turned the ringer back on.

Mike followed me in. "I was just on my way over to pick up a set of books and thought I'd drop by and see how you're doing."

I sighed. "I was just going through some of my mother's things."

He turned toward the den. "Oh? Anything of interest?"

I folded my arms. "Not really. Just some old photographs."

"Want to get a bite of supper with me later?" he asked. "We can discuss what's in the will."

My resistance flared up again. I rolled my eyes. "Well ..."

Mike started toward the door. "I've gotta go. I'll come by after work ... sometime around six. How does Wild Bill's Buffet sound?"

I stared at him with my mouth open. "But ..."

"See you at six, Juniper." Mike was already out the door, headed toward his car. I stood there with my arms still folded, thinking ... *Wild Bill's Buffet?* How were we going to discuss Mother's will in a place like that?

Later on, I heard the mailman drop the mail off and went to the door to get it. There was the usual selection of bills, advertisements and a couple of letters addressed to me that appeared to be sympathy cards. One was from the Petersons, some friends of the family that lived over in the next county. The other one was in a pink envelope with a rainbow printed across the back of it. A white return address label had been stuck over the rainbow that said it was from Rosalee Sutton. There was a post office box number and then Wade City, Colorado.

Who was Rosalee Sutton? And where was Wade City? I carried the mail to the kitchen, where I had been in the middle of preparing myself a salad for lunch. I quickly opened the envelope from the Petersons, and sure enough, it was a card expressing their deepest sympathy. Then I sat down and stared once again at the pink envelope with the rainbow on the back. The slanted handwriting, very legible, piqued my interest. It was addressed to Miss Juniper Sutton. I carefully slit it open and pulled out a letter on white linen stationery that had been imprinted with a huge rainbow across the front. The same handwriting from the outside of the envelope filled the page.

Dear Juniper,

My condolences to you upon the recent loss of your mother. Although Margaret drifted away from us, I remember she was a kind woman and carried a lot of love and devotion for her family. Both her memory and that of your father will live on in my heart forever.

Of course, none of us really dies, and I perceive a warm reception for Margaret in the hereafter, and a happy reunion with Nathaniel. I hope you will be able to get past this difficult period of sorrow. A year ago, your uncle made his transition, so I have also shared a loss.

I have a request. I would like you to come to Majestic Mountain as soon as you can. I need someone to work in my gift shop at the lodge. You are welcome to stay here as long as you'd like. I believe this will be a good opportunity for us to get to know one another, and it will certainly be a chance for you to get a fresh perspective on your life.

There is also a matter of urgency I need to discuss with you. Forgive me for not being able to disclose any details at this time.

Looking forward to your arrival.

Love and Light,
Aunt Rosalee

I vaguely recalled that Uncle Fred had been married, but I was quite sure Mother had mentioned that his wife had left him. So who was Rosalee? This woman had signed her name as my aunt. She had obviously known my mother, whom she had mentioned by name. And what was this matter of urgency that Rosalee needed to discuss with me?

I read through the letter a second time, then folded it back up and returned it to its envelope. How could someone I didn't even know expect me to drop everything and go to Colorado? True, there really wasn't anything holding me here in Kansas.

For a moment, I toyed with the temptation of taking the car and driving to Colorado. My own little compact car that I'd driven in college was no longer trustworthy. I wouldn't dare take it outside Great Bend with the transmission in such poor shape. I had used my mother's Grand Marquis to run errands and go places over the past two years. It might make a trip to the mountains, but it was a gas hog and needed new tires.

"What am I doing even considering this?" I chided myself.

Placing the pink envelope on the desk beside the photo of my father and Uncle Fred, I hesitated, then reached for the picture and studied it again. The letter had mentioned that my uncle had died a year ago. How sad that I would never meet him. Perhaps Aunt Rosalee could tell me about him and about my father. Perhaps it would help fill the void in my mind and my heart.

There had to be a reason why Mother kept the truth from me. Maybe finding out about the past would help me find my future.

2

Mike was true to his word and picked me up at six o'clock. It was the busy hour at Wild Bill's, so we waited in line and then ordered our steaks before shuffling through the crowd of buffet lovers. This was Mike's idea of eating out—not mine. I would have preferred a quiet restaurant with a more relaxing atmosphere.

"Great food," Mike commented, once we were seated.

I tasted my salad, rather annoyed with the noise, and tried to ignore the distractions. "We should have gotten carry-out," I remarked. We sat at a booth next to a family with two small children. The toddler boy wiggled and twisted between his parents, more interested in his surroundings than his meal. The little girl sat in a high chair and fussed, shaking her curls and refusing the finger foods offered to her.

Mike dug into his steak and baked potato, then looked at me through his thick glasses. "You're right. I should have thought of that." He bit into one of his three dinner rolls, then wiped his mouth with a napkin. "We could have made the evening a nice and cozy one at your house."

His words startled me and I stared at him, the fork halfway to my mouth. *Cozy?* Was Mike joking? He kept his attention on feeding his face, so I quickly made up my mind he must have been kidding. At least I hoped he was.

When we had finished our meal, Mike looked over at the dessert counter, then turned to me and said, "I think I'll have some of that banana cream pie. How about you?"

I shook my head. "No, I'm full."

"Are you sure, Juniper?"

"No, thanks, I ate too much as it is." I reached for my iced tea glass, which was half empty.

Mike was back a few minutes later with the banana cream pie and a plate of chocolate cake.

"A great selection of desserts tonight," he managed to say

in between bites. "I really like coming here."

I kept my opinion to myself.

Mike surprised me by saying, "Let's talk about the will. I'm going down to the courthouse Monday and I'll open the estate. You shouldn't have anything to worry about. I'll take care of all the details."

My nerves tightened and I clutched the cold glass in my hands. "What details?" I asked.

Mike bit into his cake. "Oh, you know ... for one thing, we'll have to transfer your mother's funds into an estate account at the bank. If you come across any papers pertaining to CDs or special savings she might have had, I want you to let me know."

"And whose name will be on this new bank account?" I challenged.

"Well, Juniper, I am the executor. I have to do it, according to law."

"But what about the bills? The utilities? My groceries?" It was so noisy in the restaurant, I had to raise my voice.

Mike waved his hand at me. "Don't worry about a thing, kid. I'll take care of you."

I felt the heat start to rise in my cheeks. My heart pounded with humiliation. "What does that mean ... you'll take care of me?"

"Just what I said." Mike cocked his head and attempted a smile. "That's been the plan all along. I'll take care of you."

This was not what I had hoped for. "Mike," I said, "I think I'm perfectly capable of taking care of myself."

He shook his head, still eating cake and now licking chocolate frosting off his large, stubby fingers. "You don't get it," he said, "do you?"

I sighed in frustration as I set my iced tea glass on the table.

"Juniper, I'm going to marry you," he said casually.

"You're *what?*" My voice must have exploded above all the noise because several people turned to stare.

Mike grinned and there were chocolate cake crumbs on his teeth. "Margaret made me promise I'd take care of you for the rest of my life. And that's what I intend to do. Juniper, don't you see? You have nothing to worry about."

I was trembling and my face felt flushed. I had everything to worry about. The last thing I wanted to do was end up in

Great Bend, Kansas, for the rest of my life, married to Mike Rollins. "I think we should go," I suggested, and dug in my purse for my tube of lipstick.

"Sure, just as soon as I finish my pie."

"I'm going to the lady's room." I stood up and marched off, unable to stand another minute.

Mike had left the tip by the time I came out. We headed outside to his minivan. I couldn't believe how laid back he was after proposing marriage to me in Wild Bill's Buffet. I sat in silence as he drove back to my house. To fill the void, he switched on loud country western music from his CD player. All the way home I stared out the window. When we arrived, I opened the door and got out.

"Juniper, wait ... I'll come in with you."

Before I could protest, Mike jumped out of the car and accompanied me to the front door. It was still daylight and a neighbor girl was walking her dog on the sidewalk. I unlocked the door and Mike followed me in.

"Why aren't you talking?" asked Mike as I put away my purse and checked the answering machine. There was one message flashing, but I didn't want to listen to it with Mike there. I turned to him and saw the flustered look on his square face. He really did believe he was going to get his way, I realized.

"Oh, Mike, it's just that ... that ..." I turned away, then faced him anew, determined to be forthright. "How can I possibly marry you? I mean ... we never ... I don't ..."

Mike stepped in front of me so quickly, I almost jumped. He grabbed my shoulders and then planted a kiss on my lips. I was so shocked, I pulled away and gasped.

"Now we've kissed each other," he said as if that act alone made everything right. "Don't you think it will work, Juniper?"

What more would he pull, trying to convince me to marry him? I wiped the moistness off my mouth. "I need to be alone right now, Mike. I need to think this over. I mean, you've really pulled the floor out from under me."

I expected him to argue, to plead, to try once again to persuade me with his insane logic. But for once, he seemed to realize he'd possibly gone a step too far and he backed off.

"I'm really sorry, Juniper. Of course I understand you need some time to think about this. I'll leave and give you your space." He started toward the door, then stopped and glanced at the telephone. "You've got a phone message."

"Yes, I know."

When I didn't make a move to turn on the machine, Mike continued out the door. "Well, okay then. I'll call you tomorrow morning. Good night, Juniper."

"Good night." I closed the door after him, then quickly locked it.

Suddenly, I felt like crying. Anger, mixed with grief and self pity, surged and forced me to surrender myself to the living room couch for a half-hour sob session. I had actually done little weeping since Mother's death. My feelings came to the surface now in a delayed reaction. Whenever I thought of living my life as Mike's wife, with him taking over the decisions and finances, I fell into a new series of sobs. And to picture myself sharing my bed with him ... it was just too appalling.

For one thing, I didn't love Mike. I still loved Sean, and Sean was dead. I wasn't even sure I could ever love another man. No one had appealed to me in these past two years, although it was true I had kept myself busy caring for a sick woman. I had forced such ideas out of my mind.

Now that I thought about it, I recalled instances where my mother had encouraged a relationship with Mike Rollins. I had always shrugged it off and she hadn't pressed, but Mike must have talked it over with her. He had said he had made a promise to her, to take care of me the rest of my life.

Well, I didn't need anyone to take care of me. Or did I? I shuddered as I looked around at the walls with their peeling wallpaper and the old carpeting and furniture. What was I going to do? Stay here and fix the place up? I'd most likely be looking for a job, and like before, perhaps I'd meet someone. I only knew one thing: I *wasn't* going to marry Mike.

It was dark by the time I pulled myself together and rose to go into the kitchen. I turned on a lamp and noticed the blinking light from the answering machine as I strolled past. I prepared a cup of hot tea for myself first, then stepped back into the hallway and played the message.

"Juniper?" It was a woman's thick-sounding voice. "I was hopin' to catch you home, darlin'." There was a trace of a Southern drawl in the woman's voice. "This is Rosalee Sutton ...

your aunt. Did you get my letter? Well, anyway, I've made arrangements for you to fly into Colorado Springs next Tuesday, if you can get away by then." There was a pause, then she said, "You can call me back, or I'll try and reach you again tomorrow." She quickly left the phone number and then the message ended with a click.

I didn't erase the message right away. I might want to listen to it again. Did everyone think they should run my life and make arrangements without consulting me first? Aunt Rosalee had a lot of nerve telling me I was flying into Colorado Springs next Tuesday. I didn't even know this woman. Yet, at the same time, there was some quality in her voice, some down-home softness that touched me. I wanted to get to know her. I really wanted to go to Colorado and see what this was all about.

As I drank my tea, I thought about the predicament I was in. If I stayed, I would have to deal with Mike and his ridiculous idea of marrying me. Aunt Rosalee offered an escape from the immediate dilemma. It didn't mean I had to stay and work for her at her lodge as she had proposed in her letter. What had she said? She needed me to work in her gift shop? What kind of a lodge did she run? A ski lodge? And why would a lodge for skiing be open in the summertime? I couldn't help but grow more curious, the more I thought about getting on that jet and going to the mountains.

When the telephone rang, I set the tea cup down and hurried to the phone. If it was Aunt Rosalee again, I wanted to talk to her, to find out more about her offer. I picked up the receiver. "Hello?"

"It's me, Juniper." It was Mike. "I couldn't wait until morning. I had to talk to you tonight before you went to bed."

My heart started to thump, but more from dread than anything. "Yes, Mike, what is it?"

"I'm such a dolt," he said. "You've got to forgive me for bringing up the plan the way I did. I forgot that women like to be charmed. I guess I'm not one for romance."

I sighed in protest. "Mike ..."

"Anyway, I really wanted to clear that up with you. I couldn't stand the thought of you being upset with me."

"I'm not upset with you," I lied.

"Well, good. I'm glad to hear that, Juniper."

"Mike, it's late and I'm tired. Let's talk about all this another time, okay?"

"Why can't we talk about it now?"

"I just said ... Look, I've got to make a phone call. I'd appreciate it if you'd ..."

"Who are you calling?"

Annoyed, I wished I had the guts to slam the phone down, but I hated when someone did that to me. "It's no one you know," I said.

"Oh ..." Mike sounded wary. "It's not another guy, is it?"

"No."

"Who, then?"

"Really, Mike, that's none of your business."

There was silence on the other end. I don't think he'd expected I would say something like that. Finally, he sighed and said, "Okay, okay ... I'll call you in the morning."

After we disconnected, I listened once more to the message on my machine and jotted down the phone number Aunt Rosalee had left. Then I dialed the number with trembling fingers. Mike had managed to rile me once more.

"Rainbow Majestic," a soothing female voice said after the third ring. "How may I help you?"

"Uh ..." I had expected Aunt Rosalee to answer, but this was obviously the desk clerk at the lodge. "Is ... Is Rosalee Sutton there?"

"Who may I say is calling?" In the background I could hear some beautiful, calming music that sounded like harps and flutes.

"This is Juniper Sutton, her niece," I said into the phone.

There was a momentary silence on the other end, and then the woman said, "Just a minute. I'll get her."

I was put on hold and the music changed to something light and classical. Half a minute passed before someone picked up. Then I heard Aunt Rosalee's low voice say, "Hello."

"Aunt Rosalee?"

"Juniper, so nice of you to return my call. You must have received my letter by now."

"Yes, and I'd like to know what all this is about," I said.

She ignored my remark. "Can you get to Dodge City early Tuesday morning? Your flight leaves at 9:20 A.M."

"Dodge City? Sure ... sure, I can drive there."

Aunt Rosalee wasn't going to take no for an answer—that was clear. "Good," she said. "I'll send Wes to meet you when you get into Colorado Springs."

"But, Aunt Rosalee ... what should I bring? What kind of weather is it there?"

She laughed. "Oh, girl, we get all kinds of weather here at Majestic Mountain. You'd better bring somethin' warm."

"I thought you lived in Wade City."

"No," she replied. "That's the closest town—about eighteen miles away. We live at nine thousand feet. This time of year we still get freezes at night." Then she added, "Don't pack too much. If you decide to stay, we can go clothes shoppin'."

"What about my ticket?"

Aunt Rosalee explained that I had an electronic ticket. All I had to do was show up with my picture I.D. She gave me all the flight information and then thanked me again for calling her back. "I'll look forward to seein' you at the Rainbow Majestic Tuesday night," she said. "I just know you're gonna love it here, just like your father did."

I wanted to ask more questions, but she was being summoned at the other end and had to go. After a quick good-bye, she hung up.

That night I went to bed and lay awake for some time, pondering the trip and trying to imagine what the mountains must be like in Colorado in June. I wasn't even sure where Majestic Mountain was in Colorado—or Wade City, for that matter. I made it a point to look up their location on the atlas in the morning.

3

"**Y**ou're going *where?*" Mike's voice boomed into the telephone the next morning. He had called me from work while I lingered over a cup of coffee at the kitchen table. I had already guessed his reaction to my news.

"Colorado," I repeated.

"Where in Colorado?"

"The mountains. I'm going to visit my aunt who lives near Wade City," I told him.

"Juniper, what are you doing?" His condescending tone irritated me and my defenses rose.

"I think I deserve a little vacation," I told him. "In case you haven't noticed, the last few months have not been exactly fun for me. After all this time, never getting to go anywhere, I have an opportunity to see some place *other* than Kansas."

If Mike took offense to that, he didn't let on. After a pause, he said, "Well, okay, I guess you're right. You have had a pretty rough haul." He grumbled something, but I didn't catch it.

"Mike, I hope you'll be generous enough to withdraw some cash for me out of Mother's account to take along," I said.

"Well, just how much are you going to need? I thought you told me your ticket's paid for."

"I need to put gas in the car," I began, "and ..."

"I'll drive you," Mike offered. "That way you won't have to spend money on parking at the airport. It's highway robbery, you know."

Oh great, I thought. I really didn't want Mike driving me to the airport, especially all the way to Dodge City. But I didn't know how to decline his offer without making him more controlling. "Fine," I said. "I have to be there at seven A.M."

"That early! We'll have to leave here at four A.M."

"Then I'll drive myself," I insisted.

"No, I'll take you. When is your return flight?"

I then realized that Aunt Rosalee hadn't mentioned a

return flight, but I didn't want Mike to find out. I told him I'd forgotten for the moment and would let him know later. Then I begged him again to let me have some travel money, all the while seething inside because Mother wanted to punish me for some imagined transgression by making Mike executor.

Tuesday morning, before dawn, I was headed south in Mike's minivan. I could tell he didn't share my enthusiasm. I tried not to show how excited I was and eager to get away from Great Bend. We spoke little and when we reached the airport three hours later, he offered to accompany me in, but I shook my head.

"No need for that," I told him. "I'm a big girl. I think I can manage." He pulled into the drive for ten-minute unloading and parked, then helped me get my suitcases out of the van.

"How can I get in touch with you?" Mike asked. "Suppose there's a question about the estate?"

I promised I'd call him after I got to the lodge. I really didn't want him to have the number, for fear he'd be calling all the time and pestering me. On the other hand, I realized it was important for someone to have my contact information.

"Have a safe trip," he said.

I slung my purse over my shoulder and picked up the two suitcases, then turned to smile at Mike. "Thanks for bringing me."

He stood there, just staring. I figured he was waiting for a goodbye kiss. But before anything like that could happen, I turned and walked rapidly toward the terminal. "Bye, Mike," I called to him over my shoulder.

"*Call* me, Juniper ... don't forget."

When I was inside the terminal, I sighed with relief, then proceeded to check in. After I'd checked my bags and gone through security, I decided to hang out in the coffee shop and eat a bagel. It was still an hour and a half before my flight. Fortunately, I'd brought some reading material along. I found my gate well in advance, took a seat, and dozed off and on. Shortly before nine o'clock, my flight was announced. A couple of minutes later, the voice on the loudspeaker called for passengers to board. I produced my pass and followed others in a line into the boarding corridor. It was a bright, sunny day with little wind, and promised to be a fine day for traveling. Not having flown for a number of years, this was an adventure for me. Just getting out of Great Bend was reason enough for exuberance.

I found my seat and made myself comfortable. I wondered what I would find when I reached Colorado Springs. Aunt Rosalee had mentioned she was sending someone—a man—to meet me. I assumed he would drive me to wherever the lodge was. I wondered how far Wade City was from Colorado Springs and how long it would take us to reach Majestic Mountain.

Soon we were in flight. I had the window seat, so had watched everything outside during take-off. I watched the patches of color in the Kansas fields below, in various rectangular shapes and hues. The fields disappeared after we climbed to a height above the clouds. Now the blue sky was a sea of infinity and the white, choppy cloud cover below us reminded me of a cotton world, a land for angels, perhaps.

I mused about my father. Aunt Rosalee had hinted on the phone that my father had loved the Majestic Mountain area. How well had she known him, and why had my mother not mentioned Aunt Rosalee's name in all these years? I couldn't help thinking there was some mystery surrounding my father and his death in the mountains.

I wished I had more vivid memories of him. I knew Mother had loved him, but she hadn't done much to keep his memory alive where I was concerned. She always managed to steer the conversation away when it got close to my father's love of hunting, as though discussion in that direction might cause her to slip and say something she didn't want me to know.

I recalled the paragraph in Aunt Rosalee's letter to me that talked about death. She had said no one really dies. What had she meant by that? And why had she talked about a warm reception in the hereafter for my mother, and a happy reunion with Nathaniel, my father? Her language seemed very strange to me. I wasn't used to people talking about death in those terms. How could she say no one dies? Obviously, both my parents were dead.

As for a hereafter, that was something I had always accepted as a myth. Even though I'd been raised in the Presbyterian faith and been taught about heaven and hell, my logical mind questioned the validity of such places. I shied away from sermons that preached hell and damnation. When the minister started ranting about fire and brimstone, quoting Bible passages, I found myself shutting down mentally and drifting off toward something I preferred to think about.

There had been many sermons in church when I had simply sat there, behaving as I should and looking attentive, yet my mind was off on a trek in a forest somewhere, looking for wildflowers or checking for animal tracks in fresh mud. One day I hoped I could live in a woods like that, where I had all those wild things at my disposal and could study them and get to know them.

A recurring dream that continued to haunt me involved a small log cabin. I had dreamed often about that log cabin in the woods, where I might have lived, and then ... the fantasy always ended there. I could never open the door and actually go inside my dream cabin. There was some kind of mental block every time I thought about it. When I daydreamed about my cabin in church—and if the sermon was still going on—I'd simply imagine myself taking another path in the woods, perhaps finding a cold, bubbling brook to poke my bare feet into, or a patch of wild raspberries that needed picking.

The other thing that puzzled me about Aunt Rosalee's letter was how she had signed it: *Love and Light*. It sounded so new-agey. I wondered why she had signed her letter to me like that and what she had meant by it. What was she going to be like, anyway? She had sounded like a genuine, down-to-earth person over the telephone. I could only hope that the time I spent at Majestic Mountain was going to be of some benefit. Just getting away from Mike and the immediate events, I suspected, would help.

Before I knew it, we began to descend and, through a smoggy sky of blue and wisps of brown pollution, I caught my first glimpse of the distant mountains. The jet circled a bit and then the pilot announced that we were landing in Colorado Springs. The temperature was a pleasant 76 degrees and the wind was out of the southwest at five miles per hour. It was also an hour earlier than what my watch said. We zeroed in, then the jet touched down with a series of slight bumps. The brakes squealed and I felt the force of the craft decelerating from a great speed.

I couldn't help it, my heart started thumping with anticipation. I had no idea how I was going to find Aunt Rosalee's driver, but if no one was there to claim me, I could always call her from the pay phone. I followed the other passengers as they slowly shuffled out, hampered by those who had to retrieve their carry-on bags from the compartments above the seats.

When I stepped into the terminal, I searched the crowd of people. In the background someone held up a cardboard sign with big printed letters on it that spelled JUNIPER. I knew that was my contact. There probably weren't that many people named Juniper, even in the state of Colorado.

I wove my way through the people toward the sign and stopped in front of a man in his early thirties, tall and lanky, with thick blond hair and blue eyes. I was struck by his good looks and startled by how much he reminded me of Sean.

He managed a shy smile, then said, "Welcome to Colorado, Miss Sutton." His casual attire consisted of blue jeans and a white T-shirt with some small green lettering on it. The words read: GO WITHIN.

My heart was racing. It took a few seconds for me to recover. "You must be the driver Aunt Rosalee sent to pick me up." I extended my right hand.

He shook it, then said, "I'm Wes Andrews." His voice was as soft as his manner, and he gazed around. "I suppose we should head for the baggage claim." I noticed a trace of a drawl in his speech.

We had only a short ways to walk. The Colorado Springs airport was not huge. Wes kept glancing at me. To cover my nervousness, I made small talk until we got to the baggage claim area.

"I guess you must work for my aunt," I said.

"Yes, ma'am."

"What do you do?"

Wes told me he had a lot of different duties at the lodge. "Mainly I'm a gopher," he said with a smile. "You know ... go for this, go for that ... Today I'm a chauffeur. Mostly I do work on the grounds at the Rainbow Majestic. Landscaping and that sort of thing."

"You're a groundskeeper then?"

"I s'pose you could say that."

"What's it like there?" I asked.

Wes's blue eyes seemed to light up. "Oh, the Rainbow is incredible. It's in such a beautiful, pristine area. Majestic Mountain is just behind the lodge, and there are awesome views in every direction."

"I can't wait to see it."

He led me over to a small crowd. "Looks like the bags are comin' through now."

"Yes, I'd better pay attention." I watched for my luggage and when I spotted my bags, I pulled them off the circulating ramp.

Wes immediately took them from me. Then he led the way out of the terminal. Once we were out in the sunshine, he stopped on the sidewalk near the exit and looked around. I wondered if he was trying to remember where he had parked his vehicle. Then he set the suitcases down and reached into a tiny brown pouch that hung from his belt. I watched him pull out and open up a cell phone.

"Excuse me one minute, Miss Sutton." Wes punched a couple of buttons on the cell and, a moment later, he said, "Drake ... Wes here. Where are you?" There was a pause, then he said, "Yeah, she's here. We're just outside the baggage claim area. Okay. See you in a few." He closed up the phone, then replaced it in his belt pouch. He shrugged apologetically. "Sorry. Drake'll be here directly. He had to run some errands for Rosalee. He took the SUV to town while I waited here for your plane to come in."

I smiled, but wondered who Drake was. Then Wes directed me over to a bench near the building. "Might as well have a seat, Miss Sutton."

"Please ... call me Juniper," I insisted.

"Okay." Wes smiled and sat next to me on the bench. He folded his arms and closed his eyes. I figured he must be tired and was trying to doze, so I waited in silence.

Ten minutes passed. Finally, a tan SUV pulled up to the curb in front of us. The man at the wheel got out and came toward us. His tall, muscular build was enhanced by long brown hair and a beard. My first impression was of a mountain man. I guessed he might be in his forties. Faded blue jeans clung to his long legs and he wore a navy blue, short-sleeved T-shirt with pockets. Right away I noticed his deep-colored blue eyes as they fell on mine. It seemed our eyes locked upon each other for several seconds. He studied me for a long moment without saying a word, then placed his hands on his hips. I noticed a striking familiarity about him that seized me, yet I couldn't remember ever having seen or met this man before.

Finally, he tore his gaze away from me. "Wes ..." he called, turning to the man seated beside me.

Wes opened his eyes, lowered his arms and expelled a long, slow breath. "Wow ... I was really out there." He rubbed an eye, then turned to me. "He's here now."

"I know." I stood up and again met the searching look in Drake's eyes as he reached forward and grabbed my two suitcases. It seemed he couldn't stop staring at me.

"Juniper, this is Drake Phillips," said Wes as he got to his feet.

"Miss Sutton ..." Drake nodded at me without smiling.

"My name is Juniper," I emphasized and followed them to the tan SUV.

Drake opened the back and shoved my suitcases in beside some other boxes. Wes opened the passenger door for me. I glanced back at Drake, to see if he preferred to ride up front, but he signaled at me to get in beside Wes.

I climbed in and Wes got into the driver's seat. Then Drake got into the back seat directly behind me.

"Get your supplies?" asked Wes.

"Most of 'em," said Drake.

Wes pulled out from the curb and headed for the airport exit.

"Do you work at the lodge too?" I tried to swing around and face Drake, but my seat belt was tight, so I couldn't look at him.

"Drake's one of the lodge managers," Wes explained.

"Oh? You run it?" I asked.

"I'm in charge of maintenance," grumbled the man behind me.

"He's just being modest," Wes explained. "Whenever somethin' breaks down, Drake's right there to fix it ... always." When Drake did not volunteer any information, Wes went on. "Rosalee counts on Drake to keep on top of everythin'."

Drake cleared his throat as if in protest. Out of the corner of my eye I caught a flicker of a smile cross Wes's face.

The two men conversed about some parts and tools Drake had obtained. I focused my attention on the gorgeous scenery as we passed grassy hayfields and grazing cattle. I could see the distant mountains against the backdrop of a brilliant blue sky with a few clusters of white puffy clouds. The air felt dry and soothing. Outside I had noticed the warm intensity of the sun against my face and bare arms.

"Did you have lunch?" Wes asked me a while later.

"Actually, no."

"We'd better find a place to stop and eat at," Drake said. "Rosalee said to be sure she ate."

"Are you hungry?" Wes asked me.

"Not really," I told him. "Not yet, anyway."

We drove half an hour longer and then Wes stopped at a little roadside café. By then I was hungry and ordered a BLT and a glass of iced raspberry tea. Drake ordered a meat loaf sandwich and coffee, while Wes found a vegetarian sub on the menu.

"Don't you eat meat?" I asked out of curiosity.

"No, I'm a vegetarian."

Drake snorted. "Not me." He bit a large chunk off his meat loaf sandwich.

Later on, while Drake was paying the ticket on our way out, I asked Wes, "What did you mean back at the airport when you mentioned you were *really out there?*"

Wes studied me as if he wasn't sure I would understand, then said casually, "I was meditating."

"Oh … I thought you were asleep."

He looked at me again, but only smiled.

"Let's get going," Drake called to us. He held the door open for me as I walked out. I felt myself tremble involuntarily. I was beginning to wonder just what it was about Drake Phillips that had me stirred up.

I found out the trip to Majestic Mountain would take five hours. We got on the interstate and drove north, then west into the foothills and up into the mountains. I was captivated by the beauty of them, still topped with some snow at this time of year. We drove through Eisenhower Tunnel and I felt chills. Several times I caught the eyes of these two men studying me and realized they must be curious about their boss's niece.

"Tell me about yourselves," I prompted at one point. "Wes, you start."

"What do you want to know?" He settled back in his seat and maneuvered the steering wheel with his right hand. He appeared at ease and undisturbed by the traffic on the interstate, which was heavy.

"Well, for one thing," I said, "your accent tells me you're from the South."

"He's from Oklahoma," Drake called out behind me.

I turned to face the man behind me, who leaned forward so I could see him better. "And where are *you* from?" I asked.

"I'm from Neptune." Drake stared at me, to see how I would react.

I didn't know what to say. I realized he was playing with me and I wished I could think of something to befuddle him the way he had me. But I was once again drawn in by those deep blue eyes of his and their penetrating darkness. My mind went completely blank.

Finally, the spell broke and I looked over at Wes. "Where in Oklahoma?"

Wes told about his life as we drove over Vail Pass. He'd lived in Tulsa and gone to college there. Later, he'd joined the Marine Corps and spent a couple of years in the Middle East during the Gulf War.

My heart thumped as his past brought the painful memory of Sean sharply into focus. Sean had joined the Marines and been sent to the Middle East too, and where Wes had survived his ordeal and returned home, Sean had not.

"Are you all right, Juniper?" Wes distracted me from my dire thoughts. "Do you wanna stop somewhere for a break?"

I recovered with a shake of my head. "No, no, I'm fine. It's just that ... that ..." I almost mentioned the reason why I was upset, but instead I shrugged it off the best I could. A lump clung to my throat for several minutes.

"That's enough about me." Wes seemed perceptive toward my reaction to his story. "Now Drake will fill you in on his life."

"There's nothing to tell that would interest anybody here," said Drake in a grudging manner. "As a matter of fact, I'd much rather hear about Juniper."

Wes brightened and smiled at me. "Go ahead. Tell us, Juniper."

"Actually," I said, "I haven't had that exciting a life, you know, living in Kansas ..."

"Hey, Kansas is a good state," proclaimed Drake. "I like Kansas."

Wes shrugged. "Aw ... Kansas is all right, I s'pose. But it's not like Oklahoma."

What followed was a debate about the two states, a discussion with which I purposely kept my opinions to myself. We drove for a long while before it was time to stop again for a break. Drake offered to take the wheel, but Wes declined, insisting he was fine and, besides, we'd be there before long, he said.

No more was mentioned about my background, which was fine with me. I didn't feel like talking about Sean or my mother to these strangers, although both of them seemed open and friendly. Wes was quiet and more subdued, while Drake had a spontaneous, daring side to him. I expected him to be arrogant, but Drake was simply a mystery to me. I kept feeling I'd known him before. The way he looked at me sometimes was a bit over-whelming. I'd quickly have to glance away.

Nothing could have prepared me for what met us at the end of our journey. Once we had traveled over the last mountain pass, with its stately aspen forests on both sides just starting to bud out, we descended into a long, narrow valley, and the mountain vistas surrounding this paradise left me in awe. I was hardly aware of the casual conversation going on between the two men in the car, so engrossed was I in the surroundings.

"That's Wade City to the south," Wes announced as he turned and took a road that headed away from my aunt's town. "But we're not goin' there today." The road we were on was paved to begin with, and wound around hills of sage, pinion and juniper.

"You'll see it one day, though," Drake promised.

Several miles farther, we had climbed higher and passed through forests of oak brush, and then we finally came into aspen forests mixed with evergreens. The pavement gave in to dirt and gravel, and the SUV left swarms of brown dust clouds as we entered the national forest. There were few cars on this road, from what I could tell, but when I asked if many people lived in the area of the lodge, Drake retorted, "Too many."

We entered another valley, which Wes called Teller Park. I saw green fields and large boulders. Wildflowers grew everywhere, and an evergreen grove was scattered here and there in the distance. Someone had erected bluebird houses on posts along the road, and I was delighted to see a Rocky Mountain bluebird sitting on a fence. A reddish-brown, cat-sized animal with a bushy tail burrowed off a rock into some weeds. Drake said it was a marmot. Just ahead, on the right, a mountain came into view, skirted by an aspen forest, and then I caught sight of it—the Rainbow Majestic Lodge—and it took my breath away.

Wes turned right into a narrow drive. A marble sign marked the entrance, with RAINBOW MAJESTIC LODGE in bold letters. Ahead was an enormous building complex that, at first, reminded me of a castle but minus the spires and turrets. It was three stories, and a balcony off to the left had huge windows and a stairway that led to the ground. The parking area in front was large but not paved. A couple of heavy machines took up space at one end. Later, I found out those were Sno-cats which the lodge used in the winter months for transportation, since the snow often fell too deep to plow. There were a dozen or so parked cars there now, and a couple of all-terrain vehicles. A small corral, off to the side, housed six horses.

Wes pulled the SUV up to the loading area in front of the lodge and parked.

"This is incredible." It was the first time I'd been able to speak since seeing the lodge. "And this setting ... with the mountain in back ... it's Majestic Mountain, right?"

Wes nodded. "That's right."

Drake sighed. "It used to be called the Majestic Mountain Lodge," he said. "Some people still believe that's what it should have stayed as." He got out of the back seat and opened the passenger door for me.

"Why did the name get changed?" I asked.

"Rosalee changed it to Rainbow Majestic when she took over the lodge last fall," Wes explained. "You can ask her about it."

I wondered how soon I'd get to meet my aunt. Drake grabbed the two suitcases and then beckoned me to follow him into the lodge. I turned to Wes, still seated behind the wheel, and thanked him. He smiled shyly, then slowly backed the SUV toward the parking lot.

We had to climb a stairway to get to the entrance, though I noted there was a ramp as well for wheelchairs for people unable to climb steps. I followed Drake and then we walked through double doors into the lobby.

Immediately, I was struck by the welcoming atmosphere. Soft pastel colors with a rose pattern in a wallpaper strip accentuated the reception area, and a counter was filled with little angel knick-knacks and pamphlets spread over it. A delicious, flowery fragrance permeated the air. I saw a stick of incense burning behind the counter. No one was present at the desk, but Drake jiggled a little silver bell that had its own holder, and the pleasant tone it displayed was not the kind that was annoying, but had instead a calming effect. Some soft new age music came from somewhere.

A moment later, a tall woman with short blond hair and bright brown eyes entered the space behind the counter from an arched doorway that led off to the side. She was probably in her late thirties, energetic and tastefully dressed in a light blue blouse and white slacks. She wore a colorful necklace of rocks that reminded me of a Hawaiian lei, and large silver earrings in the shape of six-pointed stars hung from her ear lobes. Her triangular face displayed a prominent pointed chin. She smiled, showing straight white teeth, as her gaze focused first on Drake. When her eyes fell on me, the smile diminished slightly.

"Gena, meet Juniper," said Drake.

"Hello, Juniper." Gena reached out a stiff hand, which I shook gently.

"Nice to meet you," I said.

Gena did not return the courtesy. Instead, she cleared her throat and turned to Drake. "Rosalee has arranged for our guest to be in the crystal suite," she said. I noticed a slight emphasis on her words "our guest," knowing she referred to me. It sounded a little mocking, but I might have been wrong. She reached under the counter and produced a key, which she handed to me. "Enjoy your stay," she said with a forced smile.

"Thank you." I turned and followed Drake as he carried the suitcases across the lobby toward a great room that displayed rustic furniture with big, comfortable red cushions and dark wood paneling. I noticed several mounted heads on the far wall and recalled that this had been the place where my father had come to hunt over two decades ago. Along the outside wall was a large stone fireplace with several pillows in front of it, placed upon a large braided rug.

Drake started up a wide spiral staircase and I followed. We climbed only to the second floor, and then he led me down the narrow hallway that veered to the right. I noticed the huge window at the top of the stairs that looked out over Majestic Mountain and the forest. Blue velvet drapes hung from this window with gold cord as tie-backs.

My door was at the end of the hallway. Drake set the suitcases down and waited for me to insert the key to let us in. This was an older section of the lodge, I could tell, although it looked as though new carpeting had been laid.

When I opened the door to the room, I was astounded at its size. I had expected a tiny cubicle of a hotel room, but this was a suite, and it was obvious why Gena had called it the "crystal suite." Fabulous displays of different colored quartz crystal specimens populated the front room, which was a sitting area with sofa, recliner and arm chair all in aqua. The walls were a very faint shade of blue, and a small mural of a rainbow scene was painted against an inner wall. A bathroom preceded the bedroom. When I walked in, I saw that it contained a queen bed with posts and a canopy, done tastefully in rose pink color. There was a bedside stand, a dresser in the corner, and a full-length mirror on the closet door.

I had left Drake standing out in the sitting room with my bags. He hadn't followed me into the bedroom. I went to the windows and drew open the pink and pastel print drapes to reveal a magnificent view of the east. I saw Majestic Mountain with only a few white snow spots left on it. The windows overlooked the back side of the lodge. A trail down below led from the flower garden into the woods. A pond with benches marked the garden as an inviting place to visit.

"Impressed?" Drake stood at the doorway to the bedroom.

I grinned at him, ecstatic. "I can't believe it. Are all the rooms like this one?"

Drake kept a straight face. "Not since I last looked."

"And all these crystals." I saw that more clusters and clear, colored stones lay around at various points through the bedroom.

"Why so many of them? Someone must be a rock collector."

"Your aunt uses them in lots of ways," he replied mysteriously. "She'll put someone in this room when they're in need of healing." He suddenly turned around and started to walk out.

"Wait," I called, and followed Drake into the sitting room. "Healing? What do crystals like these have to do with ... healing?"

He looked at me in a strange way, those mystical dark blue eyes getting to me again. "I think once you've spent some time in here, you'll begin to understand."

I shook my head, puzzled. "Would you care to explain that better?"

His dark eyebrows lifted, but he only nodded his head. "Just listen," he told me. "You'll be able to hear what they're saying." He turned and started out the door.

"But, Drake ..." I ran to the door and stared after him as he went down the hall. "When will I get to meet Aunt Rosalee?"

He stopped and turned to face me. "Dinner's at seven. She'll be expecting you to join us in the main dining room." Then he smiled as if to reassure me. "See you there."

I watched him disappear around the corner and closed the door to my room. A softly ticking wooden clock with Roman numerals on its glassed-in face told me it was just a little past six o'clock. I had an hour before it was time to find the dining room and face Aunt Rosalee for the first time.

4

After my long journey, I was happy to be left alone in the crystal suite. I unpacked my luggage and found ample space in both the dresser and closet. I set the small framed portrait I had of Sean beside my bed. His familiar face was both a comfort to me and a source of longing.

I had also brought along the old photograph of my father and Uncle Fred. I was looking for a place to set it when a knock on the door summoned me. I answered it, expecting to see my aunt. Instead, a bright-faced, rather plump woman with large green eyes and light brown curly hair smiled at me. She stepped into the sitting room, dressed in baggy white slacks and a peach sweater that emphasized her bosom. "Welcome to the Rainbow Majestic. My name is Taffi." She carried a tablet of paper, which she set down on the arm chair, and then offered her hand.

"I'm Juniper," I said, and shook her hand.

Taffi gazed at the rainbow mural on the blue wall. "Isn't this just too much? These are the best rooms in the lodge, you know." She wandered into the bedroom and peered out my windows. "The view is awesome, don't you think?"

I was a little surprised at her boldness. Despite her hefty figure, she was full of energy. It was almost as though she couldn't stand still. "Yes, it is," I agreed.

"I'm the resident graphologist," she explained. She led me back to the sitting room.

"What's that?" I asked.

"A handwriting analyst," she said. She picked up her pad of paper from the arm chair. "Have a seat." She beckoned me onto the sofa.

A little baffled, I sat. Taffi pulled a pen out of her pants pocket, then handed me the pen and paper. "What's this for?" I asked.

She looked at me. "Write your name there on the top," she instructed.

Reluctantly, I held the pen and studied her. "Just ... sign it?"

"Yes. Anywhere at the top. Just like you're signing your name on a check." She crossed her legs and fidgeted a little.

I took a breath, then signed my name—*Juniper Sutton*—at the top. When I started to hand the tablet and pen back to her, she stopped me.

"You're not done yet," she said. "I want you to write a couple of paragraphs for me."

I looked at her blankly. "Why? What for?"

Taffi uncrossed her legs and fidgeted. She bent toward me, her eyes gleaming with mischief. "Oh ... just write something about yourself. You might say something like this ... 'I got up this morning and had to catch my plane, so I drove to ...' You know, something on that order. You don't have to put a lot of thought into it. It's just a little sampling of your handwriting."

I slowly gave in. Apparently this was some kind of a game to her, and even though it seemed unusual, I scribbled out a quick summary of my trip to Dodge City with Mike, then my flight to Colorado Springs, followed by the long car ride to Majestic Mountain. I managed to fill half the page. When I was finished, I handed the tablet and pen back to Taffi.

She studied what I had written, and I watched her face grow serious and expressive as she scanned my sentences.

"Well ... how did I do?" I finally asked.

Taffi stood up, still studying the paper. "Hmmm," she murmured. "This is good ... very good." She nodded her head, still examining my marks, and then she tucked the pad of paper under one arm, grinned at me, and headed toward the door. "Thank you very much," she said.

"But ..." I stood up.

Taffi was already out the door. She hesitated and stuck her head back in for a moment. "I need to take this back to my room and study it awhile. I'll see you later, at dinner." Then she disappeared.

Was that strange, or what? I puzzled over Taffi's brief, business-like visit, and wondered what my handwriting had told her about me. I also wondered just what a resident graphologist did at a place like the Rainbow Majestic.

Since there was still time before the dinner hour, I decided to venture out into the hotel and walk a little. For one thing, I didn't know where the dining room was located. The lodge was huge and it wouldn't hurt to do some exploring. I took my key and left the suite. This wing on the second floor appeared to be all guest rooms. I walked down the other wing and saw that there were more rooms.

As I was walking back toward the stairway, someone stepped out of a guest room behind me. I turned around and came face to face with a tall, thin woman with long red hair and narrow gray eyes. She was somewhat pretty and looked to be about my age. She was dressed in a strapless green sun dress and wore sandals. In her arms she carried a pile of towels and three or four lotion bottles. My first impression was that she was a maid.

"Oh, hi," she greeted me with a smile. "You must be Juniper, Rosalee's niece from Kansas."

"Yes," I replied. Did everyone in the lodge know who I was? "I was just finding my way around." For some reason I felt I needed to justify why I was wandering.

"Oh, that's cool. By the way, my name's Clover ... Clover Wolff."

"I take it you work here," I guessed.

"I'm the lodge massage therapist," Clover explained. "Hey, let's go to my room. It's just down the hall. Then I don't, like ... have to stand here holding all these towels."

I followed Clover down the hall. She explained she had just finished giving one of the guests a table massage. Her room was in my wing, but as she opened the door I saw it was just a simple room and nothing fancy like the crystal suite. Clover dropped her bundles down on a table, then beckoned me into a chair. She glanced into her mirror and pulled her long red hair into a pony-tail, which she secured with a band. Turning back to me, she smiled, then sat on the end of her bed. "I was hoping I'd get to meet you. How was your trip?"

After an exchange of conversation, she asked me if I might want a massage. I gazed at her in surprise. "You mean, now?"

"No, not now." Clover laughed. "But let me schedule you in. Like ... how long are you staying at the Rainbow?"

I hesitated, recalling there had been no mention of my return flight to Kansas. "Well, I don't know," I replied. "It depends."

Clover nodded. "Okay then, I'll, like ... set up an hour for you this week. The lodge isn't very busy right now, so there are, like ... plenty of openings." Then she asked, "What do you think of this place?"

I explained that I hadn't really seen it yet.

"Who have you met?" asked Clover.

"Well, Wes and Drake picked me up in Colorado Springs," I told her. "The only other people I've met are Gena ... and Taffi ... and you." I added that I hadn't yet met my aunt.

"Rosalee's a real sweetheart. You'll love her," said Clover. Then she sighed. "Wes ... he's quite a hunk, isn't he?"

I merely smiled. "Wes is cool," I agreed. "And so is Drake."

Clover swept a stray hair aside. "Did you know Wes lived in, like ... a monastery for a few years?" No, I hadn't known that. I knew only the part about the Marine Corps and his being from Oklahoma. "Wes knew Rosalee years ago. That's how he, like ... got the job here."

"I see," I said. "And what about Drake?"

Clover crossed her legs. "Drake used to live in North Dakota, I believe. You say you met Taffi?"

I nodded.

"Taffi can be a lot of fun," Clover told me. "But watch yourself. She'll find a way to get a sample of your handwriting, and then she'll, like ... know everything about you."

"She already did," I confessed. I was beginning to wonder what kind of a place this was.

But before I could ask, Clover's face grew serious. "You say you met Gena?" When I nodded, she continued, "Some of us, like ... find it hard getting along with Gena."

I recalled the woman's guarded reaction when I'd met her, and asked, "What makes you say that?"

Clover was not one to hold back. "Gena's, like ... Rosalee's stepdaughter," she confided. "Gena Sutton Howard." She made a face as she said the name.

"What does she do here, work at the front desk?" I asked, surprised to learn that Gena was related to Rosalee. That meant she must also be related to me.

"Gena's, like ... the lodge manager. She's Rosalee's right hand assistant. She runs things when Rosalee isn't around."

I remembered Wes saying that Drake was one of the lodge

managers. "I thought Wes said Drake was a manager."

"Oh, he is," said Clover. "He's, like ... the assistant manager ... under Gena ... but Drake's the only one who doesn't let her get under his skin. We all, like ... hate it when Rosalee has to go anywhere."

"Does that happen often?"

"Fortunately, not, but ..." She was interrupted by the telephone ringing in her room. She quickly reached for the phone. "Hello, it's Clover." There was a pause, then she said, "Sure ... let me get my appointment book. Just one moment."

I stood up to leave. "I think I'll wander around some more. Thanks for the talk."

Clover smiled at me and put her hand over the mouthpiece. "You're welcome, Juniper. Hey, I think we're going to be, like ... good friends. See you later."

I quietly left the room and walked toward the spiral staircase that led down to the lobby and great room. How interesting to learn that Gena was Rosalee's stepdaughter. Clover had said her name was Gena Sutton Howard, so that must mean her father had been Uncle Fred, and she must be the daughter of his first wife. Howard must be her married name, I surmised. Slowly, I descended the stairs into the great room, where there was now a fire crackling in the stone fireplace. I realized it was cooling off, and nights were obviously much cooler at an altitude of nine thousand feet.

Looking around, I saw no one in the lobby where soft music continued to play. Then I noticed the arched doorway across the way that led toward the kitchen and dining room. I wandered in that direction and saw the dining room with plenty of round tables and ornate chairs. A girl was busy setting the tables with silverware and napkins. I turned away, now that I knew where to go.

The fireplace in the great room beckoned me and I went and stood in front of it for a few minutes, watching the curling flames lick the wood and change shape. I was studying the mounted game heads on the wall—several mule deer, elk and a mountain lion—when another room off to the side caught my eye. I wandered into a recreation room with a pool table, dart boards and a bar set up along the wall. No one was in this room either, but it led into yet another room and my curiosity coaxed me forward.

I stopped when I reached the doorway because a small group of people sat inside this larger room, which was some kind of lounge with comfortable chairs, paintings on the walls and a small fireplace burning in the corner. There were two men and two women, seated with their heads bowed and their eyes closed. One of the men was Wes Andrews, who had donned a brown sweater and wore dress slacks now instead of the jeans I'd seen him in earlier. He now sat on the floor in front of a piano, his legs crossed and his back straight. He had removed his shoes and his arms were spread out slightly on either side, palms up and index fingers curled.

In a recliner, an elderly man with a shock of white hair sat, hands folded in his lap. In the next chair was an older woman wearing a maroon robe. She was slender and her blue-white hair was stylishly cut. She, too, sat quietly with her hands folded. On a couch near Wes and the piano, a younger woman with black hair sat, dressed in red satiny slacks and a black shiny top. A large crystal pendant hung around her neck. She was slender and her thick, shiny black hair fell carelessly upon both shoulders. In her hands she held a large, pyramid-shaped crystal about the size of a grapefruit.

I stared, mystified at first, but then realized they must be in some kind of group prayer. Or was it a meditation? I remembered Wes explaining that he'd been meditating outside the air terminal when I'd thought he was dozing. Slowly I withdrew, not wanting to disturb them, and walked back toward the great room and lobby.

I decided to return to the crystal suite and freshen up before dinner. After washing up, I chose a simple blue dress from my few articles in the closet. I hoped it would be formal enough for the evening. At least it was better than wearing the same old clothes in which I had arrived.

At seven o'clock I left the crystal suite and went down to the main dining room, where a crowd of people were already gathered for the meal. I looked around, unsure of myself, and noticed right away a stocky woman in her late fifties who was seated at the table nearest the kitchen. There were flecks of gray in her dark hair that hung in a long braid to one side. She was dressed in a green mu-mu type robe decorated with large red and purple flowers. She was busy talking to a man of medium height with glasses who was slightly bald. He leaned over her table with a bunch of papers, and they seemed engrossed in some business matter. I knew without anyone telling me that she had to be my Aunt Rosalee.

Before I could advance toward her, however, Clover Wolff came up from behind me and put a hand on my forearm. "Juniper?"

I turned around and greeted her with a smile.

"Come sit with me," she invited, and led me over to an empty table.

Wes sat with the elderly gentleman from the lounge. He caught my eye and smiled at me. Drake Phillips, who had changed into a black, long-sleeved shirt and black jeans, had taken a seat at a nearby table. Suddenly, Taffi appeared at his side. In her bubbly manner, she began talking to him and pulled out a chair beside him. I noticed the uncertain expression on Drake's face and wanted to see what would happen next, but Clover grabbed my attention.

"Have you been outside yet?" she asked.

"No, not yet. You mean, in the garden?"

"There's a hiking trail behind the lodge that's pretty cool."

"Yes, I know. I can see it from my room."

Clover reached for her glass of ice water. "I heard that Rosalee wants you to work in the gift shop."

I looked at Clover in surprise. "Where's that?"

Clover pointed through the door to the dining room. "It's in a room next to the lobby. It's not, like ... all set up yet. I think it would be cool running the gift shop." Then she asked, "By the way, what did you used to do in Kansas?"

I explained to Clover how I'd spent the last two years taking care of my mother.

"Oh, yes, I heard about that." Her voice was sympathetic.

"Before that, though, I worked in a bookstore." I wanted to change the subject. The reminder of my mother caused an image of Mike's face to appear in my mind. I remembered that I had promised to call Mike, to let him know I had arrived safely at Majestic Mountain.

"Is something wrong?" asked Clover.

"No, nothing," I said quickly, and started to unroll my napkin with the silverware in it.

High-heeled footsteps clunked across the floor, and suddenly Gena Sutton Howard stood over us. "Juniper, that's not your place." She placed her hands on her hips and gazed at me critically. "You're supposed to sit over there with your aunt." Gena gave Clover a disapproving look, then waited for me to get up and follow her across the room. I felt as though all eyes were on me.

Rosalee looked up as I approached and the bald man tipped his glasses up against his nose as he examined me from head to toe. Then the stocky woman told him, "Lance, let's continue with this later." She turned to me and her face brightened as a wide smile stretched across her plump cheeks. "I want to greet my niece from Kansas." She got up slowly and came around the table to embrace me. "Juniper, welcome. I am so happy to meet you." She hugged me long and hard and I could smell a sweet, flowery perfume on her that reminded me of something exotic, yet pleasant.

"Aunt Rosalee," I said with a smile, "it's a pleasure to finally meet you."

"My ... my ..." She shook her head. "You're so grown up. Well, come sit down next to me. How do you like your suite?" I noticed her eyes were a deep brown color and she had high cheek bones.

Gena glanced at me in a grudging manner. She had taken the seat across from Aunt Rosalee at our table. "It's just beautiful," I told my aunt.

Someone else took the fourth seat at our table. I recognized the slender lady with the long, silky black hair, who wore the red pants, black top and crystal pendant, and had been in the lounge meditating. She grinned as her eyes fell on me. I noticed she wore dark eye shadow and lipstick that was a violet color. "This must be the niece we've all been hearing about."

"Starla, this is Juniper ... Juniper Sutton," introduced Aunt Rosalee. "Juniper, I'd like you to meet Starla Streber."

I reached out my hand to this dramatic-looking woman. It seemed as though everyone had taken their places, and now the lights in the dining room dimmed once, then came on. A hush fell over the room and then Aunt Rosalee stood up and addressed the crowd.

"Tonight we welcome Juniper Sutton, my niece from

Kansas. And I'm sure she'll be gettin' around to meetin' y'all ...
eventually. Juniper, why don't you stand up so everyone can get
a look at you?"

Reluctantly, I stood up. All eyes were on me.

"Juniper will be stayin' with us for a while," said Aunt
Rosalee. "Maybe longer." She turned to Starla, seated at our
table. "Starla, would you please lead the prayer?" Aunt Rosalee
then returned to her seat and I sat back down.

Starla stood and took a deep breath, then pressed her
fingers together and closed her eyes. I obediently bowed my
head and waited.

"Dear Father-Mother God," Starla proclaimed, "we honor
You in all your glorious wisdom, and call upon You now to bless
this bounty, that it may nourish our bodies and nurture our
souls. We thank You for all your gifts ... of love, of healing, of
abundance ... and we ask that we be protected in all ways,
through the Light and the Love of the Most Radiant One." There
was a slight pause and then Starla released a breath and said,
"And so it is."

When I looked up, I saw Starla's face and it seemed to be
shining. The heavy makeup she wore reminded me of a Goth
glamour queen. After she sat down, the crowd began to chatter
again. Meal servers appeared from the kitchen with carts
containing trays of food, which they brought around to the
tables. There were two entrees to choose from and several side
dishes. I learned that the lodge offered vegetarian fare as well
as a meat dish. Tonight it was vegetarian lasagna with tofu, or
roast beef with mashed potatoes and gravy.

I ate heartily of the roast beef, hungry after not having
eaten since our lunch just outside Colorado Springs, which
seemed much longer than several hours ago. I noticed a couple
of women guests had joined Clover at her table. Wes sat with
the white-haired gentleman and the striking lady in the maroon
robe who had been with him and Starla in the lounge. I knew
which entree Wes had chosen. At the next table sat Drake, in an
active discussion with Taffi. She seemed to be dominating the
conversation. The slightly bald man with glasses, who had been
talking to Aunt Rosalee when I came in, was at a table with a
round-faced woman also wearing glasses, whom I guessed might
be his wife, and a young boy about nine, perhaps their son. The

rest of the dinner crowd were strangers to me.

"Juniper, how long are you going to be with us?"

I turned my attention back to our table. Starla gazed at me. With a quick glance at my aunt, I said, "That hasn't been determined yet."

Gena sipped some water and said, "By her baffled expression, I'd say she's already seen enough of us and is ready to go back to Kansas."

Aunt Rosalee gave an impatient sigh, intended for Gena, then reached over to pat my hand. "What do you think of our lodge?" she asked.

"Well ..." I mused, feeling put on the spot. "I guess there's a lot here I don't understand yet. Are all these people here tonight employed at the lodge?"

Rosalee chuckled. "Oh, no, darlin'. Most the people here are payin' guests. We're slow right now, but we've got a big holistic fair booked for next week. I hope the lodge will be packed."

"Believe, and you will see it!" Starla grinned.

"May I ask ... what kind of a place is this?" I had noticed that the hotel was by no means ordinary.

"It's a healing and light center," said Aunt Rosalee. "It's a place where people can come and experience life-changing awakenings."

"That's what I do!" piped up Starla. "I'm an awakener."

"What's that?" I asked, puzzled.

"You'll have to have an awakening with Starla," Aunt Rosalee suggested.

"Oh, absolutely," Starla agreed. "Perhaps before you leave, I can give you one."

"I'm tellin' you ... Juniper's not leavin'," said Aunt Rosalee. "I brought her here to take over the gift shop."

Gena frowned. "*If* she wants to stay, that is."

"Well, why wouldn't she?" Aunt Rosalee looked offended.

"Did it ever occur to you that she might have a home and a life back in Kansas?" Gena studied me for my reaction.

I was feeling rather pressured at the moment. All of this talk was above and beyond anything I'd heard from anybody in Kansas. Normal conversation at the dinner table had never included things such as meditation, awakenings, massages or handwriting. Just what was I getting into here? Was this some kind of new age cult? If it was, I had better take my leave as soon as possible.

Starla noticed my bewilderment and got up from her place to stand behind me. "You've confused poor Juniper," she told the other two. "I see her aura is cloudy right now. Here, let me see if I can lift some of the confusion ..." She began to wave her hands over my head, and I glanced around nervously, feeling self-conscious.

"Just relax, dear," said Starla.

Gena clicked her tongue in disapproval. "Oh, for goodness sakes ... leave the poor girl alone."

Aunt Rosalee continued eating as if nothing was strange about a glamorous, black-haired woman with violet eye shadow performing some weird ritual over my head. Starla continued to move her hands and fingers and I closed my eyes, feeling humiliated. It was all I could do to keep from pushing myself back from the table and marching right out of that dining room. But, as I sat there—within the next few seconds—I felt a comforting warmth come over me—a blanket of soothing energy that put me instantly at ease and into a more acceptable mood. I'm not sure exactly how it happened.

When I opened my eyes, I looked directly into Drake's face across the room. He was sitting there, staring right at me, and it was as though his dark blue eyes had reached out and were delving right into the core of my being. Taffi had turned around and was conversing with someone else. Drake suddenly winked at me, then slowly a smile crept onto his bearded face.

Starla put her hands down. "There," she said with satisfaction. "Now, isn't that better?"

I looked away from Drake. A second glance in his direction showed him back in discussion with Taffi.

"Juniper? How do you feel now?"

I blinked and stared at Starla. I had to admit, I did feel less agitated. Gena was smirking, and I turned to face Aunt Rosalee. "I ... felt ... something."

"That's wonderful." She smiled. "Haven't you ever experienced anythin' like this before?"

"Obviously not," chided Gena. "The girl's from Kansas, after all."

This remark brought up my defenses, but I stifled them. "I

guess when you've been brought up a Christian, it's a little awkward to come into a place like this." I immediately regretted my words by the looks on all their faces.

"A place like *this?*" Gena challenged.

"What does being a Christian have to do with findin' all of this awkward or strange?" Aunt Rosalee asked gently.

"Don't you think some of us are Christians who come here?" Starla challenged. "Why, Lord Jesus is one of my prominent guides."

"I think perhaps later tonight I'd better introduce you to Cyril," added Aunt Rosalee.

I had no idea who Cyril was, and at the moment I didn't much care. I was not fitting in, and suddenly I just wanted to retreat to the crystal suite.

Gena seemed to be enjoying my plight, and it struck me— all of a sudden—that her plan all along had been to make me feel uncomfortable. It was almost as if she resented my presence here at the lodge and wanted me to leave. I had no clue why Gena would wish such a thing, but I had that strong feeling.

On the other hand, I felt a wave of love emanating from Aunt Rosalee. She and Starla, both, had this loving projection that reached out to me almost like a soft embrace.

I sighed and turned to my aunt. "Look, I didn't mean to criticize any of you. My mother was a devout Christian and I've always been under the impression that these things were not discussed."

"She thinks we're children of the devil," Gena cried.

"No," I protested. "No, of course I don't think that. Perhaps my mother did, but me ... I've never bought into that hell and damnation garbage."

Starla smiled at me. "There's hope for you yet, darling."

Aunt Rosalee said, "Well, I think we've talked enough about this subject for now. After dinner, Juniper, we're meetin' in the lounge to hear Taffi's presentation on handwritin'. You're welcome to join us, if you'd like. I think it will be an interestin' evenin'."

They had managed to calm me down enough so that I no longer felt I had to escape to my suite. As for joining them in the lounge, I'd go because I had already met Taffi, and I really wanted to hear what she had to say about her profession.

Dessert was brought in, along with coffee and herb tea. A cherry cobbler was on the menu tonight and I ate mine in silence while the conversation remained casual around me. I kept receiving critical looks from Gena, and—when I finished my cobbler—I decided to feel her out more.

"So ... Gena ... I didn't realize you are Aunt Rosalee's step-daughter. I suppose that makes us first cousins."

"It does ... and we are." For some reason Gena didn't sound too happy about our relationship. She went on to explain, "My parents were divorced when I was thirteen. I lived in Hawaii—for the most part—with my mother. She passed on a few years ago."

I noticed Starla and Aunt Rosalee were engrossed in their own discussion about somebody named Archangel Michael. They weren't paying any attention to Gena's and my conversation.

"I'm sorry," I murmured respectfully. "You must have come here to Majestic Mountain now and then, to visit your father," I guessed.

"I lived here until the divorce," she disclosed. "Then—once in a while—they'd send me here." She blinked her eyes nervously.

I wondered why she seemed uncomfortable. "Did you know my father?" I asked her.

Gena looked startled for half a second. "You mean Fred's brother, Nathaniel?"

I noticed Gena referred to her father and uncle on a first-name basis. I nodded.

Gena quickly turned away. "I really don't remember him that well." And with that, Gena excused herself and walked away.

5

After dinner several of us gathered in the lounge. I took a seat near the back of the room and noticed Drake seated on the hearth in front of the fireplace, off by himself. A moment later, Wes slipped into the chair beside me and smiled.

"Hi, Wes," I said.

"This ought to be a good talk tonight," he said.

"Oh, are there talks every night?"

"Well, there always seems to be somethin' goin' on here at the Rainbow."

I felt comforted that Wes had chosen to sit with me. I leaned over and asked, "Wes, who is that man with the white hair sitting in the front row?" I was referring to the distinguished, elderly gentleman I'd seen meditating in the lounge with Wes and the two women.

"Oh, you mean Cyril?" When I nodded, Wes went on. "That's Cyril Jorgensen, the well-known author and lecturer. You'll have to meet him."

"And the woman next to him? Is she his wife?" I indicated the white-haired lady in the maroon robe.

"Oh, you mean Celeste ... that's Celeste Birdwell. No, she's not his wife, but they are very good friends." Wes smiled knowingly. "Celeste is a fascinating lady. You'll like her."

Clover, who sat ahead of us a couple of rows, caught my eye and waved. Then Gena appeared at the front of the room and introduced the guest speaker for the night, Taffi Kincaid. A smattering of applause followed and then Taffi, who had changed into a red velvet dress that came slightly above her knees, dominated the room with her exuberance and lively lecture on graphology. Her entertaining way of speaking to an audience left us captivated. Her talk focused mainly on how handwriting controls our thoughts and how our thinking affects our handwriting.

Using an easel and a large tablet of paper, Taffi wrote some examples of letters and how they are formed in handwriting. She explained what the different swirls and loops and lines meant. I had to admit, I was caught up in the subject as much as everyone else in the room. It had never crossed my mind that we were taught certain ways of crossing our t's and dotting our i's as youngsters in school and that these methods were meant to keep us under control.

"Cross your t's way at the top," Taffi instructed, demonstrating with her pen how to do it. "That will boost your esteem more than anything else. And ... you want to create abundance?" She stopped and eyed the audience. "Who wants to create abundance in this room?"

A lot of hands shot up in the air around us. Wes and I were too shy to raise ours.

"I'll show you how to achieve abundance," Taffi promised, and she demonstrated how to make a big wide loop when writing the letter Y. "It's that easy! Don't believe me?" She looked around, her big green eyes scanning the crowd until she found Drake seated at the fireplace hearth. "Drake ... I know you don't believe me." She confided to the audience, "Drake and I had a big discussion about his handwriting over dinner tonight. And guess what? Drake's a skeptic."

A murmur of laughter rippled through the room. I saw Drake scrunch up his face, and I felt sorry for him. Taffi was picking on him and he knew it.

"Drake doesn't use script," Taffi explained. "He *prints*. I love it!" She giggled. "Actually, he tries to hide his handwriting from me ... but I can see right through him."

Humiliated, Drake turned away and Taffi changed the subject then and passed out some sheets of paper and pens to everyone in the room. She instructed those who wanted to participate to write a few lines that she dictated. I kept wondering what Taffi had deciphered from my handwriting sample earlier that afternoon. When the exercise was done, everyone passed their pages to the front of the room, and Taffi scooped them up and went through them, one by one. I had not seen Drake hand in a paper. He appeared bored by the whole lecture.

Taffi picked out some handwriting samples she had collected from the audience and began analyzing them. It seemed to me she was making light of them, finding humorous aspects of people's personalities and entertaining us all with her amusing interpretations.

"Wes Andrews ..." Taffi held up a page after having gone through two or three others. "Now here's an interesting bit of handwriting."

I glanced at Wes, whose arms were folded as he stared ahead, his attention on Taffi.

"Wes, you really hate long, drawn-out telephone conversations, don't you?"

The audience responded with a trickle of laughter and Wes smiled and nodded.

"You have a scar on your body." Taffi went on, pacing forward and back as she studied the sheet of paper. "A bullet wound."

Wes again nodded in agreement.

"How do you know that?" called out the elderly gentleman, Cyril, from the front row.

"It's in his handwriting," explained Taffi. I was amazed that Taffi could see that in Wes's writing. How was it possible?

Taffi sighed. "You're just determined not to make a commitment, Wes. Oh, dear ... all those poor women in your life."

A ripple of laughter erupted from people in the room. I thought the statement would embarrass Wes, but he merely smiled and shrugged.

"You've disappointed more than your share, too," Taffi accused, which brought more laughter from the audience. If any of this bothered Wes, he certainly didn't show it.

Everyone waited to see whom Taffi would read next.

"Juniper Sutton!"

My heart gave a little jump and Wes turned to smile at me sympathetically. Heads turned in my direction.

"I see you have ... *issues*," declared Taffi.

A few people in the audience chuckled.

"Someone's putting pressure on you," Taffi continued. "Wants you to make a decision ..."

"Rosalee?" called out a voice from the back of the room. I turned and saw Starla had made the comment.

"I'm not pressurin' anyone," came Rosalee's denial from across the room. People laughed.

"You've lost someone close to you." Taffi looked up suddenly, her green eyes wide with surprise. "Wait! This handwriting is too depressing ... let's move on to the next one."

No one objected—least of all me—as she started in with the next person's sample. But her mention of someone putting pressure on me to make a decision suddenly reminded me again of Mike and the fact that he was waiting for me to call. I needed to get away and make that call before it got any later. I knew he'd be worried if I didn't.

I glanced at my watch and noticed it was past nine o'clock. I realized it would be after ten in Kansas. It might be too late to call Mike if I waited for Taffi's talk to end. When I looked around, I suddenly noticed that Drake was no longer at the fireplace hearth. I didn't remember when he had left the room.

Wes must have sensed my restlessness. He put a gentle hand on my wrist and asked in a low voice, "Is somethin' wrong?"

"I need to leave," I whispered.

"If you hang around, there'll probably be a meditation afterwards," he said.

I explained that I was tired and didn't think I could stay up that late, and it was true—I was feeling the fatigue after such a long day of travel and meeting new people. It might have been fun to experience the meditation, but I still felt awkward and out of place among this group of people. Discreetly, I got up and headed out of the room while Taffi continued to entertain everyone by reading handwriting samples.

Aunt Rosalee noticed my departure and waved at me. I walked through the recreation room and on into the great room, headed for the stairway. When I reached the crystal suite, I unlocked my door and turned on the light. There was a telephone on my desk in the sitting area. I was not a carrier of a cell phone. There had never been a need for me to have one.

In my purse I had a purchased phone card for long distance calling. I didn't want to run up any charges on the lodge's line. I dialed the numbers and waited, expecting Mike to answer right away. After five rings, his answering machine came on.

At the beep, I left a brief message. "It's Juniper. I made it to Colorado. I'm staying at the Rainbow Majestic and everything is fine." I had no idea, at the moment, what the telephone number was, so I made an excuse that I'd call him in a day or two with the contact number, then hung up.

When I headed for the bedroom, I saw that I'd left the drapes open. I went to close them and I happened to look down toward the garden with the benches. A man was sitting there. The area was lit up by luminaries and I could see that the man was Drake Phillips. He sat alone, staring into the dark pond.

I closed the drapes, and then—on an impulse—got my jacket out of the closet and decided to walk down to the garden and speak with him. I just had a feeling that he might welcome some company. He had obviously left the meeting room early, and I wondered if he was upset with Taffi for teasing him in front of her audience.

When I had explored the other wing on the second floor earlier that afternoon—before I'd met Clover—I had seen a back stairway at the end of that hallway. I decided it would be quicker to take that than the spiral stairway leading to the lobby. I hoped it would lead me to a back door that would open toward the garden.

As I passed, I also noticed an open door that led to a narrow stairway going up, and I wondered where those steps led. One day, when I felt like exploring again, perhaps I'd check it out. The Rainbow Majestic Lodge was probably full of many rooms and passageways. I hurried downstairs and did find a door that led to the outside. I was glad for my jacket now, with cold, night-time air sweeping off the nearby mountain.

The path was dimly lit, with several small solar lamps stuck in the ground, and I headed toward the garden area in hopes that Drake would still be there, sitting on the bench as I'd seen him. But when I arrived at the spot, there was no Drake. He had left the garden.

Disappointed, I turned back to the lodge and stared up at the grand, palace-like structure, some of its windows glowing in the dark. I wondered if Drake had gone back inside. Most likely he had.

A glimmering light, possibly from a flashlight beam, snatched my attention as I gazed ahead at the path I'd seen that led from the garden into the woods. It was dark now and rather intimidating, but I decided to take a short walk in that direction. Perhaps Drake had gone for a stroll in the woods and

I could catch up to him.

The trees that grew on both sides of the trail were young aspens, their white trunks slender and straight, and their leaves not yet budded out. Springtime came later to these higher elevations, I realized. The trees grew close together and seemed so stately. The brush was still low to the ground, and as I walked it seemed only to get blacker. The light I'd seen was gone. There was no sign of Drake. My feet found the trail easily enough and in a couple of minutes I planned to turn around anyway.

For one thing, I hadn't changed out of my dress or high heels from dinner. I hadn't intended to take a walk in the woods. I wished now I had at least changed into my comfortable loafers. My mind rehashed the evening. I liked Aunt Rosalee. She might have some strange ideas, but she had shown instant acceptance and had welcomed me—literally—with open arms. I'm sure that she knew I was tired and understood why I had left Taffi's talk in the lounge.

Clover was friendly and someone I hoped to get to know better. There was such an open honesty about her. We would have had a good time talking had Gena not pulled me away from her at dinner to sit at my aunt's table. Starla was exotic and friendly, and I liked her despite her bold attempt to perform some crazy magic over my head.

For some reason I didn't feel comfortable around Gena. From the beginning she seemed to resent me. Here we were—first cousins—and I hadn't even been aware of her existence. Mother had never told me Uncle Fred had a daughter older than I. Why not? And why had Gena seemed nervous when I asked if she remembered my father? Why had she been reluctant to talk to me about him?

Wes had sat beside me in the lounge. I smiled to myself, fondly recalling how he had touched my wrist. He seemed like such a sincere, gentle soul, plus he was very good-looking. Clover had said that Wes had lived part of his life in a monastery. I wondered about that, and I also puzzled over the claim Taffi had made about Wes and women, and his not wanting to make a commitment. He hadn't seemed too upset about her comment, whether it was true or not.

Drake was unsettling, for some reason. I couldn't put my finger on it, but from the moment we'd first met at the Colorado

Springs airport, Drake had stirred something inside of me, and I wasn't sure it was anything good. He wasn't at all bad-looking either, although he didn't appear to be the type of guy that women would fall over.

It was obvious that Clover thought Wes was attractive, but Drake was too, in his own way. Gena had seemed drawn to him as I recalled, when he had talked to her at the front counter before taking my bags up to the crystal suite. For one thing, Gena was closer to Drake's age than either Clover or myself. Maybe there was something between the two of them. Yet Drake had not shown any encouragement toward Gena. He appeared to be a man with his own ideas about things. He apparently had not agreed with Taffi on some point they had discussed at dinner. I suddenly wished Drake had remained on the bench and that I'd been able to have a private conversation with him. Maybe it would have shed some light on why I felt so strange around him.

I halted when something in the bushes rustled in front of me. As I turned around, a bird flew up over my head and I heard it call "*Beeerrtt.*" Startled, I cried out in alarm. Looking up, I watched the long narrow wingtips of a nighthawk as it sailed across the night sky. "*Beeerrtt,*" it called again. I knew it was time to turn around and walk back to the lodge.

Just as I began retracing my steps in the dark, someone grabbed me from behind. An arm, covered by a thick jacket or some other heavy piece of clothing, circled the front of my chin and pulled my neck back so that I lost my balance. Whoever it was knocked me to the ground with a thrust that caused me to skin the palms of my hands on the rocky ground as well as my bare knees.

It was dark and I could not see my assailant. The shock had immobilized me for several seconds, but I was aware of somebody running away as rapid footsteps diminished. I couldn't tell in which direction they had gone.

Slowly, I got to my feet, my heart pounding with fear. One of my shoes had come off and I fumbled for it. I finally retrieved it and forced it on with shaking fingers. My only thought was returning immediately to the lodge with its lights and people. Uncontrollable sobs caught in my throat and I stumbled in the dark toward the lights in the garden. Tears of indignity filled my eyes. I couldn't imagine who had jumped out at me from the woods, or what they had wanted. I began to run, staggering a bit in my high heels, afraid that I might be accosted again.

When I saw the figure of a man ahead, I stopped running and cringed in fear. He was near the garden pond, because I could see the lights sticking out of the ground.

"Juniper, is that you?" a man's voice called out. He then ran forward to meet me, and with great relief I saw it was Drake Phillips, dressed in a blue jean jacket. When he was close enough to see the condition I was in, he said, "Shit! What happened to you?"

More sobs broke loose and I accepted his hand that reached out to me. "Somebody ..." I started to say, still finding it difficult to catch my breath, "in the woods ... knocked me down ..."

"Who?"

"I ... I don't know."

"Come here." Gently, he drew me close and held me as I fell into his arms and cried. How soothing it was to be held and comforted just then. His voice was soft as he murmured, "Don't worry. You're safe now."

Finally, I recovered enough to pull away, and I let Drake lead me to one of the garden benches. We sat down and he made me tell him everything that had happened. I told him how I'd come to the garden to get some fresh night air. I didn't reveal that I had seen him sitting on this bench from upstairs in my room, nor that I'd wanted to talk to him and had come for that purpose. I simply said I'd decided to take a short walk on the trail. Unexpectedly, someone had jumped out of the trees and grabbed me.

"Do you know who it was?" asked Drake again.

"No. I'm not even sure if it was a man or a woman," I told him. "But whoever it was, they were strong." I looked up at him. "Did you see anybody while you were in the garden just now?"

Drake hadn't seen anyone. I figured the person must have run in the opposite direction. He insisted we return to the lodge right away. I knew I must look a mess from crying.

The group from the meeting was breaking up as we entered the front of the lodge. I felt embarrassed being seen this way, and Drake sensed my reluctance to face people and their questions. He led me up another back stairway.

Clover met us in the hallway. She was returning to her room when she heard us and came over. Her look of concern matched Drake's. "Oh, Juniper, what happened?"

"Someone attacked her in the woods," said Drake. "Can you get her cleaned up? I'm going to find Rosalee."

Clover was more than happy to take over for Drake, and he hurried down the corridor.

"I was just out for a walk," I tried to explain. "I hadn't gone that far ..."

"Never mind that now," said Clover. "Let's get some warm soap and water on those scrapes." She led me into the bathroom of my suite.

Later on, after I had changed into my bathrobe and slippers, Clover brought me some herb tea. "This will calm your nerves and help you sleep tonight," she promised.

"What is it?" I asked, accepting the cup.

"Some chamomile, mint, and Valerian root."

There was a knock on the door, and a moment later Aunt Rosalee entered the crystal suite. She still wore her mu-mu and her cheeks were flushed, her dark brown eyes wide with worry.

"Aunt Rosalee ..." I called out.

"Juniper, thank God you're all right." She gave me a hug, then sat in the big arm chair beside the sofa, where Clover and I sat. "Drake told me what happened. He and Wes are out in the woods now, looking."

"Oh, I'm sure the man is long gone," said Clover.

"Probably," admitted Aunt Rosalee, "but just in case ... we don't want to take any chances. How are you feelin', darlin'?"

I took a sip of Clover's brew and sighed. "I'm feeling better."

"She'll sleep well tonight," said Clover.

The two of them stayed and chatted with me for a short while. By the time I had finished most of the cup, I started feeling drowsy and they both noticed it.

"We'll let you get to bed now," said Aunt Rosalee. "And don't worry about a thing. You'll have a nice fresh start in the mornin'." She stood up, then bent over me and planted a kiss on my forehead. Again I caught the sweet scent of roses from her perfume.

Clover smiled at me as they went out the door. "We'll talk

more tomorrow. Good night."

"Good night, Clover. And thanks."

I made sure the door to my room was locked, then turned out the lights and went to my bedroom. Just as I'd hoped, the canopy bed with its pink covers was just as comfortable as it looked, and in no time I was fast asleep.

6

Whether it was the cozy comfort of the canopy bed or Clover's herb tea, I don't know, but I slept well that first night in the Rainbow Majestic. Sunlight streamed through a section of the drapes as I awoke. For several minutes I basked in the tranquility of the morning, until I remembered the attack last night in the woods.

Why had the assailant fled? If someone had really meant to harm me, surely there was the opportunity to do so, being far removed from the lodge and anyone who might hear my screams. Instead, whoever it was had run away just as they shoved me to the ground. But what had been the purpose?

Clover had said breakfast was served in the dining room until ten o'clock. It was informal with a self-serve breakfast bar set up for guests and employees. I would have to hustle to make it by ten o'clock.

I showered in the antique clawfoot bathtub that had a small shower head attached and a curtain that could be pulled around the oval basin. I wasn't used to sitting in a tub to shower, but it was adequate. The surface wounds on my knees and palms didn't seem too bad.

From my limited supply of clothing, I chose cream-colored slacks and a green pullover top with a scoop neck. I slipped on my loafers and—after brushing my teeth and hair—I felt ready to see what this new day would bring. Leaving the crystal suite , I walked downstairs to the dining room.

A few people still lingered over breakfast. Starla Streber sat at a table with a spiral notebook and a pen. Seeing me, she beckoned me to join her. I picked up a plate and selected a dish of yogurt and some berries from the buffet table, then dished up a scoop of scrambled eggs and an English muffin. Coffee was served in urns marked regular and decaf. I brought a glass of orange juice with me to Starla's table.

"And how are you doing today, love?" Starla's hourglass

figure hugged a lavender velour pantsuit and her long black hair
hung straight over her shoulders as she watched me with eyes
that were thick lashed and enhanced with lavender makeup.

"I slept pretty well," I told her. "How are you?"

"Content," she replied, then looked concerned. "Hey, I
heard about your encounter last night."

I imagined everyone in the lodge must know I had been
attacked in the woods. I took a sip of orange juice.

"That had to be frightening," continued Starla. "Any idea
who it was?"

"No." I reached for the salt and pepper.

"Well, some are saying it was a hunter."

I looked at her in surprise. "A hunter? Why? Who'd be
hunting in June? And besides, it was dark out."

"Rosalee's lodge is watched."

Her words startled me. I shook pepper over my eggs and
asked, "What do you mean?"

"There are people in the valley who would like to see the
Rainbow Majestic close down," Starla revealed.

"But why?" I asked.

Starla sighed. "Some of the townspeople don't like the idea
of a light center ... or the kind of people it attracts."

"What townspeople are you talking about?" I asked. "Aren't
we miles from the nearest city?"

"Wade City," said Starla. "There are some churches there ...
one in particular ... that has a vendetta against us." She took a
sip of her coffee. "It's a group that has very narrow-minded
views and somehow they feel threatened by what we do here."

I could understand a little of what she was talking about—
intolerance of one religious group against another belief system.
"But what do you do here that would be a threat to anyone?" I
asked.

"What do you think we do?" Starla challenged.

I shrugged. "I don't really know. I'm trying to find that out.
I had no idea Aunt Rosalee had a light center. I thought I was
coming to a vacation lodge or something. I'm not even sure what
you mean by a light center." I lowered my voice, then asked her,
"Are all you people involved in some kind of cult?"

Starla laughed, then placed a hand with purple-polished
fingernails on my wrist. "I see why you might think that," she

said, then stared thoughtfully into her coffee cup. "I was once part of something like that. But, luckily, I was able to get away from it before it consumed me."

I decided not to ask any more about it. I wasn't sure I wanted to know about Starla's past.

Suddenly, Starla's eyes softened and she smiled. "We are light workers," she explained. "And, no, we are not a cult, in the sense that there is no leader who makes you give up your power. We don't force our beliefs on anyone." She grew thoughtful and added, "I suppose some may refer to us as a cult, but we are nothing more than a group of souls who have come to this planet to see what we can do to make things better. You've heard of light workers, haven't you?"

I ate my eggs, not really sure if I had. If so, I'd not paid much attention. But I wanted to know more. I wanted to understand what this was all about before I made a judgment about it. So far, everyone—with the exception, perhaps, of Gena—had been extremely friendly, open, sincere and kind. If that was being a light worker, then I wanted to know more about them.

"Well, what do light workers do?" I finally asked.

"Some of us are healers," Starla told me. "When I do my awakenings, I work in that capacity. There are lots of healers that come here for classes or retreats. We get massage therapists, Reiki masters, energy healers of all kinds. And some of us have special gifts of communication. We can bring forth information from realms beyond this three-dimensional world you see. I do some of that myself." She indicated her notebook.

"What is that?" I asked.

"I get messages from spirit," said Starla. "I'm writing a book."

"You mean automatic writing?" I asked. I had heard about psychics who allowed a spirit to take over their hand and write things the person wasn't even aware of—and often in different handwriting.

"It's a form of channeling," said Starla. "Some people can channel spirit by going into a trance and allowing the entity to speak through them, using their vocal cords. Others can write, the way I do. I simply get the message and write it down, word for word." She tapped her head. "But it goes through a filter first—my brain."

I was fascinated. Of course I'd heard of channeling before, but had always associated it with psychic phenomena, a subject that had been ignored—if not totally put down as nonsense—while I was growing up.

"Does Aunt Rosalee channel?" I asked.

"No, I don't believe so," said Starla. "Your aunt is a remarkable lady, though. She has Native American ancestry. Did you know that?"

I hadn't known, but I could see by her features that she was.

"She has always wanted to have a light center where she could bring together all these special people, hold retreats and gatherings, and help those who are just learning about all these things ... people who are just starting to open up ... like you."

"And why would a church group be threatened by this?" I asked.

Starla clicked her tongue. "I suppose because we encourage free thinking ... new thought ... searching ourselves and looking within. A lot of fundamentalist churches cling to the idea of the separation."

"The separation? What's that?" I took another bite from my muffin.

"You know ... being separate from God, or whatever name you give the Supreme Being. But we aren't separate from God. We are all one."

"I like that concept." I smiled. "I have to admit, I don't know much about it, but the idea makes sense to me."

"That's good, Juniper. You are asking questions." Starla seemed pleased with me. "That is what's important. Rosalee had a good feeling about you."

"Do you know why she wants me here?"

"You'll have to ask her," said Starla.

I looked around. "Where is Aunt Rosalee, anyway?"

"She's busy getting ready for the people who are coming in next week," said Starla. "We're expecting a big turn-out for the holistic fair. There are lots of preparations to make, and you'll probably find her in her office this morning, if you'd like to talk to her."

I decided I would do just that after I finished my breakfast.

"What happened after the talk last night?" I asked.

"We had a group meditation," said Starla. "We hold those just about every evening for whomever wishes to come. You're certainly welcome to join us, my dear."

I smiled, but didn't commit myself. After I finished eating, I carried my dishes into the kitchen, where a couple of women were working. I recognized the round-faced woman with glasses who had sat at Lance's table last night, and the young boy who had been with them was drawing on a pad of paper at a table.

"Hello," the woman greeted me with a big smile. "You're Juniper, Rosalee's niece. We've heard a lot about you." She reached out her hand and I shook it. "I'm Nadine Leachfield." She turned to the boy, who glanced up at her. "And this is my son, Max."

"Hello, Max," I told the small boy.

"Hi," said Max, who couldn't be more than eight or nine. He had short blond hair and a small up-turned nose.

"And that's Thelma." Nadine pointed to the other woman in the kitchen, who was busy scrubbing pans in a large metal sink. The woman was older, with white hair wrapped in a bun in back of her head. She didn't even turn around. "Oh, she's hard of hearing," explained Nadine. She saw my dirty dishes and took them from me.

"Was that your husband you were sitting with last night at dinner?" I asked.

Nadine grinned. "Why, yes, that was Lance. He's Rosalee's accountant ... well, his official title is bookkeeper."

"Do you live here?"

"You mean at the lodge?"

"Yes."

"Sort of," Nadine replied. "We have a house outside Wade City, but we're renting it out for the summer. It's so much easier staying here at the lodge when we're working. It's a long commute on these mountain roads."

"I can imagine," I said, and eyed Max. "And he must be out of school for the summer."

"No," said Nadine. "He's home schooled ... right here at the lodge. In fact, we've got a history lesson to do after we're finished here."

Max looked at his mother and winced. "Oh, Mom, do I have to?"

Nadine merely laughed, then went back to work. I wandered out and saw that Starla was busy writing in her notebook, so I headed for the lobby. I would ask someone else how to find Aunt Rosalee's office.

Gena was talking to someone when I approached the front desk. As I drew closer I saw that Clover sat on a stool with Gena standing over her. She spoke to Clover in a scolding tone. "You're going to *have* to clean rooms today, whether you like it or not. Housekeeping is short one worker, and it's in your agreement ..."

Clover suddenly saw me and smiled. "Hi, Juniper! How are you doing this morning?" She got off the stool and came around the counter to give me a hug.

I assured Clover I felt fine. It was obvious that Gena did not like being interrupted in her authority. She glared at me and at Clover, then turned and busied herself in paper work at the desk. Clover led me aside, out of Gena's hearing.

"Gena has me assigned to maid duty this morning," she said. "Otherwise I was going to work you in for a massage. Maybe later?"

"Maybe," I said noncommittally. "Do you know where Aunt Rosalee's office is?"

"Come on, I'll show you." Clover seemed glad to get away from Gena as she led me down a hallway that went past the dining room and kitchen. When she was sure we were completely out of earshot, she glanced back at the front desk, then confided in me. "Oh, that woman can get under my skin! I don't know why I let her to do that to me."

"You said her name is Gena Sutton Howard," I mentioned. "She isn't married, though, is she?"

"She was," replied Clover. "Gena was married before she came here, but she got divorced."

"How long has she worked here?" I asked.

Clover, I knew, loved to provide information. "Oh, Gena's been running things for, like ... quite a few months. Let's see, Rosalee changed the lodge over to a light center last August, like... right before hunting season began—and *that* was controversial. A lot of guys who had been used to coming here for hunting season were, like ... ticked off big time."

I remembered Starla mentioning hunters. "I take it Gena

runs things here?"

"Pretty much," admitted Clover. "But she's bossy and likes to step on toes. It seems she's always picking on somebody."

"And this morning it's you." I smiled sympathetically.

"Oh no, not really," said Clover. "Actually, she has it in for Wes Andrews right now."

"Wes?" My pulse picked up a bit at the mention of his name. "Why Wes?"

As we walked Clover led me around a corner into another hallway past more rooms. "He forgot to, like ... pick up some kind of garden plants she wanted for out front."

"That's *it?*"

"Yup. Working around Gena is kind of like walking on eggshells."

"You mentioned about hunters," I said. "Why were they ticked off? Do you mean at Aunt Rosalee for buying the lodge?"

"Well, you see," said Clover, "Rosalee and Fred managed the Majestic Mountain Lodge for many years. Everyone thought they, like ... owned it, but they were really, like ... just the managers. They bought the lodge, like ... two years ago, when it came up for sale. And then, Fred Sutton died last year, and your aunt turned it from, like ... a hunting lodge into a light center."

"And that upset the hunters who used to come?" I guessed.

"Well, yes," said Clover. "I mean, like ... she still welcomed hunters. Rosalee wasn't about to, like ... turn away paying customers she had known for years. But some of those hunters didn't like how she was changing things, and there were people, like ... coming here to the light center who weren't happy about being in the company of ... *killers.*"

I was starting to understand the problem now.

"Here's her office." Clover stopped outside a door that was ajar. I could see Lance Leachfield sitting at a desk with a computer when I looked in. "I have to go and clean some rooms now." Clover smiled, then hurried back down the hallway, her long red hair swinging behind her.

"Thanks, Clover," I called after her. Then I slowly pushed the office door open. Lance looked up from his work. He had the same round face as Nadine, his wife, and peered at me from behind his glasses. They seemed to be more brother and sister than husband and wife, at least in looks.

"Hello," Lance greeted me. "May I help you?"

"I'm looking for Aunt Rosalee," I said.

"Come on in, Juniper," my aunt called from an inner room, her Southern drawl evident. I found Aunt Rosalee at a spacious desk, leaning back in a recliner. Today she wore shimmery gold pants and a white, short-sleeved top with a Southwest design in turquoise and peach colors. A miniature dreamcatcher, made of leather, feathers and a turquoise stone, hung around her neck. She smiled at me and I noticed how dark—almost black—her eyes were. The long braid of hair lay casually across her left shoulder.

"I'm glad you're here," she told me. "I trust you had a good night's sleep."

"Oh, yes," I said. "The bed was very comfortable."

"You seem more relaxed this morning," she observed. "None the worse for the wear after last night's unpleasant episode."

I didn't comment on the attack. Instead, I asked her the question that had been on my mind since I had arrived. "Aunt Rosalee, when you wrote me that letter, what did you mean by a matter of urgency? What is it you wanted to talk to me about?"

Aunt Rosalee's dark eyes narrowed and her chin tightened as she grew serious. She got up and looked out the door, then drew it shut so that she could speak without Lance overhearing. Returning to her seat, she folded her plump hands on the desk and looked me in the eye. "There is somethin' I need to discuss with you," she said, "and I had planned to bring it up when the time was right."

"Well, is now a good time?" I asked.

She sighed and hung her head a moment, then looked up. "As good a time as any, I s'pose. There has been somethin' that's troubled me for some time," she told me. "It has to do with what happened almost twenty-two years ago that involved your father, Nathaniel."

I waited silently for her to continue.

"I don't know how much your mother has told you about your father's accident."

"Very little," I admitted.

"You know, don't you, that your father died from a gunshot wound?"

"Yes, Mother did tell me that. She said there had been some kind of hunting accident."

"Well, accident or not ... it happened while he was staying here at the lodge."

I drew in a quick breath. "Do you mean to tell me my father's death might not have been accidental? Was he ... was he ... murdered?"

"I'm not sayin' that," protested Aunt Rosalee. "You see, Fred took your father and some others out campin' up near Diamond Reservoir. Fred took the blame for shootin' him. He said it was an accident. He said the gun went off. Nathaniel bled to death before they could get help." The memory of the horrible event brought tears to Aunt Rosalee's eyes and she sniffed, then reached for a tissue on her desk.

I already knew these circumstances of my father's death, and wondered what else Aunt Rosalee had to say about it.

"As you know, Margaret would have nothin' to do with us after your father died."

I hung my head. "Yes, I know."

"And Fred started drinkin'. He was never charged with the killin', and the authorities were satisfied that your father's death was accidental. But it brought bad publicity to the lodge. We were asked to leave. So, Fred and I moved back to Oklahoma, where I set up my secretarial business for a few years. We managed that way, but weren't really happy. Then, about seven years ago, some new people bought the Majestic Mountain Lodge and called us to see if we'd come work as managers again. Apparently, the bad press surroundin' the shootin' was over and they needed someone who was familiar with the area and could do a good job managin' the place."

"So, you and Uncle Fred moved back here then?" I guessed.

"Yes, we did. But Fred still had his drinkin' problem, and it had grown worse. Last year, the doctors diagnosed him with liver cancer. He only lived two months." She sighed. "And now I'm comin' to the part you're wonderin' about. On his death bed, Fred confessed to me that he *didn't* kill Nathaniel."

This bit of news came as a big surprise. "Oh, my gosh," I cried. "Well, if he didn't shoot my father ... who *did?*"

She looked at me almost fearfully.

"Wait. Don't tell me my dad committed suicide. I know he

never would have taken his own life!"

"No, I'm not suggestin' any such thing," Aunt Rosalee reassured me.

"What then? What did Uncle Fred tell you?"

"He never said who did it," she said. "He was so weak. I tried numerous times to get him to tell me, but he wouldn't ... and when he died, he took his secret to the grave."

I let out a sigh. "Are you sure Uncle Fred knew what he was saying? Was he in his right mind?"

"As sure as the nose on yer face," she said.

"Who were the other people in the hunting party?" I asked.

"I don't recall. Why Fred took the blame all these years ... I have no idea."

"Why did you tell me this now?" I asked.

"I felt someone needs to know besides me."

"Have you considered going to the police with this information?" I asked.

"No, because no one's gonna believe me," she said as emotion began to raise the pitch of her voice. "The police aren't gonna do anythin'. What can they do? It's been more than twenty years."

She was probably right, I realized. But it sent a shiver up my back, thinking of the possibility of murder, and especially the fact that somebody had gotten away with it and may be walking around with a guilty conscience.

"Anyway, I felt you should know," said Aunt Rosalee. "Your mama spent all those years believin' her husband's brother shot him. I didn't want you to spend your life thinkin' the same. Fred, despite his wayward behavior at times, was a good man. Maybe he didn't deserve it, but I loved him and forgave him for his faults." She wiped her eyes with the tissue.

"Well, thank you, Aunt Rosalee, for telling me," I said.

She blew her nose one last time, then asked, "Did you have breakfast?"

"Yes, thank you." I sat up straight and smiled. "Now, tell me what I can do to help you around here. I feel like I should be doing something. How can I earn my keep?"

Aunt Rosalee's face brightened. "Well, in that case, let's not waste any more time. Let me show you the new gift shop we're settin' up. I understand you worked in a book store and already have experience."

"That's right," I admitted, amazed that she knew.

"I thought you'd be good at runnin' my little store in the lodge."

"You mean ... actually running it, not just working in it?"

"You'd be in charge of its operation, from orderin' and stockin' it, to managin' it. You could set your own hours and even hire some part-timers to help you with sales, so you're not stuck in the store all the time."

As we discussed the gift shop more, I found myself growing interested in her idea. I definitely had experience, having filled in for the book store owners many times when they were away. I rather liked the notion of running my own little shop. At the same time, though, I wasn't sure about this prospect. It was a major change for me, and I knew there were things back home I needed to take care of, even with Mike taking charge of my mother's estate.

"Naturally, I don't expect you to make a commitment right this moment," explained Aunt Rosalee. "You just got here." She slowly pushed herself up from her chair and stood up. "Let's take a walk right now down to the lobby."

I followed. When we passed through Lance's office, he was just hanging up the telephone. "Taffi's okay with changing her workshop to Saturday morning," Lance told Aunt Rosalee.

"Oh, good. And did you notify the musicians? The peace dancers are being rescheduled due to the cancellation of the aura lecture."

"I'm right on it." Lance picked up the phone as we headed out into the hall.

"Don't know what I'd do without that young man," said Aunt Rosalee.

As we walked toward the lobby she told me how chaotic it could be, planning a holistic fair with speakers calling to cancel and others wanting to be worked into the schedule.

"Is this your first one?" I asked.

"No, we had a conference last fall," Aunt Rosalee told me. "It went okay, but the turn-out was low. Not enough people knew about the Rainbow Majestic yet."

Gena saw us coming and stepped from behind the counter to join us. She followed us into a small room that was being remodeled. No one was working on it now, but I could see that a counter and some shelves had been built. New paint smell lingered in the air. There was a stepladder in the middle of the room, and sawdust lay on the tan carpeting. Empty display racks leaned against one wall, with several boxes piled to one side.

"This will be the gift shop," said Aunt Rosalee.

"The *boutique*," Gena corrected her. "It was my idea," she disclosed to me.

"It might have been your idea," Aunt Rosalee said to her stepdaughter, "but I'm still plannin' on lettin' Juniper take charge and run it."

Gena frowned. "Juniper doesn't know anything about running a boutique. Besides, she's got a life back in Kansas."

"Well, it's her decision," insisted Aunt Rosalee. Turning to me, she said, "If you want to take a crack at the gift shop, it's yours as far as I'm concerned."

Gena chuckled. "I can just see it ..."

Aunt Rosalee shot her a warning look, then smiled at me and put her hand on my shoulder as she walked me around the shop. "Don't pay her no mind. Gena does enough around here as it is. It's time she slackened the reins a little and gave somebody else a chance to do somethin' once."

With a loud sigh, Gena walked out and returned to the front desk. Aunt Rosalee poked into some boxes and showed me some wares she had been collecting over the last few months. There were wind chimes, jewelry, angel knick-knacks, packages of incense, candles, compact music discs and books. She was quick to point out that I could go through some catalogues and choose more inventory—whatever I thought might be appropriate for the store.

"Aunt Rosalee, I'm not very familiar with this kind of stuff," I confessed. "I mean, these books are all metaphysical. All this is really new to me."

"Juniper, you can order mainstream books as well," Aunt Rosalee encouraged. "Just because we're a healin' center doesn't mean we can't offer items outside the new age category. Pick out some good fiction, some nature books—some normal stuff."

I smiled when she said *normal*. This was going to be fun. I envisioned myself going through catalogues, finding things that would sell in the gift shop. "How soon do we open?"

Aunt Rosalee flung out her arms and gave me a hug. "I knew you wouldn't let me down. And I know you're gonna just blossom for me." She stepped back and grinned. "Drake only has a little bit more to do in here. We can be up and runnin' for the holistic fair next week ... with limited merchandise, anyway. In fact, we'll use the holistic fair as a trial period. You should know after that whether this is somethin' you're gonna wanna do for a livin'."

Yes, I needed to make a living, I realized. I cleared my throat, then asked, "Aunt Rosalee, how are we going to handle ... I mean, what about ... pay?" I felt embarrassed having to bring up the subject.

"For now, you'll be a wage earner, an employee of the lodge," she said.

"That sounds fair," I said.

"But after you're broke in, we'll discuss the terms of a partnership."

My mouth dropped open in surprise. Then I had to ask, "Is Gena in partnership with you?"

Aunt Rosalee picked up a package of herbs labeled White Sage. "I think I need this for my office." She turned to me. "No, Gena's not a partner, and I wouldn't have her for one. She works for me, and she's been a good manager in many respects. But ... she's not endin' up with this lodge, as much as she'd like it."

Did I detect a hint of bitterness in Aunt Rosalee toward her stepdaughter? I wondered how well they got along. Last night, at dinner, they had seemed amiable. Gena just had a way of provoking people, but Aunt Rosalee seemed to simply shrug it off.

I wanted to know what I could do now to get started. Aunt Rosalee told me to draw up a floor plan of where I wanted to set things, and then she would bring me the catalogues, so I could place my orders as soon as possible. I could start pricing the things in boxes, and she gave me a notebook to write down the inventory, the wholesale price and the retail. Later on, I might get a computer to help keep track.

She left me alone, and I roamed the shop—taking it all in— visualizing how it might look when everything was ready. My own shop! I could hardly believe it.

I worked the remainder of the morning, then wandered outside for a breath of fresh air. No one noticed as I slipped out the front doors and greeted cool mountain air, a deep blue sky and sunshine that instantly warmed my bare face, neck and arms. It was close to the noon hour and quite warm by now, with no need for a sweater. I climbed down the steps and listened to the call of a Rocky Mountain bluebird, similar to our eastern version that I knew.

Wes was bent over some shrubbery in front of the lodge, working a pair of pruning shears. He didn't look up until I called out to him. He had on baggy blue jeans, sneakers and a gray T-shirt, with a baseball cap on his head to protect him from the sun.

"Good mornin', Juniper." He stood up and grinned at me. He tipped the bill of his cap toward me.

"What a beautiful day," I remarked.

"Isn't it? Whatcha been up to?"

I told him briefly about my work in the gift shop. Then I said, "Thanks for going into the woods last night and looking for that person who knocked me down. Clover told me you and Drake went out there."

"Yeah, well, we sure didn't find anybody," said Wes.

"I haven't seen Drake yet today," I said.

"Oh, he's around," said Wes. "I think they had some problem with the garbage disposal in the kitchen this mornin'."

I smiled. Wes seemed kind of sheepish for some reason. His blue eyes kept glancing at me. Finally, I said, "I don't want to keep you from your work. I know you've got things to do."

He sighed. "That's for sure. Gena's on my case today."

"So I heard."

"You don't wanna cross that lady."

"I'll try to stay out of her way. I think she has something against me."

"Well, I can't imagine that." Wes eyed me, then held his chin. I thought he was going to ask me something, but then he shook his head and knelt over the bush he was pruning.

"I'd better let you get back to work." I started to walk away.

Wes called out my name and I turned back to him. "Would you care to take a walk after dinner tonight?" Then, he quickly added, "You know, it might be a good idea if you're with someone when you go in the woods again." His smile was hesitant.

My heart quickened. "I would love that, Wes. Sure. Let's do it."

He merely smiled, then got right back to his pruning. As I headed back up to the lodge, I noticed Gena's pointed face at one of the lodge windows, looking out at us. Poor Wes. Was everyone at the Rainbow Majestic intimidated by Gena? Well, I was determined not to be one of them. She and I were first cousins, after all, and just because she was a few years older than I—and ran the lodge—didn't make Gena Sutton Howard my taskmaster. I would answer to Aunt Rosalee, and not Gena. She didn't frighten me in the least. Not then, anyway.

7

At lunch, I was invited to sit with Clover and two of the lodge maids. I was tired and the dialogue centered around people I didn't know in Wade City. From their discussion I was able to determine that Clover was popular with many of the single men in town. I suppose she had a lot of opportunities, being in the massage profession, to get to know people. I gathered that she had dated more than a few of her clients.

My thoughts drifted away from local gossip as I recalled the conversation Aunt Rosalee and I had shared earlier in her office. I had not been able to erase it from my mind, but distracting myself with the gift shop preparations had at least postponed my thinking about it. Now I replayed in my mind my aunt's words—how Uncle Fred had declared on his death bed that he had not been the one who shot my father.

So, *who* then? And if it hadn't been an accident, what had it been? Why would anyone want to kill my father? And why had Uncle Fred taken the blame himself? Had he been protecting someone? More importantly, what was I going to do with this new information about my father? I couldn't leave it alone. Aunt Rosalee had said no one would believe her. Yet I knew she had not made this up. I needed to know the truth about my father's death. I didn't know how I was going to find out, but there had to be somebody who knew something besides Uncle Fred. The question was, who? And where could I possibly begin to delve into this impossible quest?

I finally excused myself and told them I had a slight headache, which was true. I wanted to go up to my room and lie down for a while.

"I'll bet it's the altitude," said one of the maids. "Some people have trouble adjusting at first."

"Are you going to be all right, Juniper?" Clover asked. "Can I help in any way?"

"No, I'm just tired. I think I'll try to get a nap."

"That's a good idea. Drink lots of water, too," she suggested.

Upstairs in my room I found the bed had been made and new towels hung out in the bathroom. I sat on the pink canopy bed and noticed the picture of my father and Uncle Fred that I had brought along. I picked it up off my bedside table and studied it. I wondered if I would ever know what had really happened when my father was killed. A word formed in my mind unexpectedly and I recalled his pet name for me, "Muffin." A smile was immediately followed by a tear as I set the picture back on the table, then reached for Sean's picture on the bedside stand.

I stared at his face through the glass. It was the photo of Sean in his military uniform. My heart ached as it always did when I looked at his picture. I missed him and usually went through a flurry of emotions—sadness, anger, and finally despair. I sighed and thought of how Mike Rollins had proposed to me a few nights ago at Wild Bill's Buffet. How could he possibly think I'd marry him? To Mike, it was a logical solution and a casual promise he'd made to my dying mother. Could Mike possibly be in love with me? I didn't love him—of that I was sure. At one time, though, when I was a young teenager, I had found Mike Rollins attractive, but only because he was a teen-age boy older than I, and he had paid some attention to me. But that soon wore off when he left for college.

In the last year or so, he had started showing an interest in me again, but I had never believed it was anything serious. Could I ever feel that adolescent thrill I'd once had toward him? I really didn't think so. Not after knowing Sean and loving Sean the way I had.

My thoughts turned to Wes Andrews and I ran my finger down Sean's face behind the glass. Why was I looking forward to my walk this evening with Wes? What was it about him that drew me? Was it because Wes reminded me of Sean? They had both been in the Marine Corps, and both had fought in the Middle East. That had to be it—and yet there was something enticing about Wes that had nothing to do with Sean.

Wes was tranquil and wise, so easy to be around. I felt drawn to him without knowing why, except that his presence was comforting. Wes was not one to act boldly, but when he looked at me, I could feel the attraction. He seemed to be holding back, so perhaps it would be up to me to persuade him to take another step.

My eyes grew heavy and I rolled onto my side, gripping Sean's picture frame close to my heart as I closed my eyes. It wasn't long before I drifted off to sleep. I must have eaten something at lunch that caused me to dream. I was roaming a field of wildflowers on a sunny, blue-skied day, and my familiar woods were in the dream. Birds sang and rabbits chased each other in the tall grasses. I cut across the clearing to a path in the woods, and the darkness of the pine trees closed in around me.

I heard a growl behind me, and suddenly a black bear appeared and stood on its hind legs. I screamed, then ran through the woods with the bear in pursuit. Suddenly, I saw my cabin ahead. It was only twenty yards away, but my legs started to slow down. I couldn't move as fast as I wanted and the black bear was gaining on me.

In my dream, somehow I recalled that I had never succeeded at actually entering my cabin in the woods. Every time I reached the door, the dream would end. Would I be able to get in this time and escape the angry bear?

Gasping in desperation, I finally reached the door of the cabin. I turned the knob, but it was locked. I cried out in alarm and, at that point, I actually started to awaken. Just before I opened my eyes, the door to the cabin gave way and there stood Drake Phillips, looking down at me from inside. I awoke with a start.

Those piercing dark blue eyes of his lingered in my mind as I lay on the bed, shuddering from the dream. With all the other stuff happening, I hadn't thought much about Drake today. Now I recalled his finding me after I ran out of the woods last night. Perhaps Drake's presence is what had frightened away my attacker. He must have been close by at the time.

Later that afternoon, I ventured downstairs to work in the gift shop again. But I never got that far. As I crossed through the great room, Starla Streber called my name. She sat with the elderly couple named Cyril and Celeste, who had to themselves the big comfortable red couch next to the fireplace. Starla sat in the matching red arm chair and smiled at me.

"Juniper, have you met Cyril and Celeste?" she asked.

The white-haired man stood up to extend an arthritic hand, which was textured with blue veins. "I don't believe I've had the pleasure," he said in a high, pleasant voice. "I'm Cyril Jorgensen."

I shook his hand and found it to be cold. A sign of poor circulation, perhaps? "Nice to meet you, Cyril. I'm Juniper Sutton."

"Yes, I know." His smile was warm upon thin, pale lips, and his brown eyes were bright and alert.

The frail, white-haired woman beside him did not attempt to stand, but looked up at me with sparkling blue eyes. She almost appeared to glow with her wide smile. "And I am Celeste," she said. "A pleasure to meet you, Juniper."

"Juniper, go ahead and sit down." Starla stood up and beckoned me to take her place. "Why don't you get acquainted?"

"I don't want to take your chair," I protested.

Starla winked at me. "I have to leave now, anyway. I have an awakening to prepare for at three o'clock." She started off.

"Don't be late," Celeste called after her in a quavering voice. Then she patted the arm rest of the chair Starla had occupied, insisting that I join them. I couldn't very well refuse.

Cyril crossed a leg over his knee and cleared his throat. "I understand you came from Kansas," he said. When I nodded, he continued. "I was born in Kansas, you know."

Celeste turned to him as if she had heard the news for the first time. "Really?" She laughed. "I've never been to Kansas. How interesting."

"Where were *you* born?" I asked her.

Celeste blinked her eyes and smiled. "Why, California. I've lived most my life in California."

"That should explain it," said Cyril with a smirk. If he had meant his comment to be condescending, Celeste certainly had not noticed. She was a bubbly person, almost constantly laughing and cheerful, and seemed to enjoy the small talk in which we engaged ourselves for a while.

I began thinking up excuses to leave when Cyril said to me, point blank, "What was the reason Rosalee brought you here?" His brown eyes looked right into mine with such gravity, I was taken by surprise.

After a pause, I answered him. "Well, I'm not really sure yet. I guess she wants me to work in her gift shop."

He considered this a moment, then swept a hand back through his shock of white hair.

"I thought Gena was going to run the gift shop," announced Celeste.

I smiled at her, but didn't say anything.

"I'm sure we were together in a previous life," Cyril told me.

I stared at him, a little startled. "What?"

"Oh yes, we've all been together before." Celeste gestured with her frail hand. "Many times, in fact."

"Of course." Cyril cleared his throat again and studied me closely. "But I believe ... yes, I'm quite sure, in fact, that Juniper ... yes, Juniper was my daughter."

"Oh, how lovely," said Celeste with a big smile.

I didn't know what the old gentleman was talking about. I slowly shook my head in denial.

"Don't you believe in reincarnation?" Celeste's blue eyes widened in surprise. "I thought everyone who came here to this lodge believed in it. Cyril and I were together in ancient Egypt." She nodded vigorously. "We traveled there just a few years ago, and both of us took a turn lying in the sarcophagus."

Reincarnation? I had been taught that there was no such thing. Yet these two were adamant about the subject as they began to elaborate on many of the lives they had experienced, both individually and as a couple. I listened in amusement, unsure whether to believe any of this. Cyril claimed he had lived as one of the followers of Jesus in Bible times. He spoke of the apostles as colleagues and described them and their personalities, just as though he had actually lived among them. I couldn't help being bemused by his imagination ... if that's what it was.

"You see, Juniper," Cyril told me gently, "this life experience is just another semester for us on earth. There are many roads on which to travel in life and many courses open to us. We are here to learn, to monitor and to serve."

I dared to question him. "Are you saying that I've lived before?"

"I know *I* have," he said. "What do you feel deep inside?"

This was a hard question to answer. "Well, I suppose it's

possible," I finally said. "People tell stories of how ..."

"Have you ever had an experience of *déjà vu?*" he asked.

"You mean, that feeling that I've been in a place before that I really haven't?"

"Or with a person whom you already seem to know?" asked Celeste.

"You might meet someone you are attracted to, without knowing why, because you've known them before ... in a different lifetime," Cyril suggested.

"Y-yes ... maybe," I admitted.

"Or you detest someone without having a reason."

"Okay," I said, "I know that many people believe in reincarnation. So why doesn't the church proclaim it? Why isn't reincarnation in the Bible?"

Cyril's eyes lit up. "But it is, Juniper, my child. There is evidence of reincarnation in the Bible, if you know where to look for it. Some passages were inadvertently left *in.*" He smiled at the thought.

"Didn't Jesus talk about being born again?" piped up Celeste.

"Well, sure ..."

"There are as many instances in the Bible that refer to extraterrestrial life as well," continued Cyril. "Let's take Ezekiel, for instance ..."

I sighed. "Then why doesn't the church acknowledge it?"

"You've heard of the Council of Nicea, around 300 A.D.," Cyril told me. "That's when a group of priests got together and decided what to keep in the Bible and what to delete. And they took out many, many things that they felt would allow people to think too much for themselves."

"Heaven forbid." Celeste giggled.

"Don't you know, Juniper, that religion is merely people control?"

"Oh, that's not so," I replied.

"Are you a religious person?" Celeste asked me.

"Well, I ... go to church once in a while."

"Are you a spiritual person?" asked Cyril.

I was floored. *Religious? Spiritual?* Was there a difference? What were they getting at? What was *I?* At the moment, I was excited by the whole conversation, but at the same time feeling a

little defensive. All this philosophical talk going on at the Rainbow
Majestic Lodge was new to me, and I was feeling overwhelmed and
confused.

"I have an idea," said Cyril. Once again he brushed his
shock of white hair back off his forehead. "I know some books
you might find of interest. One of them is *Lost Books of the Bible*.
I think you'll find it interesting."

"Cyril has a lot of books," added Celeste.

"They're kept in the library," Cyril informed me. "Rosalee
set aside two rooms outside the dining hall as the library for
hundreds and hundreds of books. You should go there and see
what interests you."

"I ... I will," I said, already intrigued. Then I remembered
something. "Wes told me you are an author. What books have
you written?"

Cyril puffed up like a bird ruffling its feathers. "You'll be
selling them in the gift shop you'll be running."

"How long have you been here at the Rainbow Majestic?" I
asked Cyril.

"Oh, I've been coming to this lodge for thirty years," he
said.

Thirty years! "Then you must have known my Uncle Fred,"
I said.

"Oh, yes, Fred Sutton and I were good friends," said Cyril.

"Then you also must have known my father."

Cyril nodded his head. "Yes, I knew Nathaniel as well."

"How well did you know my father?" I asked.

Cyril stroked his chin, then said, "He used to come here for
hunting season, I remember. He was from Colorado Springs,
wasn't he?"

"Yes, Colorado Springs is where I was born."

"Mm-hm." Cyril continued to nod, and I wondered what he
was thinking.

"I'd like to ask you something." After a few seconds, I said,
"What do you know about my father's death?"

Cyril looked at me, startled, then gazed around the room
without answering. "I wonder if they'll be having music this
afternoon."

"Oh, I hope so," bubbled Celeste. "I just love it when Starla
sings."

"She's giving an awakening this afternoon, remember?" Cyril reminded her.

"Yes, that's right. Well, excuse me, if you will, please." Celeste struggled to stand up. "I'm going to see if there's going to be someone else providing the entertainment." The old woman started off toward the lobby, leaning on her cane.

I turned back to Cyril and asked him again, "Is there anything you can tell me about my father?"

Cyril cleared his throat. "You know, Juniper, that's a question you need to ask your aunt. I'm afraid I can't give you an answer to that."

"I've been told Uncle Fred shot him accidentally when they were hunting," I said. "Do you know any details about that?"

Cyril began to fidget and appeared uncomfortable. "I'm sure it was an accident, if that is what you mean."

"Do you have any idea who went with them to the camp site?"

"You know, Juniper ... that was a long, long time ago ..."

"Were you staying at the lodge then?"

Cyril stared at me in shock. It was obvious he didn't want to talk about this subject any longer. He stood up. "I think I'll go see if Celeste found out what she wanted to know." Then he flashed a quick smile at me. "It's a pleasure knowing you, Juniper. Go visit the library, like I said, and take some books back to your room. I think you and I will have more to talk about next time." Then he slowly walked away, slightly bent over as he went.

I wandered down the hall past the dining hall and soon came to the rooms Cyril had mentioned. Aunt Rosalee had set up a library of metaphysical books. There were shelves on every wall and a table and chairs in the middle of the room. A huge braided wool rug of multiple colors covered the hardwood floor. Navy blue drapes hung at the windows. I spent half an hour browsing through various books with topics on meditation, reincarnation, ESP, astral travel, UFOs and subjects I'd never heard of before and selected five that appealed to me. There was a ledger on the table, with a pen for guests to write down which books they had borrowed. I signed the books out and left to return to my suite.

As I headed up the spiral stairs, Taffi Kincaid caught up

with me. "Well, hi, Juniper," she called from behind me. "I've been wanting to see you. How are you, anyway? Oh, I see you plan on doing a lot of reading in your spare time. Great! Hey, I want to talk to you. Do you have anything going on right now?"

I told her I was headed back to my suite.

"Oh, that's just great! We can talk there." She accompanied me to the crystal suite, and I compared her liveliness to Celeste's bubbly manner. Cyril had seemed more serious, more down to earth, but had been knowledgeable when we talked about the Bible and reincarnation. I unlocked my door and we entered.

"I heard you've accepted the position with the lodge's gift shop," said Taffi after we sat down. Her green eyes were as wide as always.

"Yes. I hope to give it a try, at least."

"Good. You know, your handwriting has told me a lot about you. One of the things I learned is that you're pretty good at managing your affairs."

I rolled my eyes. "There are some people in my life who didn't think so." I recalled my mother and Mike.

"Your self esteem is rather low," Taffi told me, "as evidenced by your low crossing of t's. If you'd like, I'll show you an exercise that might help improve that. But we'll deal with that a little later. What I really want to know is, who are you grieving over?"

I looked at Taffi in surprise.

"It's okay," she said. "I know you just lost your mother. But I'm not talking about your mother in this instance. I can see in your handwriting that you are hurting pretty badly over someone ... a man."

"You're right," I admitted. "My fiancé was killed in Iraq a couple of years ago." I ended up confiding in Taffi my personal experience with Sean and how it still hurt whenever I thought of him.

She was sympathetic and a good listener. She supplied me with tissues from the coffee table and then sat back in the chair, satisfied that she'd been right.

"What else did my handwriting tell you?" The tears were drying up now and I blew my nose.

Taffi crossed her arms and looked smug. "Pushy men annoy you to pieces," she declared, "especially ones that come into your life and want to take over from Day One."

I smiled. "You're good."

"It's in the handwriting."

I studied her a moment, then said, "I really find that hard to believe. I mean, come on ... there's more to it, isn't there?"

Taffi's eyes grew bigger and she smiled. "What do you think?"

I sat back in my chair. "I think you might be psychic."

"Ooh, maybe just a little," she admitted, and held up her thumb and index finger pressed together. "Maybe just an itty bitty amount of psychic ability."

"See? I was right." I smiled. "What do you do? Do you channel?"

"No." Taffi studied me a moment, then said, "You're probably not going to believe this, but ... I'm a ghost buster."

"Really?" I didn't know whether I believed her or not.

"Honest," said Taffi and her eyebrows shot up. "I can detect ghosts and—once in a while—a client calls me up to do a job."

"What kind of a job?" I probed, interested.

"For instance, if someone moves into a new place and discovers there's a ghost hanging around, causing problems, or making the occupants uncomfortable, I'll go in and talk to the earthbound spirit, and in most cases I get them to go to the Light."

My mouth had dropped open.

Taffi giggled. "The radio station in Wade City brought me in for a ghost-busting job last winter."

"Wow," I murmured, then quickly added, "Well, I'm not sure I believe in ghosts."

Taffi sighed, then said, "But, then, *all* of us are psychic, you know."

"You mean, those of you who work at the Rainbow Majestic? You ... light workers?"

"Nope, I mean everybody. You, as well."

"Me?" I shook my head. "Oh, I don't think so."

"Sure you are," insisted Taffi. "Everyone possesses some degree of psychic ability. It's just that in most people it hasn't been developed and is dormant. But you can sharpen your psychic ability. You need to open your third eye."

I laughed. "My ... what?"

"Up here." Taffi pointed to the middle of her forehead. "That's your sixth chakra, your psychic center."

I was lost and she saw that I was and laughed. "It's okay, Juniper. You're going to get your chakras aligned, and then that third eye of yours is going to open right up. Just remember to take it slow. You don't want to rush it and open it up all at once. Those books you brought up to read will get you started."

"My chakras? What are they?" I asked.

"Energy vortexes along certain points on your body," Taffi tried to explain. She pointed to the seven of them along the front of her body and named them, but I was confused. "When one or more of your chakras is blocked or closed, you can't function fully." She looked around the room, then stood up. "Let's do it right now," she said, and started to choose rocks that were displayed on shelves and table tops.

"What are we doing?" I was at once alert.

"I'm going to balance your chakras for you," Taffi told me. "It won't take very long. And don't worry, it doesn't hurt." She erupted with laughter as she gathered up different colored stones. "You don't have to do anything but just lie there."

I could see there was no way to avoid what was going to happen next. My curiosity had actually taken over any reluctance I felt, and Taffi was so friendly and vivacious, I realized I was starting to like her as much as I liked Clover.

She told me to lie down on the couch—on my back—and she pulled a pendulum out of her purse that was a clear glass ball crystal suspended on a gold chain. As I lay there, quietly staring up at the ceiling, Taffi held the pendulum above my crotch so that the glass ball at the end was suspended just half an inch or so above my body. I waited to see what would happen.

At first nothing happened, and then the glass ball began to slowly move clockwise in a tiny circle. After a few seconds, Taffi stopped it, then dangled the pendulum over my abdomen. Again we waited, and the glass ball did the same thing. Next, she moved it up higher, this time over my stomach. She repeated the action over my heart, my throat, my forehead, and above my head.

"Why did you do that?" I asked.

"I was checking to see if any of your chakras are open." Taffi sorted through the collection of crystals she had gathered.

"Oh," I said, then asked, "and are they?"

"Some," she said, "but not very much."

I watched in silence as she placed a stone between my thighs, then another on my abdomen, and on up the rest of my body, where she had dangled the pendulum. Taffi explained that each chakra had to be charged with its corresponding color. The first one was my root chakra and required a red stone, a jasper. The second chakra was located over my pelvis, and she placed an orange-colored stone, which she called a carnelian. Over my stomach, just above my navel, she placed a yellow citrine, for the solar plexus. "That's your feeling center," she told me.

Over my heart Taffi placed a large green malachite stone. On my throat she carefully placed a small blue piece of turquoise and told me that was my throat chakra. Once it was opened, I would more easily be able to speak my truth. Next, she placed a piece of dark blue Lapis lazuli on my forehead, just above my eyes. The stone felt cool and soothing against my skin. Last, she placed a purple amethyst cluster on the couch just above my head. "That's your crown center," she said with a smile, "to increase enlightenment."

"I never knew about any of these," I told her.

"Just close your eyes and relax," Taffi said. "In a few minutes I'm going to check with the pendulum again and see how they're opening up."

"You mean ... they're opening ... now?"

"The crystals are helping open up your chakras," explained Taffi. She said that if I was ever working with crystals and didn't have all the right colors, I could always substitute a clear quartz or herkimer diamond, because such stones contained all the colors and therefore could be used for any chakra. "The crystals can energize, harmonize and heal," Taffi told me. "You might consider getting one to wear at all times. After a short while, you will feel the difference."

I was already feeling calm and relaxed. It reminded me of how warm I'd felt when Starla had waved her hands over me last evening in the dining room.

Next, Taffi took the pendulum and suspended it over my root chakra. It immediately began to circle in an ever increasing spiral. "Are you causing it to spin like that?" I asked.

"No, I'm not making it move whatsoever," she said. "The

pendulum is moving on its own accord."

I watched in fascination as Taffi tested each chakra. Each one reacted the same way. The largest circles occurred over my chest. "Most people we know are wide open in their heart chakras," Taffi explained. "Light workers are usually very loving folks."

The circle was smaller over my throat and third eye, and Taffi said these weren't fully open in me yet. "Give it time," she said. "You're just learning about all this."

Then she methodically removed each stone, in the order she had placed them, and when I was ready, I slowly sat up on the couch and realized I felt refreshed and relaxed. I asked Taffi a question that had come to mind during the chakra balancing. "Do you have samples of everybody's handwriting in this lodge?"

She put away the collection of rocks around the room. "I suppose so," she said.

"Then you must know a bit about the people who live and work here."

"Handwriting has given me a broad base of knowledge. I know a lot of things that some people would rather I *didn't* know." She came and sat down. "I'll tell you one thing. I know there are some people at the Rainbow Majestic who are hiding things." She grew more serious. "Some of the handwriting I've seen reveals deep problems, and in some cases guilt and deception."

"You can tell all that from handwriting?"

"Of course."

"Taffi, I'm trying to find out what really happened to my father. Do you have any idea who might be hiding information about him?"

She was quiet for a moment or two, then wrinkled her forehead. "No, Juniper, I don't know anything about him."

"I just thought you could point out to me anyone who might be ..." I hesitated.

"Guilty?" she finished.

"Well, at least guilty of withholding the truth," I said.

"How did your dad die?" she asked.

I quickly went over the facts I'd been told, then ended by saying I had reason to believe Uncle Fred had not been the one who fired the gun. I didn't tell her that Aunt Rosalee had heard this from Uncle Fred before he died.

"I'll be happy to help you in any way I can," said Taffi.

"Thank you." I smiled in relief.

Taffi glanced at her watch. "Oops, it's almost time for dinner. How time flies. I've got some things I need to do first, but, hey, I'll see you later. Thanks for the talk, Juniper."

With that, she was out the door. I sat on the couch, puzzled, still feeling relaxed from the chakra balancing I'd received. Then I remembered that after dinner Wes and I were going for a walk together. My heart picked up a few beats as I headed for the bathroom to freshen up. I had learned a lot in one afternoon and wondered what the coming evening would bring.

8

I found myself in a restless state before the dinner hour. I was torn between wanting to delve into one of the books I'd borrowed from Aunt Rosalee's library and wandering. The desire to explore more of the lodge finally won out, so I locked my door as I left and walked down the corridor of rooms.

No one was in either of the halls as I headed for the back exit I'd taken last night, when I'd headed down to the garden after seeing Drake at my window. My curiosity to see where that stairway led prompted me to approach it. Yesterday the door to the stairs had been left open. Now it was closed and I hoped it wasn't locked.

Luckily, it wasn't. I closed the door behind me and found myself in a narrow passageway that led upwards and curved to the left. The steps were old and narrow. It was obvious by the peeling wallpaper and dust on the steps that this was a stairway not often used. It was dark and I had to grip the flimsy railing attached to the wall as I climbed.

I reached the next landing, but found the door locked that led to what must be the third floor of the lodge. The steps continued on up, however. The passageway narrowed even more and the steps curved like before. It seemed to grow darker the higher I climbed. There was a dusty smell in the stuffy hallway. As narrow as it was, someone as wide as Taffi might have trouble navigating such a passageway, I thought.

Finally, I came to a narrow door and wondered if it, too, would be locked. It wasn't. I stepped into a dark attic room filled with junky furniture, antique trunks, some metal cabinets and an old record player console. There were dust-covered book shelves and boxes everywhere. I could barely see, due to the lack of light. There seemed to be another room, so I groped my way past all the boxes until I came to an opening in the wall that led out into another narrow corridor.

Obviously, this part of the Rainbow Majestic was not used

except for storage. There was a tiny, diamond-shaped window to let in some light. The musty smell drove me back into the hallway, where I continued to explore several similar rooms and storage closets. When I came to another room, I noticed a narrow door standing open at the opposite end. As I approached it, I heard distant harp music. The sounds were not anything except random chords and strumming, but I was mesmerized. I stepped through the doorway, which was barely big enough for me to slide through. As a matter of fact, I had to crouch to go through it.

A passageway dipped downward. I felt my way forward as steps continued to drop. I had no idea where it was taking me, but I was intrigued. I wondered how many of these secret passageways were in this old lodge.

The harp music grew louder. Then I saw another doorway ahead. As I approached, the music ceased. I stepped out of the panel in the wall into a rather large, darkened room with a high ceiling. There were no windows, but dim daylight came through two doorways opposite what appeared to be an auditorium. As my eyes adjusted to the dim light, I could see a raised stage with old velvet curtains to the sides, and a horseshoe of seat rows projected out. An old smoke smell, like burnt wood, permeated the air.

I felt uneasy. I was quite sure the harp music had come from this place. Suddenly, a noise startled me. I wasn't alone in this dark auditorium. My instincts told me to squeeze back through that panel in the wall and retreat up the narrow passageway. But then I heard a loud, cacophonous strum of the harp, followed by a giggle.

"Who's there?" I called out. My voice echoed in the auditorium.

There was no answer. I waited only a few seconds, then started back through the passageway.

"Wait, it's just me," a child's voice rang out.

I whirled around. "Where are you?" I asked.

"I'm right here." A small child laughed. Then a flashlight came on next to the harp and I saw the harp's player sitting on a stool next to the instrument. I sighed in relief as I recognized Lance and Nadine Leachfield's little boy, Max, holding the beam of light.

"Did I scare you?" he asked.

"I heard the music," I explained, then stepped toward the stage to get a better look at him. "Where are we?"

Max stood up and shone his flashlight beam all around. "This is the place where they used to put on plays ... in the olden days."

I could see now with his flashlight beam that the room was in pretty bad shape. On one side, the walls were charred and black from fire damage. There were broken seats, many with their upholstery torn. Someone, at one time, had started renovating the auditorium. An old, rickety ladder stood against one side of the room, and an old chandelier had been taken off the ceiling and was on the floor near the stage.

"Wow," I remarked as I gazed around the dim room. "What part of the lodge are we in?"

"The old part," said Max.

"Do you come here often?" I asked.

"No one's supposed to," he replied.

"Does your mother know you come here?"

Max crossed his arms and shook his head. "You won't tell, will you?"

I didn't answer. Instead, I said, "You must know about the secret passageways in the lodge."

He grinned and nodded. "I've explored them all," he said. "That one you came through goes to the attic."

"Is that how you got here?"

"No, I came up from the basement," he explained.

"Wow, that's amazing," I said. "Hey, sometime maybe you can show me the other secret passageways."

He thought about that a minute, as if he wasn't sure he wanted to share all his secrets with me. "Well ... okay," he agreed.

"Show me how you came up here," I said. "It's almost time for dinner, so we should probably go now."

"Come on." Max directed his flashlight and led me behind the stage, through a doorway into what had once been a dressing room. He then slipped into a closet. I followed, and we groped our way through a narrow tunnel that slanted downward. After several minutes, we emerged into the furnace room in the cellar of the Rainbow Majestic.

The basement was dark and dirty, but Max was well

acquainted with every nook and cranny as he led me up a steep flight of steps into the kitchen's pantry area.

A bustle of activity was going on in the kitchen as the cooks prepared the evening meal. The older woman, who had been washing dishes that morning, saw me and looked startled.

"That's Thelma," said Max. "She can't hear."

I smiled at the woman, who stared at me curiously as I followed the small boy out.

"Max, where have you been?" Nadine came in from the dining room with a tray of dishes. She seemed surprised to see me.

"Just showing Juniper around," he said as if it were an everyday occurrence.

Nadine smiled, but an eyebrow shot up in question.

"We found each other," I told Max's mother. Then, with a wink at Max, I excused myself and hastened to the second floor to the crystal suite, where I freshened up before dinner.

That night I again sat at my aunt's table, along with Gena. Starla was dining with Cyril and Celeste, and I noticed Clover seated at a table with Wes and Drake. There seemed to be less people than there had been the night before.

Aunt Rosalee explained that some of the guests were on an outing and hadn't come in yet, but would be served a late supper. She and Gena discussed the upcoming holistic fair while I ate grilled salmon cooked in lemon and basil sauce, Basmati rice and delicious zucchini seasoned with Parmesan cheese.

Nadine and Lance sat at their table with little Max, who kept eyeing me as he poked at his food. My attention kept wandering to Clover's table, where she appeared to be entertaining Wes and Drake with witty conversation. I wished I could join their table, but it would have been rude to leave my aunt. Drake glanced in my direction several times, and I recalled my afternoon dream about the bear chasing me to the cabin. What had my dream meant? Only once did Wes turn to look at me. Clover pretty much had his full attention. But when he did catch my eye, Wes smiled in a gentle way that told me he remembered we had agreed to take a walk together.

Gena got up to check on something in the kitchen, and I asked my aunt, "Is there a part of the lodge not being used?"

Aunt Rosalee nodded and wiped her mouth with her napkin. "Yes. There's a wing that used to be the original part of the lodge, but it's boarded up."

"Is there a reason?" I asked.

"The old part of the lodge had a small fire many years ago," she explained. "We were workin' on restorin' the old auditorium, but the remodelin' came to a halt when Fred became ill."

"I see." I took a sip of herb tea, then asked her, "Do you plan to continue the remodeling at some point in the future?"

Aunt Rosalee stalled. I waited as she searched my face. "No, we decided to put our energy into other projects." Then she said, "The fact is, that part of the lodge is haunted."

I suddenly felt a strange chill at the base of my spine. I looked at her skeptically. "Haunted? You mean ... by a ghost?"

Aunt Rosalee's eyes twinkled with mischief, giving me the impression that she was merely putting me on. "Whoever's hauntin' that wing seems to be content to stay in the old part and not bother any of us here."

Gena had reappeared at the table and sat back down. "Talking about the lodge ghost, are we?"

"I don't believe in ghosts," I told them with a smile, and sipped again at my tea.

"Well, we only tell that to guests who are troublesome," said Gena."

"Juniper's no guest," Aunt Rosalee affirmed. "She's family. And besides, Juniper's workin' for me now, and I think she has a right to know everythin' about the Rainbow Majestic."

Gena's brown eyes peered into mine disapprovingly.

"So, tell me about it," I prompted them. "What caused the fire in the old part of the lodge?"

"The ghost ... who else?" Aunt Rosalee made light of it. "As I said, we stay out of that part of the lodge, and we don't have any disturbances."

"Well, what if somebody went in there?" I asked.

Gena stared at me, but said nothing. It made me feel uncomfortable.

"Nobody goes to those rooms. It's boarded up and I keep the doors locked," Aunt Rosalee assured me.

"That stairway in back of the lodge," I said. "The one near the rear exit ... it was open last night, and again this afternoon."

Aunt Rosalee sighed. "I thought I told the maids ..."

"Juniper, you were up there," Gena accused.

"I went up those stairs," I admitted. "I just wanted to see where they went."

"Well, there's no harm in that. They just go up to the attic rooms," said Aunt Rosalee. "But I'll tell the maids to keep it locked up from now on. I don't want anyone gettin' hurt on those steps."

Gena continued to stare at me. "You were in the attic?"

"Well, yes, there's a lot of junk stored up there."

"Where else were you?" she demanded.

"Gena, stop it," warned Aunt Rosalee. Then she turned to me and said, "Just please don't go into that old part of the lodge. That's all I ask. There's nothin' more to explain. You can't go there anyway, because I've got it secured."

I didn't reveal the fact that I had found the passageway that led from the attic room down to the auditorium, nor did I mention that Max Leachfield had been there playing the harp in the dark. Gena, however, continued to watch me, and I got the feeling she knew I had violated the rules and had been inside the old auditorium.

The program in the lounge that evening was a lecture by Cyril Jorgensen. Since I had spent time with him that afternoon discussing metaphysics, I was actually interested in attending. After dinner, Gena left to set up the meeting room and I stayed with Aunt Rosalee until it was time.

Cyril was a well respected teacher and the audience was receptive toward him. When we had come into the lounge, there had only been a few available seats left in the back. Gena gave her usual introduction and then the room lights dimmed. Cyril, dressed in a white shirt and Western tie, stood at the lectern and began to talk about how he had come to the point he was at today, entertaining the audience with amusing tales of his youth, and telling some rather incredible stories of things that had happened in his life that were beyond the experiences of most people. I found myself so wrapped up in Cyril's talk that I hadn't noticed Drake standing with his arms crossed at the side of the room, nor Wes, who was sitting beside Clover near the front of the room, until after the talk was over and the lights came on.

My heart sank a little when I saw that Clover was dominating Wes. Aunt Rosalee turned to me. "Well, what did you think of our Cyril, Juniper?"

I directed my attention back to my aunt. "He's a wonderful speaker. I've got a couple of his books up in my room. I'm going to start reading one of them tonight."

"Yes, Cyril is quite knowledgeable." Aunt Rosalee stretched and stood up. "I think I'm goin' to turn in early."

Apparently there was not going to be a meditation held after tonight's program. I was relieved. I didn't feel quite ready for that. "Okay, good night, Aunt Rosalee." I watched her as she tried to leave the lounge. Several people came up to her and began conversing, which kept her from leaving.

I sat in the chair and waited. As soon as the room cleared more, I would saunter up to my room. It was quite obvious to me that Wes had forgotten our walk.

Suddenly, someone dropped into the seat next to me. I glanced up and saw that it was Drake. "How's it going?" he asked. "You baffled yet?"

His question surprised me. "I don't know what you mean," I said.

Drake watched as people left the lounge, laughing and socializing with each other. "Did you believe what you heard tonight?" he asked me.

"I ... well, I don't know," I answered truthfully.

"Cyril paints a convincing picture," said Drake, "but don't buy it until you've done some searching of your own."

I really had no idea what Drake meant. It sounded like he was criticizing Cyril Jorgensen, and I didn't like that. "A lot of what he said made sense," I said. "I've never really thought much about these things. I'm intrigued with his views on reincarnation."

Drake peered at me, then quickly looked into his lap. "So you think you've had some past lives?" he asked.

I shrugged. "Cyril says I was his daughter once."

Drake laughed derisively and looked at me. "Cyril tells every woman he sees that they've been with him in a past life. But usually he tries to win them over by telling them they've made passionate love together. I'm surprised he didn't try that on you."

I felt a flush rising in my cheeks. The man's attitude was

uncalled for and annoyed me. "Don't you believe in past lives?" I challenged.

Drake scratched his beard. "What I believe is my own business. And I don't think it's right for people such as yourself to be taken in by scammers."

I felt a wave of resentment toward Drake. "Certainly you're not saying that Cyril ..."

He stood up to leave. "Believe what you want," he told me, "but be on your guard. Everything you see here is not all light and love." With that, he walked out of the lounge.

A surge of excitement took hold of me. I wasn't sure if it was anger I felt, or complete bewilderment over Drake Phillips, who always managed to rattle my emotions.

"Juniper."

I swung around in my seat and found Wes standing over me. "Oh, Wes. Hi."

"Still up for that walk?"

My heart started pounding as I slowly rose from my seat. "Sure."

He eyed me a moment. "Are you all right? You look a bit confused."

I shook off my stormy feelings and smiled at him. "I'm okay, really."

"Well ... good," he said. "Let's go then."

I gladly followed Wes out of the lounge. We passed Clover, who was busy talking to Taffi, and Clover reached out and squeezed my arm as I walked by. She grinned at me and said in a low voice, "Go, girl!" Taffi burst out giggling.

Embarrassed, I forced a smile and let Wes lead me out toward the lobby. We were soon outside the lodge, walking down the steps and headed around the back of the building. Some guests strolled in the gardens, admiring the faint alpenglow that remained on Majestic Mountain.

"What a beautiful night," I remarked as we walked, side by side, along the pond.

"Yes, it certainly is," said Wes.

There was a lot of silence between us, and I wondered what I could say to help pull Wes Andrews out of his shell. "Do you like it here at the Rainbow Majestic?" I asked, then realized I had asked him that before.

"Oh, it's great being here," he said.

"How did you come to meet my aunt?" I asked.

"It's a long story," said Wes, "but, in a nutshell, I met her in Wade City when I attended the meditation group led by Celeste." He explained how a friend had invited him to come to one of their weekly evening get-togethers, and discovered that he and Aunt Rosalee had both lived in Oklahoma. "And when she and her husband were livin' in Tulsa after that, I hooked up with her and she hired me to build a garage."

"So you lived in Tulsa a while," I commented.

"That's where I'm from. My family's there."

"I see." We walked toward the woods and I felt a lot safer having Wes at my side after the episode last night.

"Tell me about yourself," prompted Wes. "You never did say on our way over from Colorado Springs. Did you always live in Kansas?"

"No. I was born in Colorado Springs." I explained how my father had loved to spend time at the Majestic Mountain Lodge. "He was killed, you know," I added.

"Yes, I know about that," said Wes. "Some kind of huntin' accident."

"No one's ever told me the details," I said.

"I don't think anyone knows what they were," Wes assured me. "But it was a terrible shame. It should never have happened."

I sensed he was about to lapse into some kind of anti-hunting diatribe, so I thought of something to quickly change the subject. "You said you were in the Marine Corps."

"That's right."

"And you went to the Middle East."

"That's been quite some time ago."

"My fiancé was over there, too," I disclosed. I hesitated, then added, "He didn't come back."

Wes stopped walking and looked at me with sympathy in his blue eyes. "I'm awful sorry, Juniper," he told me in a soft voice. "Wars are senseless and don't solve problems the way some people want to believe."

I ended up telling Wes about Sean as we continued walking. Finally, we turned around and headed back toward the lodge. I was just starting to feel comfortable with Wes, and hoped we would stop and sit on the bench in front of the pond. Perhaps he would hold my hand, and who knew where that might lead? I felt a shiver of anticipation.

But before we even reached the garden, we heard someone calling for Wes. Gena ran over when she saw us and was slightly out of breath. "Wes, I need you to drive a lodge guest back to Wade City right away," she said.

"What? Now?"

"Yes, immediately," Gena insisted. "Mrs. Bailey is feeling ill and wants to leave." Gena eyed me critically.

"Well, okay," said Wes. "I'll take her." He turned to me with an apologetic half smile. "Sorry, Juniper. I have to leave."

"Of course." I nodded my head. "I understand. Do what you have to do." I watched as Wes walked back to the lodge.

I thought Gena would go with him, but instead she turned to me and frowned. "It's not a good idea to try and hook up with that one," she advised me. "You'll get nothing but heartache. Wes Andrews doesn't want a woman in his life."

Gena's words stung, and I couldn't help but become defensive. "We only went for a walk," I explained. My words sounded colder than I had intended, but I didn't like this woman—this cousin of mine—telling me whom I could or could not befriend.

"I've seen how you look at him," said Gena. "I'm just warning you, Juniper."

I felt indignant. I really wanted to tell Gena to butt out. What business was it of hers, anyway? But what bothered me the most was this uncanny talent of hers of knowing what's on my mind. She had known I'd been in the old section of the lodge that afternoon, in the auditorium. *Was Gena psychic?*

She turned to walk hastily back to the lodge, then spun around, her pointy chin more pronounced. "By the way, there was a call for you at the front desk tonight. Some man ... said he was a good friend of yours. You can pick up the message on your way up to your suite." She continued walking away.

I sighed and followed her, but at a more leisurely pace. I knew the caller had to be Mike. I had forgotten about calling him again with my contact number. Apparently, he had managed to come up with it on his own.

Somehow I did not relish the thought of returning Mike's

call tonight ... or any night ... but I figured maybe I'd better do it. He was not going to be happy when I told him I had accepted a position at the Rainbow Majestic Lodge and would be staying indefinitely.

9

I decided to give Mike a call as soon as I returned to my room. Using my phone card, I dialed the numbers and waited. After three rings, Mike answered.

"Oh, Juniper." He sounded relieved. "I was worried when you didn't call. I got your message from last night, but you'd said ..."

"I'm fine," I interrupted him. I was frankly a little perturbed, due to the outcome of my walk with Wes. "I hope everything's all right with you," I added in a more friendly tone.

Mike sighed. "When are you coming home?"

"I just got here," I exclaimed.

"Well, don't you know yet when you're leaving?"

I hesitated, then told him, "That hasn't been determined yet."

"Well, what are you doing there?" he asked.

Again I hesitated. I wasn't ready to tell Mike about the gift shop.

"What's your aunt like?" he asked.

"Aunt Rosalee's charming," I replied. "And I'm just starting to get to know her." Then I asked, "Is everything going all right with Mother's estate?"

"Yeah, for now." He was in a mood to chit-chat and told me about work and what he'd been doing the last couple of days. Finally, I cut him short. "Mike, I've got to go. I don't know how many minutes are left on this phone card."

"I'll call you right back," he offered.

"No, don't bother. I'm ... I'm quite tired. It's the altitude, most likely."

Mike insisted I keep him informed as to my plans and particularly my return. We ended our conversation, but not before he said he missed me and couldn't wait to discuss with me the plans he was making for our future.

I spent the rest of the evening reading one of the books by Cyril Jorgensen. He touched upon many topics that I found interesting, and my views on life after death began to widen. I remembered that my aunt had written in her letter that nobody actually dies. It made sense that death should be more like moving from one room into another. I liked the simple style of Cyril's writing. It was as if I were listening to him talk. He wrote about vibrations and energy. He wrote of love as having the highest vibration, and explained that as spiritual beings we are the essence of the God force, "offshoots of Divine Energy." How could there be such a thing as death when energy never dies, it only changes form?

Something stirred within me, the more I read. It was getting late. I knew I should quit reading and go to sleep. But it was hard to put down these books. Finally, I reached the point where I had to get some sleep. My eyes had grown heavy and a glance at the alarm clock showed that it was almost one-thirty in the morning.

I turned out the bedside lamp and fell almost immediately to sleep. I don't know how long I'd slept, but suddenly I was awake for no reason. A breeze swept in from the windows and I felt a cold draft. I realized I must have left the windows open when I'd gone to bed.

Then, I heard the sound of a door softly closing. My heart began to hammer as I lay there on the canopy bed, worried now that someone was in my suite. It sounded like the door from the sitting room out to the corridor had been the one that closed. Who could have closed that door? I thought I had locked it hours ago. Now I had doubts as to whether I actually had.

Next, I began to worry that perhaps someone was in the suite. That thought caused my blood to run cold and my breathing came in shallow puffs as I tried to focus on what I should do. After lying there a fearful minute, I sprang up in bed and reached for the bedside lamp.

Light flooded the room and I saw that no one was in the bedroom. The breeze rustled the curtains and I climbed out of bed to close the windows. Could someone be in one of the other rooms? The thought made me shudder. Before I reached the windows, I decided it would be a good idea to make sure no one was hiding in the sitting room or my bathroom.

Relief washed over me after I checked each room and realized I was alone. Then I ran to the door and secured the lock.

I set the security bolt, which I obviously hadn't bothered to latch before. Then I closed my windows.

As I crawled back into bed, I noticed a sheet of white paper on the table beside the lamp, which I hadn't seen before. I picked it up and saw that a note had been typed on the page, probably printed out from a computer. It read:

JUNIPER GO HOME
Save Yourself Before It's Too Late

I turned the page over, but it was blank. The words disturbed me. I didn't understand what they meant. Obviously, someone in the Rainbow Majestic didn't want me here. *Who?* And what did it mean to save myself before it's too late? It dawned on me that this note might have something to do with my attack in the woods last night. Was I jumping to conclusions?

I tucked the typewritten note into my purse and tried to go back to sleep, but the disturbance had caused me to worry, so I lay awake for a long while before exhaustion won over.

As a result, I slept late the next morning and missed breakfast. Nadine gave me coffee and made me an English muffin when I went to the kitchen. She told me I was welcome to fix myself anything I wanted at any time. "There's always left-overs in the fridge."

I thanked her and asked where Max was this morning.

"Oh, he's getting a math lesson from his dad," she explained. "Lance is better at that subject than I am."

Aunt Rosalee was busy or I would have talked to her about the note and the visitation last night. Everyone, in fact, was busy preparing for the arrival of guests coming for the holistic fair the next week. I decided to spend some time in the gift shop and went there to see what I could get done.

Apparently someone had been working on the display racks. There was telltale sawdust over the floor and things had been moved around in my shop. I spent the rest of the morning going through the catalogues Aunt Rosalee had given me and made out an order for merchandise.

Wes dropped in to see me shortly after noon. He had on a white T-shirt with sweat and grass stains, and I noticed a hole in the knee of his jeans. "I wanted to apologize for last night," he told me. "I hope you didn't hold it against me when I had to take that woman home. She was with a group and didn't have her own transportation."

I smiled at Wes as I put down my pen. "Of course not. It's your job."

"Yeah, well, you take the good with the bad." He looked at the catalogues and asked, "What are you doin'?"

"Placing orders," I replied. "I need to get them in today, if I can."

He stepped over and stood beside me, examining the catalogue from which I had been working. Crystal jewelry populated the colorful page. I was aware of his closeness to me and—for a few blissful seconds—I basked in his energy.

"Why don't you order yourself one of those crystal pendants to wear?" Wes suggested. He pointed to one of them. "That one would look nice, I think."

I recalled some of my reading and said, "I'm planning to order in several. I read that you should choose a crystal carefully. I'm sure I'll know the right one when I see it."

"And touch it," added Wes. He smiled at me in such a special way that my heart seemed to leap. For a moment our eyes locked, and I expected him to suggest going to lunch together, or perhaps a second chance at a walk tonight. Instead, Wes turned away and headed out.

I decided to be bold and called to him, "Are you heading for the dining room?"

He stopped and said, "Actually, I already grabbed a bite. Gena has some things lined up for me to do."

"Okay," I said. "I'll see you later, then."

Wes nodded, then left. I finished my orders, then gathered everything up to take to Aunt Rosalee's office. Wes puzzled me. He could be alluring one moment and distant the next. He reminded me of Sean in many ways, but I had to tell myself he wasn't Sean. He was completely different, and making comparisons wasn't fair. Still, disappointment lurked beneath the surface as I left the shop and headed for my aunt's office. I would have enjoyed sitting with Wes at lunch. But, I told myself, there'd be other chances.

"Good. I'll have Lance call in these orders after he finishes his reports." Aunt Rosalee glanced over my selections with a smile of approval.

"I can call them in, if you like," I said. "There's no reason why Lance has to do it."

"Well ... I suppose ... if that's what you want to do." Aunt Rosalee dug into one of her desk drawers and then handed me a credit card. "You can use this gold card," she said, "and return it to me when you're done." She sat back in her desk recliner and studied me. "You look tired, Juniper. Are you sure you're not workin' too hard?"

I explained how I had stayed up late, reading the works of Cyril Jorgensen. Then I told Aunt Rosalee about how I'd awakened in the middle of the night and had heard my door closing. "And whoever was in my room left me a note." I reached into my purse and produced the folded-up typewritten message.

Aunt Rosalee opened it up. A frown creased her face as she read it. Then she looked at me sharply. "Who typed this?"

"I have no clue," I said.

"This is garbage!" she cried. "I want to know who did this to you, and why." Her cheeks began to flush, then she sighed. "Juniper, I'm really sorry. This is inexcusable. I don't like this one bit ... not one bit."

"Why would anyone want me to leave?" I asked.

"I don't know."

"The part that gets me is where it says to save myself before it's too late. Aunt Rosalee, what could that mean?"

"May I have this?" she asked.

"Sure, I don't want it."

"Tonight, you be sure to double lock your door," she told me.

"You don't have to remind me. I will."

Since I hadn't had lunch yet, I stopped in the dining room and had a bowl of clam chowder and a salad. Cyril and Celeste were enjoying their meal at a long table of lodge guests. I didn't see anyone else I knew except Gena, who came into the dining room at one point and marched into the kitchen. She glanced in my direction, but didn't stop to greet me.

After lunch, I went back to the gift shop and was surprised to find Drake hammering away at some shelves. He had obviously been the one performing repairs and getting display racks ready. He turned to acknowledge me as I took my seat on the stool behind the counter.

"How long are you going to be doing that?" I asked.

Drake stopped hammering and studied me. "I've got a job to finish."

"Me too," I said, and held up my papers. "I need to phone in these orders."

He put down his hammer and strolled over to the counter, where he pulled a crate over and sat down. Then he gave me a mocking smile. "Okay, you do your job first. I'll wait."

Annoyed, I let out a sigh. "I didn't mean I had to call in the orders right this minute. I was just asking how long you were going to be."

Drake stroked his beard and looked around the room. "Nice little shop," he remarked. "A lot of folks are looking forward to it opening."

I didn't feel like chatting. Why didn't Drake go back to his hammering? And I didn't like the way he was stealing glances at me.

"Why are you nervous?" he finally asked.

I looked him right in the eye, startled. "Nervous? I'm ... I'm not. I ... I just want to get some things done."

"Do I make you nervous?" he asked.

He did, but I wasn't about to admit it. "No, Drake." I started going over the order forms again. Just what did he want?

"Well, I think I do."

"Okay," I admitted. "You're right. You do make me nervous."

"Why?" he asked.

I was losing my patience. "I don't know."

"Do I scare you?" he asked.

I looked at him, incredulous. "No, you don't scare me."

"Then what?" His voice was suddenly gentle.

"Look ... Drake ... why are you asking me these ridiculous questions?"

He studied me in silence for a moment, then shrugged and got up. "Nothing." He started for the door.

I called after him. "Where are you going?"

Drake turned to me. "I'll leave you alone, so you can make your calls."

Suddenly, I felt I'd been unfair and was sorry. "No, wait," I told him. "Please don't leave. I didn't mean to be rude to you."

Reluctantly, he sat down on the crate and sighed. "I'm

sorry that I upset you," he said.

"You didn't upset me." Then I shook my head. "Okay, maybe a little. But it's only because I'm tired. I didn't sleep too well last night."

"Why didn't you sleep last night?"

"For one thing, I stayed up late reading books on reincarnation," I told him. "And then I had a visitor come into my room when I was asleep."

Drake cocked his head. "Who?"

"I don't know." I told him about the episode and the threatening note on my bedside table.

"That's not good," commented Drake.

"Do you have any idea who might do such a thing?" I asked him.

Drake's eyes searched the room and he said, "Well, if I were to make an educated guess, I'd put my money on Gena."

The same thought had crossed my mind, but I didn't let on. "Why my cousin?" I asked.

"Well ... Gena's jealous of you. She was hoping Rosalee would let her run this shop."

"Yes. I know about that." I pondered this, then said, "And if it *was* Gena, Aunt Rosalee is going to be livid."

"You say it was a typewritten note?" asked Drake.

"Yes, printed off a computer." Then I added, "Too bad it wasn't handwritten. We could have given it to Taffi to analyze."

Drake snorted. "Taffi," he grumbled, and shook his head. Then he asked, "Were all the words spelled right?"

That seemed an odd question to ask. I nodded. "Yes, why?"

"Then it seems unlikely Gena wrote the note," said Drake. "How come?"

"Gena's extremely dyslexic. She can't spell worth a damn."

"How do you know?"

He shot me a sarcastic look. "Because I'm dyslexic, too. We've discussed it between ourselves. I have a terrible time writing anything."

I thought about this a moment. "Well, then," I said, "I suppose this also rules you out."

He caught the twinkle in my eye and smiled. A flicker of recognition momentarily threw me. I must have appeared startled. Drake stared at me curiously. "What's wrong?" he asked.

"N-nothing."

"No, there is." He peered deeply into my eyes.

A long moment passed between us in which I found myself almost hypnotized by his stare. Something stirred deep within my soul that felt like longing, except that it paralyzed me with fear.

"Think," Drake said.

"What?" I managed to whisper.

"*Remember*, Juniper." He continued to gaze into my eyes. After a pause, he said, "Long ago."

But before I could demand that he explain this new game he was playing, a commotion out in the lobby grabbed our attention. Voices had risen above the usual volume, and one of them was Gena's. Drake sprang out the door and I was on his heels.

A small crowd had gathered at the front door of the lodge, some of them guests I'd seen here and there. A large man in a suitcoat and tie and two women in long dresses stood at the lobby entrance, angry expressions on their faces as they took turns yelling at Gena.

"We won't stop until this place is condemned," one of the women cried.

"What you do here is an abomination," the second woman said. "It's the devil's work, and all of you are instruments of Satan!"

Gena's brown eyes flared in a rage I hadn't seen before. "That is *not* what we are about here," she cried. "How dare you suggest such a thing?"

"Rainbow Majesty must not be allowed to thrive!" the man in the tie stormed. "You will bring ruin and corruption to the good people of Wade City—*God's* people!"

"We are *all* God's people," a lodge guest near the door called out, and others murmured their agreement.

"And who are *you* to sit in judgment of anyone?" Starla stepped forward, dressed in one of her long flowing robes, this one a deep blue in color with shiny little silver stars in the material. Today she reminded me of a slick Hollywood star from yesteryear with her silky black hair and makeup.

"We demand to see the proprietor," the first woman shouted. "Rosalee Sutton. Where is she?"

"My stepmother is resting," Gena explained.

"A likely excuse," the man muttered.

Drake, to my surprise, stepped in front of Gena and asked, "What seems to be the problem here?" He stood as tall as the man who talked about ruin and corruption, and his large build seemed to swell in a protective way. "What is it you want?" he demanded in a deep voice that remained calm, yet commanded authority.

"We have drawn up a petition." One of the women thrust a collection of papers in front of him. "We wish to present it to Rosalee Sutton."

Drake grabbed the papers from her.

"We've collected signatures from more than four hundred people who want Rainbow Majesty turned back into the hunting lodge it used to be," said the large man.

"Who are these people?" I whispered to Starla beside me.

"They belong to the Family of God congregation in Wade City," she whispered back. "They are a group of religious fanatics who are out to destroy Rosalee."

Drake handed the petition to Gena, who read it, her eyes still blazing and her shoulders heaving with indignity. "And now that you've delivered your so-called petition, you can get the hell out of here!" Drake told them.

Starla placed a restraining hand on Drake's arm.

"I'm going to call the sheriff," Gena fumed.

The man put his hands up in the air and then signaled the two women, and they hurried toward the door. Just as they were heading out, Wes walked in from outside. He seemed startled to confront an angry crowd of people, but smiled and held the door open for them until they went through.

"Blessings," Wes told them. "We hope you'll come visit us again soon. *Namasté.*"

One of the women shot Wes a look of hatred, and he turned toward the rest of us, baffled. "Did I miss something?"

At that moment, Rosalee appeared from the hallway, accompanied by Lance and Nadine, all three of whom wore concerned faces. "What was all that commotion about?" Aunt Rosalee cried.

Everyone fell into talking at once, and as Starla attempted to explain what had happened, Gena thrust the petition into her stepmother's hands. I saw my aunt's face turn pale as she read the petition. Lance grabbed her arm and gently eased her into an arm chair.

"This is terrible," someone said. "Can you imagine? Coming here just like that?"

Another guest said, "I heard there was a church in Wade City that was up in arms about the Rainbow Majestic, but I can't see what the fuss is about."

"They're a bunch of narrow-minded fundamentalists who can't think for themselves."

"*Everyone!*" Starla's commanding voice rose above the rest and she raised her arms up in the air in a dramatic gesture, turning around in a circle as she addressed the crowd. "Everyone, *please* ... listen to me. Stop and listen!"

The crowd quieted down.

Starla spoke with control and influence. "Let's not let this incident disrupt what we are doing here. Please do not judge what has just happened."

"But those people are out of their minds," a man called out.

"How dare they call themselves the Family of God?" someone else asked. "What hypocrites!"

"People, listen," Starla begged. "We must not give them our power. Whether you believe it or not, they are on their path ... and we are each on ours. Do not let this fill you with negative emotions and resentment. Come, let's all form a circle right now—and join hands."

I was impressed with Starla's leadership skills and her ability to turn this ugly scene into an opportunity for fellowship. Before I was aware of it, Drake had grabbed my left hand, and then Wes took hold of my right hand, and we stepped back and formed a large group circle in the hotel lobby. Even Aunt Rosalee seemed to have recovered from the shock and stood up to join the circle.

Starla directed us all to close our eyes as she had us focus our thoughts on healing the disruption of the afternoon. "Know that each of you is of the Light," Starla proclaimed. "Feel the compassion in your hearts for those who would unknowingly strike out and try to stop us. Breathe deeply now ..." She continued to lead us through a meditation. Strangely enough, I began to feel myself grow lighter and more relaxed than I'd felt all day. I was aware of Drake's and Wes's hands in mine, and an energy seemed to ripple through us, growing more intense as we continued to breathe and focus on love and light.

After several minutes, Starla brought us back and told us to open our eyes when we felt ready. I felt Wes drop my hand first, but Drake continued to hold onto me, and before he let go, he gave my left hand a squeeze. I stood there, feeling slightly dizzy but energized and good. The circle of people broke up, and most of them resumed what they had been doing. I turned to find Aunt Rosalee scanning the pages of the petition at the lobby counter, Gena and Lance on either side. I strolled over.

"Don't let it bother you, Rosalee," Lance told her. "There's nothing they can do."

"The nerve of some people." Gena was clearly still in a huff.

Aunt Rosalee noticed me and drew me close for a hug. "I know what you must be thinkin', Juniper. We're a bunch of weirdos that the townspeople want to be rid of."

"I don't think that at all," I told her. I pulled away and smiled. "For the first time in my life, I'm discovering something meaningful that makes sense to me."

Rosalee had mist in her eyes as she looked at me. "I do believe the egg shell is crackin'."

"Look at this," Lance pointed out, and showed Aunt Rosalee the petition. "They didn't even get the name of the lodge right. They call it Rainbow *Majesty* ... not the Majestic."

"I noticed that, too," Gena concurred.

"That's because it's not the lodge they want to destroy," said Aunt Rosalee. "It's me they want to persecute."

I found her comment disturbing. Why would anyone want to bring ruin to a person as loving and generous as my Aunt Rosalee?

She was indeed the Rainbow Majesty.

10

The excitement died down and everyone went their separate ways. After Aunt Rosalee went back to her office, Gena settled down with some paper work at the front desk. Before I left, I happened to notice a computer monitor on the desk and looked around to see what other equipment Gena used. I was thinking of the typed note that had been left on my bedside table. The keyboard and mouse had been pushed aside as piles of paper commanded the desk space.

Gena noticed me and asked, "Juniper, is there something I can help you with?"

"No, I was just looking at your computer. Where's the printer?"

Gena swiveled in her chair and pointed to the small printer on a stand against the far wall. She waited for me to explain, and when I said nothing, she sighed. "You'll be getting your aunt's laptop to use in the boutique."

"Oh, good." I smiled, then asked her, "What's this one used for?"

Gena seemed surprised at my question. "Reservations," she replied curtly.

"What about correspondence?" I was checking to see what her reaction would be.

Gena frowned. "E-mail? Juniper, do you want to check your e-mail?"

"No," I said. "I don't have an e-mail address. In fact, I write letters the old-fashioned way." I thought I'd go a step further and said, "I prefer to write in long hand."

Gena stared at me with an odd expression on her face. After a pause, she said, "I don't like to type. In fact, I don't write letters, period."

"What about e-mail?" I asked.

"No, only if it's for business." She stacked a pile of papers in front of her, then gave me a perturbed glance. "I don't like to use the computer at all, as a matter of fact. But Rosalee wants everything high tech. So, you'd better brush up on your computer skills if you're planning to stick around here."

The telephone rang just then. Gena jumped at the chance to answer it, probably to avoid answering any more of my questions. I walked away, satisfied that Drake had probably been correct in assuming Gena had not been the one who typed that note. At least, Gena had not reacted suspiciously to my line of questioning.

On my way to the gift shop, I thought about how I had suspected Gena as the one who had typed that warning note. She certainly didn't want me here at the Rainbow Majestic. Was it because she was jealous as Drake had hinted? What was there about me that would cause Gena to be jealous? She had appeared unwelcoming toward me from the first moment we'd met. Was it because Aunt Rosalee had put me in the coveted crystal suite? Or was it because she'd asked me to run the gift shop? With all Gena had to do around here, I would think taking on the management of the gift shop would be just another burden added to her many responsibilities.

Drake had not returned to the gift shop, so I got down to business and called in my merchandise orders. By the time I'd finished, I felt tired and decided a nap was in order. But before going to my room, I had to return the gold card to Aunt Rosalee.

I passed Nadine Leachfield and Max in the hallway on my way to the office. Max grinned when he saw me. "Hi, Juniper!" he exclaimed. I stopped to greet the two of them.

"How is the gift shop coming along?" Nadine's blue eyes sparkled from behind her thick glasses. "I can't wait for it to open."

"It's getting into shape," I replied. Max began fidgeting.

Nadine tried to make him stand still. "We're going out to the garden to identify some flowers," she told me, then added, "if there are any. It's Max's botany lesson." She steered him toward the lobby. "See you at dinner."

I continued on until I got to Aunt Rosalee's office. Both she and Lance looked busy, going over some reports. But when my aunt saw me looking in, she motioned toward me.

"I just brought the gold card back." I handed it to her.

She thanked me, then said, "Why don't you take the rest of

the day off?"

"I intend to." I could see that they were engrossed in their reports, so I left.

I had gotten as far as the spiral stairway in the lobby when Clover came down the steps in front of me. She was dressed in a low-cut, bright orange wrap-around dress that came up above her knees. She wore brown sandals and a ready smile.

"Just the person I wanted to see." Clover placed her hands on her hips. "Come with me, Juniper. I'm going to give you a massage."

Apparently I had no chance to decide whether I wanted a massage or not. Clover led me up the stairway to our floor, then opened the door to her room and ushered me inside. A massage table was set up in the middle of the room. I could smell the flowery scent of lilac incense.

"I had a cancellation this afternoon," Clover said, "and you look like you could use a good massage."

"I do? You mean, it's that obvious?"

"Don't worry. I'll work those tight neck muscles loose. Just let me slip into my bathroom a moment while you get undressed." When I hesitated, she said, "Just get onto the table and pull the sheet over yourself."

I sat in a chair and took off my shoes and my clothes, folding them in a neat pile on the arm rest. Then I climbed onto the massage table and sat with the sheet pulled up to my shoulders. Clover seemed to know when I was ready and popped out of the bathroom. She turned on a cassette player on her desk, and relaxing piano music filled the room.

"Just relax, Juniper." Clover told me to lie down on my belly as she took some ointment and rubbed it on her hands. I could smell its powerful sweet scent and decided to go with the flow. Both the gentle music and the blended aromas from the incense and ointment began to work on releasing the tension in me.

I closed my eyes and was aware of Clover performing some short prayer ritual near my head. She then placed the palms of her hands on my back, in between my shoulder blades, and her touch was warm—almost hot—as she began to rub in circles, pressing gently at first. I felt immediately soothed and realized this was going to be an enjoyable experience.

"How much are you charging me for this?" I asked

spontaneously. I had limited cash with me and wanted to make sure the terms were clear before she got too far.

Clover clicked her tongue. "Nothing!" she cried. "This massage is on the house."

"What?" I lifted my head, bracing myself with my elbows. "Clover ..."

"I want to, like ... do this for you, so let me."

"But ... why?"

"Just lie back down, will you? The next time you want a massage from me, you can pay me. But this is, like ... your welcome to the Majestic gift, okay?"

With a sigh, I gave in. The music played and Clover worked her magical hands over me until I believed I surely must be in heaven. Before long, her fingers grew stronger and she began to press really hard in places that made me wince with pain.

"Breathe," Clover told me softly. "I do deep tissue massage, and it's, like ... bound to hurt once in a while. But I have to, like ... press hard if I'm going to do you any good."

"Okay," I told her.

"But do let me know if it, like ... gets to be too much."

She worked me over for a while, and I was thoroughly enjoying the music and the soothing pressure of her hands. After several minutes had passed, she asked, "How are you getting along with Gena?" Her hands didn't stop.

"Oh, I don't know." There was a pause.

"She can be, like ... vulnerable at times," said Clover.

I found her choice of words rather odd. "What do you mean vulnerable?" I asked.

"For instance, this afternoon when those people, like ... came by with the petition. Gena's not always playing the role of the king's daughter."

The *king?* As in Uncle Fred? I smiled to myself, wondering if Gena had been the spoiled child of my uncle. "She grew up here at the lodge, didn't she?" I asked.

Clover squeezed out more massage oil, then moved her magical hands to my lower back. "I don't know a whole lot about it, but from what I understand, Gena spent summers here as well as vacations. Her mother was the type that traveled a lot and did, like ... her own thing, and she had, like ... lots of boyfriends, so she was always, like ... taking advantage of the opportunity to dump Gena on Fred and Rosalee."

"Well, did Gena enjoy staying here?" I asked.

"Apparently. I think she found life with her mother a little stressful."

"You know, it's strange my mother didn't talk about Gena," I told Clover. "I didn't know I had a cousin until I came here."

Clover gasped in astonishment. "You didn't?"

I explained how my mother never wanted to talk about my father or Uncle Fred.

"How much older is Gena than you?"

I told Clover I was twenty-seven, but I didn't know how much older Gena was.

"Gena's, like ... thirty-six," said Clover.

"My dad's accident occurred when I was five," I said. "Gena would have been ... what?"

Clover paused to count. "Fourteen?"

"Yeah." I winced as Clover put too much pressure on my left buttock. "I wonder what she could tell me about it." I recalled how Gena had grown nervous and avoided my questions about my father that first night at the lodge.

"I suppose you could, like ... ask her."

"Yeah." I wondered just how I was going to do that.

"Gena has a thing for Drake, you know." Clover moved on down to my foot.

I perked up at the mention of Drake's name. Then I had to ask, "And how does he feel about her?"

"That I don't know," said Clover. "Drake is, like ... so mysterious."

"Oh? Why do you say that?"

"Drake Phillips never talks about himself."

"Do you give him massages?" I asked.

"Oh, once in a while he, like ... gets one. But he doesn't like to talk."

"He talks to *me*," I said.

"I mean he doesn't talk when he's getting a massage." Clover chuckled. "Some people are like that. Some want to carry on a conversation and others prefer just to, like ... lie there."

I could understand why. Now that we had a conversation going, I wasn't as relaxed as when we had started the massage. But I didn't mind. I was learning things from Clover. "Where did

Drake come from?"

"North Dakota, I believe."

"Oh, that's right," I recalled.

"I think he was, like ... married once," said Clover. "He and Gena are pretty close in age." Then she added, "Drake's really psychic."

This surprised me. "He is?"

"He doesn't discuss it, but we all know he is. Gena's psychic, too."

"Gena's psychic?" Somehow I had guessed she might be.

"Yes," said Clover. "Gena gives readings. She'll probably have, like ... a booth at the psychic fair."

"You mean the holistic fair coming up?"

Clover was now working on my toes. "She'll do card readings or do channeling sessions."

"What about you?" I asked. "Are you psychic?"

"Me?"

"Yes, isn't everyone who works at the Rainbow Majestic psychic?"

Clover laughed. "I suppose I've got a touch of it, just like everyone else. But mainly I'm, like ... a healer, doing what I love to do."

There was a pause as she massaged the sole of my left foot. It felt wonderful. Then I asked her, "And what about Wes?"

"Wes?" Clover let out a deep sigh. "Wes ..." she breathed. "I don't know about any psychic ability on his part, but he certainly has a strong charisma about him. Have you felt it, Juniper?" But before I could answer, Clover continued, "Well, of course you have. We all sense it. He is truly an evolved spirit, and he never has, like ... an unkind word to say about anybody. I guess that's what makes Wes Andrews so special. At least he's special to me. I've been, like ... in love with Wes since ... well, like ... since he started working at the Rainbow Majestic." She sighed again.

For some reason I didn't understand, my hopes sank and I felt my heart grow heavy. I realized that Clover Wolff had deep feelings for Wes Andrews—possibly the same feelings I was starting to have for him. I wondered how he felt about her.

As if in answer to my thoughts, Clover went on. "It's easy enough getting a guy like Wes into bed with you, but he's very reluctant about promising anything."

I had to control my misgivings. She was venturing into discussion that made me uncomfortable. "Are you ... seeing each other?" I ventured.

"In a way," said Clover.

"I mean ... have you ..."

Clover finished my sentence, "Like ... slept together?" The cassette player clicked off just then, and she walked over to the desk to take the tape out and turn it over. When she had music playing again, she returned to the massage table. "Not yet."

For some reason I felt greatly relieved.

"But ..." Clover started on my right foot. "It's only a matter of time." She worked on my foot awhile and then had me turn over onto my back.

We didn't converse at all during the remainder of the massage. I closed my eyes as she started on my head and used her fingers, well oiled with aromatic ointment, to relax my cheek and forehead muscles. The gentle music played and I soon felt thoroughly relaxed. She ended the massage by stroking my scalp and softly pinching my ear lobes, sending me into oblivion. I didn't want this experience to be over, but I was almost ready to fall asleep when she stood at my head with her hands on top of my shoulders, then walked over to my feet and held my toes.

"Okay, Juniper." Clover was smiling when I opened my eyes. Then she told me to take my time and get slowly up from the table—only when I was ready. Then she stepped once again into her bathroom, to allow me to get dressed.

I lay there on the massage table for two or three minutes, basking in the tranquility that possessed me. The music continued to play as I finally got up and sat upright for a few seconds. Then I went over to the chair and got dressed. I was just slipping on my shoes when Clover stepped out of the bathroom.

"How was it?" she asked expectantly.

"Fantastic ... thank you."

We chatted a few minutes longer and then I saw it was getting late. I left for the crystal suite down the hall. I could still smell the sweet fragrance of the oils on my skin as I let myself in and unwound for a bit. I was reading one of the books I'd borrowed from the lodge library when I was interrupted by a knock on my door.

I got up to answer it and Taffi bounced into the room. "Oh, I loved that book," she exclaimed as she noticed which book I was reading, opened and resting on the coffee table. "I see you've got a couple of Cyril's books out, too."

"Yes," I admitted. "He's quite the writer."

Taffi laughed. "The old fart. Thinks he's God's gift to women."

"Really?" Her words startled me and Taffi was amused at my reaction.

"Oh, sure." Taffi was her usual exuberant self, yet I detected a nervous undercurrent in the way she flitted about the room. There was a glimmer of something in her green eyes that I hadn't seen before, as if she had something on her mind she wanted to discuss with me.

"Well, sit down," I invited. "I wanted to tell you that I think the chakra balancing worked."

Taffi sighed and stared into her lap, working her hands nervously. I could see that her mind was not on chakras. "So ... did you hear about the disturbance this afternoon?" she asked.

"I was there," I told her.

"Oh, it really shook up Rosalee," said Taffi. "Those people from town are relentless."

"What do they want?" I asked.

"They want us all to go away."

I thought about this a moment, then asked, "You mean the light workers?"

Taffi nodded her head sadly. "They think they can wave a paper at us and ... *presto* ... we'll vanish." She perked up then, with a firm smile on her round face. "But, no way. *No way* can they shut down the Rainbow Majestic and drive us out of the valley. They may not realize it, but they need our light. They may not understand us and what we're about, but one day ... yes, one day it will all become clear." She continued to rave about the mission of her light work, and I listened patiently, wondering why Taffi rambled on and what it was she really wanted from me.

Finally, I got a word in edgewise and said, "Somebody came into my room while I was sleeping last night and left me a note."

Taffi's wide eyes grew larger as she stared at me. "Where's the note?"

I explained that I had let Aunt Rosalee keep it. "It was

typewritten," I added.

Taffi demanded I tell her what the note said, so I repeated it, word for word from memory. She stood up and began pacing the sitting room.

"Do you have any clue who might want me to leave?" I asked her.

Taffi shook her head. "Not really. But, Juniper, I think you need to look out for yourself now, more than ever."

"You must have some suspicions," I told her. "You've got everybody's handwriting samples. There must be somebody who's not happy I'm here." I was waiting for her to name Gena Sutton Howard.

Taffi frowned. "I'm afraid I don't have an answer for you. But just be careful, honey, okay? Things are not always what they seem."

"There's something I found out from Aunt Rosalee about my father."

Taffi waited for me to tell her more. I filled her in on what Uncle Fred had told his wife on his death bed—that he had not been the one who accidentally shot my father. Taffi got up from the couch and paced the floor, a worried look on her face.

"I just don't understand why Uncle Fred didn't come right out and say who did it," I finished. "Taffi, you don't think my father shot himself, do you?"

Taffi shook her head, deep in thought. "No ... no, I don't get that feeling. Even if he did, why would your uncle take the blame?"

"I need to know who was with them that day," I said. "Who might know?"

"Well, did you ask Rosalee? She might remember."

I recalled our conversation from the day before. She had mentioned that Uncle Fred, my father, and some others had gone to Diamond Reservoir to camp out. She hadn't said who those others were. I decided to ask my aunt the next chance I got.

Before Taffi left my room, she said one thing that struck me—something that I would remember later, when events would cause me to question just how much she had kept from me. "Responsibility lies with each one of us, remember. No matter what happens, Juniper, sometimes it's best to simply leave well enough alone. Don't make waves."

She then left the crystal suite and I closed the door softly behind her.

11

A t dinner that evening, Starla sat at our table and dominated the conversation. It wasn't the opportune time to discuss my father's hunting accident with Aunt Rosalee, who was in a good mood and all bubbly from Starla's entertaining anecdotes. Gena seemed more subdued tonight and less bothered by my presence at the family table. I didn't contribute much to the discussion—mostly I just listened and was relieved I didn't have to reveal what was on my mind.

Wes sat with Cyril and Celeste tonight. Clover had become friendly with a group of guests at a table across the room. Taffi was chattering away at the Leachfields' table. Nadine was engrossed in her discussion with the handwriting analyst, while Lance nodded every so often, but was more concerned with Max's restless activity. The small boy was obviously bored by the grownup talk and fidgeted with his napkin and utensils. He caught me watching him and tried to hide an embarrassed smile behind his glass of milk.

Drake came in late and went straight to the kitchen. Thelma, the old deaf woman, came out with him a few minutes later. Both carried plates of food and sat down at an empty dining table. The old lady seemed pleased to be in Drake's company, and I noticed that Drake used sign language and could carry on a conversation with Thelma with his hands. Drake caught me staring at him and shot a smile my way. I sipped my cup of herb tea and smiled back at him in approval.

There was to be a workshop on tarot card reading in the lounge tonight. Although I was curious, I knew nothing about tarot and decided to spend some time outside before it grew dark. Since my arrival, I had hardly stepped outside to enjoy the beauty of the mountains and the crisp evening air. I went up to my room after dinner to grab my jacket when someone rapped on my door.

I was surprised to find Wes smiling down at me when I

answered. I immediately felt that quickening of my pulse and had to catch my breath. "Well, hello, Wes."

"Going somewhere?" He had noticed my jacket slung over one arm.

"As a matter of fact, yes, I was just headed outside for a walk."

"Then I'll join you." He stepped aside to allow me to close the door, and then we started down the hall. We bypassed the spiral staircase that led down to the great room and lobby and continued on toward the back stairway exit.

When we got to the door, I paused to look at the closed door that opened to the off-limits stairway. Wes turned to watch me. I tried the door, but it was locked.

"No one uses it anymore," explained Wes.

"I know," I said. "But it was open the other day and I went up into the attic."

Wes shrugged. "Rosalee doesn't want anyone going into the old part of the lodge."

I let that go and followed him down the steps to the back exit. The cool mountain air met us as we stepped out into the early evening. Wes led me off to the left, where we circled around the building until we came into view of a gorgeous sunset spread across the western sky. A mountain peak jutted up in the distance. Pink and orange clouds billowed with sunbeams displayed in a projecting arc toward the tree line of the horizon. I stared in awe.

"We're overlooking Teller Park," said Wes, "and beneath that mountain is Diamond Reservoir."

When he said Diamond Reservoir, I remembered that had been the place where my father had died. We stood side by side and watched the beautiful sky for several minutes. Wes said very little. I murmured praises every once in a while, and he'd nod his head in agreement. I found myself longing to touch him, but I didn't have the nerve to try anything like that.

Finally, Wes turned to me and said, "Come on, let's walk." I'd hoped he would take hold of my hand, but both of his were stuck in his pockets. We strolled together toward the parking lot, then headed down the aspen-lined drive that led from the Rainbow Majestic to the county road that went to Wade City. At one point, we turned around and Wes pointed to Majestic

Mountain in the east, where the sunset's red glow reflected on the mountain's white peak. I had never seen anything that magnificent in my life. It was almost as though the mountain was aglow with a fiery light of its own.

Wes reached out suddenly and took my hand in his. I felt an electric thrill race through me as we continued walking toward the road.

"Tomorrow is Friday," Wes mentioned as we walked. "Drake and I are drivin' into Wade City. Would you like to come along?"

I turned to look up into his face with the blue eyes that seemed to melt into my own. "I'd love to go," I said.

"Good. I have to do some things in the mornin', but we were plannin' to go in the afternoon. Thought you might like to see Wade City while you're here."

It didn't matter to me if it was Wade City or Timbuktu. I just wanted to be with Wes. He excited me in a way I hadn't known since Sean. In the back of my mind, I remembered Clover's words earlier that afternoon, how she had confided in me that she was in love with Wes. I still wondered ... how did he feel about *her?*

We walked to where the drive ended at the county road. Again I looked at the marble sign for the Rainbow Majestic and felt happy to be here. At this very moment I was the happiest I had been in at least two years. I was standing amidst these mountains, sheltered by aspen trees with their spring leaves emerging, touching the hand of this spiritual man to whom I was attracted. And he had just indicated that he wanted to spend the next day with me.

The light of day was drawing to a close and the darkness of night fast approaching. I felt the chill of the mountain air and moved closer to Wes for warmth. It would have been the perfect moment for an embrace. But he stepped away from me.

"We'd better head back. You're gettin' cold." Instead of drawing me closer to him, he led me back up the tree-lined drive. He continued to hold my hand until we reached the lodge. Then he let go and stopped at the bottom of the steps leading to the front doors. "How long will you be stayin' here at the lodge?" he asked.

I studied his face in the fading light. The question seemed

out of place, for some reason. "Aunt Rosalee wants me to stay indefinitely and work in the gift shop."

He considered that a moment and stroked his chin. "What about your life back in Kansas? Don't you feel homesick?"

"No," I answered truthfully.

"Well, what about your ... friends?"

I hugged myself in the cool evening air. "I can take them or leave them."

"You mean there isn't some special man in your life back in Kansas?" A smile formed on the ends of his mouth. "A woman like yourself must surely have some fella wonderin' when you're comin' home."

I thought of Mike and rolled my eyes. My heart beat faster now as I understood the direction of his line of questioning. "There's no one I wish to return to." For a moment his eyes met mine and I felt a surge of emotion and wondered what might come next.

Wes appeared embarrassed. "I just thought I'd ask. You see, Gena said ..."

Gena! I should have known. Gena had probably told Wes I had a boyfriend in Kansas because of Mike's call last night. I shook my head. "Gena's wrong," I said. "My mother's executor called here, checking up on me. Gena jumped to the wrong conclusion."

"I see." Wes turned toward the steps. "Well, we might as well go in. I don't know if there will be a meditation tonight. I think I'll go meditate in my room."

"I'd like to learn," I said, and followed him up the steps too eagerly. But Wes didn't answer, although I was sure he had heard me.

He opened the door for me and smiled. "Be ready after lunch," he said. "We'll want to leave for Wade City about one." Then he turned and walked away, and I stood by myself in the lobby entrance, watching him go and wondering why he was so strange.

Cyril Jorgensen was strolling through the hallway as I passed the great room on my way to the stairs. He saw me and beckoned me over. "Hello, Juniper, and how are *you?*" He was dressed in baggy dark blue trousers and a plaid shirt. He propped his bent-over form against one of the large cedar posts. "Been outside, have you?"

"Yes, for a short walk," I said.

He sifted his free hand through his hair. "They are still practicing card reading in the lounge, if you're interested."

"Thanks," I said, "but I'll pass. Didn't you participate tonight?"

Cyril lifted his wrist to show me his watch. "It's getting close to my bedtime."

I told him that I had been reading a couple of his books, and his brown eyes sparkled as a grin lit his face. "I'm learning a lot from you," I added. "How did you ever gain all that knowledge?"

"Over many lifetimes," Cyril replied.

"Do you remember every life you've ever lived?" I asked, fascinated.

Cyril shrugged. "Not all of them, certainly. I've had well over a thousand, you know."

"What?" I stared at him.

He patted my arm and said, "Certainly not all of them were on this planet."

I wasn't sure how to take his comment, but asked, "Why don't we remember those other lives we've lived?"

Cyril cleared his throat. "You see, what's really important is the life you're living now. If we didn't have that veil of forgetfulness each time we incarnate, we'd never get anything accomplished. We'd all be too busy regretting our past mistakes, or wishing we were back doing something we used to do that has nothing to do with what we came here to learn."

I had to admit that made sense to me.

"The purpose of life, Juniper, is to experience all that we can. Only through experience do we learn the lessons we've set up for ourselves."

"Are you saying our lives are predestined?"

"Oh, it's much more complicated than that," he said. "But it's true that certain people come into our lives in order for us to balance the karma we've acquired. Take, for instance, your aunt. You and Rosalee share a special bond, do you not?"

I smiled and nodded. I did indeed feel very close to my aunt, and had taken to her from the beginning. Perhaps what Cyril was explaining might help me understand the conflict I had borne most my life with my mother. I had loved her, of course, because she had been my mother. Yet I had never felt as comfortable with her as some of my friends seemed to be toward their mothers. I suggested this to Cyril and he nodded in agreement.

"I'm just sorry I never got to know my father well," I said.

An eyebrow shot up on Cyril's wrinkled face. "Even that," he said, "was for a reason. You see, Juniper, it may have been prearranged, by you and Nathaniel—before either of you were born—that he would leave while you were still quite young, in order for you to experience what life was like without a father."

"But that's so unfair," I blurted out. "My father was *killed* by someone."

Cyril touched my shoulder in an effort to calm me. "Perhaps, in one of his past lives, Nathaniel had been the one to take a life. Perhaps it was even his brother, Fred."

For some reason, his words angered me, even though I had read about karma and soul destinies. "Well, I'm sorry," I said. "Somehow I just can't accept that. My father's life was taken from him abruptly, and ... and ..." Something stopped me from mentioning any more about it. I didn't feel at liberty to discuss what Aunt Rosalee had disclosed about Uncle Fred's death bed confession, even though I had told Taffi. Perhaps I shouldn't have even mentioned it to her.

Cyril let go of me. "You must go within yourself," he told me in a calm voice. "When you find the answer to your question, you will find peace."

Just at that moment, Celeste hobbled in from the next room, leaning on her cane, and saw the two of us conversing. "Well, there you are," she called to Cyril, her high-pitched, shaky voice full of joviality. "Juniper, dear, I'd wondered what had captured Cyril's attention."

We chatted a moment longer and then I excused myself and went up to the crystal suite. I drew a bath and had a relaxing soak before donning my nightgown. I then settled down to more reading. Tonight I made sure my door was double-secured and checked to see that the windows were fastened.

Delving deeply into the books I'd picked out was a welcome distraction from the disturbing thoughts about my father, and particularly the stormy emotions I held toward Wes Andrews and his divergent attitude toward me. Just when I'd think Wes was showing an interest in me, he'd do or say something to turn it around. Remembering what others had said about him, maybe it was best if I just gave up on him. After all, Clover had her goal set on winning him. If only he didn't make me yearn so much for Sean.

Morning came, following a good night's sleep. Even though I had resolved to play it cool around Wes today, I still found myself looking forward to the trip to Wade City this afternoon.

Aunt Rosalee knocked on my door while I was brushing my hair in preparation to go down for breakfast. I let her in.

"I hear you're ridin' into town with Wes and Drake this afternoon," she said. She held out a small leather pouch. "I want you to take this money and go buy yourself some clothes while you're there, and whatever else you may need."

I refused to take the pouch from her. "But I haven't even really started working for you yet. I feel funny taking this ..."

"Juniper, I know you didn't bring a lot with you, and I said I was goin' to buy you a new wardrobe. Now take this money and get what you want with it. If it's not enough, I'll lend you my gold card."

I felt my cheeks growing hot. Her generosity was embarrassing me. With a sigh of acceptance, I took the pouch, then went to my purse and tucked it into one of the zippered compartments. "I don't know what to say. Thanks, Aunt Rosalee."

"Just say you're stayin' in Colorado." She smiled.

I turned to her and smiled back. "Okay, I will." She hugged me and then we both went down to the dining room.

"No more threatenin' notes, I hope?" she inquired on the way.

"No."

At breakfast I sat with Aunt Rosalee and Gena, who discussed the upcoming fair and compared notes on preregistered attendees as well as the workshop schedule. I ate rye toast with a Southwest omelet and watched Clover enjoying her breakfast across the room with Wes, who sipped coffee and appeared to be involved in Clover's conversation. She flirted openly with him and I couldn't help feeling annoyed. To make matters worse, Gena kept glancing at me critically as if she knew I was more interested in what was happening across the room than in talk about the fair.

"Guests will start arriving on Thursday," Aunt Rosalee was saying. "The fair begins Friday morning. Juniper, do you think the gift shop will be ready to open by then?"

I forced my attention back to business then. "Oh. Yes, I think so, Aunt Rosalee. I don't know how much of the stuff I ordered will be in by the middle of next week ..."

"That won't matter," she replied. "We've got enough merchandise to open, and the T-shirt shop in Wade City promised the rainbow shirts will be ready to pick up no later than Thursday."

"Oh, good," said Gena.

I must have looked puzzled. Aunt Rosalee explained that she had ordered special T-shirts with the Rainbow Majestic logo on them. I was positive I could have the store ready for business in less than six days—and sooner if necessary. Aunt Rosalee seemed pleased. Gena made no comment. After breakfast I felt like getting a breath of fresh mountain air and stepped outside the lodge to greet the magnificent morning. A white-crowned sparrow sang its drowsy melody. I wandered toward the garden for a stroll. The air was chilly, but the warm sun felt soothing on my bare arms. I admired the bed of wildflowers just starting to come up in the garden. Various herbs grew here and there and a soft breeze brushed through the aspen trees along the path.

I didn't like my negative attitude that had formed around Wes and Clover. Somehow seeing them together had brought up envious feelings in me. I really liked Clover as a friend. I'd hoped we could be close friends, in fact. If that were to happen, I needed to let go of my resentment where Wes was concerned. He couldn't help it, of course, if he was such a desirable, attractive man. But it irritated me that he could invoke such stirrings in me and then suddenly close the door in my face, so to speak. I would have to deal with my own hurt and get over this senseless crush I had developed toward Wes Andrews.

When I saw Drake carrying a wheelbarrow load of firewood through the parking lot, that was my signal to go inside. I didn't feel like talking to Drake—or anyone—right now.

I worked most the morning and was making some progress at arranging things on racks and shelves. Someone had dropped off a CD player on my counter, so I plugged it in and tested some new age music selections while I worked, which helped settle my mood.

It must have been after 11 o'clock when Nadine Leachfield stopped in with a concerned look on her round face. "Have you seen Max?" she asked.

"No," I said. "Why?"

"Oh, Max has disappeared somewhere again without telling Lance or me." She may have been truly concerned about the whereabouts of her young son, but I noticed her attention was immediately drawn to some of the goodies in my shop. She began fingering through a pile of music CDs on the counter.

"How long has he been gone?" I asked. I recalled how Max liked to wander the secret passageways of the old lodge.

Nadine snapped back into the worried mom. "Oh, it's been an hour at least."

"I'll bet he's around somewhere," I reassured her.

"Yes, he likes to explore the hallways and empty rooms in the lodge." Nadine peeked into a box of books I hadn't yet unpacked.

"Not working in the kitchen this morning?" I asked as I arranged a colorful group of candles on a shelf.

"Why, yes," said Nadine. "In fact, I have to get back there. Lunch is coming up." She hesitated. "It's just not like Max to vanish for this long a time."

I looked at her worried face and abandoned my candles. "Tell you what," I said. "I'll go see if I can find him."

"Oh, I didn't mean for you to have to go looking for him," Nadine protested.

"Nonsense," I said. "I could actually use a break."

"Oh, thank you, Juniper." A broad smile spread across her face. "Max likes you. I don't think he'll try to hide from you the way he sometimes does Lance and me."

I closed the shop up behind us as we headed toward the kitchen. Gena peered at us from behind the front counter in the lobby as we passed. I left Nadine when we reached the spiral stairway in the great room. She hurried back toward the dining room and I went upstairs and headed directly for the back exit in the second corridor. If the door was locked that led to the attic, I'd have to find a way to sneak down into the basement off the kitchen, to get to the passageway Max had shown me a couple of days ago.

A maid was cleaning one of the rooms in that part of the corridor, but she didn't see me. I looked around before trying the door, to be sure I was unobserved. To my dismay, the door was locked. Now I'd have to try going through the basement. On my way past, the maid stuck her head out the door of the room she was cleaning and greeted me.

"You haven't seen a little blond-haired boy, have you?" I asked.

"No. You mean Max is missing again?"

"Yes."

She laughed and shook her head. "Don't worry. He'll appear when he's ready."

"He does this often?"

"Yes, he's a crafty boy, for sure. Knows his way around the Majestic better than anyone else."

I thanked her, then headed downstairs again. When I was sure no one in the kitchen was watching, I sneaked through to the basement steps and tried not to make any noise as I groped my way down into the dark depths. I heard Nadine talking to someone in the kitchen and Thelma rattling pots and pans in the sink. I didn't dare turn on a light, but as my eyes began to adjust to the blackness, I could make out shelves of supplies for the kitchen. I wove my way around tubs and boxes, headed toward the far corner that I remembered. It took several minutes of searching before I located the narrow opening in the concrete wall that was concealed behind a number of crates and sacks of flour and other food staples.

I was able to slide myself sideways through the doorway, which began to slant upward as I groped my way through, unable to see. I knew from my adventure the other day that this passageway led to the first floor of the old lodge, and I'd eventually come out of the closet into what had once been a dressing room next to the old auditorium. The air I breathed smelled dusty and old, and a couple of times I cringed as my probing fingers encountered thin, thready spider webs. It seemed I had explored for quite a ways, and I started feeling nervous and disoriented, as though perhaps this wasn't the right passageway Max had taken me through after all. But I knew all I had to do—if I chose—was to turn around and go back.

Instead, I labored onward and upward until finally I noticed a thin crack of daylight ahead. I was coming to the end of the passageway. In seconds, I pushed aside the panel that led from the tunnel through the closet, which was already open. I stepped into the dressing room and then made my way directly to the auditorium by way of the back stage.

An oppressive stillness enveloped me as I stood on the stage. Like before, it was dark and creepy, as if unseen eyes stared at me from the shadows, and it didn't help now that Aunt Rosalee and Gena had kidded that the old auditorium may be haunted.

"Max?" I called out and heard how my voice echoed in the large room.

There was no answer. I wondered where I'd find a light switch, or even if one would work. In the dim light from outside I saw the old harp in its lonely position next to the stage.

"Max, it's Juniper," I called out again. "Where are you?" Again my words were met with silence. I slowly stepped down off the stage and strolled the dark aisle between the seats, all the while recalling that Aunt Rosalee had made it clear to me that no one was allowed in this old part of the lodge. I wondered what was the real reason she had abandoned its renovation after Uncle Fred had died.

Clearly Max was not in the auditorium. I was glad to leave that dusty place and headed down the old, crumbly hallway. Broken furniture and junky items cluttered the floor as I peeked into various rooms, calling for Max.

With a sigh, I turned around and headed back into the auditorium. It was the only way I remembered how to get back to the main part of the lodge without taking the tunnel all the way to the basement. I hoped Max had shown up by now. At least this had given me another opportunity to explore the forbidden sections.

A shudder of dread hit me suddenly as I entered the auditorium the second time. I definitely had the feeling I was not alone, and yet there was no sound or indication that anyone else was present. My rational mind told me I was being foolish, but I couldn't help the morbid fear that was building in my core. I just wanted to get out of there as quickly as possible.

I almost tripped over an upturned stool and caught myself on a railing, then hurried to find the doorway that would take me up to the attic room. My heart beat rapidly now, and I was relieved to find the door easily enough. Squeezing sideways, I slipped into the passageway and began my groping journey upward.

When I reached the attic several minutes later, I breathed a sigh of relief and moved into the back room to find the narrow stairway that would lead me down to the locked door on the second floor. That's when I heard a scraping sound.

"Max?" I called out, my voice trembling now.

A scuffle followed and then my eye caught sight of some slight movement over to my right. I moved quickly, just in time to see the boy crouched behind an old vanity with a broken mirror.

"Max!" I cried. "Come out. It's just me ... Juniper."

Max peered up at me with wide blue eyes. I couldn't decide if he looked more like Nadine or his father, Lance. "J-Juniper?" he whimpered.

"Yes." I knelt before him. "Max, they've been looking for you down in the lodge."

"Did you tell them I was here?" he asked.

"No."

He crawled toward me, still worried as he gazed around the crowded room.

"What's wrong?" I looked around.

"I heard the ghost," he told me in a low voice.

"What?"

"Down there—in that big room," he said.

"The auditorium, you mean?"

"Yes ... there."

"Max, I was just in there. I didn't see or hear anybody."

"Well, I did." His eyes were round and big.

"What did it sound like?"

"A voice," he told me. "It was a voice."

"Well, what did the voice say?"

"It said, 'Go away.' "

"Max, did it sound like a man or a woman?"

"I don't know." His eyes began to well up with tears. "It was kind of deep, like a man ... but I couldn't tell for sure. Juniper, is there really a ghost?"

I reached out to pat the boy's shoulder. "Max, I'm sure not. At least *I* don't believe in ghosts."

"My mom does," said Max. "She says there are ghosts. But my dad says there aren't."

"And what do you think?" I asked.

Max looked around anxiously. "I heard it," he said. "It told me not to come here anymore."

Most adults would dismiss this as a child's active imagination, but I felt a chill go up my spine. Max didn't act as though he were making this up. I was positive he had heard something. That's why he had escaped up to the attic room. Yet my immediate concern was getting both of us out of here and back down to the lodge. I tried to make light of his words.

"Come on, Max, let's go down the back stairway. I think we can unlock the door from this side." I reached out my hand and he took it as he slowly stood up.

Suddenly, both of us froze. Harp music began to play from far away. The chords were coming from the auditorium down below. Max stared at me in terror. In the next second, he darted out toward the narrow stairway, and I was on his heels.

12

We reached the second floor stairwell and wasted no time unlocking the door and stepping into the main lodge. Fortunately, no one was around to witness.

"Don't tell my mom," Max pleaded with me. He no longer was frightened, just wound up. I was out of breath.

"Shouldn't we tell someone about what we heard?" I asked.

"See? There *is* a ghost," Max insisted. "You heard it, too."

"I heard somebody playing the harp. I don't know if it was a ghost, Max."

"Well, if you tell ... they'll ground me."

I gave in. "Okay, but maybe you should heed the warning. The old part of the lodge is not safe, you know."

He laughed to cover up any lingering fears. "I don't think I'll go back there—at least for a couple of days."

"That's a good idea," I agreed. "I won't go either."

He studied me, then nodded his head. "You're awesome, Juniper." Then he took off and ran down the corridor toward the spiral stairway, leaving me to follow at a more leisurely pace.

I returned to the crystal suite, where I freshened up before going downstairs for a bite of lunch. I saw Starla lingering with her spiral notebook and pen over a bowl of soup. She made room for me when I brought my plate over to her table.

"How's the book coming along?" I asked.

"I'm getting such great messages," she replied. "They're keeping me busy, that's for sure."

"Who?" I placed my napkin on my lap.

"My guides."

We discussed the upcoming fair over lunch. I learned that Starla would be giving awakenings to those who signed up. She told me I should plan to have one myself—that a lot of good could come from having one.

"Well, what's it like?" I asked. "What do you do?"

Starla pushed aside her empty soup bowl. "Each awakening

is different. Each individual experiences something unique."

"Do you delve into past lives?" I asked.

"Sometimes," said Starla. "Quite often, in fact." She studied me, then said, "You should have one soon, Juniper. We need to clear a lot of your stuff that you're carrying around."

I didn't understand what she was talking about. I finished my lunch, then ran back upstairs to get ready for the afternoon in Wade City.

It was precisely one o'clock when I came downstairs, carrying my purse and jacket. When I stepped outside the front doors of the lodge, Wes and Drake waited for me at the bottom of the steps, next to the lodge SUV. Standing there with them was Clover, and I felt a sudden disappointment as she waved at me, then climbed into the back seat. I hadn't known that Clover would be going with us to Wade City.

"Juniper, you can ride in back with Clover." Wes walked around to the driver's side. Drake stood looking at me a long moment. It was almost as though he recognized my confusion. Then he smiled in a mocking fashion and held the door open for me. After I got into the back seat, Drake closed the door, then hopped into the front seat next to Wes.

"Juniper, I thought you'd like some help trying on clothes." Clover grinned at me with her gray eyes. Her long curly red hair hung loosely over her shoulders. "Rosalee asked me to come along and make sure these guys didn't, like ... try to rush you while you're shopping."

Drake grumbled to himself and Wes made no comment as he started up the engine. We drove down the long lane with the aspen trees on both sides. The ride to Wade City was long. Clover chattered the entire way. The men in the front seat carried on their own conversation while I listened to Clover's opinions about Gena, the maids, the dinner choices, the evening lectures, and what workshops she hoped to take during the fair next week.

I stared out the window at the scenery, not feeling too talkative. I was more interested in the views and landscape than trivial talk. Every once in a while, I caught Drake glancing back at me—almost in sympathy—but inwardly I felt he was laughing at me.

My thoughts kept returning to the old part of the lodge and

the startling sound of the harp coming from the auditorium when Max and I had been in the attic room. Obviously, someone else had been in the old part of the lodge when Max and I had been there. Had they accessed the auditorium by some other means or had they taken one of the secret passageways? Who could it have been?

"You've been awful quiet, Juniper." Clover touched my shoulder to get my attention. "Is something worrying you?"

I noticed both Wes and Drake had glanced back and were waiting for my response.

"Oh, it's nothing," I said.

"Your mind seems to be elsewhere," said Clover.

I needed to steer my thoughts away from the subject of the old lodge. "I'm getting the gift shop ready. That's what's on my mind."

Clover smiled. "I'm so glad you're staying." I looked at the warmth of friendship in her eyes and could see she really meant it. But I knew there was still at least one person at the Rainbow Majestic who didn't want me there.

We finally reached the state highway and drove the short ways into Wade City, which was not a large town, but had a high school, a gas station and a recreation center on the outskirts. Wes cruised the main street, pointing out its attractions. "There's our movie theater," he indicated. "It may be a small town, but we've got a movie theater, a health food store, a book store, and lots of shops."

"There's the bicycle shop." Drake pointed out his side of the car. "Over there's our Mexican restaurant, our bar and the pizza shop."

I found the little town charming with a Victorian flair in its architecture. Summer tourism was obviously in full swing as evidenced by flocks of people visiting the many colorful shops or lounging in sidewalk cafés for a late lunch or afternoon coffee.

"We even have a radio station in town," Wes said over his shoulder.

"Lots of real estate agents," added Clover.

Drake groaned and shook his head in disapproval.

"The restaurants are good, too," said Clover.

"Drake and I need to get some things at the lumber yard," Wes told us. "Want me to drop you and Juniper anywhere special?"

I noticed the way Clover patronized Wes with her flirtatious smile. She touched his arm and said, "Perhaps you can, like ... drop us off at the Peach Pit. We'll start there and work our way down River Street. You and Drake can wait for us down by The Talisman."

"We'll be in there having a beer," quipped Drake.

"I thought The Talisman would be a nice place to have supper," suggested Clover.

Wes stared at her. "What's wrong with The Vegan?"

Drake snorted in protest. "I'm not eatin' that shit." He made a face and crossed his arms.

"They have decent food at The Talisman," said Clover. "You can get, like ... meatless dishes there, Wes."

Wes shot a helpless look in my direction, which told me he would go along with whatever we decided, even though he had other preferences. He pulled the car up to the curb and parked, then Clover and I got out. The sun was intense and felt hot against my bare arms as we headed into the store Clover had picked for me. The men drove off.

Clover was enthusiastic and helpful in assisting me shop. I quickly forgot my prickly feelings toward her with regard to Wes. She had excellent taste in choosing styles and colors that suited me, and coaxed me into trying on outfits I might not have attempted had I been shopping alone. Then she assessed whether they were right for me or not.

"This is a casual part of the country," Clover explained. "And in Wade City it's dress as you please. Nobody cares, like ... how funky you look. But I prefer looking feminine, don't you?"

I smiled at her as I gazed at my reflection in the dressing room mirror. I had on a Western skirt of blue denim and a melon-colored top with a scoop neck and long sleeves that had aqua embroidery enhanced with green and gold.

"That will be nice for the Saturday night dance," said Clover as she admired my reflection.

"What dance?" I asked. I hadn't heard any talk about a dance.

"Next weekend, when the fair is almost over," said Clover. She followed me into the dressing room. "Gena's organizing it. At first, Rosalee said no, it was too much. But Celeste and Starla—the *party girls*—must have, like ... talked her into it.

The lodge is going to hold a dance in the evening—in the great room—or else they'll use, like … the dining room and push all the tables to the side."

"Hmm." I removed the skirt. "What kind of music will they have?"

"Oh, I don't know what Gena has arranged," said Clover. "Knowing her, it could be anything. She'll probably, like … hire a DJ if she can't get a band at this late date."

"Well, that should be fun," I commented. But I had a vision of Wes and Clover, locked in each other's arms, lost in the music of a slow dance. I knew I had to stop resenting her.

"I've been noticing how Drake watches you," Clover said all of a sudden.

Startled, I pulled the shirt clear of my head and looked at her.

Clover giggled. "Oh, it's obvious. Drake's got a thing for you. Don't tell me you haven't noticed."

This was not what I wanted to hear. I wanted Wes to be the one who had a thing for me. But Wes appeared to be more interested in Clover. I knew her heart was set on winning him, and naturally she would say something to ward off any competition. Clover had to know I harbored an attraction for the same man she did. But I certainly hadn't noticed that Drake had shown any special interest in me. I decided to let her comment go, and immediately changed the subject by showing interest in a pair of designer jeans on a nearby rack.

We combed through four or five more small shops before I told Clover I had enough new clothes and was finished with my shopping. She had managed to pick out a few selections for herself as well, so we walked the remaining blocks to The Talisman, carrying our large bags and feeling quite weighted down by them.

The SUV was parked on the curb in front of the restaurant, which was situated on the river. Clover left me on the sidewalk with the packages while she ran inside to get the keys from Wes. When she came out a couple of minutes later, she unlocked the back and we threw in our stash. Then she locked everything up and led me into the bar.

I followed Clover downstairs. The restaurant part was upstairs, but it was too early to eat. We found Wes and Drake seated at a small round table off to the side. Drake had a glass of beer, but I noticed Wes had only a soft drink. Some people sat at the bar, smoking and sipping drinks, and two men in jeans and western shirts were playing pool across the room. They eyed Clover and me as we sat down at the table with Wes and Drake. Country music played in the background.

Immediately Clover scooted her chair over as close to Wes as she could get and locked her arm in his, as though she were staking her claim. He didn't seem to mind her bold gesture and smiled at both of us. "How'd the shoppin' go?" he asked.

"Juniper has a new wardrobe," said Clover. "She has good taste in clothes."

"*You* picked out almost everything," I replied.

Drake gazed at me and asked, "Wanna beer?"

I stared at him and caught that familiar look in his dark blue eyes that always unsettled me. "No, thank you."

"Then how about, like ... a glass of wine?" Clover turned and beckoned to the cocktail waitress across the room. "Do you like red or white?" Without waiting for my answer, she looked into Wes's glass and wrinkled up her nose. "What are you drinking? Why don't you order, like ... some Scotch to go with that?"

"He has to drive home," said Drake.

"Oh, one drink isn't going to matter," said Clover. She turned her face up into Wes's and flashed a teasing smile. Wes turned pink and stared into his glass, but said nothing.

Just then, the waitress appeared to take our drink orders. I wasn't a drinker, and really wasn't in the mood for wine, so I asked for a cola. Clover pouted and ordered a glass of rosé. I was surprised that Drake didn't order another beer.

"Let's, like ... do something fun while we're here." Clover certainly seemed to be in a party mood all of a sudden. She looked across the room. "Let's see if those two cowboys will let us play pool."

Drake belched as if in response. I noticed that Wes appeared embarrassed by Clover and I felt sorry for him, the way she was hanging onto him and trying to be the life of the party. She had caught the eye of one of the pool players and she shot him an enticing smile. He hesitated only a moment and then returned to his game without acknowledging her. I sighed in relief.

Wes regained his composure and focused on me. "So what do you think of our fair city?" he asked with a warm smile.

"Very nice," I answered. "I like it."

"It's growing," said Clover. "Soon they say they'll have to, like ... put in a stoplight."

Drake raised his glass of beer and declared, "And when that day comes, I'll be movin' on." He took a swallow, then set his glass down.

The pool balls crashed together and a loud groan came from one of the cowboy pool players across the room.

"*I* know," said Clover, perking up. "After dinner we can catch a movie."

Wes sighed. "That'll make too late of a night. The movie doesn't start till seven-thirty or eight."

"So?"

"It'll be midnight before we get back to the lodge," commented Drake.

"It's Friday night," insisted Clover. She tugged at Wes's arm. "No one, like ... cares how late we stay out."

I could see that neither Wes nor Drake were too excited about the movie idea.

Clover appealed to me. "What do *you* think, Juniper? Don't you want to take in the movie?"

I envisioned the four of us sitting in the dark theater, Drake on one side of me, and Clover and Wes making out on the other side. "Actually ... I'd rather not," I said with a smile. "Perhaps another time, though."

Drake reached over and patted my hand, as if to tell me, "Good girl, that was the right answer." I pretended not to notice.

Clover looked about to protest, but just then one of the cowboys approached our table. He held his cue stick and smiled down at Clover, who still had her arm locked in Wes's. She peered up at the stranger with a gleam in her gray eyes.

"Wanna play a match?" the cowboy asked her.

Wes immediately unlocked his arm from Clover's in a show of indifference. Clover grinned and pushed her chair back. "Sure! I'll play," she said, and followed the young man over to the pool table. Apparently his buddy had lost their last game and was now sitting at the bar ordering a beer.

I watched Clover in amazement. First, she'd flirted with

Wes. Now, she was making a play—or so it seemed—for a stranger. Was she purposely trying to make Wes jealous?

The waitress brought my cola and Clover's rosé, which Drake gestured her to take over to the pool table. The three of us watched the pool game get started as Clover broke. Her laughter ensued and then Wes and Drake both turned their attention back to me. I wondered why it hadn't bothered Wes that Clover had simply left us to go play pool with a strange guy. Perhaps his feelings toward Clover were not what she thought they were.

"What do you think after your first week at the Rainbow?" Drake asked me. Wes also seemed interested in my opinion.

I told them I was intrigued with everything there and had been learning a lot, both by reading books and associating with the people. I mentioned the bond I felt toward Aunt Rosalee and how I thought I would enjoy running the bookstore.

"But there is one thing I want to know," I said to them. "Why did Aunt Rosalee put a stop to remodeling the old part of the lodge?"

"You mean the section where the auditorium is?" Drake asked. When I nodded, he said, "As I recall, her husband was planning to fix all that up, but then he died."

"There was extensive damage to that part of the lodge after the fire," said Wes.

I recalled that Aunt Rosalee had mentioned a fire in the old part of the lodge. "Tell me about it," I urged.

"Several years ago, there was a fire that started in one of those old rooms," Wes continued. "I've heard Rosalee talk about it. It's a wonder the whole place didn't burn down. We're so far away from any fire station ..."

"What started the fire?" I asked.

Drake ran a finger over the rim of his glass. "There's a rumor that it was started intentionally. Those rooms were once used by the people who lived and worked at the Majestic. Back when it was a hunting lodge."

"Did Aunt Rosalee and Uncle Fred live in that part?"

"And Gena," Drake added. "It was the family quarters. The auditorium wasn't used that much in those days. But once in a while they had something special going on and they'd use it."

"Do you know what happened?" I asked.

"The fire started in one of the dressing rooms back stage," said Wes.

I thought of the dressing room I had been in—the one with the closet that opened into the secret passageway. I didn't recall seeing any charred walls except in the auditorium. "Was there more than one dressing room?"

"There were two," said Drake. "The one that caught fire is all boarded up. They apparently were able to get the fire put out before it spread, but the auditorium was damaged."

"Yes, I know." When they looked at me oddly, I decided not to reveal any more about my explorations. "You said it was intentional. Who set the fire?"

Drake shrugged. "It's only a rumor. The cause was never known."

I turned to Wes. He shook his head. "I don't know either. But if you ask Rosalee, you'll find out she's touchy about the subject. She doesn't like anyone even mentionin' the fire ... or the auditorium."

"Hmm." I took a sip from my cola. "Is that why she tells everyone there's a ghost?"

Both men chuckled. Drake said, "In her mind there probably is one."

We turned in the direction of laughter. Clover and the cowboy seemed to be hitting it off. He was now showing her how to hold her cue, and I could see she was playing up to him.

I sighed. "There seem to be plenty of secrets at the Rainbow Majestic. One of them has to do with my father, and I've noticed Gena gets touchy when I bring up the subject. And I've noticed a couple of other people seem to not want to discuss it." I was musing out loud now.

Unexpectedly, Wes reached over and took my hand in his. "What happened to your father was a terrible thing, that's for sure. But sometimes it's a good idea to forget about what happened a long time ago—and move on." His warm smile, coupled with those caring blue eyes, just about did me in.

I was aware of Drake watching. He leaned back in his seat with his glass in hand, swirling its contents, and smiled in his mocking fashion. For some reason it made me nervous and—in light of what Clover had said earlier—I retrieved my hand from Wes's grasp and pretended to straighten my hair. Both men were studying me, and confusing emotions swept over me all of a sudden.

I thought of something to quickly change the subject and asked if either of them had been given an awakening by Starla.

Wes began telling me about his experience, which had helped him come to terms with his military past. He told me that Starla brought in a person's guides and she worked with them as well as her own spirit guides, in helping you overcome any problems in your life, or even issues that arose because of past lives.

"What about you, Drake?" I asked when Wes had finished. "Did Starla help you?"

Drake shrugged. "I don't know. I can't remember. I think I fell asleep on the table."

"That doesn't mean he didn't have a profound experience," Wes explained. "It still affected him."

"I'm thinking about getting one," I disclosed.

Drake observed me carefully. He seemed to be trying to figure me out in some way. I kept recalling Clover's remark earlier—that Drake had a thing for me. Well, right now Wes was paying more attention to me than when Clover had been in our company. I was naturally flattered, but at the same time a little confused. I was strongly attracted to Wes, yet I couldn't deny the fact that there was something about Drake that tugged at my heart. But if Drake was attracted to me as Clover claimed, he sure didn't show it—at least in any way I could recognize.

Half an hour passed in which our conversation drifted to various topics. Drake finally ordered another beer. Clover was still playing pool, but two other guys had joined in the game. She appeared to be having the time of her life. When we felt it was time to go get a table upstairs in the restaurant, Wes went over to talk to Clover. He came back and told us she'd join us as soon as the match was over.

The three of us climbed the steps to The Talisman's elegant dining room, which was already filling up with patrons. The hostess led us to a table for four near the back. We decided we'd wait for Clover before we ordered, but when fifteen minutes passed and she didn't join us, Drake decided to go see what was keeping her. He had just scooted his chair back when Clover hurried toward us, a wine glass in her hand and her eyes bright.

The tip of her nose was kind of red.

"I'm sorry," she said as she approached the table. "I hope I'm not, like … being too rude. But would you mind if I, like … skip out on you? Brad and Mark invited me to the party at the radio station tonight. It's a fund raiser, and I'm sure I can get, like … someone to take me up to the lodge afterwards … and if not, then tomorrow."

I stared at Clover, astounded. Wes and Drake seemed to take her decision in stride. They waved her off as they each picked up their menus. Clover smiled at me apologetically, then turned and headed back toward the entrance. She disappeared through the door and I picked up my menu and wondered if this was typical of her.

"Well, looks like I have the two of you to myself," I said. When neither of them responded, I grew embarrassed.

"I think I'll order the steak," Drake finally said.

Wes drank from his water glass, then said, "I guess I'll have a salad."

I looked at him over the top of my menu. "Is that all? I saw some vegetarian dishes on the menu. There's something with tofu."

Drake grunted in disgust.

"A salad is all I want," Wes said quietly.

"What're you having, Juniper?" asked Drake.

I chose the barbecued chicken with a dinner salad and a roll. After we ordered our meal, I bit the bullet and asked, "Why did Clover abandon us? Does she do this often?"

"Yup," said Drake.

Wes attempted a smile, but I could tell he didn't want to discuss Clover or her actions. While we ate, I found myself wondering what it might have been like had I been sitting here at this table, having dinner with just Wes. His blue eyes often fell on my face and his expression told me he wanted to be alone with me … or was it just my wishful thinking? It was almost impossible to second-guess Wes's thoughts and intentions. But my heart would flutter every time I caught him looking at me.

Drake carried on most the conversation, mostly about the mountains and his experiences hunting, fishing or camping. I couldn't help being amused by his tales, and I noticed Wes added very little to the discussion. Before I knew it, we had finished our meal and waived dessert because we were too full. We ordered tea and sat around the table another half hour, rapt in Drake's outdoor adventures. I wondered how much of what he told us had really happened.

It was almost as though Drake had taken on a different personality when he spoke of his love for the outdoors. His knowledge of wildlife and his respect for the mountains provided a clearer picture for me. Here was a man in his element, who obviously was a skilled outdoorsman and felt more at home in the woods than in any city. Drake smiled and seemed more relaxed as he recalled many of his adventures around Majestic Mountain.

When it was time to leave, Wes paid the bill and Drake left a tip. We were walking toward the door to follow Wes out when I noticed a familiar-looking large man sitting at a table. He looked up at us as we passed and a scowl crossed his pudgy face. I recognized the big man who had come to the Rainbow Majestic yesterday with the two women and the petition. He was seated with a lady and two teen-age boys, who seemed startled by his reaction to Drake and me.

"Rainbow *scum!*" I heard him mutter.

Drake stopped and turned to him. Panic rose in me as I sensed trouble brewing. Drake had stood up to the man at the lodge yesterday. What would he do now? Was he going to cause a scene?

Slowly, the big man got up from the table and faced Drake, who didn't say a word. Yet I could feel the agitation rising in Drake. I reached out and grabbed his hand in mine, to pull him away with me. I felt his fingers clasp tightly around mine, almost as if he were trying to restrain himself. The two men's eyes had locked in a stare.

"Roy, sit down," the woman at the table told her husband. There was a tremor in her voice.

Suddenly, the waiter came by. "Is there something I can help with?" he asked.

"Dad ..." one of the teen-agers pleaded.

Finally, Drake tore his gaze away from the big man and said to the waiter, "No, we were just leaving." The next moment, his grip tightened over my hand and he led me out the door.

A great sense of relief swept through me and I hardly

noticed that Drake still clung to my hand when we met Wes out front. His eyes immediately darted to our locked hands, but Drake offered no explanation, nor did he let go of me until we had reached the SUV, where he waited for Wes to unlock the doors. Then, with a gentle smile, Drake patted my arm as I climbed into the back seat.

It was starting to get dark as we left Wade City and headed back up to Majestic Mountain. I watched a magenta sunset out the window as we climbed the winding road. I was hardly aware of anything the two men were saying in the front seat, so absorbed was I in the beauty of the mountains. But—even more—I was struck with a disturbing fear, mixed with wonder, at the remembered touch of Drake's hand in mine.

13

The next several days passed without incident. I busied myself with getting the gift shop ready to open, and during my leisure hours I spent time by myself either outside or holed up in my room, reading. I had replaced the first set of borrowed books with another set from the library. I was intrigued with every subject in the broad field of metaphysics. Sometimes I took a book with me to read while I ate in the dining room.

Clover returned to the lodge Saturday afternoon. She came by the gift shop to see me and apologize. She told me she'd enjoyed the party but drank too much. For the most part she'd had a good time. "I can't help it," Clover said as she sat in a folding chair while I priced items for sale. "I like to have a good time. I hope you don't, like … disapprove of me."

I looked over at her and blinked. "Clover, what you do is your business. It makes no difference to me."

She sighed. "It's just that I haven't, like … really been getting anywhere with Wes lately … or anybody else, for that matter. And Brad was, like … really kind of cute."

I wondered if she had slept with him. I assumed she had slept with somebody at the party.

"Well, hey, I'd better go see if I have anybody waiting for a massage." She stood up and started out the door, then came back and gave me a hug.

"What's that for?" I asked.

"Thanks for being my friend," said Clover. "And remember, if you ever need, like … anybody to talk to, I'm always available." Then she left.

Aunt Rosalee was pleased with the wardrobe I'd bought. I was afraid she'd say something about how much I had spent, but it didn't seem to be of concern to her. I wanted to talk to her more about my father, but I could see she was busy with the upcoming fair. There would be time after the event was over. She did mention that I might have to give up the crystal suite for the weekend.

"Juniper, I hate to do this to you," she told me, "but we have some guests comin' who insist on gettin' the crystal suite each time they're here. I've asked Taffi and she's willin' to let you stay in her room those nights."

I told Aunt Rosalee I didn't mind at all and that staying with Taffi a couple of nights was agreeable.

I hardly saw anything of either Wes or Drake during those days we were preparing for the fair. Aunt Rosalee kept Drake busy constructing booths and shelves for the benefit of the vendors. Gena always had some assignment for Wes. Because everyone was busy getting ready, the evening talks had been put on hold. Cyril and Celeste still insisted on holding informal group meditations in the lounge, but I did not attend. I saw Nadine and Max in the kitchen every once in a while and she thanked me for finding her son Friday morning. Apparently, Max hadn't told her *where* I'd found him. And, as far as I could tell, the boy hadn't gone exploring in the secret passageways since that day.

I often wondered who had played the harp that we'd heard. Had someone else been in the old part of the lodge that morning? And if so, how had they gotten there? Surely there must be another entrance besides the secret passageways.

I cherished the time I would spend outside the lodge—usually after supper—or early in the morning. I liked to go on walks by myself—when it was daylight—and kept on the trails as I checked out different parts of the woods, always on the alert for wildlife. The birds in the mountains were not as diverse as in the East, it seemed. I discovered Stellar jays, black-capped and mountain chickadees, ruby-crowned kinglets and a few spring warblers that I could hear singing high in the trees but could never see in the dense cover of foliage.

A pine marten appeared in the woods one late afternoon and I was thrilled to see it. I found that if I sat quietly for several minutes in one place, all kinds of forest life revealed itself to me in the aspen and evergreens near Majestic Mountain. There was a brook I found that I frequented every time I took a walk. It was a little off the trail, but not far enough to warrant getting lost or accosted. Of course, it was always in the back of my mind that I had been attacked in these woods, but

I didn't dwell on it. In fact, I had practically forgotten the incident had taken place.

Wednesday evening I was reading in my room when the telephone rang. I was in the middle of a chapter about remote viewing—a fascinating ability that some people claimed to possess—and hated to get up from the couch to go answer the call. But I thought it might be Clover or Rosalee.

To my surprise, it was Mike calling from Kansas. "Hi," he said. "Haven't heard from you in a while."

"Oh, hello, Mike." My head was still spinning a little from the subject of people who could see actual things taking place in other parts of the world, just in their mind's eye.

"How come you haven't called me?" he asked.

I paused. "Well, I don't know."

"Juniper, are you all right? You sound ... funny."

"Yes, of course, I'm fine."

"When are you coming home?"

The inevitable question had arisen again and I knew I had to confront him sooner or later. I drew in a deep breath and decided now was the time. "Mike, I'm not coming home."

There was a long pause at the other end of the line.

Finally, I had to ask, "Are you still there?"

"What do you mean you're not coming home?"

"I'm going to be running the gift shop here at the lodge for my aunt," I said. "I've decided I want to stay and make Colorado my home."

Mike exploded. "*What did you say?* What do you mean you're making ... *Juniper,* have you lost your mind? What about us? What about your home here in Kansas? How can you make a decision like that right out of the blue?"

I waited for him to cool down before I spoke again. "Mike, it's nothing personal. I've been offered a job and I think I'm going to like it here."

"But you're needed here," he insisted.

"I'm sure you can handle all the estate matters," I said. "I expect to make a trip to Great Bend in the near future—to get my belongings—but it won't be right away. I think you should go ahead and put Mother's house on the market."

He was clearly mortified by my bold words and I couldn't believe how good it felt to say them. But then he said something unexpected. "Juniper, do you have any idea how your aunt managed to purchase the Majestic Mountain Lodge and turn it into some new age ashram?"

"The Rainbow Majestic is a hotel and a light center," I corrected him.

"I've been doing some digging," he said. There was an edge in his voice now. "Perhaps you should ask yourself how a woman like Rosalee Sutton, who didn't have two pennies to rub together while she and her husband were caretakers at the lodge, suddenly came into all that money—and was able to buy the lodge and fix it up. Did you know the place almost burned down twenty years ago?"

I could feel my defenses rising. I didn't like what he was implying. "For your information, Uncle Fred and Aunt Rosalee bought the lodge together before he died, and it was only last summer that she changed its name to the Rainbow Majestic."

"You need to come home, Juniper," he insisted. "I don't like what you're involved in. People like that have a way of sucking you in and taking control of your mind. I can already tell by the sound of your voice that you've changed."

"Mike, you're wrong! It's not what you think at all." Mike had a lot of nerve accusing anyone of taking control. But—for the first time—I wondered about Aunt Rosalee and where she'd obtained her money. It was true that she appeared to have limitless funds. She had refurbished the Rainbow Majestic into a splendid convention center from a fairly conservative hunting lodge.

"Come home where you belong, Juniper," Mike pleaded. "We can make a good life together."

I didn't want to make a life with Mike. I didn't love him. But I didn't want to argue with him any more. He had already upset me. "Just give me a few days to think," I told him in order to put him off. "I need some time to consider what you've told me."

"No, you should get out of there now!"

"Mike, I can't."

"And why not?"

I told him about the fair and that I needed to stay through the weekend, to help out Aunt Rosalee. I figured if I could make Mike believe I might come home after the fair, he'd cool down and not insist on my immediate departure. It worked. His anger drained and he relaxed enough to relate some matters of concern regarding the estate. After that, we said goodbye and hung up.

I couldn't go back to my reading. I left the crystal suite and wandered down to the kitchen to fix a cup of herb tea. I passed a few guests in the hallway, but for the most part, things were quiet tonight in the lodge.

I sat down at a table in the kitchen after setting the tea kettle on the stove to boil. The kitchen help had cleaned up everything and retired for the night. I sat, thinking about Mike's accusatory remark about Aunt Rosalee and how she'd acquired her wealth. Where had Mike gotten his information? Obviously, he had been checking up on the Rainbow Majestic. He knew about the fire in the Majestic Mountain Lodge. Twenty years ago was only a short time after my father had been killed.

A sudden noise startled me. Gena stepped into the kitchen and saw me. "Oh, it's just you," she said without smiling. "I wondered who was in here. I saw the light on."

I didn't want Gena to notice that I was upset. I hoped she would turn around and walk out, but instead she strolled over and took a seat beside me at the table. She looked questioningly at the stove and the kettle.

"I'm fixing some tea," I told her.

"Good idea. Maybe I'd better have a cup, too." She watched me and then wrinkled up her face. "What's bothering you tonight? You're unhappy about something."

I was surprised at her sudden interest in me, but I didn't trust her. "It'll pass."

"It's male, isn't it?" One of her eyebrows shot up. When I didn't answer, she sighed and drummed her long, thin fingers on the table top. "I tried to warn you about Wes, you know. He likes to play the field, but you can forget about that home run."

I stared directly at my cousin. "Gena, you don't know anything about it."

A smile played along the corners of her mouth and her chin became pointy. "I'm picking up quite strongly that a man has upset you tonight."

"Are you trying to do a reading on me?" I asked.

"Well, sometimes I can't help it. The images just pop into my mind, whether I want them to or not."

"Clover says you can trance channel."

Gena looked at me. "I used to. I don't do that any more."

Now I was curious. "Why not?"

"Oh, because when a spirit takes over, I don't remember anything that was said. That can be very disturbing. I can't allow such a thing to occur."

I could certainly understand her reasoning. "Well, just how good are you?" I challenged. "Let's hear what you're picking up about me now."

Gena sighed deeply and relaxed, letting her brown eyes close slowly. Then she spoke. "I'm seeing an outdoor scene ... some peaceful woods. It's a sunny day and birds are singing. I'm seeing you standing outside a building ... a very simple structure ... made of logs, I think. It's a little cabin in the woods with a dirt floor."

My heart began to beat a little faster. Gena was describing my recurring daydream about a cabin in the woods. I waited for her to go on.

"There is something inside the cabin ... someone you're excited to see. But you're afraid."

Now I was intrigued. She had described to me just how I often felt when thinking about my cabin in the woods. "What is it?" I asked her. "Is it a past life? Who am I afraid of?"

Gena looked momentarily startled, then blinked her eyes. "It is a past life," she confirmed, "but I don't see what happens next. The fear I'm picking up from you has a quality of violence in it ... rape ... or, worse—murder." She stared at me in surprise.

"Are you suggesting I ... died then?"

Gena shook her head. "I'm not sure."

"Can you tell me ..."

Gena gasped suddenly and covered her mouth. She quickly turned away and made an effort to compose herself.

"What is it? What did you see?" I demanded. "Gena, are you all right?"

She shook her head as if trying to clear away whatever image she had seen.

"Gena," I cried, "please tell me ... who did you see in that cabin? What happened?"

Finally, she sighed and looked at me in a confused way. "I'm sorry. I didn't mean to ... oh, dear ... I didn't mean to go to pieces just now."

"What happened?" I asked again.

Gena tried to smile, but it was a poor attempt at one. " I really don't know. But now it's gone. The images I was seeing have vanished."

I tried repeatedly to get Gena to disclose to me what she had picked up, but she refused to say anything more about it. Clearly it had shaken her, but as disappointed as I was at Gena's withholding the vision, I was also relieved. Some part of me resisted knowing what I would find when I opened that cabin door. I also recalled my dream a while ago—of seeing Drake's face—and then waking up.

"That cabin was not what was bugging you tonight," Gena finally said.

I got up to find some cups for us in the cupboards and searched the cabinets for the tea. "I had a phone call from my friend Mike, in Kansas," I told her. I wanted to steer the conversation away from Wes and her disapproval of him.

"Mike's your boyfriend?"

"No!" I spun around and frowned. "He's a family friend, taking care of my mother's estate."

"Oh, of course." Gena watched me. "Margaret didn't like the Suttons too well."

I found a box of peppermint teabags and brought them, along with two cups, to the table. "No, she never would mention any of you." I decided to go a step further. "As a matter of fact, she never even told me I had you as a cousin."

If this was a shock to Gena, she didn't show it.

"Gena, how did Aunt Rosalee afford all the remodeling to fix this place up?"

"I don't know. I suppose the bank gave her a generous loan."

"How were she and your father able to buy the lodge?" I sat down. The kettle hadn't yet reached boiling.

Gena looked at me suspiciously. "What does it matter? I suppose they had saved up quite a stash over the years."

"But this place is fabulous," I argued. "It must have cost close to a million dollars. The mortgage payment on something like this has to be unbelievable."

"You're awfully inquisitive tonight," said Gena. She got up

and went to the stove. She checked the kettle and found it steaming, so brought it over.

"It bothers you when I ask questions. Why is that?" I asked.

Gena poured hot water into each of our cups. "Maybe I'm concerned about you," she replied.

"How can that be?" I asked. "I don't think you like me very much."

Gena said nothing about that as she returned the kettle to the stove. "The feeling must be mutual."

I had to think about that as I pulled a peppermint teabag out of the pink box. "Since we're being frank, let me ask you something. Were you the one who came into my room last week—in the middle of the night—and left that note?"

Gena glanced at me, then took the box of tea. "I heard about that note. And I didn't type it. And, no, I wasn't in your room."

For some reason I believed her. I relaxed a little as I swirled the teabag around in my cup. "Any idea who may have left it?"

"No," said Gena.

I sighed. "Well, obviously someone wants me to leave."

"Probably for your own good," she added.

"What do you mean?" I looked at her.

"Why do you want to stay?" she challenged. "What is here for you? What kind of life do you think you're going to have running the gift shop in this lodge? And Wade City is a remote mountain town. You're going to miss all of your big shopping centers and malls."

I had to laugh. "Shopping has never been that important to me."

"Juniper, when winter comes, we're virtually snowed in up here. The only way out of here is by snowmobile. How are you going to cope?"

"I suppose just like everyone else who lives and works here," I said.

"The people here at the Rainbow are not what you're used to. I'm surprised you've stayed here this long." She pouted and sipped at her tea.

I studied her. Why did she look so troubled? "You are right

about that. I've met some very different people here. But, you know, somehow the people I've come to know at the Rainbow Majestic are more special than any people I've ever met before. They're all so ... friendly, so ... giving, and so ... so open."

"Except me." She wouldn't look me in the eye.

I turned away. "I haven't gotten to know you ... until now."

Gena stood up with her cup. "I'm going to bed."

I wondered what I'd said. She took her tea cup and started out of the kitchen. Before she went out the door, she turned to me and said, "You really don't want to know me." Then, she added, "Remember that. And don't forget to turn out the light." Her footsteps clattered against the dining room floor as she headed toward the lobby.

I sat for several minutes, finished my tea, then headed back upstairs. For a few minutes, I had actually had a meaningful conversation with Gena and had seen a kinder side of her. But she still had this grudge she carried. There was no denying that.

14

I was up early Thursday morning. This was the day people would start arriving for the holistic fair and also the day the gift shop was opening. I met Taffi in the dining room when I picked up my yogurt, juice and an English muffin. She grabbed a cup of coffee and a chocolate doughnut and then sat down next to me.

"I hear you're being kicked out of the crystal suite," said Taffi. "Her highness, Simone Sullivan, is moving in."

I smiled at Taffi's mockery. "Oh? And just who is this royal customer?"

Taffi looked at her doughnut and made a face. "I really shouldn't be eating this, you know." Then she shrugged and took a bite from it. "Oh, well ..." She chewed, then said, "Simone is a close friend of Rosalee's."

While we ate, Taffi explained the friendship. Simone Sullivan was a reputable psychic from New Mexico, who supposedly had a following. She and Rosalee had been friends for many years, and Simone always expected the royal treatment when she came to stay at the lodge. She would undoubtedly bring her daughter along, who served as her secretary and hand maiden. I wondered what they would be like. From Taffi's tone, I gathered that Simone Sullivan did not impress her.

"Hey, honey, I may have some information you'll find interesting," Taffi said after she'd finished her doughnut. Her bright green eyes were wide with excitement as she glanced around the room, then lowered her voice. "I managed to find out for you who was in the hunting party the time that your father was killed."

I perked up. "Who?"

Taffi opened her mouth to say something, but just at that moment, Starla called to us from across the room. I never got to hear what Taffi had to say.

"Taffi! Juniper! Oh, thank goodness I found you." Starla

appeared especially theatrical this morning as she hurried toward us, dressed in a long purple gown with sequins, shiny black heels and a large amethyst crystal pendant hanging from her slender neck. Her black shiny hair was brushed to one side and fastened with a diamond-studded barrette. She wore purple eyeshadow.

"Good morning, Starla," said Taffi. "Care to join us?"

Starla's face wore an expression of concern as she sat down. "Celeste has taken ill."

"Oh, no," I said. "What happened?"

"She wasn't feeling well last evening," Starla told us. "She went to bed earlier than usual. This morning Cyril summoned Rosalee, who came and looked in on her. Rosalee thought she should go to the clinic right away, so Gena called Wes, who just left with her a few minutes ago."

"Maybe it was something she ate," said Taffi.

"I hope it isn't a stroke." Starla sighed. "Poor Celeste wasn't making much sense. She seemed disoriented."

I was thinking what a shame, having this happen on the first day of the holistic fair. Starla and Taffi fell into their own conversation, so I excused myself, eager to get the shop ready to open.

"I'll talk to you later," Taffi called after me.

I was unlocking the door to the shop when someone walked by. "Good morning, Juniper."

I turned to find Drake, dressed for work in navy blue coveralls and wearing a handyman's pouch around his waist. I smiled at him. "Good morning." This was the first time we'd talked since Friday night.

He actually appeared happy to see me. "Your aunt wants to see you in her office when you've got a minute." He peeked inside after I got the door to the shop open and switched on the light. "Looks like you've got things squared away in here," he said, and gazed around at my handiwork.

"Drake, would you mind helping me move this table?" I indicated which one I wanted to reposition, and together we lifted the table—with its assortment of wares—against a wall. "Thanks," I said, then caught the look in his eyes as he stood there a moment, studying me. I wondered just what it was Drake Phillips saw in my face, and I still puzzled over how it affected me every time he looked at me that way.

I couldn't help asking my next question: "Drake, do you have any memories of past lives?" I was recalling last night's conversation with Gena and the description of the cabin in the woods.

He folded his arms and smiled mockingly. "Now why would you ask me that?"

"I asked you a question first," I reminded him.

"Do you?" he asked, ignoring my comment.

I sighed. "I don't know."

There was a strange moment of silence between us, and then he stroked his beard and said, "How do I even know I've lived past lives? Do you have reason to believe I have?" He cocked his head slightly to one side.

"It's just ... it's just that ..." I didn't know how to put it into words. I was afraid that anything I said to him would come back at me in mockery. Finally, I said, "Oh, never mind. Forget I asked." I turned around to check out the shop.

"Juniper," he said. I suddenly felt his hand touch my shoulder. "If you've got something on your mind, maybe you should tell me."

I looked at him, then shook my head. "It's silly, really." But then I found myself explaining to him, "I had a dream the other day, and just before I woke up, I saw you."

He waited for me to continue. At least he wasn't making fun of me.

"The reason I mention it is because Gena picked up what was in my dream, and it was this cabin in the woods that I'm always thinking about and remembering. I can see it so clearly." I hesitated, then added, "And—for some reason—when I saw you in the dream, I became frightened."

"Hmmph," Drake scoffed.

"Gena thought it might have something to do with one of my past lives."

"Well, I don't know what to make of it." Drake turned to go. Then he stopped and asked, "Did Gena say I was part of it?"

"Part of what?"

"Your ... past life."

"No," I said. "She only said someone was in the cabin." I purposely did not mention the part about Gena getting upset by whatever it was she had seen. "But, you see, I've never been able to face that part. When I have the dream, I reach the door, but before I go inside, the dream usually ends. This was the first time I actually saw someone."

"And it was ... me." He seemed dubious. When I didn't reply, he shrugged, then said, "I've got to get to work." He turned to go, but swung back around. "I wouldn't put too much stock in what Gena tells you." With that, he disappeared out the door and down the hall.

I was suddenly mad at myself for telling Drake about my dream. I should have known his reaction would be to brush it off. I didn't know why I thought I should mention it to him in the first place. Maybe I had figured he could provide me with another piece of the puzzle. I really wanted to understand what it was about Drake Phillips that prompted me to react to him the way I did. He could be so aggravating at times.

I busied myself in the shop and it was nine-thirty when I remembered Drake's message that I was to go see Aunt Rosalee. I found her in her office, but she was on the telephone. Lance sat at his computer, so absorbed in it that he didn't pay attention to me until I came in and sat down to wait. As soon as he noticed me, he minimized the screen on his computer monitor and cleared his throat, then grabbed for a stack of papers on his desk.

"Here to see Rosalee?" Lance asked without looking over at me.

"Yes. Has she been on the phone long?"

"Pretty much all morning," he replied. "Mrs. Birdwell took ill and had to go to Wade City to the clinic."

"Yes, I heard about it," I said. "Have you heard what her condition is?"

"Rosalee's talking to the doctor now," said Lance. His tone told me he wanted to concentrate on his work, so I sat quietly for several minutes until Aunt Rosalee hung up the phone and called me into her room.

"Well, how's the gift shop?" she asked. "Are we ready to open?"

I told her I was ready. She reached into her large desk drawer and pulled out a cash register tray, filled with money. "Then here you go," she said, handing it to me. "Lance has counted it, and I want you to count it too, before you leave here."

While I counted the money in the till and noted the totals of each kind of bill and the coin rolls on a piece of note paper, she told me Celeste had been transported to a hospital in the next biggest town. "And the doctor at Wade City suspects a possible stroke," she added.

"I'm sorry to hear that," I commented.

"Be sure you sign up for a workshop," Aunt Rosalee called to me as I left her inner office with the cash tray. "You can register in the lounge today."

I thanked her and left, noting that Lance was still glued to his desk work. Was it my imagination, or did he seem uptight this morning?

As I rounded the corner near the front desk of the lodge, I found Drake erecting a big sign that read GIFT SHOP OPEN TODAY. I smiled in approval as I passed him, and he pointed to Gena behind the counter and said, "It's her idea." Gena looked up as I walked by, but quickly looked away again.

I put my cash register together, then checked the credit card terminal and gazed around at my little store. It was open, at last, for business. I had my OPEN sign displayed in the window beside the door, and now all I needed were customers. I turned on the CD player and adjusted the volume as colorful music filled the room. The fragrant, flowery scents of incense and candles enhanced the welcoming atmosphere of the shop. Slowly I strolled the aisles one more time, to be sure everything was as it should be.

A noise at the door caused me to turn around. A tall man with dark curly hair stood, looking in. He was about thirty, with heavy eyebrows and piercing dark eyes, and his good looks stunned me. He had a thin mustache and sideburns and a large nose that was bent just at the right angle to make his slender, tanned face most interesting. He wore a blue and white polo shirt, light blue slacks, and his skin appeared well sun-tanned. He caught me staring at him and smiled broadly as he set a briefcase down on the floor beside him.

"Hello," I greeted him with a shy smile.

"Hello." I immediately detected the foreign accent. "I see the sign. You have books, yes?"

I came closer to him. "Yes, we have lots of books. Feel free to come in and look around." I noticed his strong build and figured he must work out with weights.

"Thank you. I believe I will." He extended his hand and grinned, revealing straight white teeth. "I am Vladimir Petrovsky, *yu-fo* researcher from St. Petersburg."

"My name is Juniper Sutton," I said and shook his hand. "What kind of research did you say?"

He held onto my hand several moments before letting me go. "*Yu-fos*," he repeated.

I stared at him, uncomprehending.

"*Yu-fos*," he repeated, this time with more emphasis on the first syllable.

Then I understood he meant UFOs. Obviously, he was Russian and a researcher of unidentified flying objects. Although I'd seen many books in Aunt Rosalee's library on the subject of UFOs and extraterrestrials, I had not yet gotten to them. "Are you here for the holistic fair?"

"Oh, yes, I am here for that," he replied. He looked around as he stood in the same spot. "You have a remarkable store, *Mees* Sutton."

"You may call me Juniper."

"Ah ... Juniper." His dark eyes fell over my figure. "You are named after a *tree*?"

I laughed. "I suppose in a way I am. The juniper was my father's favorite tree."

"You are much more beautiful than a juniper tree," he said. "Please ... you call me Vlad, okay?"

I warmed to him immediately. "Let me show you around the store," I said. He left his briefcase and followed me as I led him to the corner where the books were displayed on shelves. Right away, he crouched down and began going through the lower shelves that included some books on UFOs. He pulled one out and told me he'd read it, and then he chose another and started to tell me what he thought of it. I only half listened. I was more fascinated by his foreign accent and his remarkable build.

Several minutes later, Vlad had selected four books he hadn't read yet, and carried them up to the check-out counter, where I took my position at the cash register.

"You are my very first customer," I told him as I rang up his purchases. At first he didn't understand what I meant, so I explained that the gift shop had just opened this morning.

"Oh, but this is wonderful," he exclaimed with a laugh. "I am your first customer. We must celebrate your first sale of books. Will you let me buy you coffee?"

I blushed as I glanced at his eager face. "I would, but I have to mind the store." I smiled politely.

"That is okay," he said. He dug into his pocket to produce some bills. "I understand about that. But perhaps we will have lunch together instead. You eat lunch?"

I took the bills, then made change and counted it back to him. "Lunch would be fine," I told him. "I'd like that."

He relaxed with a huge grin and dark eyes that seemed to dance and sparkle. "I come by ... at what time?"

With a glance at the clock, I said, "Oh, any time after twelve is good. I close up the shop whenever I want."

"Okay. Okay, Juniper. We will have lunch." He walked over to retrieve his briefcase, then turned to me and asked, "Have you seen any *yu-fos*?"

I smiled, amused by his accent. "No," I told him. "No, I've never seen one."

Again he grinned. "That is okay. I will show you about them. I see you after twelve, Juniper." And with that, he left.

Just as Vlad left the shop, a couple of women walked in and began browsing. I stood there, staring out the door and thinking about the Russian researcher. What a charmer he was. Of course, I told myself, it meant nothing. He was simply friendly and an interesting guest who had just arrived at the Rainbow Majestic for the fair. But he had certainly captivated me with his friendly manner and broken English. It was bound to be an interesting lunch.

I put thoughts about Vlad aside as I concentrated on helping the new customers. Before long, more people wandered into the shop. Soon I had a steady morning of sales. Most the people who browsed the shop had just arrived to register for the fair, and some were vendors who had booth reservations in the great room and lobby.

A little before noon, Starla popped in to see me, and told me she was holding a time slot open for me on Sunday morning, if I wanted an awakening. "I'm booking up fast," she explained, "but I'll write you down in that time slot, if you want."

"Well, what do you charge?" I asked.

Starla hesitated, then simply said, "We can work that out later. Juniper, I'm getting the message that I'm to give you an awakening as soon as possible."

I knew better than to ask who was giving her the message. I finally consented and said, "Sure. Sunday morning works for me."

I had just finished a sale of some incense and a pair of crystal earrings when I looked up and noticed Wes at the door, carrying a huge cardboard box. He waited for my customer to leave, then brought it in and set it on the floor, next to the counter.

"What's that?" I asked him.

"T-shirts." He stood up and smiled. "I just brought them from Wade City."

"Oh, those must be the rainbow shirts Aunt Rosalee ordered." I came around the counter and joined him. "Let's open them and see what they look like."

As he turned the box around to find where to open it, I grew aware of his nearness. Then, I suddenly remembered he had taken Celeste to the clinic. "How is Celeste?" I asked.

Wes kept working at the box. "Not too good, I'm afraid. The ambulance came and took her to the hospital."

"Yes, I heard."

"She's a really sweet old lady." Wes gazed into my eyes. "It's too bad she's going to miss this fair. She was looking forward to it—and especially the dance."

"Yes, Clover told me there's going to be a dance on Saturday night."

"Are you planning to go to it?" Wes's blue eyes continued to gaze into mine and I could feel my pulse picking up. A smile stretched slowly across his face.

But before I could answer him, a booming voice called from the doorway, "Ah, there you are, Juniper! We go to lunch now?" Vlad, the Russian, walked in, wearing a wide grin.

Wes stood up and turned around in surprise.

"Vlad, I'll be ready in a minute or two," I said. I felt the heat rise in my cheeks as I stood up. "Wes, this is Vlad from Russia."

The foreign man reached out his hand and Wes shook it, then introduced himself. "Oh, you're the ufologist from St.

Petersburg," he said. "You're speaking Friday night, aren't you?"

Yes, I am," said Vlad.

Wes turned to me. "Vlad's one of the presenters."

"Oh?" I hadn't realized who he was.

"Juniper was kind to me," Vlad explained. "She made me her first customer, so we are to go and celebrate."

I was embarrassed and said to Wes in a low voice, "It's just lunch."

Wes nodded, then turned back to the box of T-shirts. He pulled a pocket knife off his belt and sliced one end of the cardboard, then lifted the top off.

"Thanks, Wes." I stooped over and pulled one of the new T-shirts out of the box. They were all the same design, a natural beige color with a large, colorful rainbow across the front and scripty letters that read RAINBOW MAJESTIC.

"They're beautiful!" I cried as I held one up for the two men to see.

Wes smiled, but didn't say anything.

Vlad stepped over and examined the shirt more closely. "Hmm, a rainbow," he said. "Very nice and pretty. I like."

"Aunt Rosalee will be pleased." I turned to Wes, but he was already heading out the door.

"We go to lunch now?" Vlad grinned at me.

I stuck the T-shirt back in the box, then closed up the shop and locked the door behind us. I didn't know what to make of Wes's hasty departure. I wondered what he thought of my having lunch with the Russian researcher.

Vlad turned out to be talkative and entertaining. As we ate lunch in the dining room, he began telling me about his life and his work in Russia and as a student in the states. He never got to explain anything fully, however, because people kept coming up to our table and introducing themselves to him. He was charming toward everyone and obviously well versed in social graces. He was engaged in a lengthy discussion with Cyril Jorgensen, who had sat down with us, when I finally excused myself, explaining that I had to get back to the gift shop.

"I understand," Vlad said with a warm smile. "We talk again some other time, okay?"

Cyril gave me a wink as I stood up to go. Before returning to the shop, I remembered that Aunt Rosalee had told me I should sign up for one of the workshops, so I strolled through the great room and headed toward the lounge. Vendors for the holistic fair were setting up their booths in the two large rooms. A lot of them had arrived ahead of time, although the conference was not officially open until Friday morning.

I looked around for Taffi, but I didn't see her. We hadn't finished our conversation from breakfast and I was eager to learn the information she had for me. I saw Aunt Rosalee mingling with the new arrivals. She waved to me as I passed by.

I found Nadine Leachfield in the lounge, bent over a table with sign-up sheets. She looked up as I came in. "Well, hello, Juniper. I heard the gift shop is open."

"Yes, you'll have to come by," I said.

"Oh, I will," she promised. She scribbled her name on one of the workshop sheets, then adjusted her glasses and smiled as she offered me the pen. "Are you going to take a free workshop?"

"Yes, but I don't really know what there is."

Nadine showed me about ten different sheets of paper, and I could see there were various workshops on everything from healing to card reading to dowsing and hypnosis. I noticed that there was a handwriting analysis class offered by Taffi, and Vladimir Petrovsky was giving a workshop on UFOs. For a moment I was tempted to sign up for Vlad's workshop, but settled instead on an energy healing class given by some person whose name was "Chi." I had no idea what to expect, but told myself it would be fun to learn about something totally out of my realm.

"There's so much to take," Nadine commented as we walked out of the lounge together. "I wish I could take them all." She giggled. "But, of course, Lance would have a fit. They cost fifty dollars apiece. I think it was so sweet of Rosalee to give her employees a free workshop."

Before we parted, I inquired about Max.

"Oh, he's rambunctious lately," said Nadine. "He's started going off on his explorations again."

"Does he ever tell you where he goes?" I asked.

Nadine laughed and shook her head. "No, but I think that boy knows every hiding place in this hotel."

"Doesn't it worry you when he disappears?"

"Not really. Max is a good kid. He knows he'll be grounded if he's not back when we tell him."

The afternoon was slower in the bookstore, so I had the time to inventory the rainbow T-shirts and put them out for display. Some of the merchandise I had ordered last week arrived, so I checked everything over and made a mental note to ask Aunt Rosalee about getting a computer to help me keep track.

A small batch of crystal jewelry had arrived and I admired the pendants as I unpacked them. A rose quartz pebble suspended from a silver chain appealed to me, and I decided to hold it aside rather than put it on display. Perhaps I'd be able to afford it after I saw my first paycheck.

I kept hoping I'd see Taffi, Starla or Clover, but apparently all three were busy with appointments already. Several more guests arrived for the fair. This kept Gena busy at the front desk. I closed the shop at five o'clock and totaled my sales, then started to take the cash register tray to Aunt Rosalee's office.

A tall, slender woman with blond hair piled on top of her head stood at the front desk, waiting, as I came out of the shop and locked the door. She noticed me right away and asked if I worked here. I detected impatience in her voice.

"Yes, what do you need?" I asked as I approached.

The woman wore expensive clothes and makeup, although she did not overdo it the way Starla did. "I want to check in," she replied, a little perturbed at my question.

"*Gena?*" I called out, wondering what had happened to her. Apparently, Gena had stepped away for a few minutes. Turning to the woman, I said, "Gena should be right back."

"Well, I've been waiting here quite a while," the woman complained. "Perhaps you could do it?"

Just at that moment, Gena returned and smiled broadly at the woman. "Hello, Simone! How nice to see you again."

The front door opened just then and a young lady—much shorter and plumper—walked in with two suitcases. She had curly blond hair and wore glasses. Wes stepped in behind her, carrying two more bags, which he set down in front of the counter next to Simone. I caught Wes's eye and he smiled at me. I was relieved that he seemed to have gotten over any resentment he may have had over Vlad taking me to lunch.

"Linda, set those over here next to the others," directed Simone. "You do remember my daughter, Linda, don't you, Gena?"

"Of course." Gena had the situation under control now and Wes went back outside. No one paid attention to me, so I eased my way past all the luggage and continued on toward the hall that led to my aunt's office.

So that had been Simone Sullivan and her daughter, Linda—the ones who would be taking over my suite. I wondered when that was going to take place. I hadn't yet been notified to remove my belongings. I thought Aunt Rosalee had mentioned they wouldn't be arriving until Friday.

I turned the corner and was approaching the office when I heard angry voices from inside. I stopped in the hallway—just outside the door—where they couldn't see me. Aunt Rosalee's voice was loud and scolding.

"Don't try to tell me I don't know what's been goin' on," she shouted. "Those reports you did are unacceptable. How can you sit there and tell me they balance?"

Lance's voice shouted back at her, "There's a good explanation for it. If you'll just let me go through everything again, you'll see there's not a problem."

"I thought you told me you had a degree in accountin'," Aunt Rosalee fired. "We'll be darn lucky if we don't get audited for this mistake."

"I can fix it," Lance insisted.

"Oh, sure! We'll go bankrupt for certain! Lance, I don't believe in robbin' Peter to pay Paul. I can't believe you would deliberately make up figures to boost our image."

"Just—please—let me redo the reports," begged Lance.

There was a short pause then, and I stepped into the office with my cash register tray. Aunt Rosalee stood with her hands on her hips, her face red. Lance sat at his desk, looking confused and ashamed. I pretended I hadn't heard their exchange as I handed the tray to my aunt.

"Well, how'd we do?" she asked me.

"We made close to five hundred dollars our first day," I said.

Aunt Rosalee grinned while Lance swung around in his chair and covered his mouth with his hands. He stared into his computer screen. "Juniper, that's terrific," praised my aunt. She carried the tray into her inner office and set it on her desk, then picked up the tape I had printed out at the end of the day. If she suspected I'd overheard them, she didn't let on.

Before I left to go to my room and freshen up before dinner, she told me to use my own judgment about the shop hours. "I'm sure you'll want to participate in some of the goin's-on, and there's no reason why you shouldn't."

"Oh, I almost forgot. Simone Sullivan and her daughter just arrived," I said. "Do you want me to vacate my room?"

"Not tonight," she said. "Simone had her reservation for the weekend. If she's a day early, we'll just let her stay in one of the available rooms. No need for you to leave yet."

With that, I returned to the crystal suite and decided to shower before dinner. It had been a very satisfying first day for the gift shop.

15

When I stepped into the dining room later, it was full of people. Aunt Rosalee sat with Simone Sullivan and her daughter, and Starla had just joined them. Simone and Rosalee laughed and talked as two old friends who hadn't seen each other in a while. Looking around, I saw Wes and Drake at a table by themselves, and decided to ask if I could sit with them. They saw me approach and made room for me.

"How did it go in the store today?" Drake asked.

"Really good for the first day," I said.

Wes studied me intently. "And how was your lunch with the Russian ufologist?"

At the mention of the man, Drake turned his head and I followed his gaze to a distant table, where Vlad Petrovsky sat with seven others, engrossed in conversation as they awaited their meal. To my surprise, Clover was one of the table's occupants. Although she wasn't seated beside him, she was strictly focused on him, her elbows propped on the table and a dreamy smile on her smitten face.

"It was okay." I unraveled the silverware from my napkin.

Neither of them commented. The servers brought the carts of food around. Tonight we had our choice of beef tips and noodles or meatless moussaka. Drake and I chose the beef and noodles, while Wes naturally selected the vegetarian fare. There was fresh salad and whole wheat dinner rolls as well. The beef tips were especially tasty.

"Thelma's recipe," Drake murmured as though he'd read my mind.

"Thelma cooks?" I asked. I had thought she was just the dishwasher.

"She's tops," said Drake.

"How's the moussaka?" I asked Wes.

He shrugged and stuck another forkful into his mouth. I was glad I hadn't ordered it, but I noticed later that Wes cleaned his plate.

"Where's Gena tonight?" I asked. "I don't see her."

"She was busy checking in guests," Drake explained. "She's eating at the front desk."

I noticed Cyril Jorgensen seated at a table with the Leachfield family tonight. Lance and Nadine were talking softly with him while little Max squirmed, as usual, beside them, entertaining himself as best he could. Cyril looked tired and unhappy tonight. He seemed not too interested in eating. I wondered if he was upset about Celeste. I also wondered why Cyril hadn't gone with Wes this morning when he had driven the elderly woman to the clinic in Wade City. I recalled that when Cyril had sat down with Vlad and me at lunch today, he had seemed his usual enthusiastic self.

For dessert there were brownies and ice cream. While we ate, waiting for coffee and tea to come around, the subject of the dance came up. Drake had made the comment that Gena and Rosalee couldn't agree on where to hold the dance. "They can't rightly tear up the great room with all those vendors in there," said Drake. "Yet Rosalee has issues about using the dining room for the dance."

I wiped a brownie crumb off my lip with my napkin. "Too bad they couldn't hold it outside in the garden area. It would be less disruptive."

Wes's eyes lit up. "That's a great idea, Juniper."

"Nah ... it gets too cold out there at night," said Drake.

"Well, it can't get *that* cold," I replied. "It's the middle of June."

"Why don't you ask Rosalee about it?" Wes suggested.

Drake reached for his cup of coffee and sipped. "Well ... I suppose it might work. I'll go ahead and ask her."

"It should be beautiful on Saturday," I commented. "I think we're approaching full moon."

"We are," said Wes. "Sunday's full moon."

"Then it's perfect," I added.

"Bah ... I don't get excited about dances," Drake grumbled. "Don't expect me to be there."

I turned to him and moaned in mock disappointment. "Oh, Drake, why are you so hard? Dances are *fun*."

Wes piped in, "Hey, dude, who knows, you might get

lucky." He lifted his cup to his lips.

Drake's eyes fell briefly on me, then quickly he looked away and sneered. "Dances are for people who wanna show off."

"Suit yourself," I told him.

"Maybe Vlad will ask you to dance," Drake said derisively.

I blushed as I noticed Wes's interested gaze. I decided to change the subject and wondered if anyone had heard anything more about Celeste's condition. Neither of them had. Then I said, "How come Cyril didn't go to see her?"

Wes sighed. "He decided not to."

"You'd think he'd want to be with her," I added. I watched Cyril across the room at Lance and Nadine's table, staring into space as if he were lost in a world of his own.

"Well, the old geezer will go to see her sooner or later," said Drake. "When he's up to it."

Once again I noted that Drake didn't seem to think highly of Cyril Jorgensen.

I hadn't seen Taffi in the dining room tonight, and wondered where she was. Drake finally got up from the table and stretched. "I think I'll go see if anyone needs help setting up in the lounge. Isn't that Russian dude speaking tonight?"

"He's on for tomorrow night," said Wes. "I don't remember who's up for tonight."

"Well, I'll go find out." Drake carried his dishes to the kitchen, then left. As I finished my dessert, I was aware of the fact that Wes and I were alone at the table. His eyes were on me. Nervously, I put my fork down, unable to eat another bite, then drained my coffee cup. I gathered up my dishes and started to get up from the table.

Wes asked, "Are you in a hurry to go somewhere?" His voice was steady and calm as his blue eyes peered into mine.

"Uh ... no ... I just ..."

Wes gathered up his dishes then, too. "Would you like to go for a walk?" he asked.

I hesitated, then said, "Okay."

We carried our dishes to the kitchen, where Thelma and a helper were cleaning up. I caught Thelma's eye and waved at her, then said, "The beef tips were excellent."

She must have understood me—even though she was deaf—because she grinned and nodded, then returned to her duty at the sink.

I followed Wes out of the dining room. Other people moved about, having finished their meals, and either strolled into the great room or stood around talking. "I need to stop in my room and get my jacket," I told Wes.

He followed me up the spiral stairs. I hurried into my suite to get the jacket while Wes remained just inside the door. Then we walked through the corridor to the back exit, like before. He didn't say anything as he led the way. Once we were outside in the brisk mountain air, we headed for the garden and the path into the woods. I wanted to say something to break the ice, but I was content just to be walking at Wes's side again.

When we came to the garden, he turned to me and asked, "Is there some place we can sit and talk?"

I looked at the bench beside the pond and moved toward it.

He shook his head. "I mean ... without anyone else nearby."

I remembered my special spot near the stream. "I know the perfect place." I started off in that direction and Wes followed.

We hadn't gone far when he began speaking. "Juniper, I want you to understand something about me. You see, I've always had this problem ... this reluctance around women."

For a fearful second, I thought he was going to announce that he was gay. I braced myself as we continued through the brush toward the stream.

"I have this tendency to back off from a relationship. I've been this way all my life. As a result, I just can't make a commitment to a woman I care about." Wes was exposing his most private self to me, I realized in astonishment.

"Why must there be a commitment?" I asked casually.

He thought about that as we walked along. Finally, he resumed, "Most women I've known expect one. They want a lasting relationship ... marriage ... children."

"And you don't want that?"

We reached the spot beside the stream at last, and sat down on some rocks to watch the gushing flow of water. The sun was setting and darkness was just starting to creep in. "I don't know," said Wes. "I guess it frightens me. I don't want to get stuck with one person in my life until I know ... for sure ... she's the right one." He looked into my face then and managed a smile.

I watched the clearness of the moving water. A small trout darted past under the current. "Well, how does anyone know when they've found that special one?"

Wes sighed as he stared down at his feet. "That's a good question."

"I found someone once," I told him, thinking of Sean. "I was sure he was meant for me. But, apparently, he wasn't." I stared into the water, suddenly feeling self conscious.

Wes reached out then and touched my hand. I let him hold it as he looked into my face with compassion. "Juniper," he said, "I'm very attracted to you."

A sob caught in my throat. I struggled to control the emotion as I looked into his face.

"But," he continued, "I abide by this universal law I carry around with me. I don't believe in hurtin' anyone." He paused, then said, "The last thing I want to do is hurt you. I know you've been hurt before." He stroked my fingers with his own and sensations escalated, along with my emotions. "I just could never bear it if anythin' happened between us that would cause you pain."

I forced my voice to remain calm. "How could you cause me pain? Wes, you're the most spiritual man I've ever met. You're sensitive, you're centered, you're always thinking of others first."

Wes stood up and brought me to my feet. "I can't promise you anything, Juniper," he told me firmly.

"That doesn't matter," I said. "I don't want a commitment."

"Not now, perhaps, but what about later?"

I turned my face up into his and our eyes locked. "I don't care about later," I said. "This is the present moment. We're both in the Now." I knew I was reiterating some of the metaphysical philosophy that was fresh on my mind from my reading. It seemed we stood there—gazing at each other—for a long time. Then, slowly, Wes moved closer and his mouth covered mine. It was a gentle first kiss and my eyes closed as I absorbed the luxury of its impact and my blood began to ignite.

I'm not sure how long we stood there beside the stream, holding each other and kissing, but I wished time could stand still and I could always feel this surging energy. A sudden movement in the bushes startled us. In the semi-darkness, a mule deer dashed away.

"Did you see that?" Wes asked.

"Yes."

After another minute, he said, "Why don't we go back to the lodge?"

"Okay," I said with some reluctance. I drew my jacket up tighter around me. There was a definite chill in the evening air. Then I followed Wes back through the woods toward the garden. He held my hand as I carefully stepped over branches and around green growth in the disappearing light.

When we reached the back entrance to the lodge, no one was in sight and I nestled up closer to Wes. He kissed my forehead.

"You can come on up to the crystal suite," I told him softly.

He hesitated, studying me a moment, then dropped a hungry kiss upon my mouth, forcing my lips apart. His probing tongue sent alarms throughout my body—erotic sensations that should have served as warnings to me—but all I could think about was this moment and the closeness of this most desirable man—not whether it was the wise thing to do or not.

We finally entered the lodge, where we hurried up the back stairs to the second floor. My face felt flushed and my body was eager with anticipation as we crossed into the hallway toward the crystal suite, Wes holding my hand.

Just as we reached the door, it opened—and there stood Aunt Rosalee.

"Oh, Juniper, there you are," she said with a questioning glance toward Wes.

"Aunt Rosalee, is something wrong?" I dropped Wes's hand.

Aunt Rosalee closed the door and we three moved into the hallway. She glanced back at the crystal suite, then looked at me with regretful eyes. "I'm sorry, Juniper, but we had to give the crystal rooms to Simone. She was dissatisfied with the room she and Linda were in, and she put up such a fuss, I had the maid come in and make up the suite for them. Your belongin's have all been transferred to Taffi's room."

I must have looked shocked. Aunt Rosalee sighed. "I hate doin' this to you. I just didn't know what else to do."

"It's all right," I told her quickly and tried to smile, although disappointment was now coursing through my veins.

"Really, Aunt Rosalee, it's not that big a deal. Where's Taffi's room?"

"I'll take her there," Wes offered. "Come on, Juniper. Taffi's room is down on the other end of the hallway."

"Here, take the key." Aunt Rosalee deposited the room key into my palm. I noted the number on the key: 224. "Thank you, Wes," she called out as he led me down the hall.

When we reached Room 224, I unlocked the door, but paused before stepping inside. There was no sign of Taffi and the room was dark. I turned to Wes. "This is a terrible way to end the evening," I said.

Wes just shrugged. "Oh, well," he said cheerfully, "*shift* happens."

We both laughed at his play on words. Then he bent forward and kissed me lightly on the cheek. "Thanks for the talk, Juniper. I'll see you tomorrow." Then he walked away.

"Good night, Wes," I called out, then sighed and walked into Taffi's room. When I turned on the light, I saw that Taffi's room was larger than Clover's. Beside the full size bed she slept in was a rollaway that had been wheeled into the room and made up for my use. I could see that Taffi kept her room neat and tidy, and I saw that my clothes had been piled neatly on top of the vanity, and my suitcases and books were in a heap on the floor by my bed.

I went to the window and saw that Taffi's room faced the parking lot. Peeking out into the night, I noticed a few cars rolling in as more people arrived at the lodge. I sat down on the rollaway bed and thought over everything that had happened in the last hour. I still felt the magic sweep over me of Wes and the romantic moments beside the stream and his lingering kiss before we'd come into the lodge. I wondered what would have happened had Simone and her daughter not taken over the crystal suite, and I'd let him in. Would he have spent the night with me?

I thought of Clover. It seemed she had pretty much abandoned going after Wes. I had seen how she had looked at Vlad Petrovsky at dinner. I wanted to discuss everything with Clover all of a sudden. I had this female need to rehash the events and emotions, and somehow I knew Clover would sympathize. On the spur of the moment, I left the room and went down to the first corridor to knock on Clover's door. But when I got there, I saw a sign on her door that read DO NOT DISTURB. MASSAGE IN SESSION. I turned around and returned to Taffi's room.

I kept hoping Taffi would return. I wanted to talk to her about what she had learned about my father's companions on the hunting campout, in case it would shed any light on what had actually happened. After waiting half an hour, trying to watch TV without any interest in it—and she still had not shown up—I got ready for bed, then dug through my pile of library books and read for another hour.

I must have fallen asleep at some point, because I awoke with a start when I heard a key turn in the lock. Taffi entered the room and smiled when she saw me. A glance at the radio clock near her bed told me it was almost 2 A.M.

"It's all right, Juniper," Taffi said, "I won't disturb you. Go back to sleep."

I sat up and placed the book I'd been reading on the floor. "I fell asleep with the book open," I told her. Then I started to explain about Simone Sullivan moving into my room a night early.

"Yes, I already heard about that." Taffi disappeared into the bathroom, but left the door open so she could talk. "I am so wiped out. I've had appointments going on all evening. I just want to collapse into bed and forget about brushing my teeth." She appeared a moment later, dressed in a pink terry bathrobe, a toothbrush in her mouth as she checked her answering machine for messages. No one had left any.

I could hardly keep my eyes open myself. "Can we talk in the morning?" I asked.

"Sure, sweetie." Taffi darted back into the bathroom to rinse her mouth. A minute later, she emerged, then climbed into her bed. "Let's talk then. I'm just so ... wiped ... out ..." She yawned, then settled down under her covers. "Good night."

"Good night, Taffi." I reached for the lamp on the vanity beside the rollaway and turned out the light. Before I had settled into a comfortable position—with the extra pillow tucked between my knees—I could hear Taffi's snores. A minute or two later, I fell asleep.

The next morning, I was up bright and early after a restful

night. Wes had filled my dreams, but Drake had also been there and I don't know what part he played, but I kept trying to hide from him in my dreams. Then, when I'd think I had eluded him, Wes would expose me. *Very strange dream*, I thought as I got dressed.

Taffi was sound asleep and breathing heavily. My moving around in the room didn't seem to bother her at all.

I went downstairs after I got dressed and found the dining room bustling with fair guests. Aunt Rosalee and Gena had just finished their breakfast. Gena left for the lobby without greeting me, but Aunt Rosalee hugged me and again apologized for having to evict me from the crystal suite. I told her once again I didn't mind and reassured her that I'd slept well in Taffi's room.

"Good." She stood up to leave. "I have to coordinate some events. Lance has the cash tray ready for you, whenever you're going to the shop."

"Okay," I said.

"Be sure you count it all," she insisted.

I decided to be direct. "Aunt Rosalee, are you having a problem with Lance?"

"It's nothin' for you to worry about," she told me, but I detected a trace of concern in her voice. "And remember, you're not chained to that store. When you want to come out and participate in the fair, you close up the shop and do it."

I thanked her, then ate my breakfast as I watched her go out, greeting people as she went. I didn't see anything of Wes or Drake, but it was later than they usually ate, having to be at their jobs early.

I opened up the shop after getting the cash drawer from Lance. Business was good, as it had been yesterday, and the morning flew by. I was surprised when Nadine came into the store with Max later that morning. She marveled at all the beautiful merchandise and got lost in her browsing. Max wandered the aisles and didn't bother anything.

When some customers had cleared out, Nadine came up to the counter with a rainbow T-shirt for herself and a couple of books and music CDs. I rang them up.

"How are things going?" I asked Nadine.

"You mean, with the holistic fair?"

"Well, that too."

She twitched a smile as I told her the total she owed me, then she opened her purse to take out her wallet. "There are certainly a lot of people that came," said Nadine. "I think Rosalee is very pleased about that, at least."

"Nadine, is everything all right?" I had noticed she had trouble looking me in the eye.

"My dad might lose his job," Max blurted. His mother turned on him with a frown.

I took the bills Nadine handed me and made the change.

Nadine looked at me with tears in her eyes. "Lance and Rosalee had a small misunderstanding. That's all it was—a misunderstanding."

I smiled in sympathy. "You don't need to explain."

"If my dad gets fired, we won't have a place to live anymore," Max told me. He didn't seem bothered by any of this. Instead, he appeared to enjoy playing the role of informant.

"Max!" Nadine scolded.

"Your mom works here, too," I said to the boy. "I'm sure you'll have a place to live, even if ..." I caught the look in Nadine's eye, then quickly added, "But of course, no such thing is going to happen. Your dad's job at this hotel is very important, you know." Then I handed Nadine her bag of items. "Everything will be fine. I just know it."

"Yes, I know it will." She brightened, then grinned at me. "I love what you've done to the shop. Come on, Max, we're leaving."

The little boy waved at me as they went out the door. For Max's sake, at least, I hoped that Aunt Rosalee and Lance could come to terms regarding whatever financial problem was occurring with the lodge. I thought again of what Mike had mentioned maliciously to me on the phone the other night, and again grew worried about where Aunt Rosalee could have obtained the needed funds for fixing up the Rainbow Majestic.

Due to a large volume of customers over the lunch hour, I stayed in the shop and worked through the rush. Things were finally settling down when Gena stormed in. She glared at me across the counter, her brown eyes wild. I cringed. I couldn't imagine what I had done to cause her to look so angry. She seemed to be having trouble grasping hold of herself.

"Gena, what is it?" I slowly rose from my seat.

Her words gushed out, *"That man!"*

There was instant relief on my part as I realized her anger wasn't directed at me. I asked cautiously, "What man?"

Gena was in a rage. I was grateful there were no customers presently in the shop. "Roy Howard was here ... *again*," she seethed. Her fists were clenched on top of the counter top.

"Who is Roy Howard?"

Gena paced the floor. "Remember that big man who came here last week from Wade City? The one with the two church women and the petition?"

"Yes, of course I remember him."

"Well, he's my ex brother-in-law," Gena told me.

"He *is?*" Then I made the connection. Gena's last name was Howard. Roy Howard—the man from the Family of God congregation—was her ex-husband's brother. I didn't know what to say. Finally, I asked, "What happened?"

"He left." She stopped pacing. "He was obviously here to stir up trouble. But as soon as I picked up the phone to call the police, he went out the door."

"Gena, I'm sorry."

"My ex-husband and his brother are low lifes! Bottom feeders! When will it stop?"

I came out from behind the counter to stand in front of my cousin. "What's wrong? Do they harass you?"

"Don't tell Rosalee," Gena warned. "I don't know what she'd do. She's under so much pressure as it is. I just ... just had to blow off some steam. Coming in here was the only thing I could think of to do at the moment."

"It's okay," I told her.

"No, it isn't!" Gena cried. Anger still pulsed within her. "I am so sick and tired. Sometimes I just don't know how much more I can take." She glared at me then. "I really think *you* need to leave here, Juniper. You don't belong here at Majestic Mountain. There's been nothing but trouble since you arrived."

I had no idea what Gena was talking about. I braced myself and said, "Gena, what are you trying to say? What trouble?"

"Just go away! Pack your bags and leave the Rainbow Majestic ... tonight, if you can."

"I have no intention of doing any such thing," I declared.

"Well, of course not," scoffed Gena. "You think you're in love with Wes Andrews. If that's what you think, you're only falling into a deadly trap—and you're going to find out too late what kind of man he is."

"That's not fair," I started to say.

"And the way you've got Rosalee wrapped around your little finger. She's going to find out one day that she's being taken advantage of."

Now I was enraged. "I would never ..."

"Don't think for a moment that everything around you is love and light. There's deception and envy and evil that exists within these walls. Wake up, Juniper! Get off your cloud of new-found new age fluff and face reality! Get out of here while you can—before it's too late. Do it for Rosalee's sake, if not your own."

With that, Gena stormed back out of the shop and I was left standing there, shaking uncontrollably.

16

Not more than five minutes had passed after Gena stormed out of the gift shop, when Drake stopped in. "Hey," he called to me, "your aunt says you're to close up for the rest of the afternoon and come out and have some fun."

I was still so shaken, I couldn't reply.

Drake folded his arms and cocked his head at me. "Juniper? Is everything all right?"

I turned sharply away from him as my eyelids released tears of humiliation. I still could not answer and I knew my shoulders were quaking.

Drake came over and turned me around. When he saw my face, he drew me immediately against his chest and held me. "Go on, let it out."

I couldn't do otherwise. I sobbed into his shoulder, unable to hold back the dam. When I was finally able to regain my composure, I gently pulled away from Drake and reached for a tissue behind the counter. "I'm sorry." I sniffed, totally embarrassed to have him see me this way.

"What upset you? Or, most likely, *who?*"

I blew my nose, then said, "Gena was just in here."

"That definitely explains it. What did she say?"

"She was upset about something that happened," I explained.

"And she took it out on you."

"I didn't know that man from the Family of God congregation was her ex brother-in-law."

Drake frowned. "He and his brother would like to see the lodge go under."

"Why?" I demanded.

Drake went and closed the door to the shop, then turned the sign so that it said CLOSED on the outside. "Al Howard is Gena's ex ... in more ways than one."

"What do you mean?" I asked.

Drake pulled the stool over and sat down, but I remained standing. "Al Howard is also an ex-con."

I gasped. "Gena's husband was in prison?"

"Her *ex*-husband," Drake corrected me.

"Oh, right. What was he in for?"

"Grand larceny, I believe," said Drake. "I don't remember all the details. But there's a court order on him not to go anywhere near Gena."

"I can understand now why seeing his brother would upset her," I said. "But why do they want the lodge to go out of business?"

Drake stretched his legs out in front of him. "The Majestic Mountain Lodge was a high-ranking hunting inn at one time, as you know. It had a fine reputation and Fred Sutton made a name for himself by it. In fact, I happen to know that both Al and Roy Howard patronized the lodge every year. They were both avid hunters. That's how Gena met Al. The Howard brothers came to the Majestic every year to go elk hunting. When Rosalee changed it into a new age retreat, they didn't like it one bit."

"Why didn't Gena say she knew who Roy was when he showed up last week with those church women?" I asked.

Drake shrugged. "She, no doubt, had her personal reasons. She's not proud she'd married into that family. And it was quite a few years ago that Al got busted and was sent to prison. She divorced him, and now he's out and trying to get revenge."

"Revenge for what?" I asked. "For Gena divorcing him?"

"Who knows?" said Drake. "But don't let Gena get to you. She's had a difficult time."

"She blames *me* for starting trouble," I disclosed. "She wants me to leave. Drake, why would Gena accuse me of taking advantage of Aunt Rosalee?"

"I can't imagine," he said, "but maybe she's right. Maybe you should consider getting away from here."

I couldn't believe what Drake was telling me. "But I don't want to leave here," I protested. "I love it here."

He studied me, then smirked. "Living in a hotel?"

"I love Colorado," I insisted.

"But you haven't even seen it," he scoffed.

He was right, I realized. Other than the trip to Majestic Mountain from the Colorado Springs airport and our day's journey to Wade City, I had hardly left the lodge in all the time I'd been here. Yet I felt I belonged.

"Besides," said Drake. He crossed his arms and eyed me. "What about that dream of yours? About living in a cabin in the woods ... with all the trees and the wildlife and the wildflowers?"

I stared at him almost in shock. Suddenly, that uneasy feeling crept over me once again, and I was afraid to discover what he might say next. He was hitting too close to home—toward something I couldn't quite reach in my mind—something that my psyche kept pushing away. I turned and went to get my purse.

"Don't want to talk about it? Okay. Have it your way," said Drake. He waited for me as I came out and locked the door behind us, then he turned and walked away.

I needed some time alone, so I hurried up the stairs to Room 224. Taffi wasn't there when I unlocked the door and walked in, but the answering machine's red light was blinking, indicating that there was a message waiting. I wondered if I should listen to it, in case the message was for me. I hadn't heard from nor seen anything of Wes all day, and I'd hoped perhaps he would call.

Curiosity won over and I pressed the "play" button and listened to the message. A man's muffled deep voice said in slow, deliberate phrases, "Silence is golden ... the truth can be deadly. If you want to keep on reading the handwriting, you'd best keep all information to yourself. If you don't, you'll pay dearly. Heed this warning if you value your life." A loud click sounded, and the recording's mechanical voice said, "Friday ... eleven thirty-two A.M."

I quickly replayed the message and listened once again to the words that commanded my attention. I did not recognize the voice, but it sounded strained—as if the caller had purposely changed the sound of his voice to disguise who he was.

Who could have left such a threatening message? It was obviously meant for Taffi, because it had clearly referred to her handwriting practice. What information did this man not want her to convey? What could be so important that someone would actually threaten her life?

I replayed the message a third time and thought it could have been Lance Leachfield's voice—or even Drake's—but the voice had been so muffled, it was hard to tell just whose voice it was.

When the telephone rang after the third replay of the message, I jumped in alarm. Hesitantly, I picked up the receiver and timidly said, "Hello."

"Juniper, dear, it's Starla. I heard you are staying in Taffi's room." After a pause, she asked, "Are you all right? You sounded rather startled."

I relaxed. "Oh, hello, Starla. I'm okay."

"Good. I'm calling to remind you of our appointment for your awakening on Sunday morning. Will eight o'clock work for you?"

I told her eight o'clock would be fine. Then she told me a few things about the awakenings. One was to avoid any drugs or alcoholic drinks twenty-four hours before the session. She also told me to write down the issues in my life I wanted to work on, and to wear comfortable clothes and eat something light.

"I'll counsel you for the first half of the session," Starla explained, "and then you'll be on the table for an hour or possibly more."

After we hung up, I felt a pang of hunger and recalled I had worked through lunch. I decided to go down to the kitchen and see if I could fix a peanut butter sandwich. I also wanted to find Taffi and tell her about the phone message. I freshened up, then went downstairs.

People were browsing through the many booths, tables and exhibits that filled the great room, recreation room and lounge. I paused to see if Taffi was in the great room, but when I didn't see her, I walked on toward the dining room and kitchen. I almost bumped into Clover, who was coming out of the dining room, accompanied by Vlad Petrovsky, the ufologist from Russia.

"Where have you been, Juniper?" Clover's eyes sparkled with excitement. "I haven't seen you all day."

"Hello, Miss Juniper." Vlad grinned at me. "How do sales of books go today?" he asked with his heavy accent.

"Oh, of course!" Clover cried. "You've been in the gift shop working. Have you ... like, seen all the vendors? You really must take some time and look at everything."

"Thanks, I will." Then I asked, "Have you seen Taffi?"

"She's probably ... like, at her table giving readings," said Clover. "I think she's in the lounge."

"You come to my *yu-fo* talk tonight?" Vlad asked me.

"Uh ... yes," I said. "I think so."

"Vlad is so interesting!" exclaimed Clover. She grabbed his hand, which he gladly let her hold as they headed on down the hallway toward the great room. Clover called over her shoulder, "Let's talk later."

I found Thelma sitting with Max in the kitchen. She was helping the boy put together a puzzle. He looked up, having heard me walk in.

"Wanna help us, Juniper?" the boy asked me.

"I would, but I'm looking for the peanut butter. Do you know where it is—and some bread?"

Max eagerly jumped up, which startled Thelma, who then noticed me and nodded in greeting. Max knew which cupboard held the jar of peanut butter and pointed to the bread container near the sink.

"Thanks, Max. Where's your mom?" I found a knife and began making my sandwich.

"She's at a workshop," said Max.

Thelma got up from her place at the table and came over to see what I was doing.

"I missed lunch," I explained.

"I'll tell her." Max began signing to Thelma what I'd just said.

I stared in amazement at the boy. "You can sign?"

"Yes," said Max. "Thelma and my mom taught me. It's fun!"

Satisfied that I didn't need her to do anything for me, Thelma went back to the table and the puzzle.

"Been exploring the passageways lately?" I asked Max.

"Just once."

"Have you heard any more from the ghost?"

"No," he said, then added, "Maybe it wasn't one."

I looked at him as I replaced the lid on the jar of peanut butter. "What makes you say that? You were convinced it was a ghost, and we both heard the harp music."

Max glanced at Thelma, who had her back to us. "Someone goes in there," he told me.

"Someone ... *who?*" I asked.

"I don't know, but I think someone has a key and goes there a lot." His eyes grew wider. "Last time I was in that big room ..."

"The auditorium?"

"Yeah, the scary place." He rubbed his chin, then said, "I heard footsteps the last time I was there. I didn't want anyone to catch me, so I hid in the dressing room, and somebody was in there walking around."

"Really?" I stopped what I was doing. "Max, did you see anyone?"

"No, I was hiding. I couldn't see out."

"Hm." I put the bread away and would have asked him more about it, but just then one of the girls from the kitchen crew walked in.

Max put his finger to his lips to remind me to be silent, then went back to Thelma and their puzzle as another worker came in to start the dinner prep. I told Max I'd see him later and left with my peanut butter sandwich and a glass of ice water. I sat at a table in the empty dining room and ate the sandwich while thinking over what Max had told me.

Who could be the person with a key who went to the old part of the lodge? Gena? Aunt Rosalee? Those two would seem to be the most likely ones. But why? Who else would have access to a key? I recalled the first day I'd explored the old part of the lodge—how the door to that stairs that led to the attic had been unlocked.

A bitter feeling passed over me as I remembered Gena's harsh words this afternoon and her insistence that I leave the Rainbow Majestic. Why did she believe my arrival had started trouble? Last night I had come close, I thought, to befriending my cousin. Our talk in the kitchen had been personal and congenial. But this morning she had acted like her old prudish self.

Drake's strange mention of the cabin and my dream had unsettled me. I wondered just what was the connection between Drake and that woods scene that tortured my mind. What was it about the man that so intrigued me? When I was around him, there was this familiarity, yet also a fear that I didn't comprehend. He disturbed me with his brash manner at times, and yet he could comfort me as he had this afternoon, when he'd encouraged me to cry on his shoulder.

Wes had been comforting last evening at the stream in the woods, yet in a different way. Wes's energy was different than Drake's. Wes was more passive, less controversial, and he had this charismatic effect over me. But where was Wes today? He hadn't even called or come by to see me. I wondered what was up with him.

As I finished the last bite of my peanut butter sandwich, I thought again of finding Taffi and telling her about the phone message. I needed to talk with her. She hadn't yet disclosed to me what she had started to say yesterday morning at breakfast, before Starla had barged in with the news about Celeste.

I joined the fair goers, stopping at the different tables in the great room. There were a lot of people browsing and buying things. Card readers were busy counseling their paying clients, and I saw Simone Sullivan consulting with a young man in shorts and a tie-dye T-shirt. Cyril Jorgensen sat on the red arm chair in front of the fireplace, resting with his eyes closed. The elderly man didn't seem the least disturbed by the noise of the crowd, which included some gentle flute music from one of the booths. I wondered how Cyril was doing without Celeste. He must miss her. No one had said how she was coming along.

I had worked my way into the recreation room, which contained more tables and booths, when I saw Aunt Rosalee talking with some guests. She noticed me and came over when I was reading a pamphlet on ear candling.

"I'm glad to see you're takin' my advice," she told me. "We've had a great turnout and this is only Friday."

"That's wonderful." Then I asked, "Aunt Rosalee, why didn't anyone tell me Gena's brother-in-law was the man who came here with that petition?"

She sighed with impatience. "Who told you that?"

"Gena." I quickly explained how she had come into the gift shop, upset over seeing Roy Howard.

"He was here again?" cried Aunt Rosalee.

"Briefly," I said. "Gena said he left when she picked up the phone to call the police."

"Oh, good for her." She frowned. "I wonder what he was doin' here today. Prob'ly came to start trouble. Well, let's just hope he stays away from now on. We certainly don't need his kind of energy with all these people here."

"Have you seen Wes?" I asked.

"I'm sure he's busy chauffeurin'," said Aunt Rosalee. "We offered free transportation throughout the day to Wade City."

I understood then why I hadn't seen Wes. He wasn't ignoring me, I realized with relief. Why had I even doubted him?

Aunt Rosalee was being summoned. Linda Sullivan came over to tell her Simone was asking for her. With a smile and a pat on my arm, my aunt went with Simone's daughter, and I finished browsing my way through the room toward the lounge.

There were a dozen or so psychic readers positioned at tables around the perimeter of the lounge, which was set up with rows of chairs for tonight's lecture by the ufologist. I saw Taffi in the far corner with a lady seated across from her. They were discussing a paper in front of them. I didn't know how long they would be, but lingered in the shadows for a few minutes until the reading ended.

"Juniper, come on over." Taffi grinned as I approached her table. She reached behind her chair and brought out a bottle of water, from which she took a drink.

"Looks like business is booming," I said.

"I'll say." Taffi's eyes expanded. "Rosalee did a dynamite job advertising this thing. I'm floored by all the people."

"Well, I'm glad. Taffi, there's a message on the answering machine in your room. I listened because I thought it might be for me."

"That's okay, sweetie."

"I think you need to listen to it," I told her.

"Why? Who is it?"

I lowered my voice. "I don't know. Some man left a rather disturbing message for you."

Taffi's smile vanished. She stared at me, then asked, "What did he say?"

"You need to hear it," I insisted.

She stood up and grabbed her purse. "Okay, maybe I'd better." Now she appeared nervous and fidgety. She stashed a few things under the table, then spread a cloth over it before leaving.

"Are you coming right back?" I asked.

"Yes, yes, of course."

"Because we need to finish our conversation from yesterday," I told her.

Taffi seemed distracted. "What conversation was that?"

"You know ... you said you found out about who was in the hunting party that day my father was killed."

"Honey, you wait right here." Taffi glanced around the room. "Don't say anything to anyone about this. Do you understand?"

"Yes, but ..."

"If anyone asks where I went, just tell them I had to go to the restroom. I'll be back soon." She hurried away before I could ask any more questions.

I sat down in the lounge and waited for Taffi to return. How upset would she be after listening to the message? Maybe I should have gone with her.

Just then, Clover came into the room and joined me. "I'm in love," she declared.

I stared at her, then blinked. "What?"

Clover hugged herself, then laughed. "With Vlad," she said. "Oh, Juniper, he's fantastic."

"But, Clover," I said, "I thought it was Wes you were in love with."

She sighed. "Not any more. Besides, Wes is too ... too ... wishy washy." There were stars in Clover's eyes and she reminded me of a school girl experiencing a major crush.

"And how does he feel about you?" I asked.

"Oh, I think he likes me," Clover said. "He's already ... like, invited me to come to St. Petersburg." She looked toward the doorway. "And there he is."

Glancing over, I saw Vlad beckoning to Clover.

"I promised him another massage before his talk tonight. I've gotta go." She hopped up—all smiles—as she went to join the Russian.

I watched in amusement as the two slipped off together, and then was surprised when Wes came in. His eyes followed the pair upon their departure. Slowly, Wes turned around and walked toward me. I smiled at him. "Don't you think they make a cute couple?"

Wes just looked at me. "Clover and Vladimir Petrovsky? Are you kidding?"

"She said she's in love with him," I added. "But ... you know Clover."

Wes stood there for a long moment as if pondering the situation. Finally, he sat down. Then he turned to me. "Why are you sitting in here all by yourself?"

"I'm waiting for Taffi," I explained.

"Where'd she go?"

"Up ... I mean ... she'll be right back." I remembered Taffi's request to not tell anyone her whereabouts.

"Well, okay." Wes stood up to leave.

"Where are you going?" I asked.

"I'm tired. I'm going to grab a shower." He did appear rather worn out. I could imagine a day of driving that long way back and forth to Wade City would take its toll. I might have asked to go along with him upstairs, but I knew I had to wait for Taffi, so we could talk. I watched Wes stroll out, remembering the tenderness he'd shown me last night and the lingering kiss.

Why hadn't he seemed happier to see me? Had it been my imagination, or had Wes Andrews appeared preoccupied— possibly even disturbed—by the developing relationship between Clover and Vlad Petrovsky?

17

Half an hour passed and Taffi did not return to the lounge. I decided to go up to the room and check on her. Perhaps I had underestimated the effect that phone message might have on her. But when I reached Room 224, Taffi wasn't there. I did notice the answering machine had been cleared of messages. I went over to check and saw that Taffi had deleted the threatening call after listening to it. I wondered if she knew who it had been.

I went back downstairs and searched for Taffi, but couldn't find her. She hadn't returned to her table. Everything was still covered up. No one I talked to said they had seen her. In the remaining time before dinner, I went to the gift shop and checked on things. I had left the cash drawer in the register when Drake had come by earlier. I took the drawer out after running my end-of-the-day sales totals, and then locked up before taking it to the lodge office. I just hoped either Lance or Aunt Rosalee was still there.

Lance was on the telephone with his back toward me. Aunt Rosalee wasn't in the office. Apparently, Lance hadn't noticed that I had come in. I overheard his conversation on the telephone.

"I understand that," Lance was saying. "The trouble is, I don't want to be on the payroll any longer. I want out of it ... completely." There was a pause and he tapped his fingers on the desk top. "Look," he said in a strained voice, "I'm about to lose my job here because of you. I have a wife and a son to think about ... *don't* ... don't do that ... *please* ... just wait ..."

At that moment, Lance turned his head and saw me standing there with the cash tray. Without another word, he reached over and pressed the bar on the telephone that disconnected the call. Then he carefully laid the ear piece back in its cradle and looked up at me with a blank expression.

I handed him the cash tray and he stood up to take it without saying a word. I watched as he carried it into Aunt

Rosalee's inner office and placed it inside her large desk drawer. I didn't wait. I simply left the office and walked down to the dining room, which was filling up fast with guests. I had no idea what Lance's conversation had been about, but I decided I already had enough to worry about at the moment.

Clover and Vlad were seated at a round table near the window. She motioned to me to join them. Glancing around, I didn't see Aunt Rosalee and presumed she would most likely be dining with Simone Sullivan again this evening. Both Clover and Vlad appeared happy and relaxed. I sat down at their table.

"Juniper has only ... like, been with us at the Rainbow Majestic for two weeks," Clover told Vlad. "She's Rosalee's niece from Kansas."

"Ah," said Vlad, "I don't know this *Kan-zus*."

As Clover tried to explain to the Russian where Kansas was in relation to Colorado, I saw Wes had come in and was standing at the door watching us. I waved at him to join us. He paused a moment, then walked over and sat down between Clover and me. She turned to welcome him with a big smile, then resumed chatting with the ufologist.

"Wes, you haven't seen Taffi, have you?" I asked.

"No," he said.

"She never came back to the lounge," I said, "and she wasn't up in her room. I have a strange feeling about it."

Wes simply shrugged. He wasn't very talkative for some reason. I tried numerous times to engage him in conversation, but his responses were abrupt and I could tell he wasn't feeling very sociable. It made me feel tense and uncomfortable—especially considering how close I thought we had become the evening before, beside the stream in the woods.

While the meal was served, I looked around the dining room in hopes of seeing Taffi. Aunt Rosalee and Gena sat with Simone and her daughter. Starla and Cyril were with a group of guests, but Cyril seemed detached as he had last night—off in his own world. The Leachfield family sat by themselves tonight. Lance kept nervously glancing around at the guests while Nadine fussed over Max.

We were having dessert when Gena appeared at our table and spoke to Vlad, who quickly wiped his mouth with his napkin, then stood up. "Excuse me, please," he told us, "but I must now get ready for my *yu-fo* talk."

Clover reached over and he gently kissed her hand, and then Vlad followed Gena out of the room. After he was gone, Clover sighed and said, "Isn't he wonderful?"

Just then, Drake approached our table. It surprised me because I really hadn't given Drake much thought and now wondered where he had been.

"I had supper with Thelma in the kitchen tonight," Drake explained as he sat down on the other side of me.

Wes began conversing with Clover while I asked Drake if he had seen anything of Taffi.

"No," he told me, "but no doubt she's giving somebody a reading." Drake surprised me by putting his hand on mine and said, "Say, I've got an idea. Would you like to go on a little adventure? See more of Colorado?"

I looked at him quizzically. "What did you have in mind?"

"We can take one of the lodge's four-wheelers out tomorrow. I want to show you some of the wild country around here. What do you say?"

I noticed that Wes and Clover were now deeply involved in their discussion, speaking in low tones. Turning back to Drake, I said, "Sure, why not? But when? I have to work in the gift shop tomorrow, you know."

"We can go out early—just after daylight—and I'll have you back in time to open your shop," he promised. He seemed so enthused about doing this that I gave in and said I'd go. Besides, it might do me some good to get out of the lodge for a while and see more of the outdoors. I had never ridden on an ATV before and wondered what it would be like.

Aunt Rosalee stood up and announced to everyone in the dining room that Vladimir Petrovsky's lecture was about to begin in the lounge. Those who had finished their coffee and dessert stood up to move in that direction.

"Oh, we don't want to miss Vlad's talk," said Clover. "Let's go now, so we can ... like, get good seats."

Wes made a face, but I noticed he stood up at once and followed Clover out of the room. Drake and I looked at one another and grimaced.

"What's got into Wes?" Drake asked me.

"I don't know," I replied. "He's been acting a little strange today." I felt a lump in my throat. Wes had been too eager to go with Clover and had barely given either of us a glance before he left.

"You going to the lecture?" Drake asked me.

"I suppose. But I think I'll check the room first, to see if Taffi's there. I really need to talk to her about something."

Drake scooted back his chair. "Okay, then. I'll meet you downstairs in the lobby tomorrow morning at six-thirty. How does that sound?"

"You're not going to Vlad's lecture?"

"I don't know yet. I might. I got some things I gotta do first."

I agreed to meet him in the morning, then finished my dessert and then went upstairs to see if Taffi had come back to her room. No one was there when I unlocked the door and walked in, but my heart raced when I saw another message blinking from the answering machine. For a moment, I was tempted to ignore it and go on back downstairs for Vlad's lecture. But—with a sigh—I decided maybe I'd better listen to the new message.

I was somewhat relieved that it was Mike and the message was for me. "Juniper, when are you coming home?" his recorded voice asked. "Have you made the arrangements yet? If you have, give me a call. If you didn't ... well, never mind. I'll be in touch."

I erased the message, then got ready to go back downstairs to the lecture. I didn't want to call Mike. The longer I could put off confronting him, the better. Why wasn't he getting the hint?

The lounge was packed with guests when I arrived. I was worried that I would have nowhere to sit, but then I noticed Taffi sitting at her handwriting table. There was an empty chair beside her, so I went over. She motioned for me to sit down, but she didn't look too happy to see me.

"Taffi, I was worried about you," I told her.

"It's okay, honey." She tried to smile, but I could tell she was uptight about something.

"Is everything all right?" I asked her.

"Yes, yes." Her eyes darted around the room.

"When you didn't come back downstairs, I ..."

"Not now, Juniper." Taffi patted my hand, then said in a low voice, "I think the best thing we can do is sit here and be quiet."

"Why?" I asked. "What's wrong?"

Taffi stared at me almost in a hostile manner. "Don't ask me any more questions."

"But ..."

"Juniper, your life may be in danger." As soon as she said it, she scooped up her purse and papers, and then stood up to leave.

"Taffi, wait ..."

"I've already said too much." And—with that—Taffi hurried out of the lounge just as the lights dimmed with the last people taking their seats.

I sat in silence and stared after Taffi as she disappeared into the recreation room. What had she meant, my life may be in danger? Why didn't she want me to ask her any more questions? The realization hit me that the phone message earlier must have had something to do with me. But what? Did the information Taffi was going to give me about my father's hunting party have anything to do with all of this? Did that information mean that somebody in this lodge didn't want me to find out what Taffi had to tell me?

The implications were starting to mount. As Gena stood up in front of the audience and introduced Vladimir Petrovsky to the crowd, I found it increasingly difficult to concentrate on the talk. My mind whirled with possibilities. Obviously, Taffi had somehow discovered who had been present at the time my father had been shot. Someone in that party—twenty-two years ago—knew who had shot Nathaniel Sutton, my father. All these years, Uncle Fred had protected that person by not disclosing the truth and taking the blame on himself, calling it an accident.

Why Uncle Fred had done that was a mystery. He had obviously been covering up for someone, unless he had been blackmailed or bribed into it. Had there been a murder at Diamond Reservoir that fateful fall day? And the thought that the murderer was at large—possibly even housed within the walls of the Rainbow Majestic—was a frightening notion.

Now, someone—a man—had threatened Taffi into silence. She had been on the verge of telling me the members of the hunting party just yesterday morning at breakfast, and she would have if Starla hadn't come in right then with the bad news about Celeste.

As hard as I tried to focus my mind on Vlad's talk and slide show—which consisted of various photos people had taken of UFOs—my mind was in a turmoil. The next hour and a half passed in a blur. I hadn't even been aware that Clover sat in the front row with Wes until the lecture was just about over. I noticed then that Wes was holding Clover's hand.

Vlad's lecture concluded, and then Gena came to the microphone to announce that there would be a group meditation after a fifteen-minute break. Anyone who wanted to participate was welcome to stay.

I waited to see what Clover would do now that the lecture was over. Would she run after Vlad, her "newfound love," or would she stay with Wes, who appeared as though he were staking a claim on her?

What a fool I had been. Once again, I felt that swelling in my throat and realized Wes had just been using me. It was obvious who it was he cared about. The more I thought about it, I recalled that Wes had started paying attention to me after Vlad had invited me to lunch yesterday. Wes had appeared jealous of the Russian ufologist, with his extraordinary good looks and charm. Now that Clover had shown a strong interest in Vlad, Wes's attention had pivoted in her direction and—by the looks of it—his strategy was winning. Clover didn't make a move when Vlad came forward. It didn't seem to matter to the Russian. He was soon engulfed by eager questioners, and Clover soon got up with Wes and they departed from the lounge together.

I finally got up to stretch and wondered what I should do. As much as I wanted to find out more from Taffi, I was afraid I'd upset her further if I sought her out. Drake hadn't shown up for the lecture, and I wondered if I should just go back to the room.

Right then, Aunt Rosalee came toward me, dressed in a pink and blue mu-mu. Behind her was Simone Sullivan, her blond hair swirled fashionably on top of her head.

"Juniper, I hope you'll stay for the meditation tonight," said my aunt. "Simone's agreed to lead it."

I tried to look impressed by that fact, but it didn't work.

"What's wrong? Juniper, are you feelin' okay?"

I managed to hold onto my escaping emotions and nodded at her, attempting a smile.

"Oh, poor girl." Simone stared at me as if she saw right through me. "Oh, Rosalee, she's in need of some balancing. Come on, let's form a circle around her." She called to her daughter, "Linda, where are you? Starla? Can you join us too?"

Starla came right over. "Linda's outside having a cigarette," she told Simone.

"Oh, that girl," Simone grumbled, then shook her head. "Well, come over here. Let's see what we can do."

It all happened so fast, I hardly knew what took place. Suddenly, a small group of light workers had eased me into a chair, and they all held out their hands and placed them on my head or shoulders and back. Everyone closed their eyes and a silence fell over the crowd. I heard Starla's soft voice in my ear, telling me to relax and close my eyes. I'm not sure what really happened, but I felt their combined energy lift me as I let my mind go blank. A wonderful feeling of peace flowed over me, which served to bring my emotions to an abrupt halt. Even the lump in my throat had disappeared.

When it was over, they removed their hands and I opened my eyes. Everyone was smiling, and even though I was embarrassed, I thanked them. Simone then stepped in front of the room as the lights dimmed. Someone had lit candles around the room, and people took their places for the meditation.

Still basking in all that loving energy, I sat and experienced my first group meditation. Closing my eyes, I listened to Simone's voice as she directed us to imagine a flowing body of water, spilling over rocks along its course, and somewhere in the background new age music played softly, enhancing the mood for relaxation. I let my mind drift, and the peace filled me to the point that I forgot I was in a room inside the Rainbow Majestic Lodge. For those few minutes, I actually was part of that flowing river, where thoughts of Wes, thoughts of Clover, concerns about Taffi and about my father's death did not contaminate my state of being.

When the meditation ended, I blinked several times to bring myself back to the present. Starla, who sat next to me, turned to me and said, "Better?"

"Yes, much better," I told her.

"Simone's good," she remarked.

I had to admit, Simone Sullivan had helped me. Whatever

prejudices I had held about her dissipated. Aunt Rosalee seemed pleased as well, and gave me a hug before I headed upstairs.

"That was a good idea about holdin' the dance out in the garden tomorrow night," she told me before I left. "Drake told us you came up with the idea."

That's right, the dance was tomorrow night. And tomorrow morning I was going four-wheeling with Drake. I had better get to bed if I was going to meet him in the lobby at six-thirty.

I climbed the spiral steps and made my way to Room 224. I didn't know how I was going to react if Taffi was there and didn't want to talk to me. When I unlocked the door and switched on the light, I was in for a shock.

The room had been ransacked. Clothes, bedding, cosmetics and books lay scattered all over the floor. The beds had been completely stripped. Lamps were knocked over. It was as though a whirlwind had flashed through the room, upsetting everything it possibly could. I could only stand there with the door still open, unable to react.

Some guests passed by in the hallway, but they were too busy talking to notice. I finally turned around and looked down the hallway. I could hear voices coming from the stairway. A moment later, Aunt Rosalee appeared, and behind her were Simone and Linda, obviously headed for the crystal suite. I called to them and got their attention right away.

Aunt Rosalee was the first to reach me. As I pointed, she looked into the room and gasped. Then, Simone gave a cry of alarm.

"Someone's been through our room," I said.

"Lord a-mercy!" Aunt Rosalee walked in and placed her hands on her wide hips as she looked all around.

"What happened?" asked Linda.

Simone held both her hands up in the air and closed her eyes. Slowly, she turned around in a circle.

"Where's Taffi?" asked Aunt Rosalee.

I shook my head. "Last I saw of her was just before the lecture."

"She wasn't at the lecture?"

"No, she left the lounge."

Aunt Rosalee asked Simone, "What are you pickin' up about this?"

The blond woman slowly opened her eyes and said, "I sense the person who was in this room was not a thief. They were looking for something in particular ... something of value only to them."

"Shouldn't we call the police or something?" asked Linda.

Aunt Rosalee frowned, then looked to me for an answer.

I shrugged. "What if Taffi did this?"

Aunt Rosalee turned to Simone with a questioning look.

"I don't believe Taffi had any part of this," she told us.

"Well, I don't know ..." Aunt Rosalee was certainly in a quandary.

"It's probably not necessary to call the authorities about this," I reassured her. "Let's wait. Taffi might be able to explain this when she returns."

My aunt stepped over and gripped my arm. "I don't want you to stay here by yourself," she told me.

"Taffi will be here," I reminded her.

"I'll send somebody up from housekeepin' to straighten up this room," said Aunt Rosalee. "But if you want to come stay with me tonight, you come on down."

I thanked them. After a minute, they all left and I shut the door behind them. Then, I turned back to the mess and started picking up my things. I didn't have that much stuff, compared to Taffi—yet I felt violated and troubled by the disruption.

Who could have done this? And what were they looking for? Somehow I couldn't make myself believe that Taffi had torn up the room. She had appeared uptight and even frightened when I'd spoken to her last. Where was she now? And how would she react when she saw what had happened to her room?

18

B y the time the maid knocked on the door, I had assembled
all of my belongings and picked up my clothes. While she
tidied up and made the beds, I took a shower. When I came out,
the maid had left and everything was in order.

Taffi never returned to her room. I came to the conclusion
that she was avoiding me. I was sure she must have found a
friend to spend the night with, so I stayed up and read until I
was sleepy. Nothing disturbed me the rest of the night.

The alarm went off at six. I wasn't ready to get up that
early, but I didn't want to keep Drake waiting. I had packed a
pair of jeans and put them on, along with an aqua sweatshirt
with a hood, since mornings in the mountains were cold.

At six-thirty Drake was in the lobby, dressed in blue jeans
and a denim jacket. "I like a woman who's on time," he
commented. No one was up yet, except the girl at the front desk
who relieved Gena during the night shift.

Drake and I stepped out into a crisp morning of frigid air
and rosy sky. He led me down the steps to the waiting all-terrain
vehicle parked at the bottom, then directed me to climb on. He
then slid into the seat in front of me.

"Shouldn't we wear helmets or something?" I realized the
only way I was going to keep from falling off this machine was
to hold onto Drake.

"Nope," he replied. He made sure the ATV was in neutral,
then turned the switch. The engine engaged and it wasn't as
loud as I had imagined. "Just be sure to hang on good and tight."

I hesitantly placed my hands around Drake's waist as he
gripped the steering wheel. "Ready?"

"Yes," I called out.

We headed out of the parking lot. As we started down the
narrow lane that took us to the county road, I instinctively
pressed myself against Drake's back—afraid of falling off. I didn't
know what he was feeling, but I was embarrassed that my chest

and chin were tight up against him. I really didn't know of any other way to keep from losing my balance.

We reached the road and slowed a bit. Drake then made a right turn, and when I asked him where we were going, he said he wanted to check out some trails in the national forest. I had no objection. In fact, it wasn't long before I was enjoying the ride. The wind in my hair felt refreshing and revitalizing. All this fantastic beauty of the high country was right here at our fingertips. I drank in the earthy aroma of the pine forests, the aspen stands and the meadows with beaver ponds. We turned off onto a dirt road that took us deeper into the woods, and I felt exhilarated and alive.

"Warm enough?" Drake asked over his shoulder.

"Yes, fine." I was amazed at how our vehicle could so easily maneuver the bumpy path ahead of us, even crossing right over fallen trees and logs. There weren't too many puddles, but when we did find a couple of them, Drake slowed down so we wouldn't get splashed with mud.

We explored trails in several areas of the forest, and then Drake turned back onto the county road and we headed farther up the valley. When we came to a gravel road on the left, we turned onto it and found it wound around aspen trees and up over a small hill that led into a little field of evergreens.

Drake slowed and I noticed a structure on one side of a hill, almost hidden from sight by sheltering pines.

"What's that?" I asked.

Drake pulled to a stop and shut off the engine. "Come on. I'll show you." He waited for me to get off the four-wheeler first. I had to swing my left leg up over his head to slide off the right side of the vehicle. My legs felt a little wobbly after the ride. He got off the ATV and led me toward the building of peeled logs that—though incomplete —definitely indicated the makings of a cabin. Piles of lumber and building materials lay along the ground near the structure and a stack of stones had been gathered for some decorative purpose.

Drake turned to me as we drew near. "What do you think?"

I stared at the cabin, then at him. He wasn't giving anything away with his blank expression, but there was a sparkle of expectancy in his eyes. "It looks like somebody's building a house," I finally said.

"Let's go inside." He started toward the doorway.

"Wait," I said, "won't we be trespassing?"

"Not if it's my cabin," he replied.

"Your cabin?" I gasped in surprise. "Drake! You never told me you were building a cabin."

"You never asked," he retorted. There was no door on the structure yet, but he pretended there was and made a motion of swinging an imaginary door inward, then ushered me through with a wry smile on his bearded face.

Inside it was protected from the elements, even though the windows had not yet been installed. I looked around at the walls and wooden floor and noticed the cabin had an open living area that included a kitchen, a den and a ladder leading up to a loft.

"This is cozy," I said. "Are you building it all yourself?"

"Yup, that's why it's taken so long. I've had to collect every-thing as I could afford it ... or find it. A lot of the materials are recycled."

"Drake, it's awesome."

"I knew you liked cabins and I wanted to show it to you." His voice had softened.

I turned to find him standing close behind me. For a few seconds, our eyes met in a special way, but I immediately grew embarrassed and looked away. I walked over to the kitchen and noticed one of those old-fashioned hand pumps that were used in the early part of the last century, to bring water into the house. "Oh, look! Where did you get this?"

"I stole it from a museum," said Drake. I gave him a doubtful look and he shook his head. "No, it was a relic in my grandmother's estate."

"Are you going to live here?" I asked him.

"That's the general idea," he said.

"How much ground do you have?"

"I bought a ten-acre parcel off Rosalee and Fred when they took over the lodge," he explained. "I was lucky to get one of the more secluded lots."

"Then, you'll still be working at the Rainbow Majestic? You just won't be *living* there."

Drake walked over to the window opening off the living room section, his hands in his pockets. "I guess you could say I'm an independent kind of guy. I like my privacy and I love the mountains. I can't live in a hotel."

"I can understand that," I said. "I didn't realize how much I missed the outdoors until this morning. It's just so beautiful." I then found myself telling Drake about how I'd started to go to college to become a wildlife biologist and how I'd always been drawn to the woods and all living things.

We sat on the wood floor and talked for some time. He wanted to know why I hadn't continued in that direction and he didn't chastise me for letting go of that ambition. I asked him, "What's your dream? You obviously have one. You're building this."

"I'm living my dream," he told me. "I don't like to dwell on the future and what lies ahead. None of us knows what's going to happen, and the world we live in is in such a mess."

I agreed with him on that.

"The way things are going, maybe a remote, self-sustainable lifestyle is the way to go," he continued. "What's going on in my life right now is all I really think about."

"But in the past you had this vision of a cabin you'd build someday," I told him.

"Along with the beautiful young woman who is sitting in it now." Drake's eyes seemed to peer deep inside of me.

I felt a wave of confusion wash over me and found myself again embarrassed in his presence. I turned my eyes away. There was a long silence.

Finally, Drake asked, "What is it about me, Juniper, that scares you so? Why can't you ever look me straight in the eye?"

My heart started to race and I felt cornered all of a sudden. "I ... I don't know. I really don't understand why you have this effect on me," I told him.

Drake studied me. "I know I'm not as good-looking as Wes, but I didn't know I was that ugly."

I laughed to cover up my confusion and self-consciousness. "Don't be ridiculous, Drake."

"But it's true, isn't it? It's Wes you're attracted to. You think I don't know?"

I forced myself to look at him, and he appeared vulnerable to me. His mountain man armor was down and I had a glimpse of someone who tugged at my heart. Our eyes locked for a few seconds. "No," I said, "it's not true at all." Then I said something that I couldn't help—and I wasn't sure where it even came from. "Looks are only skin deep. When I look at you, I see someone I once knew ... very well."

Drake stared at me for a few seconds. Then he motioned for me to come closer. As if in a daze, I crawled toward him and he pulled me onto his lap. I nestled my head against his shoulder as he wrapped his strong arms around me and held me. His beard felt soft against my face as we sat, watching the empty fireplace across the room. The wind blew in from the open windows.

"I was married once, you know," he said.

"Clover told me," I replied.

"It was a long time ago." After a short silence, he sighed. "She left."

I didn't know what to say. I just let him talk.

"She wasn't cut out for my kind of life. She was a city girl. Life in the woods bored her stiff."

"How did you come to Majestic Mountain?" I asked.

Drake fingered a stray strand of my hair. "Through an outfitter, I heard about Fred Sutton and the Majestic Mountain Lodge. I thought I'd check it out. Fred and Rosalee had just come back from Oklahoma to run the place."

"And was Gena at the lodge then?" I asked.

"Off and on," said Drake. "She considers it her home, you know."

"How do you feel about Gena?" I dared to ask.

Drake didn't answer. "Why?" he asked after a moment.

"I can tell she has feelings for you," I said.

Drake laughed. "Can't understand how that would be. An ugly old coon like me ..."

I looked up at him in shock.

"That's mountain man talk," he chided me. "Haven't you ever heard of a coon before?"

"You're not old," I told him.

"Who says I'm not? I'm too old for you, that's for sure."

"Nonsense," I cried. "And ... you're not ugly."

He drew me close once again and buried his beard in my hair. After a short silence, he asked, "What did you mean earlier, when you said you saw—in me—someone you once knew—very well?"

I dared to look into his face and into those penetrating dark blue eyes that scared me, yet also thrilled me. They were so familiar, and yet ...

"Juniper?" His voice was deep and soft.

My heart raced. "I ... I ... I don't know what I meant by that. I ... I wish I knew." My lower lip trembled. Then I asked, "Drake ... do *you* know? What is it I'm unable to remember? It has to do with you."

"Do you really want to know the answer, Juniper?" His voice echoed compassion and a dare, both at the same time.

I could only stare at him. It seemed we sat there for a long time, not saying anything. A rush of feelings had overcome my rationality. Then, Drake glanced at his watch and said, "I had planned to drive up over to Diamond Reservoir, but it looks like we're running late. I'd better get you back to the Majestic."

With that, the spell was broken and he helped me to my feet. We left the cabin and climbed back onto the ATV.

This time, as we rode in silence back to the Rainbow Majestic, I clung to Drake and rested my right cheek against his back. Something had shifted in my attitude toward him and I was no longer afraid of the man himself. A deep sadness had replaced the confusing fear. I had glimpsed something in him—and also something about me in that brief time back at his cabin—that I couldn't explain. Now all I could do was wonder what part Drake had played in my past life. Had he a role to play in that recurring fantasy I lived over and over, whenever I thought about my dream woods and my dream cabin? How was I ever going to find out—and then deal with it all?

After we returned to the lodge, more cars had arrived for the second day of the holistic fair. By ten o'clock I was swamped with business in the gift shop. Clover dropped in to see me and said she wanted to talk, but I was too busy to take a break. She left because she had a massage to give. By noon, things started to slow down and I recalled that I had signed up for that energy healing workshop at one o'clock. I planned to close up at twelve-thirty and grab a sandwich before it started.

I was rearranging some stock on some high shelves when I heard a man's voice call from the doorway. "Hello, Juniper."

I turned around and almost fell off the step stool. Mike Rollins stood there, staring at me with a stern look on his face.

"Oh, my gosh!" I muttered.

A smile finally spread across his square face as he stepped completely into the shop and looked around at the merchandise. "So this is where you wile away the hours," he said cynically.

"Mike," I said, "what are you doing here?"

"Aren't you glad to see me?" The smile on his square face disappeared.

"Well, I didn't expect you to ... why didn't you tell me you were coming?"

"You mean you're surprised?"

"I am that."

"You're not happy to see me, are you, Juniper?"

I shook off my shock and stepped toward him with an attempt to be cordial. "I'm sorry, Mike. Where are my manners?" I went over and gave him a brief hug.

"I've come to drive you back to Kansas," he stated.

I stared at him in disbelief. "I don't think so."

"But I thought you called and told me to come get you." He looked baffled. "There was a message on my answering machine last night. I got in my car and drove all night."

I noticed he did look tired. "No, Mike, I did no such thing. I didn't call you."

"Well ... some woman called and said you were too upset to call yourself, but that you wanted to go home, and you wanted me to come right away." Mike looked confused as well as annoyed.

"No," I said. "I don't know who called you, but the truth is ..."

"Look, Juniper," Mike interrupted in an impatient voice, "it's time you gave up this mystical game you're playing and get a life. You're coming back to Great Bend with me this afternoon."

I frowned at him. "I'm staying right here. I've got a job and friends here. I don't want to live in Kansas. I'm afraid someone has sent you on a wild goose chase."

Mike stared at me in surprise. "You're not the Juniper Sutton I once knew," he said. "You've changed."

"Maybe I've grown a little," I told him. "I'm learning so much by being here."

"You mean you've been brain-washed," he challenged. "Juniper, do you know what this place is?"

"Yes, Mike, and I'm very happy here."

"It's a new age cult ... a coven of witches ... a loony bin for gurus and mystics."

"Stop!" I shouted. "It's none of those things! The Rainbow Majestic is a light center. Healers come here to work."

"You've turned weird on me, Juniper. These people are all crazy. I need to get you out of here."

"I'm not leaving, Mike. You can't make me."

The man was getting more perturbed by the minute. I knew part of it was the fact that he was tired after driving long hours to get here.

"Mike, listen," I said in a calmer voice. I grabbed a piece of rose quartz off the shelf and walked over and placed it in his hand. "You're stressed out. What you need is some sleep. I don't want to fight with you. I just want you to understand that I'm not your property. I'm not going to marry you. I'm a light worker now, and my place is here ... at the Rainbow Majestic."

He stared at the chunk of pink rock I had placed in his hand, puzzled by it. I had impulsively given it to him in hopes the stone's energy would calm him. Just then, I saw Cyril Jorgensen in the hallway outside the door, peering in.

"So this is the gift shop." The elderly man gazed around with a smile. "Very nice. Are my books in here?"

Mike stared, not knowing what to say. I nodded at Cyril. "They are," I said.

A moment later, Wes stepped into the shop, clutching his keys. "Ready to go, Cyril?" Wes shot me a smile.

The old man moved slowly these days, and now shuffled around the shop, bent forward a bit. "Mind if I pick up a little trinket for Celeste?" he asked.

"No, go ahead," said Wes. His eyes fell on Mike, then back to me. "I'm driving Cyril over to the hospital to see Celeste this afternoon," he explained.

"How is she doing?" I asked. Mike just stood there, gripping the rose quartz.

Wes stepped toward me and pulled me aside toward the doorway, so he wouldn't be overheard. Today he appeared overly caring and deliberate in his actions—quite the contrast from his aloof behavior yesterday. "The nurse called Rosalee this mornin'. Celeste's not doin' too good, I'm afraid. Cyril's finally agreed to go visit her."

"How serious is her condition?" I asked.

Wes put his arm around my waist and spoke softly. "She had a stroke and apparently she had another one early this mornin'."

I sighed and glanced back at Cyril, who was fingering through some items in the jewelry display case.

"Who's that guy?" Wes whispered in reference to Mike.

"A friend of mine," I whispered back, then added, "from Kansas."

Wes nodded knowingly, then said, "I wondered, because he looks kind of rattled. Are you okay, Juniper?"

I looked him in the eye. "Yes, I'm fine, Wes."

"I'm glad." His blue eyes looked into mine, but this time I was immune to their spell.

"Clover came by earlier," I told him.

"She did?" He raised an eyebrow.

I folded my arms and nodded. "I think you two are going to be very happy."

Wes stared at me in a troubled way. "Juniper, what are you sayin'? Didn't the other night mean anythin' to you?"

"Nothing happened that really meant anything," I said quietly.

Wes looked disappointed, but recovered quickly and bent over and kissed my forehead—right in front of Cyril and Mike. Then, he smiled at me. "I'll be back for the dance tonight," he said. "Just make sure to save one for me."

A prickle of longing rippled through me. I hadn't expected Wes to start flirting with me again. Had something gone wrong between Clover and him?

Cyril cleared his throat and ran a crooked hand through his white hair. "I've found just the thing for my lady," he announced and placed something small on the counter.

Mike stepped aside and watched as I took my place behind the cash register and rang up a little silver angel Cyril had picked out to give to Celeste. While we were making the transaction, I heard Wes conversing with Mike.

"You're Juniper's friend from Kansas, I hear."

Mike nodded. "That's right ... Mike Rollins."

Wes extended his hand. "I'm Wes Andrews. You here for

the holistic fair?"

"I'm here to drive Juniper home," said Mike.

"I see." Wes didn't act surprised. He waited while I wrapped the angel in some tissue paper and handed it to Cyril. "Well, nice meetin' ya, Mike. Come on, Cyril."

The elderly man turned and slowly started to walk out of the shop, but he stopped to face Mike. Kansas had been mentioned and now Cyril began to tell Mike about how he'd been born in that state. To my relief, Wes managed to steer Cyril out the door, and then the two of them left.

My emotions surged. First, the shock of Mike showing up and demanding that I go back with him to Great Bend, and then Wes coming in, planting a kiss on my forehead ... I was not focusing well on anything at the moment.

"Who's that Wes guy?" demanded Mike.

I looked at Mike in surprise. "Oh, Wes is the groundskeeper here. And Cyril Jorgensen is a great metaphysical author and teacher ..."

"I don't care about that right now, Juniper," he interrupted. "And why did you give me this rock?" He plopped the rose quartz down on the counter. "Can't we go somewhere so we can sit down and talk over a cup of coffee?"

I explained to Mike that I was getting ready to close the shop and go get a sandwich. "But I only have a couple of minutes because I've signed up for an energy healing workshop," I told him.

"A ... what?"

I quickly ran my sales totals while Mike ranted and raved. I paid no attention to him and finished my task, then pulled the cash drawer out and we left the shop. I locked the door and Mike followed as I led the way to Aunt Rosalee's office. We passed the front desk, where Gena stood up and watched as we walked by. There were still a lot of people milling around in the halls and great room. The dining room was filled as we passed it.

Aunt Rosalee was running some photocopies off when we arrived at the office. She noticed Mike and smiled. "May I help you?" she asked him.

"Aunt Rosalee, this is my friend, Mike Rollins from Kansas," I said.

She pointed to her desk in the inner office and I took the

cash drawer in and set it down.

Mike stood at the door, one hand braced against the wall. "So you're Rosalee Sutton," he said.

"Yes, I am." The machine continued to spit out copies.

"Then you're the one who's responsible for conning Juniper into staying here." His tone had darkened.

Afraid Mike might make a scene, I quickly stepped back into the main room. "Mike and I are going to get some lunch," I explained quickly.

"I don't know what you mean," Aunt Rosalee said to Mike. "I haven't conned Juniper into anythin'."

Before any more could be said, Starla burst in from the hallway. Today she wore a teal pant suit and had streaks of teal paint in her black hair that draped her slender shoulders. "Rosalee, no one has seen Taffi. She's missed all her morning appointments and her handwriting analysis workshop is supposed to begin in half an hour." Starla turned to me. "Juniper, have you talked to Taffi today?"

"No, she never came back to the room last night," I told them. Now I was really worried. Where was Taffi?

Aunt Rosalee left the copy machine and picked up the telephone at Lance's desk. "Gena," she said after a pause, "call up to Taffi's room, would you please? I want to see if she's there."

Starla fretted. "I don't have a very good feeling about this, you know. Taffi was worried about something yesterday. It's not like her to just go off like this without telling someone."

I told Starla that the room looked as though it had been broken into last evening during Vlad Petrovsky's lecture. Her heavily made up eyes grew large and she shook her head in dismay. "This is not good."

All this time, Mike just stood there in the doorway, staring at Starla and saying nothing. Aunt Rosalee put the phone down and said, "She's not there." Both women stared at one another in alarm. "I say we give her another half hour," Aunt Rosalee finally said. "Maybe she left the lodge to ground herself. She'll probably show up."

Starla threw her hands up in the air in one of her dramatic gestures, then left the office.

I noticed Mike was fading from fatigue. "Aunt Rosalee, are there any rooms left for Mike to stay in? I think he needs to get some sleep. He drove all night to get here."

"I think we can arrange it," she said, at once forgetting that the man—only moments ago—had accused her of conning me. "I can always get Wes and Drake to double up in order to make space."

Mike was too worn out to argue, so I escorted him to the dining room, where we got something to eat and some coffee for Mike. I had tea. Then I led him to the front desk to get registered. I noticed that I was going to be late for the energy healing workshop.

Gena had just been on the phone with Aunt Rosalee and was expecting us. She seemed cheery and helpful as she took care of Mike. I excused myself to go to the lounge, where the energy healing workshop was being held on one side of the room, which had been partitioned off for that purpose.

The class had already begun and I slipped into a seat. I was surprised to find Nadine Leachfield at this workshop. I knew she had been to one yesterday, when I'd found Thelma watching Max in the kitchen. Later, when we had a chance to exchange a few words, Nadine told me she'd been to three workshops already. This surprised me, since she had hinted that the workshops were expensive and she couldn't afford to go to any except the free one given to her by Aunt Rosalee.

A little dark-haired Asian woman in her forties was the teacher. She called herself "Chi" and she demonstrated on each of the workshop participants how she used the energies around us and the electromagnetic fields of the earth to heal our bodies. She called it polarity balancing and also mentioned the use of Reiki as one of her tools.

I found the workshop interesting. When it was my turn to lie on the table and experience a treatment, I could actually feel heat from Chi's hands and the movement of energy shifting through different parts of my body. When the workshop ended after two hours, I checked with the front desk to see what room Mike was in, but decided not to waken him. Instead, I headed upstairs to Taffi's room.

Clover came out of her room just as I reached the top of the stairs. She beckoned to me, so I turned and headed over.

"I wanted to talk to you." Clover pulled me inside and closed her door. "You look stressed out. Here, sit down and let me, like … work on your neck and shoulders a little."

"You don't have to," I protested, but Clover ignored me and gently pushed me into a chair. She moved behind me, so she could massage my neck. It felt better than anything at that moment.

"What did you want to talk about?" I asked. "Vlad? Or Wes?"

Clover sighed, still working my tight muscles. "Juniper, I don't know what to do. I, like … thought I was doing really well with Vlad. He and I just sort of, like … clicked. You know what I mean?"

"Well, what happened?"

"Wes suddenly, like … started showing interest in me again. Now I can't make up my mind."

I hesitated before I asked, "So what do you want *me* to do about it?" It sounded colder than I had intended it to.

Clover sighed again. "I just wanted to, like … talk it over with someone," she said, "and you're such a good listener."

"Are you in love with Vlad?" I asked.

"I don't know."

"Well, are you in love with Wes, then?"

"No … yes! Oh, Juniper, I think I'm, like … in love with both of them." She halted the mini massage and sat on the couch, a glum look on her face.

"How do they feel about you?" I asked.

"I'm not sure. Vlad can have, like … any woman he wants. I'm sure he'll soon get tired of me."

"And what about Wes?"

She sighed. "It seems like Wes shows an interest in a woman only when there's, like … competition. You saw how he was around Vlad."

I nodded. I certainly had noticed how Wes behaved around other men. This morning—in the gift shop—had he considered Mike to be competition? Was that the reason he had paid me special attention? I didn't mention my own experiences with Wes to Clover. I thought it was better to say as little as possible about my own feelings when it came to men … especially now that my attitude had shifted toward Drake. I hadn't been able to get him off my mind all day. Now I suddenly wished I could talk to him. Drake would know exactly how to handle my new problem with Mike.

"I heard Taffi took off," Clover said. "She didn't, like ... show up for her class this afternoon."

This news disturbed me more. "Where would she have gone?" I asked, but Clover shrugged.

"Gena's ex-husband was on the grounds yesterday. Did you hear about that?" Clover asked. She had shifted from self pity to gossip mode.

"Her ex-husband?"

"Yes, Al Howard," said Clover. "I guess he, like ... tried to see Gena."

"What did he do?"

"I heard Starla talking to Simone and her daughter about it at breakfast this morning," Clover revealed. "Gena's ex isn't, like ... supposed to come anywhere near her, but they were, like ... seen together out by the garden last evening—just after Vlad's talk."

"But Gena was at the meditation," I recalled.

"She met Al during the break," said Clover. "Linda, Simone's daughter, was near the garden area, having a cigarette, and saw them talking. Apparently, Gena and Al didn't know anyone was nearby. Linda said they kissed, and then Gena hurried back inside and never noticed Linda sitting there in the dark."

This was strange information. Yesterday morning, Gena had come into my shop, upset because her brother-in-law, Roy Howard, had come into the lodge—allegedly to cause trouble. If she was so repelled by her ex-husband—so as to have a court order against him coming near her—then why did she meet him in secret and even *kiss* him? It didn't add up.

I stayed and chatted with Clover a while longer. She soon changed the subject to the dance and what she was going to wear. Her dilemma over the men in her life seemed to dissipate as we discussed other things. Finally, I had to leave. It was getting late, and I wanted to freshen up before it was time to go to dinner and then attend the dance.

As expected, there was no Taffi in the room when I let myself in. Everything seemed to be in order, except that the answering machine was blinking. I went over to it and saw that eight messages had been left. I played all the messages back.

Each one of them was for Taffi, mostly clients wanting to know why she hadn't kept her appointments. One was Gena from that afternoon. There were no mysterious calls—no one with a warning message. I left the messages alone, then freshened up and changed into my outfit that Clover had recommended for tonight's dance.

There was still a little time before dinner, so I reached for one of Cyril Jorgensen's books that I'd just started reading. As I opened to the page that was bookmarked, a small extra piece of paper fluttered out onto the carpet. I reached over and picked it up and noticed it had been folded in two.

Right away I saw that my name had been written on the outside of the note. The writing was in Taffi's hand, so carefully executed because of her expertise. But before I could open up the scrap of paper, someone knocked on my door. I thrust the note into my purse beside the bed, and then went to see who was at the door.

19

I opened the door and there stood Mike, still rather sleepy-eyed. "Can I come in?" he asked.

"Sure, Mike." I let him in and closed the door.

"Wow, that's some outfit." He looked me over. "What are you all dolled up for?"

I explained about the dance being held tonight in the garden, then invited Mike to sit down. I noticed he appeared calmer, but I still didn't trust him to accept my position. I kept my guard up.

"We need to talk," said Mike.

"If it's about my leaving the Rainbow Majestic, you can save your breath," I told him. "I've already made up my mind. I'm not going back to Kansas with you."

Mike looked defeated and hung his head. "I don't think you understand everything that's going on here, Juniper."

"I'm learning new things every day," I told him.

"No, I'm talking about the lodge itself," said Mike. "I've been working on your mother's estate while you've been gone. There are a few things I think you ought to know. One of them is how your uncle and aunt acquired this property. There's been some shady dealings in the past in regard to the Majestic Mountain Lodge."

"I don't know what you're talking about," I replied.

"Well, of course you don't. That woman has kept things from you."

"You mean Aunt Rosalee?"

"She might seem to you to be your sweet and loving aunt, but ... Juniper, the truth is ... she may not even own this lodge."

"Mike, what are you saying?"

"How can I put this so it doesn't shock you?" He stood up and started pacing the floor. "I've done some digging, and there is a group of investors who have a big stake in the lodge. They are the ones who put up the money for them to buy it—and to get the place renovated."

I disbelieved Mike and was a little miffed at his attempt to undermine Aunt Rosalee's image. "Okay, who are these so-called investors?"

"That's something you need to ask your aunt," he said.

"You mentioned Mother's estate," I said. "What does the lodge have to do with that?"

"Before your Uncle Fred died, he contacted your mother. This was when she still had a few of her faculties left. There was a letter in Margaret's safe deposit box at the bank that you didn't know about."

"What did it say?" I sat up straighter.

"Your uncle wrote to her and told her that in his will he was leaving his share—his interest—in the Majestic Mountain Lodge—to you, because of the guilt he had carried over the shooting death of your father."

"Mother never told me this. Neither did Aunt Rosalee," I protested.

"Your mother either literally forgot, or ... she didn't want you to know."

"Well, if she didn't want me to know about it, why did she keep the letter and place it in her safe deposit box?"

"I, too, am puzzled why she didn't simply throw the letter away," said Mike, "but we have to remember her state of mind at the time."

I knew how much my mother had loathed anything to do with Uncle Fred and Majestic Mountain. Even in her demented condition, she had managed to keep this from me. But what about Aunt Rosalee? If it was true—and Uncle Fred had willed me part ownership of the lodge—why hadn't my aunt told me as soon as I arrived here?

"What bothers me," said Mike, "is that you weren't personally notified by your uncle's attorney after his passing."

"Could Mother have prevented that?" I asked.

"It's highly probable," said Mike.

"Maybe it's not even true," I challenged. "Just because there was a letter from Uncle Fred—saying he *intended* to leave me part of his estate—doesn't mean he carried it out. I'd have to see his will."

Mike frowned. "You're right, he could very well have

changed his mind. Maybe Margaret changed his mind. She was good at telling lies toward the end."

I remembered well enough how the brain disease worked and nodded my head sadly. Then I asked, "Tell me what you meant by 'shady dealings.' What were you referring to?"

"Your uncle didn't have the money to purchase the lodge, so he relied on more creative means."

"Mike, come on—stop baiting me. Just tell me."

"He had contacts through his many years of outfitting for rich clients. He was able to finagle his way into convincing some investors who were connected to the mob to lend him the money."

"The mob!" I cried. "Mike, you can't be serious. I don't believe it."

"The investors who loaned them money were known for starting up gambling casinos in out-of-the-way towns. They were ... and I should say, *still are* ... active in pursuing their goal with the Rainbow Majestic."

"What! No way!" But I was recalling the phone conversation I'd overheard when I'd walked in on Lance yesterday afternoon. I also was remembering the argument Aunt Rosalee and Lance had been involved in over financial reports.

"The best thing you can do, Juniper, is pack your bags right now and leave with me. You don't want to get involved with gangsters."

"Aunt Rosalee is not a gangster," I told Mike. "In fact, I don't believe any of what you've told me."

"Suit yourself. I'm leaving for Great Bend in the morning." Mike stood up and started for the door. "I expect that sooner or later you'll see that I'm right." Without waiting for a comment from me, Mike went out the door and closed it behind him.

I was so upset by Mike's visit that I could only sit there— stewing—for the next half hour. The information he had given me seemed preposterous, yet doubts and suspicions seeped into my mind. I wanted to talk this over with someone. I knew that now was not the time to consult Aunt Rosalee, but I made up my mind I would talk to her about Mike's claims the first chance I got.

I found myself again wishing I could talk to Drake. He might be able to provide some answers. He had known Uncle Fred and Aunt Rosalee at the time they had purchased the lodge property, because he had told me just this morning that he'd bought the ten acres from them at that time.

Just who could the infamous investors be, to whom Mike referred? And was it truly possible that they owned a large interest in the Rainbow Majestic and wanted to reclaim it from Aunt Rosalee and turn it into a gambling casino? The horror of that happening was just too much to bear.

I finally got up and retouched my makeup, then went downstairs for dinner. Tonight Aunt Rosalee insisted I sit at the table she shared with Simone Sullivan and her daughter. There was little chance of discussing anything with her in their company. I looked around for Gena, but apparently she was busy getting things set up for the dance, which was being held after dinner.

I was lost in my own thoughts as I ate, barely aware of the friendly chatter going on between Simone and Aunt Rosalee. Across the room were scattered the people I'd come to know and love. Clover was laughing and enjoying herself with a table of guests which included Vlad Petrovsky. Starla was entertaining another table of guests, who were obviously captivated by her exotic manner. No sign of Wes or Cyril, so I assumed they hadn't returned yet from seeing Celeste in the hospital. Drake was nowhere to be seen, but I figured he might be in the kitchen with the old cook, Thelma. The Leachfield family had joined another party of guests this evening. Little Max caught me staring at him and he waved at me. I waved back, wondering about Lance and his connections.

Now, if only I could see Taffi sitting at someone's table— discussing their handwriting—I'd feel better. It mystified me that she had disappeared. I wondered if Starla and Aunt Rosalee had taken any action to try and locate Taffi. Perhaps Taffi had notified them this afternoon. No one seemed too concerned about her at the moment.

Mike had not come into the dining room. I guessed he had gone back to bed. I was grateful, at least, that he had not caused a big scene. Thinking over his visit to my room earlier, I suddenly remembered that when he'd knocked, I had been on the verge of looking at the scrap of paper with Taffi's handwriting on it. I reached for my purse and opened it, searching for the note. I pulled it out and opened it up in front of me. It contained a list of names:

> Fred Sutton
> Nathaniel Sutton
> Gena Sutton
> Cyril Jorgensen
> Roy Howard
> Al Howard

Six names were listed. What did they mean? Obviously, Taffi had purposely stuck this scrap of paper into the book she guessed I was reading—in hopes that I'd discover it. Was this the list of persons who had been in the hunting party at Diamond Reservoir the day my father was killed? It had to be.

Gena had been there—and so had Cyril. Gena would only have been a girl. She couldn't have been more than fourteen at the time. Why had she been included in this list? The two Howard brothers were also listed. Drake had told me they used to be regulars at the hunting lodge in those days—and so had Cyril. All of them must have been present on that fateful day, if Taffi's findings were correct. And one of them had fatally wounded my father. But which one?

"What's that you've got there?" Aunt Rosalee's voice startled me out of my musing. I was suddenly aware of her glancing at the note in front of me. I made an instinctive move to cover the names with my hand.

"Juniper?" Aunt Rosalee looked at me curiously. "Is somethin' wrong?"

When I looked up, I noticed Simone staring at me, a disturbed look in her eyes.

"Uh ... no, nothing's wrong." I tried to fold up the note, but my fingers trembled.

"What's that piece of paper?" she asked.

"It's ... it's nothing. Just ... just something I had in my purse." I was afraid she was going to snatch it from me, but she simply sighed.

"Prob'ly a love note," she joked. "I'll bet I know who from, too."

Simone's gaze remained fixed on me. "No," she said, "it's not anything of the kind. Is it, Juniper?"

I swallowed and started to place the note back in my purse. When I looked into Aunt Rosalee's face, I made an instant decision and retrieved the note and handed it to her. "Maybe you can make sense of this," I said.

Aunt Rosalee opened the scrap of paper and studied it. She didn't seem upset by what she saw, but she asked, "Where did you get this?"

I told her how the note had fallen out of the book by Cyril Jorgensen.

"His name's on the list," she remarked. "I wonder if he wrote this."

"It's in Taffi's handwriting," I confessed. "Taffi left it for me to find, I'm quite sure."

Aunt Rosalee handed the note over to Simone, who scrutinized it with Linda straining her neck to get a glimpse.

"Does it mean anything to you?" I asked my aunt.

"I'm not sure," she replied.

Simone set the paper on the table and held the palms of both her hands over it a couple of inches. "There's a feeling of desperation here," she told us. She closed her eyes, then opened them again. "I can sense some kind of fear coming from Taffi when she wrote these names."

"My God," breathed Aunt Rosalee. She turned her dark eyes back to me. "All of those people on the list were at Diamond Reservoir that day ... the day of the accident. I can't be absolutely sure, but I believe both Howard boys were along on that campout."

"And Gena too?" I asked.

"Yes, Gena went along with her father. She always wanted to go along. Gena would beg Fred to take her along—and he'd say she could go if she'd be the camp cook."

"So she was there ... then she must know ..." I mused.

"Gena's never talked about the accident," said Aunt Rosalee. "She was in the cook's tent, where she slept, and Fred always claimed he and Nathaniel were cleanin' the guns outside when the rifle went off." She looked at me fearfully. "But what I don't understand is what Taffi meant by givin' you this."

I was reading Aunt Rosalee's look that told me not to disclose what the two of us had discussed earlier—about what had been said before her husband died. I took the hint and simply said, "I don't know. We'll never know, unless we find Taffi."

Simone handed the note back to me with a sigh. "Well, I'm not picking up anything about it," she said. "I'm drawing a blank."

"What, Mom, are you losing your touch?" asked Linda. She had meant it jokingly, but Simone shot her daughter a venomous look.

To change the subject, Aunt Rosalee stood up from the table. "I believe the DJ has probably arrived by now for the dance. I'm goin' to go check on things out in the garden patio."

"I'll come with you," I said quickly. To my relief, Simone and her daughter stayed behind. Once outside the dining room, I said, "Aunt Rosalee, we need to talk. I'm terribly worried about Taffi, and I'm concerned about this note, as well as some other things that have been brought to my attention."

"Where's your friend from Kansas?" asked Aunt Rosalee.

"He's probably in his room asleep."

"Are you plannin' on returnin' home with him?"

I looked at my aunt in surprise. I had never seen her as worried as she was now. "No. Mike told me someone called him and said I wanted to go back to Kansas. That's the reason he showed up here. But I have no intention of doing that."

"Oh, thank goodness." Aunt Rosalee sighed in relief. We headed outside. "Juniper, I can't talk about it right now, but I have some disturbin' news I need to discuss with you. What are you doin' tomorrow mornin'?"

I told her I was meeting with Starla at eight o'clock for my awakening.

"Well, come to my suite after lunch," she said. "It's down the hall from my office. You can't miss it. We'll talk then." She smiled. "And don't look so gloomy. You're goin' to the dance, not a funeral. All those dashin' young men are gonna wanna sweep you off your feet. If only I were twenty years younger."

The outdoor patio and garden area was all lit up when we stepped out the back door. Gena and her helpers had decorated with luminaries around the pond, candles and torches stuck in the ground, and solar lanterns placed along walkways. Music was already playing into big speakers. People were gathering around, talking and getting festive. The sun was setting in the west while the sky in the east—over Majestic Mountain—reflected a magenta alpenglow with wisps of pink clouds. Although cool, the air felt refreshing and vibrant. Aunt Rosalee wandered over to talk to Gena and the DJ, who was adjusting his equipment.

"Hi, Juniper." Clover came over, her arm linked in Vlad's. "Ooh, the skirt looks awesome on you."

Vlad grinned at me. "Yes, you are lovely lady tonight," he said in his heavy Russian accent. "I dance with you later, okay?"

I smiled at them both. "Have you seen Drake?" I asked Clover.

"No, but I'm sure he's around somewhere." Then she asked, "Where's Wes? I didn't see him at dinner."

I explained how Wes had taken Cyril to see Celeste in the hospital, but that he'd promised to be back for the dance. The two of them drifted away and then Starla came over, dressed up in a long-sleeved, sparkly black gown with sequins and a low neckline. A silver chain with a beautiful turquoise stone hung from her slender neck.

"Remember, eight o'clock," she told me.

"I haven't forgotten," I replied.

"Oh, Celeste would have loved this!" Starla spun around in a circle. "Having the dance outside was certainly one of Gena's brighter ideas."

"Gena's?" I made a face, but didn't disclose that it had actually been my idea to hold the dance outdoors.

The music changed all of a sudden. The DJ spoke a few words of welcome and invited everyone to start dancing. Then, a moment later, some rock music from the '70s blared out of the speakers.

"Too loud!" several people shouted. A few seconds later, the volume was lowered.

Starla grinned at me. "Enjoy yourself tonight, Juniper. Don't worry about anything, just let yourself be free." She caught sight of somebody in the crowd. "Oh, there's Daniel, my friend from Wade City. Excuse me, will you, dear?" She streaked away.

More people had moved outside now and couples were starting to dance. For a while I just stood and listened, watching and basking in the gaiety of the evening. The DJ had brought a wide mix of tunes. A country melody came on next, followed by some Reggae. I found myself falling into the beat as I wandered slowly through the crowd.

The almost full moon appeared over Majestic Mountain, adding heightened excitement to the evening. Several people had noticed it and were pointing and exclaiming over the sight. I peered at the huge sphere of golden light and suddenly wished Drake had come to the dance. I remembered earlier that day when he had drawn me into his lap on the floor of the cabin. How good that had felt.

Then, suddenly, I felt someone tap my shoulder. Turning around, I came face to face with Wes—his blue eyes smiling down at me. A lively Latin dance had just begun to play.

"Come on, Juniper, dance with me," said Wes, and pulled me into the circle of dancers.

Surprised, but pleased to see him, I protested, "I don't know how!"

"Try it," he begged. "It's not that hard."

"But, I've never ..."

Wes took hold of me and gently steered me next to the pond. "Don't worry. There's nothin' to it. Just let me lead you around a bit. Move your feet backwards when I go forwards."

I laughed to cover up my clumsiness and embarrassment. Wes laughed too, but held onto my waist firmly as we moved into the circle. It wasn't long before I started to get the hang of it and was able to fake my way through the number. I was relieved when the music ended and Wes led me over to the walkway next to the path by the woods. He still held my hand. "That wasn't bad ... for your first tango."

"Is that what we were doing?" I laughed. "You're a very good dancer, Wes."

He looked around. "I thought your friend would be here with you."

"You mean Mike? He's probably sleeping," I said. "Besides, he's leaving in the morning."

"I see," said Wes.

"How's Celeste?" I asked. "And how was your trip?"

"Everything went fine. Celeste's hangin' in there. She's a dear old lady." He shook his head sadly. "Cyril managed to comfort her a little, I believe. He's pretty much out of it now, though. He went up to bed."

I was disappointed because I had hoped to catch Cyril after he returned and ask him about being one of those in my father's hunting party.

Wes had spotted Clover dancing with Vlad to some new music—this time an old Elvis Presley number. Clover was doing a version of the twist—really putting herself into it—and Vlad laughed and clapped his hands. All the dancers were doing their own thing. I noticed Wes staring at the two of them, and suddenly I had the feeling I had lost his attention completely.

I let go of his hand as my spirits sank. Then I looked around, trying to find some excuse to wander away from him. I was disappointed in myself for feeling elated because he had danced with me and held me. Now, I knew without a doubt—he was pining for Clover.

Then I saw Drake sitting by himself on the bench beside the garden. He was watching the crowd and turned to look at me as I walked over to him. "Hello, Drake."

"Juniper," he grumbled. He didn't seem very happy.

I sat down next to him and watched people as we both remained silent for several moments. Then I said to him, "What are you doing here? I thought you didn't like dances."

"I don't," he muttered. Then he turned to eye me. "Why aren't you out there dancing?"

"I was."

He studied me and rubbed his beard. "That's a really becoming dress."

"Thank you."

"I would think every eligible man out there would be wanting to dance with you."

"I guess I'm more the wallflower type," I said. "But I enjoy the music and watching the people." Now there was a slow dance number playing. I watched Wes approach Clover—who had been mingling with some people—and she turned and met his look with a smile. The next moment, the two of them were dancing in the circle of couples.

"Wouldn't you like to be out there now?" asked Drake.

My heart beat a little quicker as I wondered if Drake was

building up courage to ask me to dance. But right away he spoiled it.

"*You* could be the one in Wes's arms right now—instead of Clover," he said derisively.

Defiance swelled within me. "Well, I'm not. I'm sitting here with *you*."

He turned to me with a mocking smile. "But you'd rather be in her place. You think I don't know?"

Anger and hurt juggled back and forth. I could feel my face turning red. I had not expected this streak of jealousy in Drake. How could I make him believe that in actuality I preferred *his* company to that of Wes? But at the moment I felt tongue-tied and insulted by his presumption. I stood up.

"Where are you going?" asked Drake. "Don't tell me you're going to cut in?"

Humiliation rose to a peak. I was just about to lash out at Drake when I heard someone call my name. Nadine Leachfield came running from the back door of the lodge, holding up her long yellow dress. "Juniper! Oh, Juniper, come quick! We need your help."

I immediately followed Nadine as she turned back toward the lodge. Drake got up and followed me, perhaps sensing something was wrong by the look on Nadine's face.

"It's Max," she cried as we hurried through the hallway, past the lobby and on toward the spiral staircase.

"What's happened?" I asked. Drake was at my heels and I was aware of guests looking up at the three of us in surprise as we passed.

"I don't know!" Nadine was close to tears. "He won't tell us. But he asked for you." She led us up the stairs to the second floor and down the corridor that led to the back stairway and the closed-off section that was supposed to be locked.

We found Max huddled in a corner of the stairwell—hiding his face in his lap—with his knees drawn up. He whimpered while his father, Lance, knelt beside him, unsuccessful in his attempts to get the small boy to tell him what was wrong. When we approached, Nadine crouched in front of her son and said, "Max, Juniper is here now. Please, will you talk to her?"

I knelt beside the boy and he uncovered his face, which wore a look of horror. "Max? What is it?"

"Juniper ..." His lower lip trembled. "You've got to go in there ... now ..."

"Where?" I looked at the door that led to the narrow stairway to the attic room. "You mean ... up there?"

"No ... the room ... with the ... the harp." He covered his face again, as if thinking about it was too much to bear.

"The auditorium?"

Lance made a face and looked at Nadine. "That part of the lodge is closed off."

"Was Max in there?" Nadine asked me.

"We both were," I confessed. "Max, I'll go, but can you tell me what you saw?"

He shook his head vigorously, still covering his face. The boy was clearly traumatized.

"I'll go with you," said Drake.

"I don't know if you can squeeze through the passageway," I said. "It's very narrow in places."

Lance stood up while Nadine wrapped her arms around Max to comfort him. "I'm going to find Rosalee," he said. "She needs to know about this." He sauntered off.

"We may need a flashlight," I told Drake.

"You're right," he replied. "The electricity's been shut off in the old wing."

"Is there another way to get into it?" I asked.

"I believe so. Come on." He turned around and said, "Nadine, you bring Max."

I followed Drake back down the hallway. We wound through hallways I hadn't explored and through a door that I had thought was just a storage room. Drake switched on the light and we came to another door that had a sign that said: NO ADMITTANCE. When he tried to open it, it was locked.

"I'm sure Lance or Rosalee has the key," said Drake. "This door will take us down a flight of stairs—straight into the burned area."

"Can't we get there from the first floor?" I inquired.

"No, it's boarded up and nailed shut," explained Drake.

There was a commotion in the hallway outside the storage room. A moment later, Aunt Rosalee, Lance and Starla entered the room. Aunt Rosalee was furious. "No one is supposed to go in that part of the lodge," she commanded. "How did the boy get into the auditorium?"

"He used the secret passageways," I said.

Aunt Rosalee looked at me, startled. Then she examined a ring of keys, trying to find the one that would open this door.

"I'm afraid my curiosity got the better of me," I said apologetically. "Max showed me the secret passageways and—when I got a chance—I explored them."

Aunt Rosalee held her temper, but I could tell she didn't approve of what I had done. She couldn't find her key and was getting frustrated. Finally, Lance produced the right key to the door that opened up into the old stairway.

"Drake, bring that flashlight that's on the shelf over there," said Aunt Rosalee. "We're gonna need it. The electricity's off in that part of the lodge."

Drake found the light and then led the way down the stairs and into the charred corridor that was part of the old lodge. Aunt Rosalee followed after him, while Lance, Starla and I tailed them. As Drake played the flashlight beam over the blackened walls, I saw where the fire had done damage to some of the rooms on the first floor. I realized these must have been the living quarters of Uncle Fred, Aunt Rosalee and Gena at that time.

The dressing room to the auditorium was ahead, where the fire had purportedly started, but we turned a corner into a main hallway that used to lead to the first floor lobby. Drake had said this exit had been boarded up at the other end. When we reached the auditorium entrance, we all stood in the aisle by the doorway as Drake directed the light over the shabby seats and the curtains at the side of the stage. His light rested a second or two on the harp, which had been overturned and now lay on the floor.

Then, as Drake's light beam swept over the stage area, Starla let loose a blood-curdling scream. On the floor of the proscenium—face down—lay a plump woman with short brown hair, her hand outstretched in front of her, stiff and curled. A gold cord from the stage curtains was wrapped around her neck.

20

It took me several seconds to recover from the shock of seeing Taffi's dead body in the auditorium. Starla continued to shriek and carry on. Aunt Rosalee teetered, but luckily I was standing close enough to grab her or she might have collapsed.

Lance and Drake simultaneously rushed over to the stage floor to kneel beside Taffi.

"Don't anyone touch her," commanded Aunt Rosalee.

"She's been here awhile," said Drake. "She was strangled, by the looks of it."

"Lance, you'd better go call the police," directed Aunt Rosalee.

Lance stumbled to his feet and came to stand beside us in the doorway. Starla continued to wail.

Aunt Rosalee said to Starla, "Go with Lance." Then, turning to me, she said, "Juniper, take Starla somewhere and get her calmed down."

I could hardly find my voice, but nodded my head and led Starla back down the charred hallway after Lance. The only light came from the storage room upstairs, through which we had come. Starla kept sobbing, "Poor, poor Taffi," and "Who could have done this to her?"

Nadine and Max, along with a few other people, had gathered outside the hallway near the storage room. Nadine gasped when she saw our faces and Max's eyes were huge. I realized the boy had been the first one to find Taffi's body. It must have terrified him so much that he couldn't tell anyone—and since he knew that I could get into the auditorium, he had asked his parents to get me.

"What happened?" demanded Nadine.

Lance took her aside to tell her, so that no one else in the hall could hear. But Starla's outbursts sent a wave of panic into the guests. One of them pulled out a cell phone to call "911" while Lance comforted his family.

What followed was confusion. Word of Taffi's death spread through the Rainbow Majestic and in no time at all people crowded the hallways and frantically speculated that there was a psychotic killer on the premises. This was the last thing Aunt Rosalee needed. Many of the light workers banded together and decided to do something to calm everyone and bring about a sense of peace.

I was surprised at how quickly Starla let go of her shock and fell into the role of pacifier. She right away organized a spontaneous group meditation in the lounge. People were congregating for it half an hour later, when the police and ambulance crew arrived from Wade City.

"Juniper, we just heard!" Clover—with Wes behind her— hurried toward me outside the lounge. "How awful!"

"Hey, you're shakin'." Wes placed a gentle hand on my shoulder. "Are you all right?"

"I'm ... okay."

Clover looked around. "What can we do?"

"You can help Starla get everyone calmed down," I said. "The police just arrived. I'm sure Aunt Rosalee doesn't want a panic."

"We'll do what we can," promised Wes. He led Clover into the lounge.

As soon as I knew Starla had herself and the majority of lodge guests under control, I went back to the second floor entrance to the old part of the lodge. Drake had somehow managed to reconnect the electricity. Now there were lights to that part of the building. Lance stood guard at the storage room entrance, to keep people out, and Nadine had taken Max back to their room. I found Aunt Rosalee in the auditorium, now confronted by the sheriff's deputies. It was clear she had been crying. She dabbed at her eyes with her sleeve.

Drake appeared quite suddenly at my side. "How are you holding up?" he asked me.

"I'm not sure," I admitted.

He found my hand and squeezed it, then let go of me.

Aunt Rosalee told the police what she knew—how we had found Taffi—while a couple of EMTs examined the body and covered Taffi with a sheet. The questioning came next. Two detectives—a man and a woman—took testimony from those of us who had discovered the body. I explained my connection to little Max and told them he had been the first to find Taffi. Lance was asked to summon his wife and son for questioning, so he left to bring them.

"No one is to leave the premises," ordered one of the deputies.

"Well, I'm afraid several of them have left already," said Gena, who had joined us. "There are people checking out as we speak."

A deputy was sent downstairs to the lobby to keep guests from leaving. "Those who absolutely need to leave must write down their contact information," the detective ordered. "We will need to question those who had any contact with Miss Kincaid."

"I'll go downstairs and help with that." Gena quickly left.

"Miss Sutton." I turned to face the woman detective. "I understand you roomed with the deceased. Do you recall anything unusual that occurred in the last two days?"

Aunt Rosalee began to make faces at me. I couldn't tell if she was trying to warn me, or if it was simply concern for me after all that had happened. I felt I had to tell them about the break-in that had occurred last evening, and I also mentioned the threatening telephone message from Friday afternoon. The detectives took careful notes. However, I did not volunteer any information regarding Taffi's list of names that had been tucked into Cyril Jorgensen's book. I wanted to talk to Aunt Rosalee about it first. I only hoped I wouldn't be accused later of withholding incriminating information.

When the police questioned Max, I stood close by to catch every word. The boy was in his pajamas and had calmed down somewhat since I'd last seen him, but the incident had left him shaken. He clung to his mother's hand.

Max told everyone he had slipped into the passageway from the basement after the dance had started. He wanted to follow his route to the attic room, and had taken his dad's flashlight with him. Thelma was supposed to be watching him, but she was busy in the kitchen with the clean-up, and his parents had already left to go to the dance.

"I walked into that room ... with the stage," Max explained, "and I saw someone had knocked over the harp. I was gonna set it back up ... if I could ... and that's when I saw the lady on the floor."

"What did you do then, Max?" the man detective asked.

"I ran up the passageway to the attic ... because it's quicker. Then I came down those back steps and went out into the hallway. The maid saw me and scolded me." He began to sob now. "She ... she called my mom then." He covered his face and cried.

Nadine hugged her son, while Lance turned hard eyes on the detectives. "He's had enough questioning for one night."

"Thank you, Max," the woman detective said gently. "We won't ask you any more questions tonight."

"Nadine," said Aunt Rosalee, "why don't you take Max down to the kitchen and have Thelma make him some hot chocolate?"

This idea seemed to appeal to Max. He rubbed his eyes as his mother led him off.

"We'll need to have access to this area the remainder of the night," one of the deputies told Aunt Rosalee. "Forensics will need to be in and out, to collect specimens and take plenty of pictures. Do you have any idea who did this?"

Aunt Rosalee frowned. "I've already told y'all what I know. I have absolutely no idea who wanted to kill poor Taffi."

"It's too bad someone erased that message on the answering machine," the man detective told me. "It's the best lead we have right now to go on."

"Do you have any recollection of whose voice was on that message?" asked the woman detective.

I told them no, and that Taffi herself must have erased the message after listening to it. I had nothing more to offer them. We were all exhausted from the horrendous events of the evening.

"You'll spend the night in my suite," Aunt Rosalee insisted. She put her arm around me as we left the auditorium and the milling team of police. "They've already taped off your room, but we can stop there and collect the things you'll need for tonight."

Sure enough, we found yellow police tape stretched across the doorway of Room 224 after we returned from the old part of the lodge. I didn't remember when Drake had left us. Lance stayed behind to help in any way he could as they put up police tape in the back hallway. I was allowed to retrieve my toilet articles and some clothes, then followed Aunt Rosalee downstairs to her suite, feeling exhausted.

We met Starla talking with some people in the great room, and she turned to me. "Juniper, about the awakening ..."

"It's okay," I told her, "we can reschedule ..."

"No," she insisted. "No! I'm still up for it, if you are, dear. Now—more than ever—I think it's important that we do it." There was a look of urgency on her face, now streaked from the mascara which she hadn't bothered to wash off. "Eight o'clock, Juniper—in Room 207."

I managed a smile. "Eight o'clock it is," I said, then followed my aunt to her suite. At that point, I was so drained, I couldn't have argued if I wanted to.

The next morning, I awoke on Aunt Rosalee's daybed in her sitting room. It was a cloudy morning for once, and I realized neither of us had set an alarm. Glancing at the clock, I saw I had half an hour to get dressed, eat something and meet Starla for my awakening. Aunt Rosalee was still asleep in her bedroom and I didn't want to waken her, so I quickly pulled on a loose pair of slacks and my new rainbow T-shirt, then found my loafers. I felt groggy and spent. My mind was heavily laden from the awful memory of seeing Taffi's body in the auditorium. It still seemed so unreal. How could that jolly, vivacious young woman be dead?

Today was the final day of the holistic fair. It was early and only a couple of people were up, roaming around. Tables lay draped with covers or sheets over them as I looked toward the great room on my way to the dining hall. I was struck suddenly by the memory of Taffi's covered table in the lounge, and a sick feeling hit me.

I wasn't that hungry, but Starla had instructed me to eat something before the awakening. I sat at a small table with coffee and a bagel when Mike wandered in and saw me. He poured himself some coffee, then joined me at my table.

"What happened here last night?" Mike asked. "I heard sirens."

I quickly told him the events without giving too many details.

"I gather this woman was a friend of yours?" he guessed.

"We were roommates for the weekend." I lifted the half-empty coffee cup to my lips.

"Oh, I'm sorry," he mumbled.

My mind was numb and I didn't feel like talking to Mike. He seemed to sense this and drank his coffee quickly, then said, "I'm leaving for Kansas. You coming?"

I stared at Mike blankly. "No." Then I said, "And you may not be able to leave right away. The police have the lodge under investigation and said nobody could leave."

"What do you mean I may not be able to leave?"

"Check with Gena at the front desk," I said.

Mike swore under his breath.

I rose and grabbed my purse. "If you'll excuse me, I've got an appointment this morning."

To my surprise, he didn't ask what I meant. I climbed the spiral staircase and passed a sheriff's deputy coming down. I found Starla's room on the second floor and knocked on the door.

Starla opened it right away and greeted me with a smile. "Good morning, Juniper." She was dressed in a comfortable pink pants outfit and her black hair was gathered behind her head with a clip. She hadn't bothered to put on her usual makeup this early. "You look worn out. Did you sleep at all?"

"I must have. I don't remember."

She invited me in to a large, though modest room that had maroon drapes and carpeting. It was a large enough room to hold two queen beds, but one of the beds had been removed and in its place was a table around which, I presumed, she performed her awakenings on people. A sectional divider gave the awakening area a sense of privacy.

"Come over here, dear, and let's talk." Starla led me over to a desk, where she told me to sit while she pulled another chair over for herself. On the desk was a large blank sheet of drawing paper and a large box of crayons. I couldn't help but wonder what their purpose was.

She began by asking me a few questions about myself and my life before I arrived at the Rainbow Majestic. I found it was easy to talk to Starla, and she seemed interested in what I disclosed. I told her about my engagement to Sean and how he'd been killed in the war overseas, and then I told her about my mother's illness and how I'd taken care of her until her death only three weeks ago. It seemed now as though it had happened a much longer time ago.

We discussed my feelings about my mother's illness, how my mother had treated me toward the end of her life, and how she had treated me during my childhood. This led into the past that dealt with my father's accident, and how my mother had always kept me from knowing too much about him or his relatives here in Colorado.

Starla made no comments about my life. She merely asked questions, then scribbled notes to herself on a small pad of paper. "Okay, darling," she said with a smile, "I want you to draw me a picture while I go make things ready for your awakening."

"Draw a picture?" I scrunched up my face.

She indicated the crayons and paper, and nodded. "Yes, draw me a picture of anything you want. Whatever comes to your mind. I'll be right back." She stood up, leaving me to puzzle over what it was I should draw on the blank paper.

My mind was still full of last night's events. I thought about drawing the horrible scene in the auditorium, when we'd found Taffi, but I shook that idea away as I reached for a green crayon. I lifted the crayon to my nostrils and sniffed it. The memory of that wonderful waxy smell tugged at childhood pleasures—of being young, innocent and free of troubles and responsibility.

Suddenly, I felt carefree and imaginative—if only for that short time in Starla's room—and I began drawing a woods scene with evergreens and hills and a blue sky. I then drew in the log cabin, using burnt sienna and brown umber. To top it off, I put mountains in the background, and a man and woman looking out the front window of the cabin. I wasn't much of an artist, but I was fairly pleased with my colorful depiction of my recurring dream.

Starla returned then and picked up the drawing. She sat and studied it, then placed it down again in front of me. "That's really sweet, Juniper," she told me. "Now, tell me who that man is with you inside the cabin."

I stared at my drawing, then up at her. "I don't know."

"Yes, I think you do." She smiled. "But it's okay. You don't need to tell me. But before we move to the table, perhaps we need to talk about more of your issues." She crossed her legs, then asked, "What is it you want out of life, Juniper?"

I had to stop and think before I answered. "I suppose I want to experience love and a family ... and to know peace."

"Do you consider yourself not at peace now?" she asked.

"How can I be at peace when so many people I know have died?" A tremor of emotion ran through me.

"Death is only an illusion. Don't you know that?"

"I understand about our souls," I replied. "I know that when we die, we are merely stepping out of our bodies. I don't doubt that we go on, and even though I was raised to believe otherwise, I do believe our loved ones who departed are still with us."

"Tell me, what makes you believe that?" Starla challenged.

I sighed and stared into my lap. "I don't know ... maybe it's because I have dreams. I've dreamed many times of seeing Sean. I've dreamed about my father, and I think the other night I even dreamed I saw my mother." I looked up at Starla.

"Sometimes dreams are an important way in which our loved ones who have crossed over can communicate with us," said Starla.

"But I still miss them." A sob escaped. "And it seems so unfair that people die so young and unexpectedly. Sean had his whole life ahead of him." I burst into tears and began to cry hard now. "Even my father ... I barely knew him ... and now Taffi!"

Starla let me cry, and then she handed me a tissue. "We'll work on that this morning," she told me. "And now, tell me about this man named Mike, who is here. How do you feel about him?"

I looked at her, startled. "Mike's going back to Kansas. He thought he was going to marry me, but I don't love him. Mike can be very controlling."

"And you don't like that in a man?" she guessed.

I shook my head. "I don't like that in anybody."

"What qualities do you find attractive in a man?" Starla asked.

"Sensitivity," I replied right away, thinking of Wes. Then, thinking of Drake, I said, "Honesty ... and protectiveness."

"What about physical attraction?"

"I suppose that's what draws most people at first," I admitted, "but looks are only superficial. It's what's inside a person that counts—and how they feel toward me. Really, Starla, I've had so little experience with men. Sean was my first and only love."

"Until now?" she prompted.

I blushed, feeling as though she could somehow read my mind. It seemed more people were able to do that here at the Rainbow Majestic Lodge than not. "Okay, I'll admit it. I've been attracted to a couple of guys since I've been here." I waited, then asked, "Must I reveal their names?"

"No, dear." Starla stood up. "I think I've got enough to work with now. Let's go in here now. I'm going to start by washing your feet."

Starla turned on some soft new age music. I saw that she had lit candles near the table, where she told me to sit. I removed my shoes as instructed, and she took a bowl of warm water and bathed both my feet, then dried them with a towel. She then told me to lie back on the table, which was covered by some kind of cream-colored comforter that felt cozy and warm. I adjusted my head on a pillow, and then Starla asked me to close my eyes and just rest. She placed some crystals on top of me and then stood at my head and recited a prayer, calling upon her guides—as well as my guides and angels—and announced that the awakening was now to begin.

The music continued to play as I just lay there with my eyes closed, feeling more and more relaxed and calm. I could hear Starla moving around the table. I wasn't sure what she was doing, but I could feel the sweeping of air and the sound of something—like a huge feather being swished over my head and body. I could sense the placement of crystals on and around me, and I soon found that my mind wanted to wander.

Feeling completely relaxed and content, I began to get pictures in my mind's eye. I didn't fight them—I just let them appear—and then vanish. At first, all I saw were flashes of people or scenes from the Rainbow Majestic, the tables and exhibits I had visited downstairs during the fair, the therapists giving chair massages, the readers sitting and spreading cards out for clients. I relived a couple of sales that had occurred in my gift shop, and then I drifted to the lobby, where Gena was talking on the telephone at the front desk. Next, I was headed outdoors, floating down the steps to the parking lot.

I saw Wes in shorts and a yellow T-shirt, weed-eating along the side of the building, and then I saw Drake waiting for me on the ATV parked out front. As I climbed onto the back of the four-wheeler, I turned and watched Wes stare after us. He stopped weed-eating a moment and shaded his forehead, watching as I rode away on the ATV with Drake, holding onto Drake's back.

My reverie continued with the tree-lined landscape, the blue sky overhead and the mountains skirting the background of this lovely dream scene as I watched the road shoot under us and felt the wind blow through my hair. There was such a feeling of freedom, and holding onto Drake made me feel secure and safe. Then, he stopped at a place that was in the woods with evergreens. At first, I thought we had arrived at Drake's cabin, but instead, the landscape changed abruptly into a winter scene.

Naked aspen trees—mixed in with evergreens—stood in snow, and as white flakes fell from the sky, I saw an open area where three tents were pitched. They were large tents, made of canvas—like tents of long ago—and a column of smoke drifted out of the top of one of them. Suddenly, Drake was no longer there with me and neither was the four-wheeler we had been riding. I was standing in the snow—which was up to my knees—and I could hear voices arguing from the tents ahead. The sky was dark and gray, and I realized it was evening. Camp lanterns glowed from inside the tents, and the wind blew in cold gusts around me. I was suddenly cold and began to shiver. Not only that—I was afraid.

"Drake!" I shouted. "Drake, come back!" I was feeling panic stricken that he had left me here alone in these snowy woods at night. "Drake, don't leave me again ..." I began to sob, remembering now that sometime in the past I had felt abandoned by him. *When and where had that been?*

Suddenly, an explosive gunshot cracked through the frigid atmosphere and caused me to jerk, lying on Starla's table. I heard a girl scream and men's voices shouting from inside the tents. I watched as two male figures darted out into the dark, headed for an old pickup truck that was blanketed with snow. They frantically began brushing the snow away and shouted at each other as they attempted to start the engine. I walked toward them and the tents, and realized the two were just young men in their twenties.

Unseen, I hurried toward the opening of the tent, but just before I entered, a man stepped out of the tent flap and put his hands on my shoulders. "Juniper, it's all right now," he told me. He crouched down—because I was very small—and he smiled into my face, his green eyes twinkling. "I'm going home for a while." I recognized my father's face, which had such a serene look.

"Daddy," I cried. "What happened? Where are you going, Daddy?"

"Don't worry, Muffin," he said. "You'll be fine. I'll watch over you, but you won't be able to see me. One day you'll understand." He bent close and planted a kiss on my cheek. "I love you, Muffin. Goodbye." Then, suddenly, he walked off and left me in the snowstorm, which was swirling from so much wind and flakes that I could no longer see the camp nor the truck, or hear the voices and the girl's sobs. *I felt so alone!*

My father! I had just talked to my father at the scene of his death ... yet he had been so complacent and nonchalant. It was as though I really had been there ... I, the little five-year-old girl whom he used to call Muffin. Gut-wrenching sobs gushed forth as I began to cry on Starla's table.

The music played on and I heard Starla whipping that feather fiercely through the air, as if she were trying to sweep away—with fury—my negative emotions. When my sobs quieted, my mind lapsed once again into a relaxed state. I might have slipped off to sleep, except that suddenly—there in my mind's eye—was the cabin of my dreams. I saw quite clearly the surrounding woods, the blue sky and the little house of logs as I walked up the path toward it on a summer day, swinging a small basket at my side that contained freshly picked blackberries.

A fearful tension gripped me and I stopped. The dread I'd always felt upon approaching that cabin was strong, but now I could hear my father's voice behind me, serene and casual. "Go ahead and open the door, Muffin," he told me. "I'm here with you, and nothing can happen to you now. There is nothing to fear. Open the door to the truth."

My breathing came rapidly and I felt a cold sweat as I placed the berry basket down on the grass beside the door. My fingers trembled as I reached up to turn the doorknob, then stopped. "I can't," I cried. I shook my head from side to side on the table. "I don't want to open the door."

"Yes, you can," Starla's voice rang out. "Open the door, Juniper."

"No," I sobbed. "No ..."

"Muffin, I'm here to protect you." My father's soothing voice was as clear as if he really were in the room. I felt a sudden overpowering glow of love, like a wave of warm energy moving over my body, and it gave me new strength.

"Go ahead, Juniper," Starla told me.

Slowly, I turned the doorknob. The door swung inward and—at first—everything inside was dark. I waited for my breathing to return to normal, then picked up my berry basket and stepped in. Light from outside the cabin filled the inside room, and I saw a man lying on the bed.

I was no longer afraid as I recalled that this was my new home—and this was also my wedding day. The man, asleep on the bed, was my husband, and we were homesteaders who had come West with our families in a covered wagon. Drake had been a farmer's son and had fallen in love with me, the daughter of a preacher. We had been married that morning, and tonight would be our first time together. While he rested, I had gone to the woods to pick some berries to go with our supper. A big smile spread across my face and I was just getting ready to call his name.

Suddenly, a big strong arm grabbed me from behind the cabin door. I tried to scream, but the hand covered my mouth and nose as I struggled in the arms of an Indian man. The fear I had sensed before opening the cabin door now came back in a rush. I screamed and thrashed around on Starla's table, reliving the horrible scene. As I fought for my life, I caught sight of Drake lying in the bed, one bloody arm hanging down off the side. He had been scalped. In my last breath during the struggle with the Indian brave, our eyes met and he raised the knife in his hand above my head.

At that point—in that lifetime—I must have fainted, because the next thing I saw was my body in a heap on the dirt floor of the cabin, the blackberries scattered in every direction and an oozing puddle of my blood began to flow across the room. I was no longer in my body, but a spirit hovering near the ceiling of the cabin, and I felt my father take me lovingly in his arms and pull me away.

The reverie ended at that point. I opened my eyes and sat up on the table. Starla stood beside me. She watched me a moment, then set down her eagle feather and said a quick prayer in front of me.

"Juniper, that was awesome," said Starla. "How do you feel?"

Surprisingly, I felt calm. My tears ceased and I awoke to a new understanding as I looked around the room and blinked. "I'm ... okay," I told her.

"Do you want to talk about it?" she asked.

"In a minute."

"You take your time, dear. Lie back down and rest a bit, and when you're ready, we'll talk."

I took her advice, only because I felt emotionally exhausted. The warm glow of new understanding was with me, and I basked in that gentle energy for several minutes more as the music continued to play and to relax me.

Finally, I sat up. Starla came over, dragging a chair with her. I told her everything I had seen and she grew excited, because she had seen some of the same scenes. She told me I had successfully peeled away several layers of myself, shedding old energies that no longer served me. She said I should take it easy for the rest of the day—not do anything strenuous—just do what I felt like doing.

"Starla, I never expected the awakening to be ... such an awakening," I told her as we sipped herb tea half an hour later. She had made us a couple of cups in her personal coffee maker in the room. I was still struggling with the realization that Drake had been my husband in the frontier life with the cabin. But he—and I—had been killed before we had even come together as man and wife.

"Now you must learn to forgive," Starla told me.

I looked up at her. "Forgive who?"

"Drake ... for not protecting you then."

"How could he? He had already been scalped."

"And yourself ..."

"Yes," I breathed. "Now I understand what it's like to ... die."

"And ... someone else too," said Starla.

"Who?" I asked.

"You know who," she said with a smile.

"You mean ... the ... the Indian ... the ... the man who ..."

"Yes." Starla nodded and sipped her tea.

"Who was he?" I asked.

"I think you already know the answer," she said.

"Starla ..."

"You only need to remember," she said. "You're blocking it, but I saw too."

"Tell me who it was, Starla."

"No, it's up to you, darling."

I sighed in frustration. "I can't remember. I saw his face, but ... but I didn't recognize him."

"You don't want to admit it," she said. "But don't worry, Juniper. When the time comes, you will remember. And when you do, you must forgive."

21

Still feeling halfway in that "other world," I left Starla's room and returned to Aunt Rosalee's suite. When I got there, Simone Sullivan was just leaving. A frown crowded her face. She barely acknowledged me as my aunt welcomed me inside.

"Don't pay any attention to Simone," said Aunt Rosalee. "She was interrogated by the police this mornin'—and she's livid."

"Why is she so upset?" I asked.

"Somehow she blames me for what happened." Aunt Rosalee sighed. "And she's probably right. I should have been more concerned when Taffi disappeared. Maybe we should have called the police after your room was ravaged."

"Don't go blaming yourself," I told Aunt Rosalee. "Have the police been able to find out anything?"

Aunt Rosalee went to her door and peered out, then closed it again and locked it. She seemed worried to me—more than usual. "The sheriff's deputies came up with some disturbin' evidence," she disclosed. "Apparently Taffi had a great deal of money in her bank account."

I shrugged. "I really don't see what that has to do with anything. Just because..."

Aunt Rosalee interrupted me. "It was over five hundred *thousand dollars*," she exclaimed.

I winced. "Wow..."

"They'll check it out, of course, with the bank in Wade City when it opens tomorrow," said Aunt Rosalee, "but they asked me if I knew anythin' about it. The deposit was made just the day before yesterday."

"Well, do the police think there's a connection between the deposit and what happened to Taffi?" I asked.

"I don't know, Juniper." Aunt Rosalee sighed once more. "I think they've pretty much concluded their interrogations, at least. They're startin' to let people leave."

"What a shame the holistic fair had to end this way," I said. "Just think, if it hadn't been for Max, who knows how long it would have been before Taffi's body was found?" I shuddered at the thought.

Aunt Rosalee beckoned me over to the couch and we both sat. "I've got some things I want to discuss with you, Juniper. For one thing, I discovered my key missin' that goes to that hallway through the storage room."

"You mean, that entrance we went through last night to get to the auditorium?"

"Yes," she said. "Lance has a key, and I'm the only one who has the other."

"Gena doesn't have one?"

"No."

"So, what does this mean? Did someone take your key and gain access to the old part of the lodge? Do you think Taffi ...?"

"Someone who knew I had the key took it," said Aunt Rosalee. "I kept the key in the drawer of my desk. And they must have talked Taffi into goin' with them. Taffi considered herself a kind of ghost buster, you know. I used to tell people we had a ghost in that auditorium, so they'd stay away. I finally had to block off the old part with the addition of the storage room, in order to keep people out of there."

"But Max went there," I said. "He discovered all the secret tunnels. And I discovered them that day I found the stairway on the second floor that goes to the attic. The door was unlocked then."

"The maid was careless and didn't lock it back up," said Aunt Rosalee.

"But why would it have been unlocked then?"

"I suppose Gena had ordered some things to be moved up into storage."

That sounded plausible to me. Then I asked, "So, who could have taken your key and lured Taffi there? And did they mean to kill her? That would make it premeditated murder."

"The police said Taffi was strangled with that gold cord off the stage curtain. It would have to have been someone fairly strong. Taffi was a big woman and could handle herself."

"You're suggesting it was a man, then?"

Aunt Rosalee shook her head. "I just have no clue who

would want to do such a thing, or why any information was so important that someone would murder Taffi."

"That list of names I found," I said. "Taffi told me earlier she had found out who the people were that had been with my father at Diamond Reservoir the day he was killed. Besides my father and Uncle Fred, there was Gena, Cyril—and the two Howard boys."

"I didn't want you to tell the police about that list," said Aunt Rosalee. "I didn't want them jumpin' to conclusions. And I don't want you doin' that either, Juniper. For one thing, we don't know for sure that those *were* the members in the huntin' party. We're only guessin'."

"Well, Cyril ... or Gena ... should know."

"Yes, I think we need to talk to both of them," she agreed. "I just wonder how Taffi found out that information."

I thought about this, then said, "Someone may have told her, or ... maybe she picked something up by reading their handwriting." Then, I asked, "Aunt Rosalee, what caused the fire in the old auditorium?"

I had caught her off guard. Her dark eyes were wide as she glanced at me, then turned away. "If you must know—and you certainly have a right to—it was Gena," she told me.

"Was it intentional?"

"No," she said quickly, "though some people think so." She sighed. "Gena had a difficult adolescence. It's no wonder with the kind of mother she had. But it was from a cigarette left in a waste basket. Gena used to hide her smokin' habit from us by goin' in the dressin' rooms."

"Why did you stop the repairs in that part of the lodge?" I asked.

Aunt Rosalee shook her head. "It was too disturbin' to Gena. She convinced us to board up that part of the lodge for good, and since there was extensive damage, it made sense. Does that answer your question?"

"I suppose." I imagined that Gena had personal reasons that exceeded her stepmother's knowledge, but I accepted the explanation and let the subject rest.

Aunt Rosalee settled back on the couch. "Another thing I wanted to discuss with you was the gift shop. How do you feel about it so far?"

I told her I loved working in the gift shop, and so far I thought it had done remarkably well. She told me sales had been greater than she had hoped, but she also reminded me that business wouldn't always be that good, since the Rainbow Majestic wasn't booked with fairs and conferences all the time.

"We managed to actually turn a profit with this fair," said Aunt Rosalee. "That's the good news. But there's also a piece of bad news."

"What's that?" I asked.

Aunt Rosalee sighed. "The lodge's finances look grim. I just found out we're operatin' in the red. There's a balloon loan payment comin' up soon, and if I can't pay it, I might lose the Rainbow Majestic."

"Oh, Aunt Rosalee! Certainly with summer here and the tourist season ... and hunting season just ahead ..."

"That's my biggest dilemma," she said. "I know that if I open the lodge up to hunters this fall, we'll be all right. The trouble is, people like my friend Simone, who say I can't run a light center and also cater to hunters. She insists I'll go under—that no light workers will come here any more."

"That's ridiculous," I said. "Do you truly believe that?"

Aunt Rosalee studied my face. "You reminded me so much of your father right now." She chuckled. "But Simone also says that hunters won't come here on account of it bein' a new age retreat."

"I don't see why not," I protested.

"Accordin' to Roy Howard from the so-called Family of God congregation, the Rainbow Majestic is bein' boycotted. And he's doin' everythin' in his power to give us a bad name."

"Well, if that were true," I said, "then how do you account for the tremendous turnout you had for the fair?"

"I would tend to agree with you, Juniper, except that I'm afraid this latest event with a murder in the lodge is goin' to keep hunters away—as well as light workers. You could say it was the final nail in the coffin."

We both hung our heads. I knew what she was saying. It was all too true that scandalous events and murders could be detrimental to a destination resort such as the Rainbow Majestic. And with its being on the brink of bankruptcy, it would take a miracle to keep the lodge from having to be sold. I recalled the things Mike had told me about the rogue investors and the people who wanted to take control and turn the Rainbow Majestic into a gambling casino.

"Well, how did your awakenin' go with Starla?" Aunt Rosalee asked, interrupting my thoughts.

"I'm still reeling from it," I said. "It was an eye-opening experience."

"They usually are. Did you get into any past lives?"

"Yes," I said. "It answered a question I've always wondered about ... and that lifetime ended tragically ... but, somehow, I feel detached from it now."

"That's good," said Aunt Rosalee. "It does none of us any good to dwell on those things in the past. It's what we do in *this* lifetime that counts."

"I ... I spoke with my father," I told her.

Aunt Rosalee reached over and patted my hand. "And how was that?"

Instead of answering her, I thought of an important question I'd wanted to ask. "Aunt Rosalee, what did it say in Uncle Fred's will about the lodge?"

The question obviously took my aunt by surprise. But, before she could say anything about it, there was a loud knock on her door. Aunt Rosalee jumped up to go and unlock it.

Gena entered the room. She fixed her gaze upon me. "Juniper, your friend, Mike, says he's leaving now."

I stared at her. "Okay," I finally said, but made no effort to stand up.

"Aren't you at least going to see him off?"

I sighed. "I really have nothing more I want to say to Mike."

"He drove all this way to see you, and you've treated him like dirt." Gena placed her hands on her hips. "I've tried to talk him into staying another night."

"Why?" I asked. "So he can convince me to go back to Kansas with him?"

"Well, it wouldn't be a bad idea," said Gena.

"*You're* the woman who called and told him to come here ... and that I wanted to leave the Rainbow Majestic," I accused her. I heard Aunt Rosalee groan in protest.

Gena merely frowned at me. "You still don't believe me

when I say I think it's in your best interest to leave."

Now Aunt Rosalee spoke up. "Gena, I'm surprised at you."

"Yes, I made the call," she admitted hotly, "but not for the reason you both are thinking." She turned and started to leave, but Aunt Rosalee stopped her.

"Gena, wait. Juniper has another question for you." Aunt Rosalee closed the door so Gena wouldn't leave—as if that gesture could stop her. She turned to me. "Go ahead, Juniper."

I stood up to face my glowering cousin. "Gena, I know you were at Diamond Reservoir the time my father was shot. Can you tell me what happened? Do you remember how he died?"

Gena's lower lip trembled and she turned away, so we couldn't see her face. She placed her palms against her cheeks and walked toward the window. "Please don't ..." She was close to tears. "Don't make me remember that time."

"So you *were* there," I said.

Aunt Rosalee looked from me to Gena, then back at me. "Maybe now is not the right time for this."

I gave in and sat back down. With a loud sob, Gena ran to the door and out into the hall after Aunt Rosalee opened it for her.

"Why don't you go say goodbye to your friend?" Aunt Rosalee suggested.

Reluctantly, I left the suite and wandered down to the lobby. Gena had vanished and her assistant was checking out Simone Sullivan and Linda as I approached the front desk.

Simone looked at me without warmth. "I'm sure you'll be glad to get your rooms back," she snapped at me. She closed her purse, then motioned to her daughter and they left. Apparently, their luggage had already been taken out. Linda glanced back at me before going out the door and shot me a quick, apologetic smile and waved. I smiled back.

I didn't see Mike anywhere, but Clover came out of the great room with Vlad Petrovsky, who carried his bags. Clover smiled and was saying her goodbyes to him. They stopped at the desk, and Clover gave Vlad one last big hug, then she retreated back down the hallway with a wave and a smile at me.

"Ah, Juniper!" Vlad grinned at me while the desk clerk printed out his receipt. "What a gr-r-reat time was had here. I enjoyed very much! Even though you don't see *yu-fos*, I enjoyed meeting you."

I smiled. "It was good meeting you too, Vlad."

"I come give talk next year, okay?"

"Sure," I said, then wondered if the Rainbow Majestic would still be in operation for another holistic fair.

"You give hug?"

"Sure."

He wrapped his muscular arms around me and squeezed. *"Dah-svee-donya,"* he told me in Russian. I was afraid he was never going to let go.

Voices in the hallway behind me caused me to turn and I saw Wes walking in with Cyril Jorgensen, who carried a navy blue windbreaker in his arms. Wes had seen Vlad's bear hug and I recognized the familiar interest in his blue eyes.

"Hello, Juniper, and how are *you?*" Cyril had a twinkle in his brown eyes today.

"Fine, thank you. Are you two going to see Celeste again?" I asked.

"No, Cyril wants to go for a ride," Wes explained. "I thought I'd take him for a jaunt. Have you been over to see Diamond Reservoir yet?"

Diamond Reservoir? My interest was piqued. "Why, no, is that where you're headed?"

"Come with us," invited Cyril.

"Can you get away right now?" asked Wes.

I looked around, still searching for Mike, but apparently he must have given up on me and already left. "Sure," I said. "I'd love to go. And I've been wanting a chance to talk more with Cyril, anyway."

The old man offered his arm to me. "Well, come along then, young lady. It's a beautiful day for a ride in the mountains."

I felt I should at least tell somebody where I was going, but the girl at the desk was busy with Vlad, and there were others waiting to check out. Before we went out the door, I caught sight of Gena returning to the desk from the back room. She watched us as we left the lodge. I was convinced she knew something about my father, but didn't want to tell me. Oh, well, maybe I'd have better luck with Cyril.

Outside the day was cloudy and cool. So far, there had been no rain, but the surrounding mountain tops were blanketed with dense cloud cover and there must have been rain or possibly snow happening in the high country. I noticed Drake outside in the parking lot, talking to a group of people who were getting into their vehicle. He turned his head and saw the three of us as we made our way to the lodge's parked SUV. I hesitated while Wes helped Cyril into the front seat of the car.

Drake left the group and walked over. "Anything wrong?" he asked.

I stared at him, the memory of my experience on the awakening table still fresh in my mind. I was recalling the violence that had led to our deaths, and I couldn't answer right away. Finally, I said, "N-no."

Drake glanced over at Wes, then started to turn away.

"Drake, wait!"

He turned to me with impatience. "I've got to get back to work," he growled.

"Come with us to Diamond Reservoir," I said quickly. Out of the corner of my eye I watched as Starla and the Leachfield family headed from the lodge to a parked car—obviously Lance Leachfield's vehicle. Lance was unlocking the doors.

Drake searched my face. "Why?" His look softened for a moment.

"You wanted to take me there yesterday morning," I told him. "Remember?"

Drake made a face. "Well, now you've got Wes to take you. I don't need to be a fifth wheel, and besides—I've got some people I need to help with their luggage."

His words stung. Across the parking lot, Starla and Max Leachfield climbed into the back of the car as Lance and Nadine got in front. Their car started up and I watched it begin to roll away. I waved at Max, who watched me from the window.

"Come on, Juniper," called Wes. "Get in, if you're coming along."

Drake sauntered off and I turned with a sigh and got into the back seat of the SUV. A few cars were leaving with guests who had just checked out. I hadn't seen in which direction the Leachfield car had turned, but most were heading toward Wade City.

Cyril was in high spirits this afternoon as we drove up the county road. I'd heard the reservoir was about ten miles farther up into the mountains from the Rainbow Majestic. Some light rain had begun to smatter the windshield, but Wes didn't turn his wipers on right away. Cyril carried on a metaphysical discussion with Wes in the front seat, which I only half heard.

I was remembering the last time I had ridden in the SUV—with Clover, Wes and Drake—on our excursion to Wade City. I was a bit curious as to why Clover hadn't insisted on coming along just now. Wes was attentive toward Cyril, but acted almost as though I weren't in the car with them. I wondered why he was so strange, and then recalled that he had seen Vlad giving me that big goodbye hug back at the lodge. Well, if he was jealous of someone like Vlad, it was just too bad. My attraction to Wes had dwindled rapidly in the last couple of days.

I still didn't know what to make of Drake. My feelings toward him were now stronger than ever. The relived scene from our mutual past life had given me new insight. I wanted to talk it over with Drake, and wondered how he would react to what I had witnessed on the awakening table. I was afraid he would disbelieve everything and chock it all up to my imagination. I felt he was rejecting me, especially after our bitter moments at last night's dance, when he had made that remark to me about dancing with Wes. I realized Drake was probably jealous of Wes, but he didn't know that my feelings had changed, and that something deep inside of me yearned for him. Drake had no idea that I was ready to discover if there could be anything meaningful between the two of us in *this* lifetime.

I stared into my lap, dejected at the thought that it was probably too late for Drake and me. We were two completely different individuals. Our common interest had been the mountains and the wildlife. I longed to develop that part of me that had been suppressed all these years, the instinct for the enjoyment of the outdoors—fishing, hunting and camping—all those things I might have grown to enjoy had my father lived. And now with the Rainbow Majestic on the brink of going bankrupt, what future was there for me here? Yet the thought of returning to Kansas and my old life had no appeal for me. My life path had changed at the Rainbow Majestic. I had become a light worker and I wanted—more than anything now—to be of service to others.

We had been traveling about fifteen minutes when Wes asked, "What do you say, Juniper?"

I snapped out of my sullen thoughts and asked, "What?"

"We were talking about the lodge murder," Cyril explained.

"What do you think happened to Taffi?" asked Wes.

I hadn't realized the direction their conversation had taken. "I don't know," I replied.

"Why do you think she was stopped?" Cyril asked.

"Stopped?" I echoed.

"She was onto something," Wes said.

I sat up straighter and leaned forward to hear better. Wes had pulled into a long driveway, surrounded on both sides by evergreen trees. The road headed toward a large body of water. Rain continued to come down and he had the windshield wipers working now. "What do you mean?" I asked.

"She knew too much," Cyril agreed, and he nodded his head. "Taffi had knowledge of some facts somebody didn't want to get out."

"Please tell me what you're talking about," I told him. "Wes, can we stop and get out? I'd like to see the lake."

"It's drizzling," he complained.

"That's all right, Wes," said Cyril. "Pull the car over here. We can get a good view of the water."

Wes pulled the car close to the water's edge, but not where we could get stuck. I noticed another car around the other side of the lake, driving slowly along. There was a campground on that side. A few camping trailers and tents were set up far away, under the trees on the beach side. No one was around where we were parked. Wes continued to let the car engine idle, and he put the wipers on intermittent.

"Do either of you know who killed Taffi?" I asked. For some reason my nerves were on edge. I don't know why, but these two men friends I had trusted suddenly seemed like strangers to me. A gnawing fear began to grow inside of me.

Cyril watched out the window. "That question is irrelevant, considering that the answer you really want goes back more than twenty years ago." He turned to look at me, and I couldn't read what his emotions were.

"Cyril," I said, surprised that I sounded more confident than I was, "you were in the hunting party out here at the reservoir when my father was shot. Do you know who shot him?"

Wes glanced at me quickly, then over at Cyril. He seemed

surprised I would ask such a question of the elderly man.

Cyril chuckled and shook his head. "What difference does all this make now? It's something that happened long, long ago, and it won't bring your father back to you."

I braced myself. "But Taffi *died* because of what she knew about it. I know that Uncle Fred didn't shoot my father. He confessed to Aunt Rosalee on his death bed. But he didn't say who did. And if he didn't ... *who did?*"

The old man swept the white hair back off his forehead. "All right," he said. "You're right, I was there. I didn't fire the shot that killed your father—but I might as well have."

"What does that mean?" I asked.

Just then, another car pulled up beside us. We all looked over and saw Clover climb out of the passenger side. Gena jumped out of the driver's side and ran over to us. Wes rolled down his window.

Gena's eyes were wide with fear. "Have you seen Lance?" she cried frantically.

"No," said Wes.

"They left in their car a little while ago," I said. "Starla was with them. Why?"

Clover approached and looked worried as did Gena. "Rosalee sent us out to look for him," Clover said. "She's convinced his life is in danger."

"Lance?" questioned Wes. He reached out the window and took Clover's hand in his.

The rain had subsided a little. I looked across the water at the campground and saw some people moving around on the beach. A small blond-headed boy was near the water with a woman who resembled Nadine at this distance. A tall, lean man and a short, dark-haired woman were standing by the car, and I wondered if it was them. "Look over there." I pointed across the reservoir.

Everyone looked in that direction. I opened the car door and stepped out. "Why is Lance's life in danger?" I asked Gena.

She shook her head without answering and wandered over to the water's edge. I followed her, and then I heard Cyril laboring to get out of the SUV.

"Gena," I said, standing beside her as the rocks separated the water from the shoreline, "talk to me ... please."

"I don't want to talk right now," she protested. She wandered along the shore, away from me.

I turned and called to Clover and to Wes, who had also gotten out of the SUV. "What did Aunt Rosalee mean about Lance? What's going on?"

"They see us," Wes called out. The group on the other side of the lake seemed to notice us then. Wes waved both hands to call the Leachfields over.

Clover picked her way over beside me and said, "I think Gena's, like … on the verge of a nervous breakdown. But she insisted on coming out here after she saw you leave with Wes and Cyril. When Rosalee came down to the desk, she asked us to find Lance. She'd just, like … gotten a threatening phone call. Someone in the lobby said they overheard Starla and Nadine talking about taking a drive out to the reservoir."

Wes helped Cyril over to the shore. The old man—leaning on Wes for support—called out Gena's name. She turned to stare at him, but didn't move.

"Gena, come over here," Cyril called to her. "The game's over. I can't go along with this charade much longer."

Gena shook her head at him. Tears were streaming down her cheeks. "Leave me alone!"

"You and Juniper must know the truth," Cyril insisted. He tried to move toward Gena, but Wes held him back. Gena stood there—waiting—hugging herself from the cold.

Cyril turned to me, his face now grayish and pained. "Juniper, Fred Sutton was a good friend of mine for many years. So was Nathaniel, your father. That night in the hunting camp, the three of us sat and drank in our tent … until we were far from sober. It was Fred, Nathaniel and me in one tent … the two Howard boys in their own tent beside us … and, of course, Gena had her own tent in the cooking camp. Your uncle would get so tight … he'd start saying things he didn't mean." Cyril hung his head. "I guess we all did. Only your father … Nathaniel … managed to maintain his sobriety."

The old man brushed his arthritic hand over his forehead again and continued. "That night some awful things were said. Fred accused me of sleeping with his ex-wife, Janet. He called me some lousy names … which I won't repeat here." Cyril cleared his throat. "Of course, it was true … Janet and I had once been close.

We had an affair while she was still married to Fred. But, if you knew Janet, you'd understand ... she liked men ... and she thought —at one time—that I was some kind of handsome Harry."

I saw that the Leachfields and Starla were walking the shoreline—headed toward us—and had made it about halfway already.

"Well, Fred and Janet had been divorced for a number of years, and I had managed all that time to keep the affair to myself. How he learned about it, I don't know. But, for some reason, he decided to take it out on me that night."

"*I* told him," Gena said. She sniffed as she slowly turned toward us. "Mother often bragged about her conquests. I told him she and Cyril had had an affair."

"It doesn't matter," said Cyril. "What matters is what I'm going to tell you next."

"Why? *Why* must you tell them?" demanded Gena, and she grew angry again.

"Please, Gena ..." Wes pleaded. "Let him finish."

Cyril sighed. "A quarrel developed between Fred and myself. It soon turned into a fist fight, and then Fred reached for his rifle. I don't know if he meant to shoot me, or merely to frighten me. But, at that point, Nathaniel stepped in and tried to stop the fight. He tried to get the gun away from his brother, who was screaming that he wanted to kill me before I went after Rosalee." Cyril's lip trembled in shame. "To think that I would ever bring harm to that wonderful, spiritual woman ..."

"And what happened?" I asked.

Cyril looked at me. "While they were struggling over the gun, someone had stepped inside the tent. And then ..."

"*I shot him!*" Gena shouted.

Everyone stared at her.

"I heard what was going on, and I was scared to death somebody was going to get killed. I picked up the nearest rifle— and it was loaded. I walked in and aimed, and before I knew it, the gun exploded ... and Uncle Nathaniel doubled over." Gena fell onto the rocky ground and completely fell apart, sobbing hysterically.

Cyril broke away from Wes and stumbled over to Gena's side.

"*You* shot Nathaniel?" Wes cried in astonishment.

"But surely it was, like ... an accident!" Clover rang out.

"Yes, it was an accident," Cyril affirmed, growing sad.

"Then why did Uncle Fred say *he* shot my father?" I asked.

Cyril knelt beside the woman on the bank and put his hands on her quaking shoulders. "I convinced Fred to take the blame," he said. "I did it because ... because I wanted to protect ... my daughter." He indicated Gena.

22

The woman on the shore turned her head and stared into the elderly man's face. "You?" She shrank back in alarm. "*You are my father?*"

Cyril nodded gravely. "Yes, Gena. Fred Sutton was incapable of siring a child. When your mother became pregnant, Fred Sutton accepted it, and decided to claim you as his legal heir. I certainly had no objection. He was not a resentful man. I know he loved you as if you were his own."

The rest of us were silenced momentarily by this startling news on the part of Cyril Jorgensen. I noticed but paid little attention to the new blue pickup truck that rattled by on the road beside the lake. Lance and his family—along with Starla— hurried toward us now, no doubt wondering why Gena and Cyril were kneeling beside the water's edge.

So, Gena was Cyril's daughter! My cousin was not my blood cousin after all. My heart suddenly went out to her as I could imagine what she must be feeling right now. But there were still questions to be answered. For one thing—who had killed Taffi? And what had Cyril done to convince Uncle Fred to lie about the accident? Gena had only been a girl of fourteen at the time. Surely the authorities would have treated this purely as an accidental death. Why had these two men protected Gena all these years?

"Everybody okay over there?" Lance's voice called out as they approached.

Before anyone could respond, the loud crack of a gunshot exploded. Both Clover and Nadine screamed, and I cringed. Then I heard Gena yell, "Lance! Watch out!"

I then saw a tall, slim man wearing a camouflage suit with a hood dart out from behind the blue pickup that was now parked behind some trees nearby. Starla grabbed Nadine and Max and pulled the two of them toward a pier used for fishing and boat launching. The three of them crawled underneath between the water and the steep embankment of weeds.

Wes quickly tucked Clover and me down among the tall grasses, to keep us hidden. I watched as Gena rose to her feet and looked around.

"Al!" Gena yelled. "Al, don't do it!"

"How does she know who it is?" asked Clover.

I didn't answer.

Then another man stepped out of the blue truck's cab sporting a rifle. He was a larger man and also wore camos and a hood to disguise himself. I put two and two together and realized the slim man with the handgun must be Al Howard, Gena's ex-husband. The man by the truck had to be his brother, Roy Howard from the Family of God congregation.

"We don't wanna hurt anyone," the large man called out. "Just give us Lance Leachfield. Hand him over to us now, and nobody gets hurt."

Lance, who had crouched near the shore, slowly rose to his feet with his hands on top of his head.

"No, Lance! Don't go!" Nadine screamed.

The slim man walked slowly toward Lance, his gun raised and ready. "That's right, Leachfield. Cooperate—and your family lives. One false move and it's over ... for all of you!"

Nadine began sobbing and Starla scolded her to keep quiet. Lance continued to step slowly toward the blue pickup while the rest of us watched, not daring to speak or move.

Suddenly, a red car approached from the direction of the county road. I heard Clover whisper to Wes, "That's Rosalee's car."

The two men in camouflage suits and Lance had noticed the car too. The larger man rushed forward and grabbed hold of Lance's arm. The tall, slim man helped drag Max's father toward the truck. A struggle ensued in which Lance attempted an escape, but the large man managed to jab him good with the butt of the rifle. Then the two men pushed Lance into the front seat of the truck. The large man climbed in beside him.

Aunt Rosalee's red car screeched its brakes as it halted between the SUV and the truck. Drake leaped out of the driver's side. Then I heard Aunt Rosalee shout at him in protest. "Drake, they've got guns!"

A shot rang out again. This time we heard the bullet

ricochet off Aunt Rosalee's car fender. Drake ducked and ran to an evergreen tree, where he took cover.

Nadine screamed for Lance, and Gena shouted, "Al, stop! Please!"

I could hear Aunt Rosalee's voice in the car, frantic and frightened.

Wes left us and began zigzagging toward Aunt Rosalee's car. I watched—my heart pounding from fear—and thinking that Wes must have learned that maneuver from being in combat. But my main concern at the moment was for Drake, who was taking a terrible chance as he tried to reach the blue pickup, where the tall man—apparently Al Howard—climbed into the driver's seat. I could see Lance inside, doubled over in the middle of the cab. I couldn't bear it if something were to happen to Drake. I realized deep down inside just how much he meant to me.

Wes and Drake took turns as they moved furtively toward the truck, but we all could see that they were never going to be able to overtake it. Al had started up the engine and was now backing up.

"We've got to stop them," Gena shouted. "They'll kill Lance! There's a contract out on him."

Cyril stood up and waved his arms at the truck, but the gesture was futile. Clover looked at me. "Juniper, only a miracle will stop this."

I agreed with her, but I didn't know what to do. Then—unbelievably—a miracle did occur. A huge motor home had just rolled in from the road. Aunt Rosalee's car was blocking the space where the blue truck would have passed in its escape. The motor home came to a stop and the driver stuck his head out the window.

Drake reached the truck first and tried to open the passenger door. Roy Howard reached out the window and knocked Drake to the ground. Al, who was behind the wheel, could see that he was trapped between the motor home, Aunt Rosalee's car, and the reservoir.

Meanwhile, Wes had crept up beside Al's side of the truck and tried to get that door open, but Al—who had the truck in reverse—shot backwards and rammed into the front end of the motor home. There was no escape for the two men in their camos, yet they were still the ones with the guns.

Drake was on his feet once again, but Roy Howard had pulled his rifle through the open window, prepared to shoot. Just as he pulled the trigger, Lance managed to bump the large man enough to send the bullet's aim into the air.

Drake had the door open now and—although he was no match for the big man—he was successful at dragging him out of the truck. They struggled with the rifle until Roy dropped it, and then the two men fought—rolling on the ground, which was now muddy from the rain. Wes struggled on the other side of the truck with Al, who appeared to have the upper hand.

Clover and I wasted no time scrambling to our feet. We ran over to the scene. Aunt Rosalee had gotten out of the car, and now Nadine and Starla—with Max—ran toward us from the pier. Gena helped Cyril, who could hardly walk. The driver of the motor home hopped out, talking into his cell phone, and the rest of us stood back—uncertain what to do in the double brawl outside the truck.

Al Howard struck Wes to the ground, then took off into the woods while Wes groveled in his attempt to recover. By the time he was back on his feet, Lance had jumped out of the truck and ran over to where Drake and Roy Howard were battling. He grabbed the rifle off the ground before Roy could get his hands on it again. Wes staggered over and helped Drake get control of Roy, whose hood had come off, revealing his identity. Each gripped one of the large man's arms and pulled him to his feet. A trickle of blood ran from Roy's nose.

Within fifteen minutes, a sheriff's deputy car pulled into the reservoir, its lights circling. Apparently, they had been over at the Rainbow Majestic—doing more investigative work—when dispatch had gotten hold of them. The two deputies apprehended Roy Howard, but his brother had escaped into the woods. We were sure Gena's ex-husband was well out of the vicinity by now, but another unit was called in to comb the area for him.

Aunt Rosalee insisted that Lance be put under protective custody and told the officers about the call she'd received that afternoon. The motor home was finally permitted to proceed to the campground. The rest of us returned to the Rainbow Majestic. Aunt Rosalee told us all to meet in the lounge.

When I walked into the lobby behind Clover and Wes,

Gena's desk clerk called to me. "The crystal suite is being prepared for you," she told me. "Your clothes and other belongings have already been moved out of Taffi's room." She handed me the key.

I thanked her, then turned to Clover, who said, "You know, all those crystals in there need to be cleansed and recharged ... especially. like ... after Simone's stay in that room."

I sighed. "What should I do with them?"

"I'll help you. We'll soak all the crystals in sea salt. Then we'll rinse them off and recharge them in the sun." When she saw my flustered look, Clover smiled. "Not now, of course," she said. "Like... after the meeting." She turned to Wes, who smiled at her and squeezed her hand.

I was surprised to find Mike sitting in the arm chair in the great room, next to the fireplace, reading the Sunday paper. He looked up at me as we all trudged past on our way to the lounge.

"I decided to stay another day," he told me, and stood up to walk beside me. "Hey, what happened?" He had noticed Lance, who was holding his side—and Drake, whose face had been smudged and his hair ruffled and clothes muddied during the fight with Roy Howard.

I quickly filled Mike in on the events that had occurred out at Diamond Reservoir, and then we all grabbed seats in the lounge and pulled our chairs close together in a circle.

Aunt Rosalee said a prayer of thanks for everyone's safety, then turned to her bookkeeper and said, "Lance, suppose you begin and tell us just what you think you were doin'."

Lance—still nursing his bruised side—composed himself, then began his story. He said that a while ago—he wasn't sure exactly when—he'd been approached by the spokesman for the group of investors who had handled the loan to renovate the lodge. He had been asked to report to them periodically and let them know certain details that had to do with the Rainbow Majestic's income and bank records. They had offered him a tempting remuneration for this information, and he had complied—against his better judgment—because he needed money. He and Nadine had debts to pay off that their combined salaries did not cover.

"And then they wanted me to start cooking the books," Lance admitted. "I refused at first, but then they said if I didn't do what they said, they would see that Rosalee found out about my spying. I had no choice but to do their bidding."

"Y'always have a choice," drawled Aunt Rosalee bitterly. "What did they want you to do?"

Lance swallowed. "They wanted me to draw up false reports that showed the lodge was losing money. They figured if you saw the lodge was not making it, you'd be willing to sell it to them."

Aunt Rosalee frowned. "What else?"

"When that didn't seem to work, they wanted me to get the lodge into trouble with the Department of Revenue by not making the tax payments. I refused at that point. Now they've come up with this scheme of calling in the loan ... the balloon payment you have coming up. There's nothing I can do about that, I'm afraid."

"And now that you've defied them, they're out to get you," said Aunt Rosalee. She turned to Cyril. "And Cyril, I want to hear what you've got to say."

The elderly man looked about ready to collapse, but he leaned forward in his chair and repeated the story he had told us at the reservoir—about how he and Fred Sutton had gotten into a fight the night my father was killed. Cyril explained about his earlier affair with Janet Sutton and ended with the announcement that Gena Sutton Howard was actually his daughter.

Starla and Nadine Leachfield looked startled when they heard this.

"Well, I'm really not surprised," said Aunt Rosalee. "I knew Gena wasn't Fred's. But he never told me who her real father was."

Everyone looked at Gena, who sat beside Cyril, dotting the end of her nose with a tissue. I had never seen her look so defeated.

"Well, I'd like to know something." I looked directly at Cyril. "I'd like to know why you and Uncle Fred protected Gena all these years. She fired the gun that killed my father, but it was an *accident!* Why didn't you tell the truth and tell the authorities what really happened? Why did Uncle Fred carry the blame all those years?"

Cyril cleared his throat and sat back in his chair. "Let me

tell you something, honey," he said in a calm voice. "Gena was in a terrible state of mind when she realized she had shot your father ... her uncle, if you will ..."

At this, Gena let out a sob and covered her face.

Cyril went on. "I did not want my daughter to grow up with that stain on her. I told Fred that if he didn't say it had been he who shot Nathaniel, I would go to the authorities with the information I had ... and reveal to them all those illegal hunts he had taken rich clients on ... and all the outfitting he had done without a license."

"Fred was a legitimate outfitter!" protested Aunt Rosalee.

"Not until later years." Cyril chuckled sarcastically. "Not on your life ..."

There were a few moments of silence as Aunt Rosalee absorbed this disturbing fact about Uncle Fred. Then she looked around the room at each one of us and said, "Perhaps now it's time for me to make a confession to ya'll." Her eyes rested on me. "Juniper, you asked me this mornin' what it said in Fred's will."

I noticed Mike perk up in the chair beside me.

Aunt Rosalee continued. "When Fred died, the lodge was under joint tenancy, which means that the lodge automatically became mine. But he also mentioned in his will that after I passed, the lodge would go to his niece—Juniper Sutton."

A murmur of surprise rippled throughout the room and I felt people's eyes on me. Mike smiled at me smugly, his arms folded across his chest. Drake appeared shocked at the news.

"Juniper, when I asked you to come to the Rainbow Majestic, I had every intention of tellin' you about this," Aunt Rosalee said to me. "But just before you arrived, I learned that the Rainbow Majestic was close to bankruptcy. I just didn't think it was fair to say anythin' to you at that point. I was afraid I was goin' to lose the lodge."

"And I was afraid she would break down and tell you anyway," said Lance. He looked sadly at me. "I'm the one who typed that note and took it up to the crystal suite when you were sleeping."

"You?" Aunt Rosalee looked alarmed "Why, Lance?"

He stared into his lap. "I could see there was going to be trouble with her being here. I figured I could try and frighten her away."

Again there was silence in the room. I looked over at Gena, who was huddled in her chair, sniffling.

"Didn't Uncle Fred leave anything for Gena in his will?" I cried. I suddenly felt sorry for the woman I'd thought was my cousin.

"He did leave her one of his vehicles," said Aunt Rosalee, "and she was the beneficiary of a small insurance policy. She wasn't left out completely."

"But why did he want to leave the lodge to Juniper?" Gena cried out in anger. "I'll never understand it."

Mike explained then about the letter Uncle Fred had sent my mother—the one she had never shown me—but had kept hidden in her safe deposit box. "He felt responsible, I suppose," said Mike. "He wanted to do something to make up to his niece because she didn't have a father."

I looked over at Mike, surprised at his sudden stab at sympathy. Suddenly, Mike didn't seem the same to me. Had he been influenced since his arrival at the Rainbow Majestic? Had some of this love and light penetrated his hard core?

"I was devastated when Fred said he wasn't leaving me the lodge," Gena said. "I couldn't believe he'd do that to me. But now I know why. I wasn't his flesh and blood ..." She sobbed into her tissue a moment, then said, "Al—my ex-husband—contacted me about a year ago, when he got out of prison ... and he learned about the outcome of Fred's will. He could see I was furious. He told me if he could make Rosalee give up the lodge, he and his associates would buy it—and I'd get it back ... that is, if I went back to him."

"Gena, you wouldn't!" Aunt Rosalee reprimanded.

"Al is a horrible man," Gena said, "but when Juniper showed up, I was afraid. I wanted her to go away. She was asking all sorts of questions about her father's death ... and I knew Rosalee was grooming her to be her partner ... something I'd never see." Bitterness crept into Gena's voice. "I could tell Juniper wasn't going to give up on her quest. She managed to talk Taffi into finding out information for her."

"Did you kill Taffi?" I blurted out, and everyone stared at me.

"No!" Gena cried. She broke down again, then said, "But Taffi had somehow read my handwriting and knew I had killed someone ... even if it was an accident ... and she suspected I was plotting against Rosalee to take over the lodge."

"But how did Taffi come up with the list of six names?" I asked, then had to explain that the list named who had been at the hunting camp that fateful night.

"Maybe she found the old police report," suggested Nadine.

"Or maybe somebody told her," said Cyril. "Taffi had a talent for uncovering information. I believe I am the one who supplied her with those names, although—at the time—I had no idea why she wanted to know."

"Then was it you who left the message on Taffi's answering machine?" I asked Cyril.

"No," he replied.

"Gena, do you know?" asked Starla.

Gena merely shook her head, her face buried in her tissue. She had said all she was going to say, although I suspected she knew more than what she was telling.

Shortly after that, the meeting broke up. Clover and Wes left to gather up all the stones in the crystal suite so they could cleanse them for me. I hesitated when I saw Drake was still seated near the fireplace, deep in thought. He hadn't said a word during the entire meeting. I ventured over to him while the others sauntered out. Mike lingered behind me.

Drake looked up at me as I approached. I could see the longing in his eyes and my heart began to beat faster. "So you're now part owner of the Rainbow Majestic," he mumbled.

"Not really ... not yet," I answered shyly.

"Well, congratulations." He didn't smile. In fact, he suddenly seemed rather resentful of the idea.

I told him, "Unless Aunt Rosalee can pay off the loan, I'm afraid neither of us will own the Rainbow Majestic."

Drake shrugged. "Oh well ... rainbows appear—and then they vanish. They're only an illusion ... I'm sure the Majestic Mountain Lodge will be back in business in time for hunting season—and will do just fine after the Suttons."

I couldn't believe Drake's attitude, all of a sudden. "How can you say that?"

"I just did," he quipped, and then he eyed Mike. "And what do you think of all this mess you've walked into? Do you think Gena got the shaft on this deal?"

So, that's what was eating him. *Gena's loss.* I should have known all along that Drake cared for Gena. It was obvious now where his affections lay. I backed off—deeply hurt.

Mike replied to Drake's question. "If you want my opinion, I think it's time Juniper returned home to Kansas and let the Rainbow Majestic go."

"Well, I totally agree!" Drake stood up, defiant. He didn't look at me at all. He said to Mike, "Go on and take her home where she belongs. Maybe we all would have been better off had she stayed there in the first place." He marched out of the lounge then.

So now it was all *my* fault! I was so choked up with emotion, I couldn't talk, or I might have said something in retaliation to Drake. I looked into Mike's smug face and couldn't take any more. Hot tears spilled from my eyes and my throat constricted. I turned and fled from the lounge—passing an oblivious Drake—and rushed up the spiral staircase to the crystal suite.

I had no sooner got inside the newly cleaned rooms than my sobs gushed forth. I collapsed upon the rose-colored bed in my room and picked up the photograph of my father, Uncle Fred and the deer. How I wished—with all my heart—I could feel my father's arms around me now, comforting me in my unbearable pain. Letting the old picture fall against my pillow, I wept—long and hard.

23

I must have fallen asleep after my crying spell because—when I awoke—it was dark and the dinner hour had passed. I got out of bed and turned on the bedside lamp, then went to wash my face in the bathroom. I noticed as I looked around the suite that every crystal had been removed. Apparently, Clover and Wes were still working on them. The room felt devoid of its usual placid energy.

Moonlight streamed in through my windows. I strolled over to look out at the full moon that had just come over Majestic Mountain. Its golden light was bright and inspiring, but my heart was heavy from all that had transpired. I now wondered if perhaps the best thing to do was for me to return to Great Bend with Mike. The last two weeks had been beautiful and transforming to my spirit, but what if Aunt Rosalee lost the lodge? What then?

And now it seemed as though I had lost those I cared about ... Wes had finally found Clover—but somehow I was happy about that. They belonged together and I no longer got mushy around Wes. Drake was another matter ... my feelings had grown toward him and I had been so afraid for him during his fight with Roy Howard. The awakening I'd experienced with Starla that morning had brought things to light for me, especially where Drake was concerned. I had loved him deeply in that other life, and I felt drawn to him now—more than ever since the arresting fear had dissolved in my understanding of what had happened when I entered that cabin so long ago.

Looking out my window—over the woods and garden below—I saw a figure sitting on the bench near the pond. My heart seemed to skip a beat as I recognized Drake. He was sitting there alone, just as he had that first night I had arrived at the lodge and I had looked out this very window. That had been the night I'd been accosted in the woods.

For a moment I hesitated. My common sense was telling

me to stay put. Drake had made it very clear he didn't want me around. Hadn't he told Mike to take me back to Kansas? But my heart knew differently.

"Listen to your heart, Muffin," the voice said in my head— my father's voice. "Life is short and life is precious. Go to him."

I never questioned what I'd heard. I didn't think about a jacket—or my key. I slipped on my shoes and ran out the door, down the hallway to the second corridor to the back stairway. The only thing I could think about was the man sitting on the bench outside in the garden. This time he would be there, and I'd open my heart to him. I'd convince him that he was the man of my dreams and that I needed him.

But when I got outside into the cool night air and the moon-light, the bench was vacant. Like before, Drake had apparently gotten up and left. My heart raced from my run down the steps, and I stood—looking around—wondering where he'd gone. I would find him, if he hadn't wandered far.

The moon, still full, was partially covered by clouds, but still gave plenty of light as I set out on the path into the woods. I was determined to find Drake and I didn't think about the fact that I could be in danger. All I could feel was the pain in my heart for that man who had held me in his lap inside the partially built cabin. I only wanted to go to him and make things right between us again. I had to at least give it my best shot.

Then, a man's voice called to me from the trees beyond the garden. A loud whisper called out, "Juniper ... over here ..."

"Drake?" I called out in desperation.

"Yes ... I'm over here," the voice whispered. It wasn't far away.

I stepped toward the woods, but everything was silent. "Are we playing games?" I called out.

Suddenly, a tall figure leaped out of the bushes and grabbed me. "There won't be no more games," he said harshly, and dragged me over into the bushes. His hot hand covered my mouth and forced my head back. I struggled, frightened to death as I realized this was not Drake. It was Al Howard!

"We're going for a ride," he told me wickedly, "and it's a one-way ticket for you. Gena deserves the lodge—not you—and she's getting it! You're in the way!"

As much as I struggled, it was no use. He was much

stronger than I was, and he was adept at moving through these woods in the dark. Where he was taking me, I couldn't see. I wondered if he had been the one who had shoved me when I'd been in the woods that first night at the lodge. Suddenly, someone else was with us.

Gena stood in the moonlight with a gun in her hand, and suddenly I was terrified of them both. Al Howard held me fast, and even though I fought, I couldn't move.

"Don't do this, Al," Gena pleaded with him. "Once was bad enough. Let her go!"

"Quit joking around and help me get her into your car," Al ordered.

"Release her, or I'll pull the trigger," commanded Gena in a shaky voice.

I then realized Gena had the gun pointed at Al. She was trying to save me.

"You bitch!" he roared, and in the next instant Al threw me to the ground and lunged at Gena. "Give me that gun, you cunt."

I looked up and could see the two of them struggling with the gun. I rolled into the protection of the trees, scared to death for Gena. She shrieked as this brute of a man punched her.

When the gun went off, I screamed. Seconds passed, and then—out of nowhere—Drake was on the scene. He must have been close enough to have heard the voices, and then the gunshot had directed him to the exact spot. I watched him pounce upon Al Howard as Gena crumpled to the ground, obviously shot. The two men fought with grunts and punches and groans, until somebody showed up with a flashlight. By then, Drake had managed to wrestle the other man to the ground and the gun lay beside them.

More people approached, drawn by the commotion. I heard somebody call out to get Rosalee, while someone else said to call an ambulance. The man with the flashlight was a guest at the lodge. He helped secure Al Howard, with Drake's help, until police arrived on the scene sometime later.

As soon as I was able, I crawled over beside Gena, who was now surrounded by two women who had come out to the garden. Gena was bleeding from a wound in her shoulder. She looked at me and said, "Juniper ... did Al hurt you?"

"Don't talk," I told her. "Help is on the way." I applied direct pressure on her shoulder to stop the bleeding. One of the women who had come to help said she was a nurse. She took her scarf and pressed it over the wound. When I took my hand away, it was covered in Gena's blood.

"Al ... Al killed Taffi," she disclosed, finding it hard to get her breath.

"Yes," I said, "but he's not going to get away with it."

"I ... took Rosalee's ... key," she confessed. It seemed important to her to tell me.

I waited in silence—not wanting her to use up the last of her strength by talking.

Gena moaned, swallowed and continued. "Al made me ... get it ... Al wanted to ... stop Taffi ... told her to come ... with him ..."

"Don't talk anymore," I pleaded.

"He wanted to ... to stop ... you."

It seemed like the ambulance was taking forever to get here. Wade City was eighteen miles away.

While we waited, Gena insisted on telling more. "You and Max ... I knew you were in the auditorium that day," she said. "I ... got Rosalee's key and went in ... hoping to scare the both of you ... wanted you to ... to leave."

"It's okay, Gena," I told her. "I understand your reasons."

"But ... I was wrong ... about you," she said. "The night we talked in the kitchen, I saw ... I saw ... *oh, my God* ..." She started to cry harder, and I reached out to comfort her.

As I sat there with Gena, I suddenly had a flashback of her with blood on her hands. My eyes grew wide with instant terror as I recalled the Indian brave who had killed Drake and me in the frontier cabin. He had been *Gena!*

I then remembered Starla's words: "You must forgive him."

Gena's eyes had finally closed in weariness. I placed my hand on her head and swept back a lock of sweaty blond hair. "Gena, I forgive you," I said in a low voice. "The scene in the cabin came back to me when I was lying on Starla's awakening table. I now know it was you. But you see, it doesn't matter now. What's in the past is over and long gone. I truly do forgive you for taking our lives then."

I didn't think she had heard me, but her eyes fluttered open and she whispered back to me, "Thank you, Juniper." Then she slipped into unconsciousness.

When the EMTs arrived, they attended to Gena. The police

came and took Al Howard into custody. By that time, Aunt Rosalee and a crowd from the hotel were there in the woods near the garden.

"Juniper, thank God you're all right." Aunt Rosalee gave me a hug, then said, "Why don't you go inside and clean yourself up?"

I realized that I was a mess from the scuffle with Al Howard and I still had Gena's blood stains on my hands. Looking around, I didn't see Drake anywhere. Clover, Wes and Starla were giving statements to one of the sheriff's deputies next to the pond. I quickly made my escape into the lodge and found the nearest restroom.

By the time I came outside again, the ambulance had left and the crowd of guests had broken up. Most of them had moved back inside the Rainbow Majestic. I noticed the chill in the night air and hugged myself as I strolled into the garden to see if I could find Drake anywhere.

"Juniper," said a man's voice.

I spun around and faced Mike, standing next to the back door of the lodge.

"Oh ... Mike." I went toward him.

"Are you all right?" he asked.

"Yeah ..." I looked around at the garden. Everything was quiet and there was no sign of Drake.

"Listen, kid, I'm sorry about all this," said Mike.

I stared at him, puzzled. "Why?"

Mike removed his glasses and wiped the lenses on his jacket sleeve. "I've been an asshole."

I had to stifle my reaction to Mike's words. "Whatever do you mean?"

Mike sighed. "These people ... your friends ... and Aunt Rosalee ... I didn't mean what I said, you know." He put his glasses back on his square head and attempted a smile. "I'm definitely leaving tomorrow morning. And I'll understand if you don't want to go back to Kansas with me. But just know ... if you decide to come along ... it's cool."

Mike *had* changed. I smiled at him and then reached forward and gave him a long hug. "I'm not sure yet what I'm going to do," I told him. "It's possible I might be going with you." I sighed as he let me go. "It all depends ..." I stared at the ground and felt a tear spill down my left cheek.

Mike smiled at me, then jerked his head toward the garden. "I think there's somebody you need to discuss it with," he said.

I followed the direction of his eyes and saw Drake lingering beside the bench in the garden, his hands in his pockets, looking out over the pond. Mike motioned for me to go over, then he turned around and stepped inside the lodge.

For a moment I stood, watching the man in the blue jean jacket with the long hair and beard. Then I stepped forward and shouted, "Drake!"

He looked up as I ran over to his side. His face did not give anything away.

"Drake, I came down to talk to you earlier. But you were gone. Then I thought it was *you* calling to me from the woods. I didn't know it was Al Howard."

Drake saw the concern in my eyes. Without hesitation, he took hold of my hand and led me over to the bench. A light mist had started to fall and the mountain air felt cold. Drake sat me down on the bench and then pulled me into his arms. "Juniper, I'm sorry for the awful things I said to you earlier."

It felt so good to be right where I wanted to be—comforted in his strong arms. "Drake," I said, "I've got so much to tell you."

He wasn't listening. "I didn't mean to say those things," he told me. "I've just been a little mixed up lately. I haven't been able to figure out where you were coming from." He then looked into my eyes and I saw love and caring, and I wasn't afraid to look into their blue depths any more. "You remember now, don't you?" he asked.

I knew to what he referred and nodded. "I relived it in the awakening today," I told him, finding I didn't even have to explain. "Drake, I want to be with you."

"Why?" He looked at me oddly. "Why would you want *me?*"

I tugged at his beard. "Now just why do you *think?*"

Suddenly, he buried a deep kiss upon my lips, and pulled me tighter against him. The moonlight played over us and I knew—in that moment—that Drake was the man I wanted to live my life with. I also knew—without a doubt—that he wanted me as well.

24

An eventful week passed. On Saturday morning—one week after Drake and I had taken the ATV out and he had shown me his cabin—we found ourselves there again. We had packed some yogurt, coffee and cinnamon rolls from the lodge's kitchen and carried them on the ATV. While Drake checked on his well, I sat on the wood floor inside the cabin and pulled the food items out of the pack.

Over the course of the week, a lot had come to light. Gena was slowly recovering in the hospital from the gunshot wound in her shoulder. Even though she had lost a significant amount of blood, she was gaining strength and was going to be all right. This was a big relief to all of us at the Rainbow Majestic.

Aunt Rosalee had found out from the police investigation that the huge sum of money—five hundred thousand dollars, in fact—had been deposited into Taffi's checking account in Wade City just the day before she had been found strangled to death in the old auditorium. It had been drawn on a foreign bank in the Caribbean—payment from a questionable source. None of us could believe that our beloved Taffi had been working with the mob.

When Gena was out of Intensive Care, Aunt Rosalee and I visited her at the hospital, and she was able to talk to us about her involvement with Al Howard. She had already disclosed everything to the police and was satisfied that her ex-husband would be going to prison for life.

"It was a set-up," Gena told us. "Al was the contact for the mob. They were determined to get hold of the Rainbow Majestic and turn it into a gambling casino. All they had to do was convince you, Rosalee, to sell the lodge."

"Then what Mike told me was true," I said.

"It would be a cold day in hell before I'd sell the lodge to those crooks," commented Aunt Rosalee.

"They already had Lance on their payroll," Gena continued. "When Taffi became a threat to them ... for knowing too much ... they tried to bribe her."

"I can't believe she'd do such a thing," I said.

"Actually, she didn't agree to it," insisted Gena. "Taffi refused to go along with them. She turned the money down."

"But ... the money was in her bank account," protested Aunt Rosalee.

"It was electronically deposited without her knowledge," revealed Gena. "They figured she would either cave in and go along with them, or they could make it look like embezzlement or money laundering. They knew that amount of money would raise questions and that Taffi would be scared to death."

"You said Al killed her," I told Gena. "What happened?"

Gena told us that Al had made her give him the key to the storage room entrance into the old part of the lodge. Then he had tricked Taffi into taking him into the old auditorium so she could demonstrate how she communicated with disembodied spirits. He somehow convinced her that he was a paying customer, but first needed to test her ghost-busting skills.

"Taffi's other specialty was being able to tap into the fourth dimension," said Aunt Rosalee.

"But when he got her into that isolated area, he ... did her in." A sob caught in Gena's throat. She laid back against her pillow and closed her eyes.

"You just rest now," Aunt Rosalee said softly. She fussed with Gena's blankets. "You have to get well so you can come back and run the lodge."

Gena's eyes opened in surprise. "Do you really want me back?" she asked.

"Well, of course," insisted Aunt Rosalee.

A noise caused me to turn toward the doorway to Gena's private room. Cyril Jorgensen stood there. With a smile he shuffled toward us, carrying a vase of brightly colored flowers. "How's my girl doing?" he asked.

"What? Are those for me?" Gena smiled as her father walked over.

Cyril explained that he had just come from visiting Celeste, who was on another floor. He had spent a lot of time in the past week at the hospital, visiting both Celeste and Gena, and their father-daughter relationship was blossoming. Later, Aunt Rosalee had told me she hoped Gena would continue on as general manager at the lodge after her convalescence.

A memorial service had been held on Wednesday for Taffi at the lodge. Al Howard was charged with first-degree murder and Gena was willing to testify, even though there was a risk that she might be convicted of being an accessory to murder. Aunt Rosalee's attorney assured her that most likely any such charges against Gena would be dropped. Al's brother, Roy, was out on bail, but was being convicted on racketeering charges, and his church group had completely ostracized him. The DA was investigating the band of investors the Howards were associated with and who had dealt with Fred and Rosalee Sutton when they had purchased the lodge.

Once Mike understood that I was in love with Drake, he did as he had said and returned to Kansas on Monday morning. He told me that he could handle matters with the estate by himself. His final revelation—which was the true reason he had stuck around—was to tell me that my father had left me a legacy that I didn't know about. My mother had kept it from me all these years—apparently in her effort to maintain control over me—and in all those years it had built up substantial interest. Now, suddenly, I was a modestly wealthy woman, and I decided to become Aunt Rosalee's partner and offer some of my money to pay off the debt on the lodge.

The Leachfield family left and found work outside Wade City. Aunt Rosalee had been willing to keep Lance on as her bookkeeper, but he felt compelled to leave. He and Nadine wanted their son, Max, to grow up in a more traditional environment, where he didn't have to rely on secret passageways to amuse himself.

Starla was delighted that Drake and I had gotten together. Wes and Clover were an item now, and Wes had decided that committing himself to a woman wasn't such a bad thing after all as Clover doted on him constantly.

Drake walked into the cabin and we sat on the floor and enjoyed our pilfered breakfast from the lodge kitchen. After he finished his cinnamon roll and was stretched out on the floor beside me—cup of coffee in hand—he looked around at the log walls. "Guess I'd better get windows put in here soon," he said.

"It might help keep the flies out," I said, and brushed one off my roll.

"Then you can get some curtains to put up," he said.

"That would be nice," I agreed.

"And, while you're at it, you can pick out some furniture for your new home."

I sat up straight and stared at him. "What are you talking about?"

"Oh, here … I almost forgot." He reached into his pocket and pulled something out that was hidden in the palm of his hand. "It's something I thought you ought to have."

"What is it?" He placed in my hand the rose quartz pebble connected to the silver chain—the one I had admired in the gift shop and tucked away to buy for myself. My eyes grew wide as I stared at the lovely crystal pendant.

"It's yours." His voice was gentle as he searched my face.

"How … how did you … Drake, how did you know?" I asked him in wonder.

He helped me with the clasp as I put it around my neck. "Mountain man's secret," he said. "Oh, I know it's not a diamond ring. You'll get that later."

I could only stare at him. "I think you'd better explain …"

Next, he reached over, grabbed me and kissed me—mountain man fashion. "You are going to marry me, aren't you, Juniper?"

There was no having to think it over. I had made up my mind a week ago. I looked into those mystical blue eyes and asked, "What do *you* think?"

He pulled me onto his lap and we laughed and rolled upon the wooden floor. Outside the windows of the cabin the blue sky of Colorado outlined the peak of Majestic Mountain with its white specks of remaining winter snow—and a Rocky Mountain bluebird sang from a tree stump nearby.

About the Author

Ann Ulrich Miller received her Bachelor of Arts degree in Creative Writing from Michigan State University. Originally from Monona, Wisconsin, her writing career began at age 15 with the sale of her first short story. The mother of three grown sons, she has lived half of her life in Colorado, where she won a full scholarship in 1982 to the Aspen Writers Conference. She has had articles published in newspapers and has had short stories published.

Her stories appear in two of Arielle Ford's anthologies, *Hot Chocolate for the Mystical Lover* and *Hot Chocolate for the Mystical Teen-age Soul.*

She is the author of a Space Trilogy, which includes *Intimate Abduction, Return To Terra,* and *The Light Being.* She also wrote a romance mystery, *Night of the November Moon,* and has published three mysteries in her young adult Annette Vetter adventure series set in the 1960s.

Her favorite genre is romantic suspense. She writes novels for both adults and young people, with most of her writing reflecting her search for a higher purpose in life. Since 1987 she has published a monthly metaphysical newsletter, *The Star Beacon.* Her spiritual autobiography, *Throughout All Time,* tells about her esoteric life with her husband and soul mate, and how she dealt with his passing.

Currently she is director of a nonprofit learning center in Pagosa Springs, Colorado, and at work on her next novel.